W9-BHU-074

Ace Books by J. Ardian Lee

SON OF THE SWORD

OUTLAW SWORD

SWORD OF KING JAMES

SWORD OF
KING JAMES

J. ARDIAN LEE

ACE BOOKS, NEW YORK

SWORD OF KING JAMES

An Ace Book / published by arrangement with
the author

PRINTING HISTORY
Ace trade paperback edition / July 2003

Copyright © 2003 by Julianne Lee.
Cover art by Dan Craig.
Cover design by Judy Murello.

Check out the ACE Science Fiction & Fantasy newsletter!

Library of Congress Cataloging-in-Publication Data

Lee, J. Ardian.
    Sword of King James / J. Ardian Lee.— Ace trade pbk. ed.
        p.   cm.
    ISBN 0-441-01059-8
    1. Matheson, Dylan (Fictitious character)—Fiction. 2. Scotland—History—18th
century—Fiction. 3. Highlands (Scotland)—Fiction. 4. Time travel—Fiction.
5. Jacobites—Fiction. I. Title.

PS3562.E326S95 2003
813'.6—dc21

                                                                    2003041926

ACE®
Ace Books are published by The Berkley Publishing Group,
a division of Penguin Group (USA) Inc., 375 Hudson Street,
New York, New York 10014.
ACE and the "A" design are trademarks
belonging to Penguin Group (USA) Inc.

PRINTED IN THE UNITED STATES OF AMERICA

10   9   8   7   6   5   4   3   2   1

For Dale

ACKNOWLEDGMENTS

The following have my heartfelt gratitude for their generous help: my agent, Russell Galen; swordmaster F. Braun McAsh; Russell Handelman of the Philipsburg Manor Upper Mills, Sleepy Hollow, New York; Ernie O'Dell and The Green River Writers of Louisville, Kentucky; Gaelic language instructor John Ross; native guides Gail Montrose and Duncan MacFarlane of Glenfinnan, Scotland; Teri McLaren; Trisha Mundy; Diana Diaz; Betsy Vera; Dona Morgan; and always, Ginjer Buchanan.

AUTHOR'S NOTE

Events in *Sword of King James* are not meant to represent neopaganism in any way. Any similarities to practices of neopagans are coincidental. The treatment and representation of faeries in this work are issues that are strictly between me and the wee folk.

Though this story is based on historical fact, the fictional characters are not actual people, and any resemblance to historical or contemporary persons is coincidental. Glen Ciorram and its people are imaginary, and no fictional character is meant to represent a historical member of the Matheson, Bedford, or Ramsay families.

However, the nonfiction characters and events are as true as possible to what is known about them.

On spelling: In the early eighteenth century, spelling was a dodgy affair any way one looks at it. Standardized spelling in English didn't come along for another century at least, and for Gaelic it didn't happen until the latter part of the twentieth century. The spellings for Gaelic words in this book are from *MacLennan's Dictionary*, which tends to the archaic and therefore lends itself to the period. All other words (except, of course, for the Spanish) are either English or dialect words used by

English-speaking Scots, and for the sake of internal consistency are spelled according to American usage.

E-mail J. Ardian Lee at ardian@sff.net, or visit *http://www.sff.net/people/ardian/*.

CHAPTER 1

The fire on the hearthstone rose and fell with the low, monotonous sound of chanting. Flames licked over sharp-smelling pine that burned brightly, crackling, casting lively shadows against the walls of the underground lair. Living tree roots lined the walls of the centuries-old home, gnarled and entwined, looping in and out like Celtic knots. Trees lived in the space, residents as rightful as the faeries themselves. Candles burned here and there, set along those roots and across a wooden table nearby, its top thick with melted beeswax. The sweet smell of the candles, burning wolfclaw, and nettle mingled with the scents of wood-smoke and earth.

The faerie Daghda—An Daghda Mór to those who once worshiped him—lounged naked beside the fire, comfortable on silken feather pillows, drowsing as Morrighan cast her spell. But, comfortable as he was, he tired of waiting. He stirred and propped himself on one elbow to watch. She was dawdling; he knew it. He was being ignored, and he hated that. More than anything, he hated being ignored.

"Come," he said. "Lie with me and forget the damned mortal." He held his hand out to her in invitation. His *ball mór* swelled as he gazed upon her flushed, glistening skin. The sweet ache made him shift position, and he raised his knee. It had been far too long since she'd last shown interest in him, and the longing was no longer tolerable.

She declined to reply, ignoring him still, and lifted the sword over the fire to cense it in the smoke. Her words were in the Old Tongue, muttered under her breath. He couldn't hear what she said, though he lay quite near. She was shutting him out on purpose now. Anger rose, and he sat up on the pillows.

His voice took on a petulant tone, though he hated it and coughed first to clear it from his throat. "What might be the purpose of it? If it's the blood lust ye desire for him, he's human and therefore filled with it already. Or is it fear in yourself? Do ye think his powers are greater than your own?" He knew her well and wouldn't hesitate to prod her most tender places.

That brought an evil look, and a smile touched his mouth as she paused in her chanting. Smoke drifted past the blade of the aging sword—a worn Scottish broadsword with a heart-shaped basket hilt of pierced steel. "He's but a mortal." She sneered, but he thought there was more to it. Such as lust of her own. Jealousy rose again in Daghda, and he spoke more firmly this time.

"Exactly as I said, *mo caraid*."

"It might interest you to learn, he calls his dirk Brigid after your daughter."

That did nothing more than irritate him further, and whether he felt it toward the mortal or toward Morrighan, Daghda couldn't say. Nor did he care. He replied, "All my daughters and sons are dead. He's welcome to consecrate his dirk as he likes. Also, the goddess of war holds the life of every man, save the cowardly who are of nae account in any case. Leave him be, and come to me."

Daghda refrained from mentioning his own powers, for his best days were far behind him. Any more, he was happy enough merely to not age like a mortal, for that was nearly the only power left to him now that the *Sidhe* were dwindling. Only a few scattered faeries remained in the isles, hiding from the increasing numbers of men and their new powers of construction and destruction.

The pleasures of Morrighan's flesh were his only joy in life anymore, and her waning interest tore at him. Longing filled him for the day he'd first seen her, straddling a burn, washing the heads of men slain in battle. Her thick black hair had draped over her face and shoulders, and she'd eyed him with such a bright, hot look of lust, he'd taken her on the spot. In the flowing water, surrounded by the spoils of her triumphant day, he'd taken her to him and made her his own. At least, he'd thought of it that way. It had been a glorious coupling, recounted through the centuries in story and song. Remembering the mindless joy, her excitement for the death all around, the heat and strength of her body, his skin warmed, glowing red in the firelight.

Morrighan spoke, a low growl of anger, and her lip curled as she struggled to retain her concentration on the work at hand. "He knows things I cannot. He speaks to the *Tuatha De Danann* without fear. He hears the tree spirits, and they attend to him. They do his bidding. I must ken what he has seen and understand his power. Where it lies. How it might be had. I must have it."

"And if his power is naught but luck?"

A crooked smile crept over her bloodred mouth, and her cold eyes made him shiver, warrior though he once had been. "In that case, he'll need luck beyond imagining simply to live." With a quick flurry of words she finished the spell, her red-clad breast heaving and her skin ruddy with power. She held the sword aloft, and the blade glinted in the firelight. Aloud, she cried, "Let the will of the great art be done!"

The sword disappeared amid crackling, sparkling air as the fire leapt. The hairs rose on Daghda's arms, and he rubbed them down. Morrighan sighed and stared at the now empty space, satisfied.

Daghda let a smile lift the corners of his mouth as Morrighan's gaze wandered over him. A fine sheen of sweat covered her, and her eyes were wild, dancing. He said, his voice husky with longing, "Seeing you like this recollects me of the day I came upon ye with yer feet spread wide and yer skirts tucked up to your waist, letting the burn run between your legs all free." Lying back on the pillows, he touched his tongue to his lip.

She smiled. Her eyes glittered in the high, hot firelight. In one movement she dropped her crimson robe from her shoulders and came to kneel between his splayed knees. His blood surged and he reached for her involuntarily, wishing to have his mouth on hers. Or any part of her. His hand slipped behind her neck, and she slithered the length of him, skin on skin, until her hips pressed hard against the insides of his thighs. He moaned, deep in his chest as the ache in his groin sharpened to sweet pain. Her mouth found his as she straddled his hips. As she claimed him and he surrendered to her, he thought that perhaps he would like her to cast a spell such as this every day.

CHAPTER 2

Dylan Matheson slipped his arms around his wife and snuggled deep into the musty feather mattress. In that netherworld between sleep and waking he hovered, treasuring the warmth of her, the smell of warm skin, and of warm linen and wool in their bed. Cait made a contented sound, like a sigh, and pressed herself back against him as she drew his arms tighter around her. He buried his nose in her hair and filled himself with her scent. For him, the dizzying, heady earthiness of her meant lust, longing, home, and the other half of himself. He would never forget the way she smelled—always remember the warmth of her, the sound of her breathing. He would never forget—

Sharp awareness invaded, and pain. Awakening, impossible to forestall, came and Cait disappeared, collapsing to nothingness in his arms. Dylan groaned as the joy of her turned to grief. He moved his hand over the mattress as if it might be possible to find her there somehow—that she was merely misplaced. Cait was dead. She had been for seven months. Murdered in July. Raped and left on the table in the next room with a bayonet in her throat. Since then the wood of the tabletop had been sanded clean of blood, but it still bore the deep gouge left by the blade point. There was no sanding deep enough to make that go away.

He sat up in the solid darkness and rubbed his face awake. It was nearly dawn, he knew, though there was no window in the room and no sound of birds in the winter-locked glen outside. Even the yard chickens would be still huddled among the bushes by the sheep enclosure for another hour or so. Nevertheless, he knew it was time to get up. Lying abed after waking wasn't his habit, for even in February there was always more work on the farm than could be done by one man with two children. Work was his salvation. Keeping his body occupied helped ease the pain of thinking too much.

A deep breath lightened his heart, but not completely. He hated that dream. Hated waking up to find it was a dream, then spending the day lugging around a heart blackened with pain. For a moment he held in his fist the gold ring he wore hung around his neck alongside his crucifix. Cait's wedding ring. Like a talisman, it seemed to carry a power to heal him. Then he pulled his top woolen blanket around himself and slipped from the bed.

Reaching under his bedclothes, he found the linen sack that held a smooth stone about the size of a shoe. On his son's bed, casting about under the comforter sewn from rabbit skins, he located another stone in another sack. Then he retrieved a third from beneath his small daughter's blankets in the lower bunk.

His joints—knees, hips and shoulders—ached with the cold. He was thirty-five now, pushing thirty-six, and winter nights stiffened him as they hadn't before. For the first few years after his arrival from the twentieth century he'd acclimated well to the northern cold, but now the small aches and his various injuries—wounds and broken bones acquired over the years—conspired to make him favor his left leg slightly as he made his way through the darkness to the bedroom door. He pushed open the straw wattle door of the bedroom and went into the sitting room. His collies—a white bitch named Doirinn and a gangly, half-grown black puppy he'd named Fionn—rose from the floor by his bed and padded after him.

The sitting room was nearly as dark as the bedroom, but the dim red glow of embers guided him to the hearth, where he dumped the three stones from their sacks into the ashes near the fire. By bedtime that night, the heated stones would be returned to their sacks, then slipped into the beds. There they would again warm the feet of himself and his family in the winter chill.

Kneeling by the hearth, on the dirt floor covered with dried reeds and bracken, he placed some kindling wood on the embers, then a rush light soaked in pitch straight into the coals, and leaned down on all fours to blow gently so the embers would throw more heat. Fionn came to sniff at what was going on, poking his nose in Dylan's face. "Go." Dylan snapped his fingers and pointed away. Fionn, eager to please now that he was catching on to his training, went directly to where Doirinn stood, and lay down beside her. Dylan returned his attention to the task at hand. The rush light caught, and he encouraged the wood to burn. Once it also had caught, he next set two dried peats on it. The peats wouldn't produce any better light than a dim glow, but the steady heat would be right for making breakfast when Sarah arrived. He lit a candle from the burning wood and set it in an iron holder next to the hearth. Then he rose and turned his attention to the pressing matter of his bladder.

Though he'd been in this century for several years, his origins in twentieth-century Tennessee were still with him in many respects. The chamber pot of his household was not kept in the bedroom as were pots elsewhere in Glen Ciorram. Cait had always thought him strange and shy for it, but for the sake of privacy he insisted the lidded pot go on a stool behind a curtain in the corner of the sitting room.

Now he made his way past the shadows of tools and household utensils hung on the wooden wall of the byre, carefully avoiding the malt bin upon which the faerie, Sinann, was most likely curled up, asleep and invisible. In his old life he'd never lived with this much clutter, having kept a large loft apartment and few things in it. But here tools were necessary, they needed protection from the weather, and space indoors was limited. He leaned sleepily against the stack of bags containing seed corn as he peed into the pot, then let down the hem of his nightshirt and set the pot on the floor for the kids to use when they would awaken.

Sìle was almost two now and just learning to use it by herself, inordinately proud each time she left something in it. The bigger the better for her, and it was hard to not be just as pleased as she when she crowed, giggling, and clapped her hands over a scatological accomplishment. Ciaran had just turned four, and though he was an old hand at going potty, he was still too short for the stool. Leaving the wooden pot on the floor was safer than hoping the kids would set it down and lift it back up by themselves without spilling the contents.

The fire was now warming the air in the house, though slowly, since it was a battle against freezing temperatures outside. It had snowed the day before, and now the ground was covered with a thin blanket of pristine white. Dylan hoped he wouldn't find more snow on the ground this morning. He should have manured the fields by now, which would have protected the ground from freezing, but now he would have to throw the compost on top of snow. He went to the bedroom to dress, still followed by his dogs.

The nightshirt pulled over his head went onto a peg, and he shivered in the freezing darkness as he pulled on both of his sarks, which hadn't been washed in two months. Today he belted his kilt around his waist without pleating it first, a quick-and-dirty arrangement for the sake of not having to fool too much with the enormous yardage of plaid. The free length of wool he wound tightly around his body for warmth, rather than draped loosely as he would in summer. Trews went on and tied around his waist, though he hated the itchy wool on his legs, two pair of knee-length stockings in addition, then his sheepskin leggings with the silver-hilted dirk named Brigid strapped to the right one. Finally he brushed floor dirt from his stockings before pulling on his boots. These were twentieth-century, ankle-high suede boots with rubber soles, his last remaining tie to his life before being brought to the eighteenth century. But they were about worn out. He'd reattached the soles so many times they were growing ragged at the edges and now were nearly worn through in the middle. It was getting to feel like wearing moccasins. He would soon have to wear brogues indigenous to the century, and say good-bye to arch support.

As he ran his fingers through his hair to get it off his face, he began to feel almost human again. Almost. That dream was going to stick with him for the rest of the day, creeping into the corners of his soul and darkening them. But there was work ahead, something to keep his mind off the grief.

Dylan then drew on his black wool coat, picked up the wooden bucket from the table, and ducked through the low, leather-hinged door. The pre-dawn was icy, and the wind buffeted, but no more snow was on the ground than had been last night. He took a deep breath of the winter air and woke up completely, then caught himself as he slipped on a patch of ice. The dead grass crunched under his feet as he walked. Looking out across his fields, the mountains at the far end of his small property rose, bare and rocky shadows. Above them, the sky was just turning purple.

For a moment, he was struck by the majesty of the mountains and the vast stretches of time in which they had been—and would be—unchanged. It was no accident he was in this place on this day, he was certain of that.

Out of all the millennia past and future, all the thousands and millions of years in which this planet existed and would exist, he lived now. No accident, and he was glad of it.

Doirinn and Fionn cavorted in the dooryard, each running and sniffing the ground for a good spot to pee after the long winter's night. Fionn leapt on Doirinn, wanting to play, but the older dog swerved away, ducked when he leapt again, and went on sniffing the ground as if the puppy weren't there.

At the burn running from the spring in the southern slopes, Dylan filled the bucket to carry the water to the house. Carefully, with no sloshing, or he would have to work all day in cold shoes. By the hearth, he filled a three-legged pot and set it over the small fire. It would be steaming by the time Sarah got there, and she would start the parritch boiling.

Sinann's sleepy voice came from atop the malt bin, "Good morning to ye, lad." She sat cross-legged and leaned against the byre wall behind.

Dylan only grunted.

"*Och*, ye had the dream again, I see." Her short white hair was mussed, but she fluffed it a bit with her fingers and it fell into its proper, feathery arrangement.

His voice low, so as to not awaken the children, he said, "I'm all right. Let me make it through another day, and maybe I'll wake up tomorrow not feeling sucker-punched." The daily routine was comforting in its familiarity. Like putting one foot in front of the other, step by step he moved on.

"A living wife would take some of the pain from it." Her voice was entirely too cheery.

Dylan sighed and poked the fire to encourage more heat; then he squatted on his heels to watch it. "Not today, Tinkerbell. Please. I'm just not in the mood to hear it." Everyone in the glen, including the nitwit faerie—especially the nitwit faerie—expected him to marry Sarah. The poor woman had been in love with him almost since his arrival in this century, thanks to a love spell Sinann had put on her. By the time Dylan had realized Sarah's predicament, he'd already fallen in love with Cait.

Sarah, magically besotted as she was, had behaved badly at the announcement of his betrothal to Cait, but to her credit there had been no outbursts after that. During his marriage she'd been a good friend and kinswoman to Cait and himself. Since Cait's death, she'd been employed by him as part-time housekeeper and caretaker for his children, and their relationship remained perfectly decorous. He liked it that way. No fuss, no muss, and he could sort out his grief and his life without Cait on his own.

"She's already maintaining the household; it's time you allowed her to do a bit of maintenance on yerself."

"Tink—"

"She loves ye still, lad."

He sighed. "I know." He held a hand over the water to see if it was making progress yet. It wasn't.

"Ye cannae go on supporting two families forever." In that, Sinann was right. It was expensive to hire Sarah, for she had two sons of her own, and he couldn't expect her to take up the slack in his household without being willing to make sure she wasn't shorting herself of food and clothing in her own home. In addition to the work she did for Dylan, she worked in the castle in payment for the single room among the castle servants she shared with her boys. Since coming to work for him, she and her small family were clothed and fed breakfast by Dylan but slept at the castle and took lunch and supper there. Sarah was cousin to the Laird's wife and was also the widow of a cousin to the Laird himself. As a close cousin to the Laird and therefore a kinsman to Sarah, Dylan had more responsibility to her than an ordinary employer, regardless of what he could afford to pay.

In addition to the cost of hiring Sarah, he'd needed to hire a boy from the village to tend the sheep. Dylan's barter goods—wool thread, excess oat crop, eggs, and such—were running out fast this winter, and he stood the risk of having to sell some of his whiskey before its time. His first distilling wouldn't be ready for another year yet, though, and bringing out the casks from 1717 this year would blow his plan to produce the first truly aged whiskey in the Highlands. He wasn't willing to do that.

But neither was he willing to remarry soon. Maybe he never would be ready. Replacing Cait was inconceivable. Though the pressure from all sides to hook up with Sarah was monstrous, he stood up to it, reluctant to marry anyone just because it fit everyone else's idea of what should be.

Nor would he hand the kids over to the Laird and Lady, their grandparents. Iain and Una were eager to take Ciaran and Sìle into the castle with them, but Dylan was adamant they stay with him. He'd struggled too hard to establish his household with Cait and be a father to his children; he wasn't going to give up now.

In an effort to get Sinann off his back about Sarah, he said, "What about Ena? She's been giving me the goo-goo eyes, too, you know."

The faerie made a sound of disgust and said, "She's also the least comely lass in the glen. At half yer age, her smile is already blackened and ragged, and she's nae chin to speak of. That's nae wife for you. Let her marry Coinneach."

A wry smile crossed Dylan's face. Sinann sounded positively offended he could even think about marrying an ugly girl. "I don't know," he said, "Coinneach doesn't seem interested, and he's still a boy besides. There's something to be said for having a wife nobody else wants. I'm thinking low maintenance might be the way to go."

Sinann, appalled into speechlessness, snapped her fingers and disappeared.

Snickering to himself, he stood, picked up his bear-head staff, and went back outside for his morning workout. Leaning the staff against the outside wall of his house, he then stepped into his dooryard to assume the horse stance—feet parallel and at shoulder width, knees slightly bent—and begin the warm-up. Doirinn and Fionn sat nearby to watch, wearing big, happy dog grins.

Dylan shook himself out all over, back straight and shoulders back. He took a deep breath and crossed himself, touching fingers to forehead, torso, left shoulder, then right, saying, his words coming in a faint, silvery cloud in the starlight, *"In nomine Patris, et Filii, et Spiritus Sancti. Amen."* Then he leaned forward, back flat and hands on hips, to bounce his torso, stretching the leg muscles. *"Pater noster qui es in caelis . . ."*

By the time he'd finished the rosary he was well warmed, the ache in his left leg was gone, and the sun was turning the sky pink. He took the staff in hand and paused a moment to empty his mind before starting the kung fu form. Segueing from Western devotional to the Eastern "no-mind" took strict mental discipline, which he found an advantage in this time and place where calm had saved his life more than once.

He'd not been born Catholic, nor had he been particularly religious in his old life. But here, where disease was unstoppable and the weather influenced the death toll each winter, Dylan had acquired a deep appreciation for belief in an orderly universe where everything happened for a reason.

Most days in his workout he was either unarmed or used the staff, for it was far safer these days than bringing out one of the swords he'd hidden inside his roof thatching. The Disarming Act of 1716, made law after the last Jacobite uprising, had made it illegal for him to own a sword. Not to mention that one of those weapons was a cavalry saber taken from the commander of the garrison in Glen Ciorram. He'd already weathered one recent search of his house by hiding his weapons in the cave where he kept his still. But Sinann couldn't keep track of every dragoon and alert him of every approach. He'd been lucky that once. It wouldn't be too smart to be waving the swords around unnecessarily.

Even carrying Brigid around out in the open was a dodgy proposition, though he got away with it. Technically, even the knife was illegal, but some leeway was given for dirks. In the Highlands knives were a necessary tool for daily living, much like the pitchfork and peat spade he owned. That sort of tool could also be a perfectly deadly weapon and had often in the past been carried into battle. For the past year or so, the *Sassunaich* at the Queen Anne Garrison in the lower glen hadn't given the Mathesons and the surrounding clans much grief over dirks used for cutting meat, leather, and cloth, and for carving wood from which almost everything was made. It had been more than three years since the last uprising, and the dragoons stationed in Ciorram had settled into a pattern of casual harassment meant to keep the Matheson clansmen cowed without too much work on their own part.

The clansmen responded by acting cowed, while resentment grew.

As Dylan exercised, the sun rose enough to show itself over the mountains to the east. For a moment he turned his face toward the warmth but tensed to see a red-coated dragoon on horseback, silhouetted against the sky at the end of his property. The figure faced Dylan's house, as if poised to charge down the hill at it. Irritation rose at the sight of an English soldier on his land, and Dylan stood to face him, taking deep breaths, his no-mind destroyed. His thoughts raced with his hatred of the English Army. He stayed where he was and watched. The dragoon was still as a statue, watching also.

The door behind creaked, and Dylan looked to find his son standing in the yard, watching him watch the soldier. Dylan left off staring at the *Sassunach* and tucked the staff behind his right arm as he turned to the boy.

"Maduinn math, athair," said Ciaran as he rubbed sleep from his eyes. Even for such a small boy, he had a good strong voice. He always spoke with conviction, just as his mother had. His plaid dragged the icy ground,

not tucked, and his cheeks and the tip of his nose were turning pink with the cold.

Dylan ruffled the boy's longish hair. "In English, son."

Ciaran blinked a couple of times as he retrieved the correct words, then said, "Good morning, father."

Dylan's knowledge of the future had always been more often a burden than a blessing. But in this case Dylan was glad he had foreknowledge enough to make sure his children would be bilingual before the time came that Gaelic would be all but outlawed. He reached over to straighten his son's plaid and wondered whether Ciaran's inability to dress himself completely might be purposeful. It seemed he always left something to be done by his father. The boy's ruddy cheeks reddened more, and he tugged on his coat.

"What're you doing up so early?"

That took a moment for Ciaran to decipher, but he replied, "I'm wanting you teaching to me. Kung fu." He chopped the air with a knife-edged hand, which made Dylan smile as he squatted on his heels to be at eye level.

"Think you're ready?"

Ciaran's eyes went wide, and he nodded with the enthusiasm Dylan had seen often when he'd taught martial arts to kids in Tennessee. A wide grin lit up his face. "*Och, tha!* Aye! Teach me, Da!"

Dylan nodded. It was time. He'd taught boys as young as four, and there was no reason Ciaran shouldn't know how to fight like his father. "Okay, come." He stood and waved his son to the center of the dooryard. "Stand here." Then he looked up at the hill to the east.

The dragoon was still there, watching. Dylan wanted to know what was so damned interesting.

He faced Ciaran and knelt. Reverting to Gaelic for the sake of clarity and expedience, he said, "All right, son, put your feet like this." He set the little feet parallel to each other, at shoulder width from each other. "First I'm going to teach you how to stand. We won't do anything else until you've learned this. You've got to forget everything you know about standing, even though you've been at it for three years and are very good at it. Aye?"

Ciaran nodded, and they began. Dylan took his son through the basic lesson on how to stand in such a way as to make it difficult for an opponent to knock him over. Once Ciaran mastered the art of standing with his weight balanced, Dylan began to teach him to punch. Though little boys always seemed to want to learn the kicks first, and Ciaran was no exception, Dylan had always insisted they learn to punch properly. *Wrist up at the hip, extend the arm, wrist down at the very last moment.* Again. And again. Right, then left. Maintain balance, back straight, punch without leaning forward. "Without leaning forward, I said." Ciaran corrected himself, and Dylan nodded. *"Balach mhath."* Good lad. Ciaran barely spared a moment for a quick grin, then went back to punching the air in dead earnest.

Dylan kept the first session short, for he knew the lessons would stay with Ciaran better if each ended with him wanting more. The boy attended well to the lesson, alert to instruction and willing to cooperate when corrected. Dylan forced himself to not smile too much, for it would be interpreted by Ciaran as laughing at him, nevertheless it was difficult to hide his pleasure at teaching his son the thing he did best.

He concluded with the speech he always gave about never choosing to hit if redirection would solve the issue, and never choosing to draw blood unless it was necessary. Little boys tended to come away from their first lesson wanting to practice their new skills, looking for someone to punch, so Dylan taught his son the difference between aggression and defense.

It was time to stop when Sarah and her sons approached from the trail to Ciorram and went into the house. Dylan sent Ciaran inside for breakfast, and Sarah waited by the door for him. The dogs followed. As Dylan watched his little boy go, nearly swaggering with his newfound knowledge of fighting, the pride swelled him and a smile curled the corners of his mouth. He'd dreamed of this day since he first opened his dojo in Tennessee. A piece of his soul clicked into place, and there was a warm feeling of rightness in the world.

"Ye're wanting to make of him a warrior, then?" Sinann appeared to his left, visible and audible only to him. "Good for you."

Ciaran ran to take Sarah's hand, and Dylan avoided her gaze by turning to eye the distant dragoon as he spoke to Sinann. "I'm wanting to help him stay alive once he's grown and I can't protect him any more." As he spoke, the distant *Sassunach* turned his horse and proceeded on his patrol of Dylan's property, disappearing down the other side of the hills.

"As I said. It's a warrior ye're raising, who'll grow to protect himself and his people."

He cut the faerie a sharp glance, then turned to pick his staff up off the icy ground. "He's my only son, Tink. Probably the only one I'll ever have. I'm going to do my level best to make sure he doesn't end up cannon fodder for either the Jacobites or the English. Nor his sons, nor their sons." He poked a mound of snow with the staff. A whiff of cold wind blustered across his face and numbed the tip of his nose. He rubbed it warm.

"But the lass from the future said—"

"He won't die at Culloden." Dylan stabbed the ground again in punctuation, then started for the house.

She flew along behind him. "Ye cannae change history. You've said it yerself."

"My son can't be the only Ciaran Robert Matheson in the Highlands." He turned back toward Sinann and set the end of the staff hard into the ground. She touched down, crossed her arms, and tilted her head. "There are distant cousins in Sutherland we don't even know."

"They're nae in support of the cause. The lass said he would be a Jacobite. 'Twas in the book she read."

"We don't—" Dylan spotted something stuck in the ground, right behind the faerie, he hadn't noticed before. "Hey . . ."

He reached behind her. "Look, it's my old sword." Sinann turned and made an inarticulate noise of warning, but not quick enough to keep him from touching the sword. He pulled it from the frozen sod but regretted it instantly. The hilt was warm. *Too* warm. He recognized the feel of enchantment.

"Oh, no. Tink—" As the magic swept up his arm, he expected to black out and find himself in a different time and place. Several years before, he'd picked up a claymore and had been transported five thousand miles and nearly three hundred years from his home. His life in Tennessee had ended on that day. Alarm surged. "Tinkerbell, what did you—"

The magic filled him. Goose bumps rose all over him until he gasped, then the energy settled in his groin. "Whoa!" He set the tip of the sword in the ground and held himself up with his staff. Then, laughing, he said, "Hey, that felt pretty good. Do it again." He straightened and flexed his grip on the hilt, trying to get back that feeling.

Her voice was tinged with alarm. She shook her head and took several steps back. " 'Twas nae myself that did it."

Dylan shuddered and stood upright again. "What was it, then?"

She shook her head, worried. "I cannae say."

The sword was no longer warm, and he looked it over. It was his, all right—a rather old and worn Scottish broadsword with a heart-shaped steel basket hilt. "I lost this coming back from Perth about three years ago. Seumas and I were bringing casks of smuggled sherry, and we were attacked. In the middle of the fight on the wagon my sword went over the side, and I never saw it again."

"It's nae the one the English took from ye, then?"

He shook his head. "It's the other one. The one I . . . the one I won." It was the weapon he'd taken from the first man he'd killed in a sword fight, in which he'd carried only the small *sgian dubh* he wore under his arm. Now he switched the tip of the sword back and forth, then whirled it in a mulinette to the side, remembering the feel of it in his hand. It was a good weapon, despite its age, and had done well for him in the past. "Well, whoever sent this back, I'm glad they did."

"What was that ye felt when ye touched it?" Her frown made it plain she didn't like this. She crossed her arms as if afraid to touch the thing herself.

He shrugged. "A charge. Maybe sort of a thrill." *Orgasm* was the word he would have used, were he inclined to volunteer that sort of information to Sinann. Had the enchantment gone on much longer, it would have been obvious.

Sinann fidgeted, very agitated. "It isnae good. Someone powerful did this. One of the *Sidhe*, at the very least. Someone whose powers have not weakened as have mine."

Dylan grinned. "Someone more dangerous than yourself? God help us."

But Sinann didn't laugh, and that finally caught his attention. She said, "Oh, aye. Someone *far* more dangerous than myself."

Then it came to him. The wolf he'd dreamed of shortly before he'd lost this sword, which had been a faerie in disguise. He nearly groaned. "The Morrighan."

CHAPTER 3

"**B**itch!"

Barri Matheson ducked but was then blindsided by a slap from her husband's left. She reeled. "Ken, don't." He was drunk again, and there was no talking to him, but she tried anyway, even as she untangled her feet from the chair legs and tried to stand. "Please, stop." He picked his plate up from the dining table and threw it at her. The china made a low, musical tone as it bounced off her shoulder and hit the carpet. Food went everywhere.

"Dammit!" He rose and punched her face again with a closed fist. Her vision exploded in stars. Staggering as she retreated, she had a vague realization he was cornering her. A dodge to the side to get away from him, and he sidestepped with her, growling, herding her farther into the dining room, toward the kitchen.

She didn't even know what had set him off this time; he'd simply hauled off and clobbered her at supper. Now she was backed up against the china cabinet, cringing against it, trying to make herself as small a target as possible. Dishes in the cabinet chimed and clanged against each other as he attacked her again. The ugly smell of his supper he'd thrown at her made her retch. It was all over her, cold and sticky now as it dripped from her face and hair.

"Please . . . stop this . . . Ken!" She wept as he pummeled her back. Something snapped inside, and blinding pain shot through her entire torso. She screamed and collapsed onto the floor.

He finally stopped hitting her and stepped back, panting from exertion. Her own breathing was shallow, each breath like a knife in her chest. She remained on the floor, still as a rabbit, and hoped he would leave her alone now. If she could just stay here a moment and catch her breath, maybe the pain would go away. If he would just let her alone for a moment . . .

The doorbell rang, then there was pounding on the front door. Kenneth staggered away toward the table, saying, "Someone's at the door. Go answer it."

Weeping, Barri couldn't move. The pain was too much. Breathing hurt. She couldn't catch a full breath. Kenneth spun on her. "The *door!*" When she wouldn't look up, he came back, one fist cocked again. *"Answer the fucking door!"* She could only huddle on the floor, crying. Kenneth uttered a sound of disgust and went to collapse into his seat at the table. He threw back some more whiskey, then stared into the middle distance in a stupor for a moment. Then he reached for a piece of pot roast on the platter in the middle of the table.

The pounding on the door stopped. A moment later, Barri heard, "Good God!"

"Who let you in here?" Kenneth scowled at the intruder. He now had a mouthful of the pot roast, and his words were muffled.

"Mrs. Matheson! Are you all right?" It was Cody Marshall, six months pregnant, and she came to kneel next to Barri, balancing herself against the cabinet. "Come," she said, "Let's get out of here."

Barri shook her head, still huddled on her hands and knees. "I can't." She knew Kenneth wouldn't let her go, and if she tried to leave, he might hurt Cody. She took quick, shallow breaths, and still the pain was piercing. Cody tried to take her arm to help her up, but moving her arm hurt too much.

Cody said, "You're hurt."

Barri nodded. The smell of gravy in her hair was nauseating, and she tried to wipe it away. That only made it worse, with the gravy now all over her fingers.

"She fell," said Kenneth, though he surely knew nobody ever believed that anymore.

Cody held both her hands and said in a low, soft voice, "I'm taking you to the hospital."

"Can't." Barri shook her head, terrified of being talked into something she knew would be a mistake. She was afraid to leave the house. What if Kenneth didn't let her back in?

"You need to go." Cody held her unwieldy belly with one arm as she rose to a crouch, holding out her hand to Barri. "Let me help you into the car."

Each breath stabbed. Tears streamed down Barri's face. If she could just lie down for a while, she'd be all right. Kenneth would pass out soon. She would figure out what had set him off this time, then would avoid doing it anymore.

She stalled, speaking between shallow, panicky breaths. "Why . . . did you . . . come? Did you . . . find something?" Cody was a lifelong friend of her son, and for the past two years, since Dylan's disappearance, had been researching the Matheson ancestry. Specifically, she was looking for information about the Scottish highwayman for which Dylan had been named.

"Mrs. Matheson . . ." Cody took Barri's hand, but stopped pulling when she realized it was hurting her to move the arm.

What had brought Cody here? "Did you find something?"

"Yes, I found something. Now, come. I'll tell you if you'll let me take you to the hospital."

That moved Barri. Dylan's last wish before his trip to Scotland had been that she learn more about that "Black Dylan" fellow, or *Dilean Dubh*, as Cody said it in Gaelic. She'd never paid much attention to the rather lurid story of the Scottish namesake, but Dylan had seemed to think it terribly important. Now she and Cody thought of Black Dylan as a way of keeping in touch with her missing son. *Dead* son. Not missing. She knew he must be dead. It had been two years. He would have come back by now if he were able.

She struggled to her feet, each movement a jolt of pain. Kenneth rose from his chair. "Just you wait a minute, missy . . ." He took a step toward Cody, his arm cocked.

Without an instant of hesitation, Cody pulled a drawer in the cabinet, grabbed a steak knife, turned, and held him off with it. "Stop! Do not take another step!" The point of the blade was unwavering. She'd been one of

Dylan's students and held the knife as surely as a practice foil. Everyone in the room knew she understood how to use an edged weapon.

Kenneth froze, staring at it.

She said, "I'm taking your wife to the emergency room. You're not going to stop us. You're not going to *try* to stop us. If you attempt to keep us from leaving, I will put this knife in your throat."

"Go ahead." He shrugged, belligerent but afraid. He flinched, looking at her sideways. His fist clenched and unclenched. "Try to cut me. I'll kill you, bitch!"

"I've stabbed a man before. Don't think I'll hesitate to do it again." The tone in her voice was no-nonsense. Barri, breathless with alarm, was sure Cody meant exactly what she said. Half of her wished Kenneth would force it, and the other half was terrified of it. A small voice in the back of her mind wondered what man she'd stabbed, but the voice went ignored.

Kenneth backed down and sat again in the chair to sulk, muttering, "You're just like him."

Cody set the knife on the floor, out of Kenneth's reach, then turned to help Barri and muttered also, "I'll call that a compliment." Barri had to smile through her pain.

It was a struggle to make it to Cody's car. Kenneth yelled after them that they should leave, get the hell out of his house, and never come back. This was his favorite way to save face, to demand she do something she was about to do anyway, and pretend she was obeying. Usually it angered her, but this time she didn't care.

The drive to the hospital was an appalling adventure in pain. Barri spent the trip panting shallow, agonizing breaths and not getting nearly enough air. Leaning against the door, it was still impossible to keep from jarring as the car moved through the streets. She began to cough, and soon tasted blood in her mouth. Cody pulled up to the emergency entrance of the hospital and left the door of her car standing open as she went for help. Soon Barri was lifted onto a gurney by several strong men and rolled into the building.

Somewhere in the confusion and hurry, Cody disappeared. Barrie asked about her but was told to relax, and she never received a definite answer. She would have to wait to find out what Cody had learned about Black Dylan. Other things were more pressing. A nurse administered something for the pain with a needle. There were X rays, long hours of waiting, and a bit of sleep on the gurney in a dimmed hallway. Someone came to clean the gravy from her face and clothes, and her goopy hair took a good rinsing in a basin. It was a relief to not smell like a garbage pail anymore.

Eventually it was determined a broken rib had made a small tear in one lung. She was admitted and taken to a room, a private one with flowered wallpaper, soft linens, and fluffy pillows. There she slept, in fits, waking frequently through the night to think and listen to the rattling of the room heater by the window.

The place was strange. Too warm. Everything around her had a surreal quality to it. Colors were different. Shapes were not quite right. Gradually, as she thought about going home, she realized nothing familiar would be quite the same ever again. The security she'd clung to for so many years had turned out to be an illusion. There was no security. There never had been and probably never would be.

Images of Kenneth turned in her mind, a constant nudge that kept her awake in spite of drugs and exhaustion. Kenneth with a closed fist or a handy blunt object. Kenneth railing at her for things she couldn't control, or ridiculing her just for fun. The past thirty-five years had been filled with those times, and the sober moments when she could glimpse the real Kenneth Matheson had become fewer and farther between with each passing year.

The hours passed slowly. The moon outside the window rose above the frame and disappeared. The darkness seemed eternal. The world empty. She may have dozed, but couldn't be certain. Her limbs were stiff with tension and inactivity, causing her to shift restlessly for relief.

When the new day arrived, the sun made bright patches on the ceiling as it rose on the horizon. It warmed Barri's face, and its brightness made her lower her lashes against it. Alone in the hospital room, she reflected on the world and her place in it. For decades she'd awakened next to Kenneth in the morning, afraid to disturb him lest he wake up with a hangover and a mouthful of sharp, ugly words. It had been years since she'd dared to go to bed before he was asleep or passed out, for it left her vulnerable to attack. More than once he'd taken a belt to her for the effrontery of sleeping before he was ready for bed.

Even worse, a small part of her believed Kenneth had chased Dylan away—that her son had gone to Scotland to flee his father. There he'd met his death at the hands of robbers. After that, it was a short leap of logic to feel Kenneth had killed their son, and as she realized she felt that way she also realized she could never forgive her husband. She'd forgiven everything else he'd done, but losing Dylan was the one thing she couldn't bear. Now she was at the end of her endurance.

She'd lived far too long fearing each day. Today, as the sun rose on a day more beautiful than any she could remember, she realized she wanted to be a part of a world where sunrise was a good thing.

Cody arrived at midmorning. She poked her head in the doorway. "Hello?"

"Come in." Barri began scooting to sit up, then remembered the buttons to adjust the bed. She fumbled to find the control and began the tedious process of bringing the bed to a sitting position. She picked at and arranged her hair in an effort to be presentable, but it was hopeless. No shower, no fresh makeup, no comb—she wanted to hurry home to clean up, but Kenneth might be there. She couldn't face him yet. There was too much else to do first.

But Cody, bless her heart, came into the room carrying a plastic bag from the drugstore. "I brought a few things I thought you might need."

Inside the bag were a hand mirror, a new hairbrush, some bobby pins, and a lipstick. The shade wasn't exactly Barri's, but it was close enough, and she could hardly complain. What a sweet girl Cody was! A pang struck her as she wished once again Dylan had married her. If only he had been married, he might not have gone to Scotland . . .

Barri shook her head to take herself off that self-destructive train of thought. "If only" never helped anything.

Cody eased into the chair next to the bed and sighed as she took the load off her feet while Barri set to brushing out her hair. There was a tiny glob of dried gravy still in it, and she picked at the spot until it was all out and rolled up neatly into a little ball. She placed the nasty wad carefully aside on the nightstand. When her hair was all brushed out, she readied it for a bun at the back of her head. Tying it up was the only way to bring this black-and-silver mess under control without curlers. She fussed and clucked at it as strands escaped and hung in wispy corkscrews over her forehead.

Cody said, "Don't worry about it. You look fine."

Barri sighed and continued to pull her hair straight. "It's so disorganized. It's so . . ." She thrust some pins into it so it would stay and examined the result in the mirror, which she moved around her head to see from different angles. "It's undignified."

"Undignified?"

"I'm too old to wear my hair down anymore. When I was young I did, but now I would look silly. I just can't be comfortable if my appearance isn't neat." Barri opened the lipstick and applied the color expertly, though it was a new tube and not yet worn to the shape of her lips. "I learned a long time ago that if you look respectable, people will treat you that way. Then, pretty soon you feel as good as you look." She slipped the cover back onto the lipstick tube and smiled brightly at her visitor.

Cody said nothing, but sat back with a thoughtful gaze. Her eyes narrowed, which made Barri's smile falter. Then Cody said, "Dylan once told me you used to be a hippie."

Barri smiled again and flushed with a mixture of nostalgia and embarrassment her past had been revealed. "Oh, that was so long ago! But, yes, that's what they called us. When I was young. Back when I first met Kenneth, and we were young and rebellious, and . . . well, silly." She folded her hands on her lap, around the lipstick tube.

Cody's eyes went wide. "You think that was silly? I think it's fascinating. I think it would have been exciting to live back then."

Barri chuckled. She'd heard before from young folks who thought it must have been exciting to have lived a life free of convention. "We were out to change the world." It was an apology for failure.

"And you did." Cody sounded sincere, but Barri shook her head.

"We thought we could change human nature. What we discovered was that throwing away the rules only made for confusion, hurt feelings, and unhappiness. So new rules fell into place. Some of them worked, some didn't. We grew and we learned, and instead of changing the world, the world changed us."

A shiver ran through her as she recalled those years before Dylan had come and she and Kenneth had then married. It was difficult to explain to Cody the terror of realizing how irresponsible everyone around her had been. For some of their friends, the old value systems were eventually replaced by new ones, and that was all right. But many people she had known rejected all standards, sneering at those who lived by rules of any kind. For several years she and Kenneth had lived in chaos. Friends died of overdoses of heroin, or never quite came back from trips on LSD, or simply lived in self-inflicted poverty, accomplishing nothing.

During that time she and Kenneth had lived in his van, sleeping in the cold, eating bad food—or no food at all—moving from place to place in a cloud of pot smoke. It had been exciting to meet new people and see new places, but after a while she realized her life was filled with people she didn't know, who drifted in and out of her existence like a bad TV signal.

Then, in the fall of 1969, she'd learned she was pregnant, and suddenly rebellion for its own sake seemed like a bad idea. That was when they'd finally come home to Tennessee, married, and Kenneth had gone to work for his father.

Cody's eager face made it clear she wanted to know about those days. But Barri had no wish, after more than thirty years, to speak of them. Instead, trying not to be too depressing, she mentioned the one thing she'd done that interested everyone. "You might not believe this, but we went to Woodstock." As she spoke, she fiddled with the lipstick tube, turning it end to end in her fingers.

Cody giggled. "Dylan told me. He also told me he was conceived there."

Barri's cheeks burned at that, and her gaze went to the lipstick. The blush crept down her neck and under the hospital gown. "Yes. Well—"

There was a twinkle in Cody's eye as she touched her fingertips one by one as if counting on them and said, "If one does the math, it really is easy to believe Dylan was conceived on a blanket in the woods—"

"If you must know," Barri's voice lowered and she glanced at the door in hopes that nobody was listening, "it was on a mattress in the back of Kenneth's van." The memory of that weekend made her smile in spite of herself. "He was so handsome. He had a beard back then, and his eyes were so beautiful they just made my heart race. They were so blue. . . ." Her voice went even softer. "I loved him so much. . . ."

"You weren't married yet."

Barri straightened, struggling to recover the dignity she felt slipping away. "Of course not. Married people don't go traipsing off to rock concerts for an entire weekend. At least, not back then they didn't. We didn't think we were the type of people who got married and settled down in a bourgeois establishment household. But . . . well, once Dylan made himself known, everything began to look a lot different. Suddenly it was important to have food every day, and to have a place to sleep every night. I couldn't raise a baby in that van. So we forfeited our status as rebels and got married." She thought for a moment, then added, "We were fated."

There was a tense silence, and Cody said softly, "Mrs. Matheson—"

Barri brightened and said, "That's quite enough about me. So, how are you this morning, Cody? You look like you might not be feeling well."

Cody sighed, then replied, "Oh, I'm just a mite wore out. I'll be glad when this baby comes."

Barri chuckled. "You'll be a great deal more glad of it by the time he does finally come. You've got, what, two or three months left? I remember with Dylan, I thought he would never get here."

"That's about how I feel now. More than two months . . . I don't know if I can stand it." For a moment she watched Barri fiddle with her hair some more, tucking in some ends, then she said, "Are you feeling any better?"

"I'll be all right. They gave me a drug to help the inflammation from the tear in my lung, but other than that, there's not much they can do for a broken rib. They'll be sending me home today, most likely."

Cody looked over at her. "Are you going home?"

Barri laid her hands in her lap and stared at them. "I can't."

A sigh of what might have been relief escaped Cody. "You shouldn't. I know he's hurt you before. Dylan told me he's put you in the hospital twice before."

It had been more than twice. There had been a third time Dylan didn't know about, and Barri didn't tell Cody now. Instead, she said, "I keep hoping he'll realize what he's doing to me—to our marriage."

"You can't believe he doesn't know what he's doing to you." Cody's eyes glinted with anger. She was a feisty one. As a little girl Cody had always been right there by Dylan's side, slashing pirates with plastic cutlasses or mowing down soldiers with imaginary machine guns.

Barri said, "Not when he drinks. He doesn't know what he's doing when he drinks."

"That's not an excuse. He shouldn't drink if he can't do it without hurting people."

"He can't help himself."

But there was a silence as Cody's eyes narrowed.

Barri sighed, and a jolt of pain ran through her back. "Yes, I know. I need to leave him." Saying it out loud made her go cold. She ran her thumb along the lipstick tube, pressing hard against the cold, ridged metal.

Cody leaned forward in her chair, cradling her belly in her hands. "Yes. You do. You also need to have him arrested for assault."

That brought a small gasp and more pain. "Cody, no!"

"I'm serious, Mrs. Matheson. What he did is a criminal offense. He belongs in a jail."

"They wouldn't put him in jail." The thought of filing a complaint against her own husband and having him arrested was mind-boggling. She'd never dared to raise her voice to him, lest he become even more angry and violent. If she were to put him in *jail* . . .

"He'd kill me." She trembled at the knowledge it was not an exaggeration. "Or he'd kill himself."

Cody sat up. "Has he threatened suicide?"

"He tried it once." Barri hurried to elaborate when she saw the narrow look of skepticism in Cody's eyes again. "Yes, he did. Many years ago, when Dylan was very little. We were . . . well, we were fighting." Her ears warmed at having to say it aloud, but she laid her fingers on her chin and continued. "He punched me. He caught me just right on my chin, and I was knocked out. When I woke up, he was passed out on the couch. There was glass all over the floor, from the picture over the mantel, and in the middle of the mess on the floor was the revolver we kept. Well, it was his, actually. I never wanted a gun in the house, because Dylan was only three at the time, and I was terrified he would find the thing and hurt himself with it. So I'd taken the bullets out of it. Kenneth didn't know it. I expect when he tried to shoot himself with it and discovered he couldn't, he threw it against the wall and passed out."

"What did he say when he woke up?"

Barri shook her head. "Nothing. I think he was ashamed of trying to kill himself. He never mentioned the gun again, and I got rid of it. And I thank God every day for giving me the courage to have emptied the gun. He would be dead now if not for that. I couldn't have him arrested. It might kill him."

"When you leave him, what if he comes after you? Wouldn't it be safer for you if he were in jail?"

Barri hadn't thought of that. But Cody was right. It was certain he'd be angry. Then a horrible feeling of being trapped closed in as she thought of something else. "They couldn't keep him in jail forever. He'd be let out eventually, and then he'd be that much more angry with me."

Cody sighed and slumped in the chair. "What're you going to do? You can't go back to him."

It was true. If she returned home, eventually her husband would beat her again. It was entirely possible he would one day beat her badly enough to kill her. Slowly, in a very low voice as if saying it too loud would bring down the wrath of God, she said, "I suppose I should call the police."

Cody replied in an equally soft voice, "Yes."

Cold fear crept in as Barri considered what she was about to do. Cody handed her the phone for her to call the police.

Later that day, Kenneth was arrested and charged with battery but released on bail immediately. Barri also called a lawyer and had him file for divorce that day. As soon as she was released from the hospital, Cody and her husband, Raymond, drove her to the house to pack some things.

Barri was terrified. Though she gripped her arms with both hands, the trembling wouldn't stop. She took deep breaths as she mounted the porch steps, but she couldn't quit shaking. Cody was beside her, and Raymond was close behind.

Raymond was not a large man nor a skilled fighter like Dylan, but he was a steady sort—no nonsense. When Barri let them in the front door with her key, he entered the house first and placed himself between her and Kenneth, who was coming down the main stairs in the foyer.

"Get out!" said Kenneth, snarling. He didn't seem drunk, but was flushed with rage, and his blue eyes were rimmed with red. He wore a faded T-shirt over an old pair of jeans, and his feet were bare. A brief concern flickered across Barri's mind that he'd gone to jail and been seen in public dressed like that, but she reminded herself she didn't care anymore what he did in public. He wouldn't be her husband much longer, and what he did no longer reflected on her.

"I'm here to pick up some things," she said. Her voice was as firm as she could make it, but it trembled nevertheless.

He fairly vibrated with fury and came at her, pointing toward the door. "I said, get out! Get the hell out of here, or I'll throw you out!"

"Kenneth—"

"Out!"

"Mr. Matheson," said Raymond as he stepped forward and placed a restraining hand on Kenneth's arm, "stand aside, please." Kenneth threw off the hand, and Raymond continued, "Mrs. Matheson is going to pack some clothes, and you're going to let her." His voice was firm and even, and lower than his normal speaking voice. "If you don't let her, you'll go to jail again. Only this time the bail might not be so affordable."

"Fucking pansy." Kenneth spat the words into Raymond's face, close enough and vehement enough to make him blink, but he didn't make any further threat. Kenneth stood where he was, an ominous but unmoving presence, as Barri, Cody, and Raymond passed him on the stairs.

Barri felt cold, and Kenneth's infuriated, red-rimmed eyes shook her to the core. She strode quickly into the bedroom, where she pulled her suitcase from the closet and began filling it.

"Papers, Mrs. Matheson," Cody reminded her. "Don't forget your important papers. Birth certificate, passport, titles on vehicles, insurance policies, that sort of thing."

Barri nodded and continued packing clothing.

Kenneth, downstairs, shouted obscenities at a safe distance, calling names and denigrating her as a person and her performance as a wife for the past thirty years. Raymond stood by the bedroom door, silent as a sentry at Buckingham Palace. Barri fought back tears as Kenneth cut her with no knife.

"You killed Dylan!" he screamed. "You clung to the poor kid until he had to run away to Europe to get away from you!"

Poor kid? The last time Kenneth had been in the same room with Dylan, he had called his son a "little prick." But though Barri knew what Kenneth said wasn't true, a small part of her accepted the accusation. Her heart clenched and guilt choked her. She took deep breaths as she secured the suitcase and tried to lift it. Pain stabbed her, and she gasped.

"Raymond . . ." Cody called, and her husband came in to lift the case.

"The office is downstairs," said Barri, and Raymond led the way past Kenneth on the stairs.

"Bitch!" Kenneth was still in his spot on the bottom step, and when he saw Barri was headed for the office, he let out an inarticulate roar and shouted, "Nuh-uh! No you don't!"

He made a grab for Barri. Raymond intervened and pushed Kenneth away so he stumbled against the foyer wall, then set the suitcase on the floor to ready for another assault. He put up his fists as if he were in a boxing ring.

"I'm serious, Mr. Matheson. I will call the police if you come near us again." Raymond's voice was beginning to show strain. Having no inclination to fight, he was facing an angry, self-righteous, and violent man. Everyone present knew Raymond was ill equipped to defend himself, and it was plain to Barri only Kenneth's cowardice and doubt kept the situation from erupting into a brawl.

Not waiting to see what else Kenneth would do, Barri ducked into the office. The oak file cabinet was jammed full of three decades' worth of accumulation generated by marriage and parenthood: warranties and manuals for household appliances, tax records, bank records, bills, and certificates of ownership. She pulled a bank statement, savings book, the title for the green SUV in her name, and her birth certificate and passport.

As her fingers plucked the birth certificate from the file, she found Dylan's behind it. Without a moment of hesitation and with trembling fingers, she took it and the hospital birth record, with its tiny black footprint. Then she reached into another drawer for a manila envelope and slipped the papers into it.

Kenneth was still braying at Raymond as she returned to the foyer. Without any further exchange, the three left the house.

Raymond took the suitcase to his own car, and Cody accompanied Barri to the SUV.

"You're not taking that car, Barri!" Kenneth screamed at the top of his lungs for the entertainment of the entire neighborhood of tract mansions surrounding the antebellum Matheson house. He declined to venture down the porch steps, where Raymond might engage him in the yard, but rather shouted out across the circle drive, waving his arms and swaying so much it looked as if he must fall down the porch steps.

Barri cringed. Why did he have to make it so plain to everyone around what was happening? She fumbled with the keys, trying to put them in the door lock of the SUV, but her hands shook too much. She dropped them, and when she picked them up, she dropped them again.

Cody came. "Here, maybe I should drive." She held out her hand for the keys.

Barri nodded, relinquished the keys, and hurried to the other side of the car, away from Kenneth. As Cody drove her away from the house that had been her home for over thirty years, Barri did not look back. She swallowed her tears.

The sun was setting when they arrived at Dylan's dojo. He'd once made his living teaching martial arts and fencing here. Raymond set the suitcase on the pavement by the front door as Cody asked Barri, "Will you be all right now? I could stay for a while if you like."

Barri stared at the double glass doors, unable to reply.

Cody said, "If you think it's going to be too much—"

"No." Barri finally said, her voice shaky, "I've got to do this by myself. It is too much, but I really think I'd rather be alone."

"You'll need help taking the bag inside."

Barri shook her head. "I want to just stand here for a moment. I'll be all right."

"Call me if you need anything. And if he comes, call the police."

Again, Barri nodded. Cody hugged her, carefully, then she and Raymond left her alone.

In his will, Dylan had bequeathed to her—only her, not his father—the building and most of the martial arts school it housed. His former employee, Ronnie, had received a sizeable piece of the school and now ran it, but the apartment above the offices had been unoccupied since Dylan's death. Now Barri gazed at the words painted on the storefront windows on either side of the glass doors: Matheson Fencing and Martial Arts. The letters were painted in red and gold, Dylan's name the largest in an arc over the others.

Barri's heart clenched. It was a struggle to keep her composure. For two years she'd avoided this place. Though Ronnie still taught classes here, the apartment had gone untouched, and as far as Barri knew, nobody had even been upstairs. Now she trembled at what lay ahead. Seeing the dojo without Dylan here, without his voice echoing from the mirrored walls, without his life filling the place, she knew would be unbearable. But it was time. She had no place else to go. She went inside, dragging her suitcase by many short tugs.

The sun was almost down, shooting orange streaks and black shadows through the blinds in the windows of the storefront. The orange light dimmed as the glass door shushed closed and the panic bar clanked shut behind her. Barri looked around. The exercise floor and black, angular weight machines stood beneath fluorescent shop lights suspended from a cathedral ceiling. The place had a slight whiff of the public showers in the back, mildewy and dank, beneath the polish on the hardwood floors and lubricating oil on the exercise machines.

She avoided looking at herself in the wall mirrors, for she didn't want to see in the reflection of her own eyes what she was feeling. Leaving her luggage on the floor by the door, she went to the stairs that led to the apartment above, built on a balcony over the offices.

Up here, dust lay in a thick, untouched layer over everything. *Ashes to ashes; dust to dust.* Dylan's things seemed forlorn, their master long gone. A dusty throw pillow lay on the floor, and she picked it up to restore it to its place on the dusty couch. A thin cloud rose and hung in the air, motes drifting lazily. A few kung fu magazines lay on an end table, men on the covers engaged in dramatic flying kicks. The corners of some of the pages had curled in the varying humidity, and one of the covers had curled completely into a tube. Against one wall was austere steel shelving, containing Dylan's television and stereo, cluttered with a number of music CDs and tapes. Against the opposite wall were another few shelves, but these were wooden and filled with books. The titles were all nonfiction: mostly history, especially Scottish history.

Barri's chest tightened more. Breathing became very painful. She swallowed hard but couldn't get the knot from her throat.

The rest of the apartment was as spare as the steel shelving. Aside from the few books, magazines, and CDs, there was little to tell who her son really had been. Over the low wall of the balcony she could see the exercise floor, the equipment, racks of wooden sticks and practice swords, and display cases filled with old-looking swords that were just for display. Down there had been Dylan's life. The teacher was the man he'd been— the man she'd raised.

She went to the bedroom, which was even more spare than the living room. White walls bore no decoration of any kind. The sheets on his bed were plain, pale blue, and the comforter navy. A blue towel was draped over the single wooden chair by the bathroom door.

The window had no curtains, only a yellowed, cracked shade. A few shirts and jeans hung in the closet alongside one charcoal gray suit. Some shoes lay scattered on the closet floor, including one old, alarmingly worn-out pair of leather high-tops that were covered with something black. The heels were soaked in it, and the toes bore spots and splashes.

He'd been gone a long time. This place, his things, seemed to have given up waiting for him to come home. The room felt desolate. She sat on the bed and held a blue-cased feather pillow to her chest.

It smelled like him. God help her, she could smell her son on the pillowcase. Stunned, she held it to her face and took as deep a breath as she could. Memories swarmed. She closed her eyes and could see him again. Tall and athletic, with kind eyes like his father's had been before the whiskey destroyed them.

She remembered how protective he'd been, how the last time they'd talked he'd tried to convince her to leave Kenneth. It had seemed a silly, impossible idea at the time. But now she wished she could have that day to do over, for she would say yes, she would leave Kenneth, if only Dylan would not go to Scotland. Anything to make him stay. If only . . .

She brought to mind the time when Dylan was a boy. He'd begged her for kung fu lessons. He'd insisted it be kung fu and not karate, because kung fu was what that man in the movies did. And the swords! The light in Dylan's eyes when he'd talked of this sword or that, and she couldn't have known a saber from a foil, but she'd loved to listen to him explain it all because it made him happy.

She remembered his soccer games when he had been littler, all the years watching him play and sharing in his excitement when he won.

She remembered Christmas long before—the year when he had still believed in Santa Claus and sat up most of Christmas Eve to catch the jolly old elf.

She remembered the day he was born, so small and helpless. When the joy of his safe arrival had been tempered with the awful knowledge that by bringing him into the world she was responsible for everything that would ever happen to him. Each scraped knee had been her fault, each disappointment. And, ultimately, his death.

Curled up on her son's bed, she hugged his pillow to her face and remembered until she slept.

CHAPTER 4

Dylan went to his house and shoved the broadsword deep into the thick straw and bracken of the roof thatching with the others. He would have to make another scabbard for it, since he'd long since sold the original. But it would be simple enough to sew a leather scabbard to slip onto his baldric, as he had for the cavalry saber. Easier, really, since the broadsword wasn't curved. He went inside his house.

By the fire, Sarah bent to tend the iron pot filled with steaming, gray parritch. It was a large pot, to provide breakfast for two adults, three active boys, and a small girl. Butter and salt waited on the table to flavor the oatmeal, but there was no milk because the cows, ewes, and Ginny the goat were still breeding and wouldn't have milk for a couple of months yet.

Little Sìle ran to her father, and he swept her into the air to make her giggle. Then, cradling her in his arms, he growled loudly into her tummy, shaking his head until she was breathless with screaming laughter and kicking her little legs as hard as she could. Then when he let her down onto the floor, she held up her arms and jumped up and down, making begging noises for him to do it again. He obliged once more, then told her no when she begged him a third time.

Sarah's sons, Eóin and Gregor, who were eleven and nine, were sitting at the table, arguing about something concerning the new school.

The Laird had just that year managed to entice a Catholic tutor from Aberdeen to teach in Ciorram. The practice of Catholicism was against the law, and especially the teaching of it was frowned upon by the Crown. It was very risky for the teacher if Major Bedford at the garrison should catch wind of the new school. But many, including the teacher, thought the risk worthwhile, for their religion demanded it.

To Dylan, raised in twentieth-century America, the simple solution might have been to hire a Protestant tutor and demand he provide the children with a secular education while religious tutoring was accomplished at home. But even Dylan realized in these times there was no education separate from religious schooling, and teachers never lost an opportunity to denigrate religion that was not their own. In recent years an organization called The Society in Scotland for Propagating Christian Knowledge was making it difficult for Catholic families to educate their children in public schools. Using textbooks titled *Dangers of Popery*, *Protestant Resolution*, and *Funeral of the Mass*, they gave Catholic families a lose/lose choice between an actively anti-Catholic education and no education at all.

Luckily, Ciorram's remote, mountainous location and its almost wholly Catholic population, coupled with the Laird's allegiance with other Catholic lairds and his own inherited jurisdiction, made it possible for Mass, wedding, and funeral rites to take place in Ciorram without serious disruption from the soldiers. Other Catholic schools were in operation under the protection of some Catholic Lairds, such as the Duke of Gordon, but in this tiny glen, under the thumb of King George's army, the practice of Catholicism was not without danger. Father Turnbull risked arrest and deportation each time he traveled to and from the glen, carrying rosary, holy water, and other accoutrements of his vocation. His comings and goings were always under cloak of night or deception.

Therefore, the new tutor kept as far away from the Redcoats as possible, for he risked the same punishment. School sessions took place in the castle rather than the church, and even in that stronghold the soldiers were entitled to search and root out evidence of illegal activity. They were quite happy to do so, for remote Ciorram was a boring post, and harassment was diversion.

So the classroom was a windowless space behind the pantry over the kitchen. Where there had once been three cisterns for rainwater, there were now two, and some tables and chairs had been set up in the dank, mildewy area. Though harassment was low-key and haphazard, it was persistent. Along with their lessons in reading and mathematics, the children learned lessons in hating the *Sassunaich*.

While Eóin and Gregor discussed their lessons, Ciaran was trying to interrupt to brag about his kung fu lesson. Eóin was unimpressed, probably because he'd taken such lessons with the men on Sunday nights since he was eight. He ignored Ciaran, who wasn't nearly old enough for school and therefore not part of the conversation. But the little one persisted. Gregor went so far as to whack Ciaran on the head to get him to shut up.

"Hey!" Dylan reached over to grab Gregor's arm. "You want to hit someone, pick on a boy your own size. Only a coward hits little kids."

Gregor frowned at him and yanked his arm away. Ciaran stood to the side, frowning and silent as he rubbed the back of his head.

Dylan jabbed a finger at Gregor. "All right, boy. Be that way. But if you hit him again, I'll tell the whole glen that the only fight you can win is with a four-year-old."

After that he was ignored, but Gregor refrained from hitting Ciaran again.

Coinneach Matheson stuck his head in the door to announce his presence and call the dogs. The energetic teenager took Dylan's bear-head staff from beside the door and ran with the dogs to the enclosure where the flock awaited. There he would nudge the sheep out to whatever grazing might be found that day on the hills of Dylan's land.

Most Highland farmers kept their sheep housed in the byre with the cattle all winter, but some of the Ciorram men had begun to appreciate Dylan's success with his outdoor sheep enclosure. Others were now keeping their flocks outside through the winter, allowing their sheep to grow a heavier fleece in the cold. Also, though it required spending time in the cold themselves, they supplemented winter fodder by putting the sheep out to graze whenever possible. Much to the surprise of everyone in the glen, in three winters there had been no losses from the cold, and wool production had increased significantly.

Dylan took the chamber pot outside to empty it on the manure pile at the far corner of his dooryard. After flinging the waste then shaking out the pot, he muttered a curse, hawked an enormous wad, and spat on the huge mound of manure, garbage, and dead leaves as he had every morning since the day he'd avenged the murder of his wife. Then he walked to the burn to rinse the pot, and returned it to the stool behind the curtain.

By now the fire on his hearth was high and the parritch nearly ready, and the room warm enough for Dylan to remove his coat. He hung it on its peg by the door and set about rearranging his plaid to be a mite more presentable. He needed to bring fodder to the hungry cattle in his byre—they were already stomping and lowing for it—but he sat for a moment with his daughter, listening to her fractured nonsense chatter as she pretended to talk, with the boys arguing in the background.

Sìle favored him in looks, as did her brother, with dark hair and blue eyes. But unlike her brother, she also showed a goodly amount of her mother. Her smile, lit up by a fine row of baby teeth, would one day echo Cait's. Also like her mother, her skin was so pale as to show blue veins here and there, and she had the redness of lip that ran among Cait's female relatives. It was anybody's guess, though, where the curliness of her hair had come from. Since nobody in the glen and nobody in Dylan's immediate family back in Tennessee had such a mass of corkscrew curls, Dylan figured it must be someone distant on his side.

They sat at the table for breakfast, the boys perched along the bench and Dylan and Sarah in chairs at either end. Dylan sat Sìle on his knee while they ate, because she was too little to see into her bowl if she sat on the bench and that made for frequent accidents. Also, attending to Sìle gave him an excuse to not look into Sarah's heart-struck eyes across the table. It wasn't his fault the woman was so in love, and certainly not his fault he couldn't return the devotion, but he somehow felt guilty for it anyway. The boys' chatter covered the lack of conversation between the adults. Dylan ate quickly.

After breakfast he rose from the table and tied a linen kerchief around his forehead to keep the wind outside from blowing his hair around his face during the day's work. Though he supposed he could wear his hair short if he wanted, he'd never much cared for very short hair and in any case preferred to fit in with the other clansmen who would think him strange for too-short hair. Also, shaggy locks tended to keep his ears warmer than without. He did, however, keep his hair only collar length and his beard more neatly trimmed than any other in the glen. Too much hair was a pain in the ass to comb and clean, nits being what they were and keeping clean such a laborious job.

He pulled his coat back on, then fed the kine in the byre with straw from the recent threshing and hauled water from the burn for them. He looked at the sack of milled oats, hefted it, and decided to hold off threshing more. In a few weeks there would be milking to do, and that would be his job. Sarah would make the cheese and butter and take home for her labor a portion of what she made, to consume or trade as needed.

Dylan put that out of his mind, though, as the memory of Cait humming a light tune while she churned butter by the fire rose to mind. He was unwilling to dwell on Sarah taking over more of Cait's work, and so shook his head and went on with his own.

Having finished the daily chores, he lifted his pitchfork, wooden shovel, and heavy mallet from their pegs on the wall and went back outside for the winter field work. He threw the tools into his two-wheeled wooden cart, then hitched one of his garrons to it. The white, pony like horse was fractious this morning, having had little to do since the harvest. Stamping and tossing his head, he then tried to take a bite out of Dylan's thigh. But Dylan dodged, bopped the garron's fuzzy nose with the back of his hand, and spoke to him in low, soothing Gaelic until the horse calmed. Then he led the garron and the cart to a spot by the manure pile and began digging with the shovel to throw the rotted refuse into the cart.

It was an enormous pile, a year's worth, and it stank horribly as gases were released from beneath layers of compost. The first year he'd done this, he'd nearly passed out while digging, and now was careful to step away for fresh air whenever nausea rose or the world went fuzzy.

Every so often he would come upon a beef or mutton bone, and would pause in his work to set the piece on the hard ground at his feet. With the mallet he pounded the crumbling bones to powder and tiny chunks, then shoveled them into the cart with the rest of the fertilizer.

The cart was nearly full, and a deep dent made in the pile, when Dylan's shovel encountered something that broke with a hollow *pock* sound. He grunted. *There it is.* With a hard shove, he dug out the broken object and tossed it onto the ground. It rolled, then wobbled before going still. A human skull, its forehead caved in.

Connor Ramsay's skull, to be precise, which for Dylan cast doubt on the humanity of the thing. Ramsay had been Cait's first husband and was also the man who had murdered her.

Sinann appeared, perched on the side rails of the cart. She'd probably been watching, waiting for this. Over the years, Dylan had become accustomed to being spied on and so was not surprised by the sudden arrival of the white faerie. She said, "You should have thrown the Whig dandy in the bog and been done with it."

Dylan shook his head. "He'd just be dug up later by someone cutting peats. The way those bogs preserve dead things, anyone digging him up would have recognized him. I couldn't have that." The skull was darkened, but showed a graininess that indicated it was soft.

"Nae man would blame ye for the killing. They'd have done the same, had they known."

"Yeah, and then they would call my children bastard because Cait's first husband was still alive while we were married." He stared down at the broken skull, its mandible hanging from one side by hard, black remnants of flesh. It seemed as if Ramsay were screaming, driven mad by seven months of burial in excrement. It was all he'd deserved, and the thought made Dylan's heart a bit lighter.

"No man kent it. You had no way to know he was alive."

He leaned on his shovel and tilted his head at her. "That surely wouldn't have mattered. The children would still be declared illegitimate and myself a criminal and an adulterer. Iain Mór has been none too thrilled with me since Cait died, and with the marriage vacated and the children illegitimate, he could claim them to raise them himself."

"He doesnae wish it."

That brought a laugh, and Dylan straightened. "His wife does. Una wants to raise those kids herself. She's said more than once she doesn't think I can do it by myself. Being 'just a man,' and all."

Sinann had to nod, conceding the point. "There's truth in that, lad. Ye are just a man."

Dylan's eyes narrowed.

The faerie hurried to add, "It willnae be easy to convince Lady Matheson of yer competence."

He grunted, then leaned on his shovel again, toward Sinann, his voice lowered lest he be caught talking to the invisible faerie, and continued, "And then there's Father Turnbull. He'd have had a hissy fit over me having married a woman whose husband was still alive, and quite possibly he'd have excommunicated me. And the children."

"He wouldnae!"

His head tilted, questioning, "Wouldn't he, though?" On reflex he took a look around for the priest, though he knew Turnbull was nowhere in the parish. Speaking of the devil made him nervous. He turned back to the compost heap and began picking out the rest of Ramsay's skeleton. "I think he'd leap on the opportunity to kick me out of the church." Which, in this glen, was tantamount to forcing him from the clan. "He's been giving me the hairy eyeball since he came to the Highlands." Dylan looked slantways at the faerie. "He hears tell I talk to invisible demons."

Sinann giggled, then made a disgusted noise at what Turnbull might do. "Let him do what he will. The clan wouldnae turn their backs on ye."

"Nope, I've got to do better than just not be shunned if I'm going to help the clan through the next uprising." A femur landed next to the skull.

Sinann's eyes lit up, and she fluttered a few feet off the cart. "Ye've decided to change history, then? You're ready to save yer people?"

Patiently, Dylan reiterated what was beginning to feel like a litany. "No, Sinann, history can't be changed. But there are things that must be done, and Artair isn't going to do them. He's going to inherit the lairdship from his brother one day, and when he does the first thing he'll do is let out a blood-curdling war cry and lead the clan right into the teeth of the *Sassunaich*. If the Mathesons are meant to continue living in Glen Ciorram, it won't happen by Artair's wise leadership. I've got to do whatever I can to keep the clan and my children safe."

The faerie settled once again on the side of the cart, her thin arms crossed over her chest.

Dylan shrugged and continued, "And, besides, even if the clan wouldn't condemn me for killing Ramsay, there's the issue of what the Crown would have to say on it if the truth were known."

"But Bedford watched you kill him, and he's said naught to the Crown, nor to anyone else. He has just as much reason to keep Ramsay's true death a secret, seeing as he's the one what staged the official one two years before."

"Which is the only thing that's keeping him from arresting me for it." His patience was running thin now, and tension crept into his voice. "He'd then have to explain to the Crown how I managed to murder a traitor to the Crown who had supposedly died in the Major's custody. Neither of us wants anyone to know how Ramsay really died, and don't think I'm not boggled by the irony of sharing a secret with that asshole."

Dylan shook his head again and muttered, "Wouldn't he just love to catch me on something else, though." He stepped back and hauled off with the mallet, then swung. The skull flattened. Splinters of bone flew. Another swing, and the rotting skull became stinking brown-and-white mush.

"It doesnae bother you to have his body give sustenance to the fields in which you grow food for your children?"

"Nope. He's nothing more than a couple pounds of chemicals now. Nothing more nor less than the shit I spread on those fields."

"And if his ghost should trouble ye?"

That gave Dylan pause, and he set the head of his mallet on the ground. He believed in ghosts, just as he now believed in faeries; he'd seen the ghost of the white dog, for which the castle, *Tigh a' Mhadaidh Bhàin*, got its name. But he shrugged and said, "Ramsay is in hell. Far away from here." He then knelt and sifted through the mess to find the teeth.

"*Och*, he's taking trophies now." Sinann wrinkled her small nose.

"Nope. The teeth won't crush, and they're recognizable as human. I'd rather not be plowing them up again year after year, so I'm going to throw them into the loch. I don't want to see them ever again." He counted out twenty-seven teeth, most of them with black cavities of varying size, and one root with the entire crown rotted off. His tongue absently felt of the gap where he'd had one of his own teeth extracted by the blacksmith a few years before. Then it touched a jagged spot on the other side, and he knew he would lose another before the year was out. He untied the kerchief from around his forehead, shook it out, and laid the teeth in it. Then he tied it and the teeth into a tight bundle and slipped it inside his sark. To keep his hair off his face now, he made two thick braids of it on either side.

With a sigh, he picked up his shovel to dig out the rest of the skeleton for crushing.

He spent the remainder of the morning scattering manure over his fields with the pitchfork. At midday he scrubbed his hands in the burn with lye soap and took a break to eat, seated on a three-legged stool in his dooryard where he wouldn't track excrement into his house, then resumed the job. Lunch weighed on his stomach uneasily, for his boots and leggings were covered in fertilizer and the methane gas he'd been inhaling all morning was nauseating. This job, like the plowing, would take several more days, for there were many acres to cover. It was one more thing Cait would have helped with, guiding the garron as he shoveled compost from behind while the cart moved over the field. He closed his eyes and tried to stop missing her so much.

Near sunset, he picked the braids from his hair and scrubbed all over in the burn with the lye soap, clothes and all, though the water was bitch cold and turned his skin red. Then he went to the house to dry out by the fire and eat the supper Sarah had prepared and left for him.

During the afternoon she'd returned to the castle with the children to accomplish her work there. Ciaran and Sìle would run and play with many of the village kids in the Great Hall, for all the adults in the clan looked after all the children and there were many eyes and hands about the castle. Ciaran and Sìle, being the Laird's only grandchildren, would be especially privileged, but every child at the castle was looked after as family. Because, however distantly related, they were family. By the same token, any Ciorram children at play in or near Dylan's house would be supervised by him as if he were their father.

After eating, and when his clothing was more or less dry, he banked his fire, pulled his coat back on, and walked down the track toward the castle.

Glen Ciorram was not a large glen, but was still several times larger than Dylan's little hollow in the mountains. It was situated lower but ran mostly east to west like his property, with a bit of a crook at one end where sat the already ancient stone church, Our Lady of the Lake. The church stood, tiny but intact, against a wooded hill. Just beyond, at the very end of the crook where the glen petered out among steep granite mountains, was the Queen Anne Garrison where the English dragoons were quartered.

Over the past five years the English presence in this part of the Highlands had grown from an independent company in a low stone barracks to a full regiment in a many-storied, fortified structure. To the locals, the building was seen as both good and bad. Bad in that the garrison and its outbuildings and animal enclosures required ever-increasing amounts of land that otherwise might have been farmed to feed Mathesons. Bad in that it meant a constant presence of bigoted, red-coated *Sassunaich* in the glen. Bad in that the commandeering of food, fodder, and horses was a burden on the Mathesons and surrounding clans. Nevertheless, it was deemed good in that the barracks meant the dragoons had their own beds and fires, and the clansmen weren't required to billet in their homes the occupying forces of what many considered a foreign power.

Darkness was nearly complete by the time Dylan made his way into the village, his hands plunged deep into his coat pockets and the black wool collar turned up to his ears against the winter air. The sky was still light, though the glens and forests had darkened. Brilliant colors streaked across it in cloud patches overhead, but they were cold. A cathedral for Beira, the queen of winter. She was a goddess Dylan didn't care to meet personally.

As he made his way past the peat bog, nearby trees rustled in the wind high above the ground. Dylan stopped to listen, attending closely to what the spirits would say.

"They're restless," said Sinann, fluttering and listening.

Dylan nodded. "Something's got them riled." He picked up his pace, boots crunching the ice-locked path on his way to Ciorram.

In the glen, a gathering of men, some with torches in hand, stood near the drawbridge that crossed from the mainland to the island in the loch where stood the gray, towered *Tigh a' Mhadaidh Bhàin.*

They seemed be gathered around Dùghlas Matheson, who was Coinneach's older brother.

Also in the midst of the group, as always louder than most, was the Laird's young half brother, Artair. Angry voices drifted to Dylan on the wind off Loch Sgàthan, and he caught snatches of heated discussion.

"*. . . creach . . .*"

". . . MacDonell . . ."

". . . if we're nae to starve . . ."

As Dylan approached, Robin Innis saw him and called to him. "*Och,* Dylan! The MacDonells have sneaked in and made off with all three of Dùghlas's kine!" Everyone knew the MacDonells had a fresh vendetta against the Mathesons, what with Artair having recently despoiled their prettiest daughter. In addition, some other grievances between the clans went back centuries, and in fact the first man Dylan had ever killed had been a MacDonell.

Red anger over the stolen cattle rose in Dylan, as if climbing his spine with hot claws and settling to burn in his head. "Damned MacDonells; we should kill the lot of them."

Several of the Matheson men nodded agreement, but Dylan blinked and hauled in a deep breath as he wondered why he was so enraged over three kine. He felt hot. Itchy. There was a buzzing inside his head. He shook back his shoulders, but the anger wouldn't clear. Artair declared they should go after the stolen cattle, and Dylan found himself agreeing with more enthusiasm than was reasonable. Just then the thought of putting Brigid into someone's throat sounded like fun.

He looked at the ground and shook his head. *No, not fun. Sometimes necessary, but never fun.* He took deep, slow breaths and calmed himself. All his life he'd had a bad temper, much to his shame and annoyance, but until today had usually succeeded in controlling it.

Artair's energy was so high he bounced on the balls of his feet. He addressed the men. "We'll need arms and provisions. Each of ye go to yer homes for what ye've got in the way of weapons, and meet at Dùghlas's. The track across the snow should be easy enough to follow, and those MacDonells are all stupid enough to leave a trail straight to their lands." The last wasn't true, but Artair had a jingoist manner of leadership that was easy to follow mindlessly. Tonight Dylan didn't argue, because he was as hot to chase down those thieving MacDonells as everyone else.

But as Artair spoke, a thundering of horses came along the track from down the glen. The cluster of Scots stepped away from each other, to not look so much like an assembly. A double line of dragoons rode toward them at a gallop, all thudding hooves, creaking leather, rattling sabers, and jingling bridles. The twin lines separated and surrounded the Ciorram men before anyone could get far enough away to not be seen. Major Bedford led the Redcoats, with Lieutenant MacCorkindale just behind.

"Halt there, you!" the Major shouted at one of the fleeing men and fired his pistol in warning. The other riders lowered their muskets to bear on the men on foot.

The Ciorram blacksmith, Tormod Matheson, was nearly to the draw-bridge. He obeyed and halted, and stood to listen.

The Major, straight as a ramrod on his fidgety mount, gave the order for the muskets to return to ready, then addressed with precise, cultured enunciation the loosened cluster of Scots. "This is an illegal assembly. Understand, all of you, that by rights every man here should be arrested immediately."

He paused a moment to let that sink in, strong chin lifted, staring down his long, straight, aristocratic nose at the men below. The Scots waited patiently, each man wishing he were anywhere but within earshot of this English swine. Bedford drew a deep breath and continued, "Furthermore, I am aware of the reason for this gathering. Be advised that anyone attempting to recover stolen property in my jurisdiction will be deemed as operating outside proper authority." As he spoke, his focus found Dylan and his eyes narrowed. "Anyone found doing such while in possession of banned arms," he glanced at the dirk strapped to Dylan's legging, "will be arrested and prosecuted under the strict terms of the Disarming Act."

The Matheson men said nothing, keeping still and gazing as blandly as possible at the *Sassunach*. Tormod stared at the ground. Seumas Glas MacGregor, whose willingness to laugh in tense moments usually brought pleasant relief, had only a slight curve at the corners of his mouth tonight, and an ugly light in his eyes.

Dylan stared back at Bedford and dug his fingernails into his palms. He shrugged one shoulder to feel the pull of flogging scars at his back—a reminder of an earlier encounter with Bedford. Dylan despised the English Army with every shred of his soul, and this Englishman in particular had personally done him incalculable damage. Dylan's arm twitched to draw Brigid, but he refrained. Instead, he broke eye contact with the Major and stared into the middle distance. It was all he could do to keep still. The rage continued.

Bedford continued, "A detail of dragoons will be sent out tomorrow to search for the thieves. With luck, your cattle will be returned to you."

Artair snorted, sullen and ornery. He was in his early twenties, but often behaved like a beardless lad.

"Something to say, Artair?" It was an invitation for Artair to hang himself. The tone in Bedford's voice was one of anticipation.

The belligerent young man tossed his mop of strawberry blond hair from his eyes and puffed out his chest. "More than likely, if the *spréidhe* make it back to Ciorram, it will be in the bellies of your detail."

Dylan cut him a sharp glance, wishing that brat would shut the hell up, but Artair paid little heed to anything beyond his own need to be the center of attention. He only glared up at the Major. Now it was Artair Dylan wanted to kill, and the itching inside his skull was maddening. He flexed his fingers.

Bedford sniffed in response to the young man's comment, reined in his nervous mount, and said, "Since you Mathesons seem unwilling to cooperate with His Majesty's duly appointed keepers of the peace, I have no choice but to impose a curfew on this God forsaken dale for the next week." Again, he addressed Dylan rather than Artair, and there was a note of triumph in his voice. It was apparent he'd counted on Artair to give him an excuse for a curfew and was pleased to have been obliged. "Any man, woman, or child seen outside his or her hovel after sunset will be arrested and held at the garrison for no less than one month. I will not tolerate lawlessness. The only way to put a stop to this thievery is to make you savages desist retaliating by more thievery and killing."

The Major's horse fidgeted again. It was a large animal, a dark thoroughbred with four white legs that caught the attention as he pranced. The Redcoat continued, "God knows you Mathesons have stolen enough MacDonell cattle in the past; I expect you people may even have owed them those three."

Bedford didn't need to tell them that, for it was understood by all the clans that keeping track of who had reived more cattle from whom was pointless. Starving clans stole from those who had surplus, knowing that when fortunes reversed, they themselves would become targets. The system of reiving had worked as social welfare for centuries, and nobody in the Highlands was willing to give it up. There was no alternative safety net in a world where cattle meant the difference between life and death for a clan.

Artair spoke up again. "If we let them go, they'll be back for more."

Bedford finally addressed Artair. "They'll be back for more in any case, you fool." His well-bred voice carried all the contempt of the wealthy for those less important.

Artair started to say something else, but Bedford spoke over him. "Because I am a reasonable man, I'll allow each of you to make your way home. Go directly home, for the patrols will be heavy until the curfew is lifted. Anyone who ventures back outside tonight will be apprehended."

Damn. Ciaran and Sìle were in the castle. Dylan was going to have to smuggle them home or stay the night. Even more now, he wanted to kill Artair and his unruly mouth.

There was a silence. Nobody moved. Then Bedford ordered his men, "Disperse them."

The muskets were lowered to hang by their baldrics at the dragoons' sides, and a dozen sabers were drawn in a flurry of singing metal. The cavalrymen urged their horses forward. The Ciorram men ducked between the horses and hurried to scatter, chased halfheartedly by the soldiers who laughed at the fleeing Scots. Dylan let himself be herded to the drawbridge, where he, Dùghlas, Seumas, Robin, and Artair then headed for the castle.

Under his breath, Artair muttered to the others, " 'Tis a disgrace to scurry from the *Sassunaich* like insects. Matheson men arenae to be taken so lightly." He scowled at the ground, then at the men who walked with him.

Dylan couldn't help but agree. It curled the edges of his soul to obey Bedford, but the alternative at that moment was a bloody confrontation they couldn't win, nor even survive. He walked on behind Artair.

The young man then added, "Follow me, men." He ducked as if to dodge off the gatehouse path, but Dylan grabbed him by the coat and threw him back onto the track. Artair staggered and shook off Dylan's grasp, then raised a fist in warning.

Dùghlas, who was about Artair's age, muttered an objection to the treatment, but Dylan ignored it and said to Artair, "Are you mad? There's a dragoon watching you." Artair and the others looked over their shoulders, but Dylan refrained from staring at the soldier that had reined in his horse just short of the drawbridge. Artair opened his mouth for a loud insult to the Redcoat, but Dylan hauled him back around and shoved him forward. "Keep going."

"Ye forget who I am." Artair's voice was low and ominous.

"I wish. Just keep going, or I'll kick your butt."

Artair kept going, because he knew Dylan could make good the threat. But he couldn't resist an insult along the way, if not to the dragoon, then to Dylan. "Listen to you, all the big talk coming from a man who lets his wife's killer live."

Red-clawed anger took Dylan again, and he gave Artair another hard shove as they passed the gatehouse and entered the castle bailey. Artair stumbled heavily. "Shut up," was the best comeback Dylan could manage just then.

Artair recovered from his forward stagger and turned to begin bouncing on the balls of his feet, sneering. "Why Bedford is yet alive, is what I dinnae ken. I recall yer promise to kill him if we would stay our own hands. Ye promised her father, and now ye've reneged. 'Tis shameful, I say. Would ye nae say also, Dùghlas? Robin?" He addressed the other men, who drifted past, not wanting to be involved with this but also not wanting to offend Dylan or Artair by walking away.

Dùghlas muttered an "Aye." Robin didn't reply, for Dylan had once saved his life, and he was a loyal friend. But Dylan could tell he was also wondering why Bedford had not paid for the murder the entire glen assumed he'd done. Seumas was silent as well.

Ranald Matheson, a young retarded man, came from the Great Hall and spotted the men walking through the bailey. In particular, he spotted Sinann flying behind Dylan.

"The faerie! The faerie!" he squealed, pointing and leaping about. His feet were bare, but on this cold night he wore a tattered kilt over his sark, wrapped and draped about him like an unbelted toga. One end of it dragged the ground. He followed the group of men back through the heavy doors and into the Great Hall. Ranald was just a year younger than Artair but had the intellect of a small child. Nobody claimed him as a son, but everyone cared for him, and he stayed at the castle. Though Dylan had lived in this glen for years, he still had no clue who Ranald's parents were or had been, for the retarded man was believed to have been a changeling left by faeries as a child.

Dylan knew this to be untrue, for Sinann was mortified by the very thought that Ranald could be one of the *Sidhe*. His presence irritated her, and her inability to hide herself from his sight frightened her. Nevertheless, the clan believed he was a faerie child and treated him like one. He earned his keep, more or less, by accomplishing as much unskilled labor as he could be talked into. Which was little, since it was easier to just feed him and let him go play than to teach him anything. Right now he was leaping around behind Dylan, pointing at Sinann and squealing in a cracked voice to make eardrums bleed.

Talking over the racket, Artair picked up steam against Dylan. "Aye, 'tis a cowardly thing to stand by and let the man who killed yer wife walk the glen, terrorizing others, all the womanhood of the clan a-wondering whether they'll be next."

They passed through the entry to the Great Hall, where supper was nearly cleared away and most of the trestle tables had been taken up. By the hearth was a small group of men in close conference, and a few words in English drifted over. Artair continued, loud enough for his voice to echo from the rafters and therefore be heard by the other group of men, "I say ye shrink from the duty because ye're afraid to have your hands bloody. Especially as it might be yer own blood. Admit it."

Dylan's tongue touched the ragged scar on the inside of his cheek, where Ramsay's rapier had caught his face. He had swallowed quite a bit of his own blood that day. His beard was exactly the length required to hide the mark on the outside so nobody would see it and ask about it.

Whenever the subject of Cait's murderer came up, he turned it aside, unwilling to explain why he hadn't tried to kill Bedford.

Sinann stood behind Dylan and tried to hide from Ranald, but it was hopeless. The retarded man circled Dylan and pointed, laughing.

Among the group by the fire were Laird Iain Mór and a bewigged fellow in the plain breeches and wool coat of a Lowland peddler. Incongruously, the Laird wore his very best sark and kilt, and at his side hung the shining, silver-hilted sword passed down with the lairdship for over a hundred years. It had been a gift from James I, the first Stuart king of England. Sight of the precious and illegal sword, outside of Iain's sanctum, gave Dylan pause, for even before the Disarming Act it had rarely left Iain's office. Also, the soft-looking visitor seemed a bit familiar, which also piqued Dylan's curiosity.

Old Malcolm Taggart, who was Iain's right hand—*fear-còmhnaidh*—and first cousin through a female line, sat on a bench nearby and leaned against a trestle table. He appeared to be asleep, but Dylan figured he was listening quietly, according to his habit.

Dylan decided it was time to put Artair's razzing to rest, now that there was no longer any danger of someone identifying Ramsay's body. He turned to Ranald and laid a finger against his lips. That silenced the young man, who leaped onto a trestle table and crouched on his bare heels, still staring at Sinann, though he was now quiet and his mouth was pressed against his knees. Then Dylan turned to Artair and finally said, loud enough for his own voice to carry across the room and into the talk before the hearth as Artair's had, "Cait's murderer is dead."

Iain held a hand up to his guest to stay the conversation for a moment. The group of men fell silent. He leaned back in his chair to listen for what else Dylan might say, and set a hand on the pommel of the King's sword as he stared at Dylan.

Artair crossed his arms over his chest and said in a tone of ridicule, "He isnae dead. He's out there even now, giving orders to arrest us."

"No. I've killed the man who killed Cait. The real murderer returned the day after the funeral, looking to kill me and the children. We fought, he died."

Not entirely certain now, Artair said, "Easy enough said."

Robin looked to Dylan, hopeful. Seumas was expressionless.

"It's true. Here." Dylan opened his coat, reached inside his sarks, and pulled out the small bundle of teeth. "This here is what's left of him." He tossed the bundle to Artair, who frowned as he caught it and hefted it. The contents rattled.

Artair snorted. "Aye. Some buttons, I expect." He untied the kerchief. "Cut from an old—" His eyes went wide with bald surprise. Even Artair didn't have a smart remark for this. Dylan glanced at the group of men by the fire, who attended closely to Artair's reaction.

Robin looked into the kerchief draped across Artair's hand, and said softly, "Och . . ." Seumas wore a wide grin, his faith in Dilean Dubh nan Chlaidheimh, his former comrade in arms, restored.

Dylan retrieved his kerchief and the teeth, and tied them into a bundle again. "Off with you, wee Lairdie. Get away from me before I decide your ass needs kicking after all."

Artair, sullen now, went to sit with the men by the fire as Dylan flagged down Gracie, who was in charge of the castle staff. Quietly, he let her know he and the children would be staying the night, and she went to prepare a room for them.

On their way to sit with the other men, Robin asked him, "Who was it, then, if not Bedford?"

Dylan shook his head. "It doesn't matter who he was. What matters is, he's dead, killed by the bayonet he used to murder Cait."

Robin nodded, approving. His step seemed just a little lighter.

By the hearth, one of Iain's tenants vacated a stool by the fire for Dylan to sit and went to perch atop a trestle table with Robin, Seumas, Dùghlas, and some other tenants, where he could see over the heads of those on stools. Dylan accepted the honor of the seat, for it was called for by his status in the clan.

He was understood to be Iain's first cousin through a male line, because he'd presented himself to the clan five years before as the son of Roderick Matheson, Iain's uncle.

Of course, though Dylan truly was a direct descendant through the male line, even he didn't know exactly how many generations there were between himself and Roderick. Maybe fifteen or so, but he sure couldn't tell the clansmen that. He'd arrived in this century with nothing more than the clothes on his back, sparse knowledge of his Scottish ancestry, and a story cobbled together on the fly about having been shanghaied by a press gang. But by virtue of perseverance, luck, and his skill with a sword, he was now the second-largest landowner in the clan and the father of the Laird's only grandchildren.

There had been a short time when he'd been considered Iain's heir, and according to tradition his claim to the title was nearly as solid as was the Laird's half brother's. Dylan knew there were as many who wished him to succeed Iain as there were who wanted to see Artair Laird, and everyone knew Dylan would be a threat to the young man's claim. Dylan had been in danger from Artair since his betrothal to Cait, a truth made obvious by the nick a ball from Artair's pistol had taken from Dylan's right ear two days afterward.

Tonight, as Dylan unbuttoned his coat and warmed himself by the high fire, he eyed the Lowland visitor who sat opposite, beside the Laird. The man spoke entirely too well to be a merchant, and he seemed in fear for his safety. He was far too walleyed to be anything but a fugitive of some sort. Ruling class ... fugitive ... he was probably a high-ranking Jacobite. The man looked familiar, but Dylan couldn't say why.

Smiling, the Laird addressed the Lowlander in English, "My lord, here are two brave men you should meet." He gestured to Artair, seated to his right. "This is Artair, my brother." Then he indicated Dylan, "And my uncle's son here, Dilean Dubh, was among your forces at Sheriffmuir."

The missing name fell into place in Dylan's mind, and hatred rose again, reddening his vision. He said, his voice low, "Mar."

CHAPTER 5

The visitor was John Erskine, 6th Earl of Mar. Dylan had never seen in person and close up the leader of the Jacobite forces in the last uprising, but now recognized him from a photo of a portrait he'd seen in a history book what seemed an eternity ago. He'd always thought Mar, with his sharply defined lips, poorly defined jaw, and dark shadows under his eyes, all topped with a large, curly wig, looked like Rodney Dangerfield in drag, and now saw that in a shorter, more discreet wig the Earl looked like a *young* Rodney Dangerfield in drag.

Mar smiled and nodded. "You were with us in 1715?" His accent was the highest of upper-class English and plump with the most rounded of syllables, sounding far too much like Bedford for comfort.

Dylan had a strong urge to snatch his former commander by the throat, but kept his seat. He took a deep breath and held it. The buzzing in his head grew louder. The itching felt like it was inside his skull, and he touched his fingers to the back of his neck, wishing he could scratch. Finally, he said, "I was."

Mar seemed taken aback by Dylan's odd reaction, but continued, "Terrible business, that. Many brave men fell. Far too many."

"Not nearly enough." It was out before he could stop himself. He bit hard on his lower lip, but knew it would do no good.

Mar frowned. "I beg your pardon? You would have had more butchery?"

"We lost. Those men died for nothing."

Sinann rose into the air beside Dylan. "What is it ye're after, lad?" She sounded alarmed. "This isnae a good direction ye've taken the conversation."

An edge came into Mar's voice, and he shifted in his seat. "Half the men ran." His hands gripped hard on the arms of his chair.

Iain's voice was low with warning, "Dylan . . ." He shifted his large bulk as if readying to restrain Dylan by force if necessary.

Dylan glanced at Iain's reddening face, but he couldn't help but continue. His own face flushed with rage. He gripped hard the stone face of the fireplace beside him. "You quit the field and left us there!"

"No, Dylan! Are ye mad?" Sinann waved her hands in his face to catch his attention, but that only angered him more. In a second he was going to snatch her out of the air so he could see Mar's face. She fluttered away at the look in his eye.

He continued, "Argyll had us backed up against the river. The men on the muir with you had hardly fought, having spent the day chasing a few Redcoats hither and yon. By the time you got back, we were demolished. You, on the other hand, were fresh. You could have attacked them from the rear."

"*Och!* Will ye control yer tongue, man!"

Dylan ignored her. "Instead you let them dig in. You let them have us. When you left the field, the Redcoats were murdering the wounded, systematically walking among the fallen men and running them through with bayonets. Those of us who escaped were left without our baggage. No kilts and no food. The rising was over. We had no choice but to go home."

Mar's pale face was turning a blotchy red, and his eyes darkened.

"Dylan, that is enough!" Iain warned. His voice made it clear he would swing on Dylan rather than speak again. The other men were now muttering amongst themselves.

Sinann slapped Dylan's face, then dodged as he grabbed for her. Finally he regained some sense of what he was doing, and nearly gasped. Still enraged but gaining control of his mouth, Dylan sat again. "I apologize, my lord. But I, myself, was wounded in that battle and nearly died."

Sinann settled on one of the trestle tables, frowning, legs crossed and arms akimbo. Her eyes flashed with anger.

Dylan opened his coat and his sarks to reveal the scar made by an English cavalry saber. Having been run completely through, all that had saved him from death had been transport by Sinann to the turn of the twenty-first century and emergency surgery. After his recovery, he'd been returned to the midst of battle. Now he revealed to the room the entrance wound. The scar on his belly brought an exclamation from Mar.

Dylan continued, "There was no running, only a retreat after hope was gone."

"Yes, I see." Mar was regaining his composure, though his mouth retained an angry set. "However, you couldn't have been terribly alert while backed up against the river, could you? So badly wounded as you were."

Dylan's face flushed, and his ears warmed as he buttoned his clothing again. Unable to tell of the historical account he'd read at home while recovering from surgery, or that he'd experienced the last of the battle in reasonable health after six weeks of recovery, he said, deflated, "No. I suppose not."

"Dylan Dubh," said Mar, "You must understand that an ordinary soldier cannot know the reasons for every decision made on a battlefield." His voice carried the tone of the experienced, battle-hardened commander Dylan knew he was not. It was plain there would be forgiveness if Dylan let him continue with the lecture and support the fiction. "Sometimes there are considerations not obvious to the lowly foot soldier."

Dylan rankled at the word *lowly*, but held his voice level. "Such as?"

Mar's eyes narrowed. "Such as the need to not waste men in tidying up a conflict we considered won."

Dylan swallowed hard the urge to point out that the battle had not been won, and merely nodded.

"You can understand, then, why I didn't give the order to charge."

Again, Dylan nodded. He understood why—that Mar had not possessed the balls to attack, or had not been able to correctly assess the situation below the muir. It had been a fatal mistake and that battle had been the final failure that had cost the Jacobites the war.

Dylan also knew from history that because the uprising had been such an equivocal loss there would be another, to begin in a month or two, and it would come much closer to home than had the one just past. It would fail in Glen Shiel, in the Northwestern Highlands.

In fact, the coming uprising turned out to be the reason Mar was risking arrest by his presence in Scotland. As Iain spoke again and the previous conversation picked up where it had left off, Dylan realized the Earl was rallying support for the troops that were expected from King Philip V of Spain. With hostilities between England and Spain having broken out the summer before, Spanish leaders were conspiring with Scottish ones to coordinate a large Spanish attack on the south of England with a Jacobite uprising in Scotland. The rising would be supported by a small contingent of Spanish troops, numbering three hundred or so.

What the Earl of Mar and the Laird of Ciorram couldn't know, and Dylan didn't dare tell them, was that the Spanish assault on England would never happen. An unforeseeable storm would wipe out the Spanish fleet, and the Jacobite forces wouldn't learn there'd been no invasion until it was too late to stand down in Scotland. It was to be a disaster even more humiliating than Sheriffmuir.

But telling what he knew would surely do nothing more than bring accusations of witchcraft once his predictions proved true. He'd learned long ago history couldn't be changed. Even his presence wasn't change; having been named for himself—as far as his parents knew, a distant cousin in the dim history of the old country—he knew he'd always been meant to live in this century. Nothing he did *could* change anything, because he was part of the past that was meant to be.

He watched Mar's face, wondering whether the Earl really believed what he claimed. Did he truly think the Jacobites could prevail over the English with Spanish help? What did he figure would happen once Philip V had conquered England? Did he expect Scotland to then be at war with Spain for control of England? Did he expect Spain to install James III on the British throne? Mar was known throughout history as "Bobbing John" for his opportunistic politics, and now he was an outlaw in Britain. His only hope of ever returning home was for a sympathetic ruler to wrest the throne from King George. Dylan knew it didn't matter to Mar whether that ruler was Philip or James, so long as Mar was on the good side of the winner.

Dylan knew Mar would fail on both accounts.

A teenage boy burst into the Great Hall, skidded on the reed-strewn stone floor, and called out, *"Iain Mór! An Sassunaich!"*

Iain cursed and took Mar by the elbow as they all rose from their seats. Ranald sent up a squeal of excitement. The group of men by the fire scattered every which way, lest they be caught in assembly. Most ducked into the kitchen, to either escape through the animal pens or hole up in the schoolroom. Robin and Seumas scurried to set up a chess game at the other end of the room, and Malcolm shushed Ranald before sending him out to the bailey. Iain took Mar toward the hallway that led to the North Tower. Dylan headed toward the kitchen in search of his children, but Iain called to him.

"*A Dhilein!* Come. Artair, you as well." Dylan obeyed, puzzled. The four of them went to the passage at the other end of the Great Hall. Mar was panting with fear and deathly pale at the prospect of being arrested, for he would then be hung without delay.

They passed Gracie in the hallway as she carried linens, and she accepted the fuss with her usual composure. She was a veteran of many a search by the English, and her appearance of calm was an asset to the entire castle in these situations.

Iain grabbed a large candle from a sconce, then led the men into his office on the ground floor of the North Tower. "Get the door," Iain told Artair, who shoved the heavy, carved oak door shut so it latched. Then Iain lit the five candles set in a candelabra on his desk and doused the one in his hand before setting it down.

The Laird's office was well appointed, furnished with upholstered chairs, a large oak desk, and cases of shelves. Some of the shelves contained ledgers and books bound in leather, and others held racks of wines and brandies. Opposite the desk hung a tapestry depicting Iain's father and a white faerie only Dylan knew to be Sinann. Though it was common knowledge the tapestry was an enchanted gift from faeries, Dylan was also the only one who knew the nature of its enchantment.

He looked closely at the faerie in the picture and saw it move, following the men in the room with its gaze. Sinann was watching, but wasn't in the room. He frowned. She should be looking for his kids, not engaging in stupid faerie tricks.

Iain went to a set of shelves against the wall, found finger purchase at one side, and pulled. The shelves, which had appeared built solidly to the wall, swung out like a large door with the low scraping sound of wood against rock. Though the Laird was tall and muscular, it took several hard yanks to pull it entirely open wide enough to admit a man. Carved stone steps led down into a pitch-dark tunnel, barely wide enough for a man's shoulders. Iain handed the candle to Mar and said, "This passage ends hard by the burn that runs from the wooded hills. Follow the water upward, past the faerie tower, and ye'll come upon yer men there."

Dylan warned, "Bedford has imposed a curfew. There's been a *creach* on the glen, and we're to be prevented from having justice from the MacDonells."

Iain made a disparaging noise, then said to Mar, "My lord, be cautious. The soldiers will be out in force tonight and looking for blood if they dinnae make an arrest in this search." A fearful light came into his eyes. "And whatever ye do, dinnae stop at the *broch sidhe*. Ye ken what devils the wee folk can be."

Mar nodded, having taken seriously the warning of faeries. Then, without a word, the Earl entered the passage. Iain lifted the baldric from his shoulder and hung the King's sword from a peg behind the bookshelves. Though the sword had once been proudly displayed on the wall behind the Laird's desk, for the past three years it had only been safe when hidden. He then shoved the bookcase to and closed the passage with a heavy, scraping sound.

Iain Mór turned to Artair and Dylan and reverted to Gaelic now that the English-speaking Earl was gone. His voice was grave. "Attend me, the both of ye. Until now, I was the only one to know about this passage. Before me 'twas my father, and before him his father, as long ago as there have been Mathesons living in this castle. One of you will be Laird of this glen one day, and I expect the both of ye to honor the trust I've put in ye and keep the secret to pass to the next laird after you."

Dylan was stunned. Artair cut him a glance, furious, then glared at Iain. But they both nodded.

"Swear it. Artair, on the grave of your mother; Dylan, on the grave of your wife."

They both swore, readily.

Artair then said, "Why is it ye're telling us both this?" His displeasure at discovering he was in competition for the inheritance was plain on his reddening face and in the white line of tension around his mouth.

Iain gazed at him for a long moment, then at Dylan. His pale, beetled eyebrows came together in a single, straight line as he considered. A glance at the door, where there was not yet the sound of searching soldiers, then he took a sharp breath, having decided. "Come. There's another thing for the two of you to see." He went to the shelves behind his desk and pulled out a ledger. Spread on his desk, the heavy pages fell open to a place where two folded papers had been inserted.

"I'm most likely a fool for showing ye these, but you have a right to ken where ye stand, and a need to understand how it will come about in due time." He peeked inside one of the papers, then handed one to each of them.

Dylan unfolded his, and by the light of the candelabra on the desk scanned the elaborate handwriting. It was difficult reading, with all the *S*s looking like *F*s, but at least it was in English. By catching the highlights, he could see it was a transfer of property. Iain Mór had signed the entirety of his estate over to him. Dylan's heart skipped a beat but steadied when he realized what the other paper must say. One glance at Artair's face, flushed with happiness, told him what he already had figured out: that the other paper was an identical transaction, signing the estate over to Artair. It was obvious why they had been written.

Dylan said, "You can't just bequeath your property, because we're Catholic." Iain nodded, and Dylan continued, "It's against the law for a Catholic to inherit. So you have to sign your estate over before you die, thereby making someone else Laird. But you don't know yet which one of us you want to pass the jurisdiction to, so you had two papers written up. One naming Artair and one naming me."

Artair made an inarticulate noise of disappointment and looked over Dylan's shoulder at the other paper. "Him the Laird? It's myself has the rightful claim! I'm the son of a laird, and this colonial prodigal but a grandson. By rights, the property is mine!"

Iain's face clouded with anger. "The *property*, my brother, is mine. *Och.* Property, ye say. If yer thought were for the responsibility, or for the leadership of the clan, then I'd have nae doubts. But I must consider the welfare of this glen, even after my death. I cannae simply do nothing, as was done in the past, and trust the clan leadership will pass to the one as can hold the people. For if I failed to make the transfer beforehand, the land would then go to the Crown under the anti-Catholic acts. I must decide which claimant to the title will keep the clan whole and safe."

Iain reclaimed the two papers, saying, "Both papers will be in safe-keeping until either I choose or I die. If I die before I've chosen, Malcolm will be the one to decide which transfer will be made public."

Artair muttered, "It's the *Sassunach* way of doing things. With papers and all that."

"It's the *Sassunaich* who force us to engage in this cowardly subterfuge in order to bequeath property to our kin. 'Tis only right we should use their soulless system against them." Iain's eyes flashed with anger. Whether at the degenerate *Sassunaich* or at Artair's dull-wittedness, Dylan wasn't certain. Dylan had to smile at the plan. The old man was pretty wily.

"So now the two of ye understand my intent. These will be put away, safe, until one of them is needed." He put them back in the ledger book, and the book onto the shelf.

Dylan wasn't sure what to think about this. It was plain Iain considered Dylan once more in the running as his heir. Furthermore, by revealing the secret passage to them both at the same time, Iain must not only assume one of the claimants would be dead by the time the other succeeded to the lairdship, but more than likely intended to encourage the conflict. *Let the best man win.* Darwinian theory in action.

A shouting went up in the Great Hall, heard dimly in Iain's office. They were English voices, demanding to know of the Laird's whereabouts. Iain, Artair, and Dylan hurried from the room. The Laird ordered them to split up—Artair upstairs and Dylan out of the tower and down the corridor past the servants' quarters—and Iain himself returned to the Great Hall to present himself to the Redcoats as puzzled and offended over the intrusion.

Dylan ducked through the door to the passageway along which the servants' rooms were situated.

Sinann popped into view. "Have ye gone mad? What did you mean by addressing Mar the way ye did?" She was aghast.

He didn't want to hear about it. "Never mind, Tink."

"I've never seen—"

"I said, put a cork in it, Tinkerbell!" he said in an ugly hiss. "Not now!"

There was the pounding of boots along the wood floor above, echoing like thunder in the long corridor, and Dylan paused in the hallway. Should he go or stay? He burned to know where Ciaran and Sìle were, but wanted to stay away from them if he might be arrested.

Doors opened all along the hall—curious servants looking to see what was going on. Dylan shook his head, gesturing for quiet up and down the hall and to close the doors. Most of the servants obeyed, but Sarah stayed.

"Go!" Dylan waved her back inside and turned to proceed.

"Come. It's safer in here." She sounded terrified. He stopped and turned back. She waved him in.

He realized she was right. If he weren't found wandering the halls, he would be less a target for arrest and questioning. But he shook his head. He had to find his children, to know they were safe. "No, I'll be all right. Get inside and be quiet. Be civil to them when they come. It'll—"

The door at the far end of the passage opened. Dylan fell silent and faced the intruder, struggling for an insouciant air he did not feel. He'd just aided the escape from English justice of a man wanted for treason, and in so doing had committed treason himself—an obvious and unforgivable violation of the terms of his pardon. Even if the English didn't know for certain, they must at least suspect Mar had been there, or they wouldn't be searching the place. Someone was sure to be arrested tonight just for the sake of form. Given Dylan's precarious relationship with Bedford, he was a likely candidate for that honor. He watched the door open, wanting to flee but knowing he'd never make it out of the corridor unseen.

A man entered the hall. It was just Artair. Dylan relaxed, but alarm surged again when the young man drew his dirk and said, "Traitor! 'Tis you passing word to the *Sassunaich!*"

Dylan drew Brigid from his legging scabbard. It took only an instant to figure out what was going on here. Artair was taking this opportunity to make an easy accusation and get Dylan out of his way.

"Don't make me kill you, lad." Denying would be a waste of breath, for he knew even Artair didn't believe what he said. "If you want the lairdship, you'll be needing to stay alive to inherit, and I guarantee you won't if you don't stand down right now."

Artair came at him with his dirk, like a bull, full-on speed but with his weapon dodging deceptively. Dylan scurried backward, just enough to throw off his opponent's timing, then clashed dirks and attacked. Suddenly on the defensive, Artair stumbled backward. Recovering, he parried, but there was nowhere to go but backward. Dylan forced him down the hallway. He had no intention of killing the young punk, not with a garrison commander at the door who would be oh, so eager to shoot him now and ask questions later. But he put a scare into Artair, forcing him closer and closer to the door at the end of the corridor.

Dirks clashed and flashed under the flickering light of the sconces, and Dylan hit harder with each thrust, careful to barely miss Artair each time.

Then, just as the younger man tripped over the threshold at the end of the hall, Dylan gave him a shove with his boot and closed the door on him. He scabbarded Brigid in his legging and turned back down the hallway.

English soldiers raised a shout on the other side of the door. Artair was in custody.

Then Dylan ran to Sarah's door and slipped inside just as the passageway door from the West Tower opened, and the sound of leathersoled boots on stone echoed in the hall. He silently closed the door and looked around Sarah's quarters.

The single room she shared with her young sons was dim, lit only by the fire in a small hearth. Two bunks were stacked against one wall, and a table and chairs stood in the middle of the room. Eóin and Gregor sat on the top bunk, wide-eyed at the excitement. Sarah stood next to the hearth and opened her mouth to say something.

Dylan cut her off, his voice urgent but hushed. "Boys! Under the covers! Now! You're asleep!"

Both boys dove under their blanket and lay still as logs. Nobody needed to tell the children of Glen Ciorram how dangerous the English were. There was not a sound from either of them.

The soldiers were just outside, moving from room to room in their search.

Dylan grabbed Sarah and pulled her down with him onto one of the chairs to sit on his lap, just as the door burst open and two Redcoats entered. One, a sharp-eyed Private, carried a bayoneted musket, and the other was Bedford's Lieutenant, Niall MacCorkindale. Relief washed over Dylan. The Lieutenant was from Skye and suspected to be Catholic, and despite his utter loyalty to the Crown, was not entirely unsympathetic to his fellow Scots.

"*Och,* said Dylan, struggling to appear embarrassed. He was flushed and breathless from the fight, and so didn't need to feign excitement. "MacCorkindale. What's going on?" He eased Sarah from his lap, and she stood to the side. Dylan could see she did not have to fake embarrassment. Her face and neck were bright and hot. She reached for a shawl and drew it around her shoulders, her gaze hard on MacCorkindale's black riding boots.

The Lieutenant addressed them in Gaelic. "Dylan Dubh. I'm surprised to see you here." He gestured to the very small room. It was crowded with the belongings of three people, as servants' quarters had never been meant to house more than one or two.

Dylan stood. "Aye. Well, I'm a mite surprised myself." He glanced at Sarah, hoping it would appear a leer, and stepped closer to the Lieutenant. "I'm hoping you'll keep this to yourself. If the Laird should learn of it . . ."

MacCorkindale gazed blandly at him for a moment, and alarm surged the Lieutenant might make an arrest just for aggravation value. "Make love in yer coat, do ye?"

The reply was immediate, on reflex, "Of a cold winter I do, until the moment I find myself under the blanket with a warm and generous woman." Then Dylan's voice went low, "A man can't spend every winter night alone, *you well understand*." His tone was to remind MacCorkindale of the Redcoat's own visits to Nana Pettigrew, who made the greater portion of her widowed living servicing the soldiers from the garrison.

There was but a shrug from the Lieutenant, then, "It's nae my business where ye sleep or whose servants ye niggle. Have ye been here all evening, then?"

"Since you last saw me. With the curfew, I don't dare take my children home." Where were Sìle and Ciaran? Blind anger rose, and he took deep breaths to calm the urge to draw Brigid and get these *Sassunaich* out of his way. "We'll be staying the night in the castle." He held out his wrists as if to accept shackles, and said with a cutting edge to his voice, "But if ye must arrest me again, it's your privilege. I've no other wife to be murdered in my absence."

MacCorkindale cut Dylan an equally edgy glance, pursed his mouth, then turned his attention to Sarah, who appeared close to tears.

Dylan reached for her hand and pulled her to him, then said to the Lieutenant, "If ye please." She pressed her face to his shoulder, and he continued, "She's frightened."

The Redcoat's eyes narrowed. "Has she cause for fright?"

Dylan's ears warmed and his head buzzed with the flaming rage. "The English Army murdered her unarmed husband before her eyes. I call that cause enough to be frightened of a Redcoat at any time."

MacCorkindale grunted. "All right, then." He nodded to the private, who began searching the small room. He stuck the bayonet into dark corners, under the bed, and threw the blankets from the bunks. Eóin and Gregor looked up.

"Go back to sleep, lads," said Dylan. "It's all right, the soldiers just want to look."

The boys lay back down on the straw mattress, and the Redcoat proceeded with the search. Once satisfied the Earl of Mar was not hiding in Sarah's room, MacCorkindale left with his private and closed the door behind them.

Sarah collapsed against Dylan and began weeping into his coat. He held her for a few moments. She muttered, her teeth clenched and her voice a low growl, "I hate them. I hate them with every bit of my soul. God help me, I would kill every last one of them if I could." Her fist gripped the black wool of Dylan's coat, and she said through her teeth, "I hate them. I hate them. I hate them."

"It's all right," he whispered. "They're gone."

She lifted her head to wipe her face with ineffective fingers. Dylan dabbed at her tears with the plaid slung over his shoulder. She muttered in a voice made gummy from weeping, "They'll be back. They'll always be back to kill us. They want us all dead, and they won't stop until they've murdered us all."

He wished he could tell her different, that the future promised safety for them from the English Army, but he knew it did not. The killings and arrests and evictions wouldn't stop until the Highlands were almost entirely depopulated, more than a century from now.

Sìle and Ciaran. "I've got to find my children," he said. *Where are the kids?*

Sarah stepped back from him and wiped her eyes. "They're in the guest chamber in the West Tower. Cait's bedroom." Then she tried to wipe the dark spot of tears from Dylan's coat, but he held her hand to keep her from fussing over him.

He squeezed it, thanked her, then slipped from the room to find his children.

CHAPTER 6

The sounds of searching Redcoats were dying out and the uproar in the servants' rooms was winding down as Dylan made his way to the West Tower. He murmured, "Sinann, you here?"

She popped into view. "Aye. Always." Her wings aflutter, she hovered over his left shoulder as he walked.

"Did you know about the escape passage?"

"*Och,* of course I did. 'Tis nae for naught I gave Iain's father the tapestry through which I can spy from a distance when I've a mind."

Dylan swallowed a wisecrack about Sinann ever having had a mind and asked, "So how come you never told me about it?"

"Well, for one thing 'tis a secret only to be disclosed by the Laird, and who am I to defy tradition?"

"I could have used it to get back into the castle to find Cait."

"When? When could you have used the passage while unwelcome here, that ye wouldnae have been killed as soon as ye did? Did ye happen to notice where the passage begins? A grappling hook in a garderobe would have been far safer."

Dylan considered that a moment, then grunted in grudging agreement. Then he said, "What do you think about what Iain did? I mean, Cait never even knew about that tunnel, and she lived in the castle almost her whole life."

"As close as she was to her father, how are ye so certain she wasnae told?"

"She came to me in secret one night when the English were out to arrest me, and she was soaked from having swum from the island. Gracie had let her down with a rope ladder through a garderobe. Only the Laird knows about the bolt-hole, or Cait would have come through it that night. What do you figure it means that he told both Artair and myself about it?" He hauled open the door to the West Tower, then shut it behind himself and Sinann. "I mean, he made a *point* of it."

She giggled. "I'm thinking ye're a-going to become Laird Dylan Robert Matheson of Ciorram, and save yer people from the English, as I've said for the past five years and some months."

He grunted but then said, "Seriously. What's his plan?"

Her voice turned grave. "I expect he's wanting a fight."

Dylan nodded. He started up the spiral stairs, and she followed. "Which, of course, Artair is most obliging on that account." He blinked back red anger once again, then said, "You figure Iain is truly putting the succession up for grabs, or is he just using me to teach Artair a lesson? Or even just to put the fear in him? I mean, if Artair ends up dead, will I have to fight Iain?"

The faerie shrugged. "I surely dinnae ken."

After a moment of deep thought, he said, "You know I don't want it."

"Of course, ye do."

"No, I don't. Being the laird would be like painting a big, red target on my back. You know what's coming. Another uprising, then twenty-five more years of English oppression before the final uprising. And that's when the fun will really begin. After the '45, the clan system and its inherited jurisdictions will be outlawed. Some lairds will start thinking of themselves as mere capitalist landlords because—guess what—they will be. Then begins a century of political and economic evictions that will only end when there's nobody left to get any work done."

"So ye must wrest the lairdship from Artair."

"Not if Iain is only fooling. If he's only interested in teaching Artair a lesson, I'll most likely end up dead. And then where will my children be? And their children? I need to know what Iain's up to."

"I dinnae think it matters, for ye must take the lairdship from Artair. Aught else will be death for the clan. Even I can see that."

Dylan sighed and nodded again. As much as he hated to admit it, even to himself, she might be right.

Cait's childhood bedchamber in the West Tower, now kept for guests, had been refurnished since her marriage to Dylan. Her feather bed and trunk having been moved to the peat house in the upper glen, the bed was replaced with an elaborate, carved piece with many curtains of silk. A large, new armoire stood against the far wall.

The kids weren't there. Dylan's breath stopped cold and cold sweat broke out.

He took the candle from the wash stand to look under the bed, panic rising as he remembered the soldier with the bayonet poking it under Sarah's bed. "Ciaran?" But there were no child-sized shadows. "Sìle?"

"Da!" Both the children appeared from nowhere, huddled against the wall next to the bed, wearing nightshirts. In the boy's hand was the Matheson crest brooch Sinann had made into a talisman of invisibility. It had saved Dylan's own life more than once, and Ciaran's once before when Bedford had threatened the boy's life. Tonight, he'd pinned it on his sark and held his sister, both of them keeping still in order for the magic to work, and were hidden from the red-coated soldiers as they searched the room for Mar. Sìle burst into tears and ran into Dylan's arms.

"She wasnae crying, Da, I swear it. She dinnae cry until she saw you. She was quiet when the soldiers came. I told her nae to be crying."

"I know, son. You took good care of her." He knelt to hold his daughter close, lifted Ciaran in the other arm, and rose to sit them on his lap at the edge of the bed. Both kids were now crying quietly.

"Were they coming to kill us, Father? Like they did Mother?" Ciaran lived in terror of the Redcoats, having witnessed murderous behavior in them all his life.

"No. They were looking for a man. They didn't want you. They didn't want me, either. You're safe." He hugged them tighter. "You're safe."

Dylan held his children for a long time, swaying gently back and forth, until the crying diminished to little hiccups. As they began to settle and drowse in his arms, he let them down onto the mattress to curl up and sleep. Quietly, he stood and pulled the bed curtains shut.

Sinann flew to the top of the bed to perch, as Dylan went to an arrow loop and opened the shutter to look out on the castle bailey below. By the torchlight he could see only a couple of women talking by the animal pens near the kitchen. There was no sign of Ranald. The English soldiers had moved on, either satisfied with an arrest of a Matheson in lieu of Mar, or given up. The castle was quiet again.

He replaced the shutter, then sat on a stool by the fire to remove his boots, his stockings, and those damned, itchy trews. For a moment he scratched his thighs where the wool had irritated, eyelids drooping with the blessed relief. Then he stood and unbelted his kilt to let the massive drape of red plaid drop to the floor on top of his boots. The small bundle of teeth fell from inside his sarks, and he left it there on the floor next to his clothes. Then he peeled off the sarks one by one, and the dirtiest one joined the pile on the floor. The less dirty one he hung from a hook on the armoire.

Gracie had left a ewer, basin, and towels on the washstand, and Dylan set to bathing. Though he'd done a thorough job in the burn earlier, he liked a good scrub just before bed each night. To him, going to bed clean was a sign of the difference between civilized life and the life he'd led as an outlaw before marrying Cait. These days, continuing the habit helped him feel not everything had gone to hell since she died.

Tonight the chilly water on his skin seemed to cool him inside as well, calming the itchy heat inside his head and the fiery anger that seemed to crawl under his skin. Cool trickles ran down his back and his legs, and as he wiped himself down, the cleansing felt more than skin deep. Gradually, the angry claws in his back let go and he began to feel human again.

Fully washed, he ran his fingers through his hair in an attempt to organize it. Then, having dressed himself once more in just the less dirty sark, he slipped through the gap in the bed curtains and slid under the covers next to his kids. It was a large bed, but he still had to nudge Sìle a bit to make room. The two-year-old made a whimpering noise, then woke up enough to realize he was there. As he settled in, she climbed onto his chest and he held her. There she fell back asleep, curled up in his arms with her head pressed over his heart. Ciaran shifted position, then settled down to continue his little-boy snoring. Dylan drifted off to sleep, to the comforting sounds of his children breathing.

The woods were warm, and alive with tiny creatures buzzing and flitting through the air. Dylan looked around but didn't recognize the place.

He'd never been here. It was Scotland; he could tell by the tall-crowned Scotch pines and the dark green moss everywhere. Toadstools stood in faerie rings, like circles of spinning tops in the grass, their dancing frozen in time. The warmth of the day made him remove his coat and drop it on the ground. *Where am I?* A rabbit hopped into view, peering at him from under a spray of bracken. Dylan wished for his bow and quiver, for it had been far too long since there had been fresh meat in the pot at his house. But then he saw a strange light in the animal's eyes, as if it knew who he was and what he was thinking. It owned an air of superiority Dylan found unsettling. The rabbit twitched its nose at him, then hopped away, in no particular hurry.

Dylan wandered through the trees, hoping to figure out where he was and how to get home, and found himself on the verge of a clearing. Shafts of sunlight came through the branches above like Jacob's ladders, brightening patches of grass dotted with clumps of heather. Tiny purple blossoms were sprinkled here and there. It was awfully pretty. More beautiful than any place he'd ever been. Even more beautiful than he'd ever thought possible.

A woman lounged on the ground, dressed in a shimmery white gown of fabric like the dress Sinann wore, but far more sheer. It draped over her breasts and hips, concealing nothing, and slithered over her pale, perfect skin as she sat up to greet him. "Dylan Dubh." Her hair was nearly black and cascaded over her shoulders in smooth waves. Bloodred lips parted, and the tip of her tongue ran over them. Black eyes revealed the depths of the abyss. The buzzing in his head renewed, and every hair on his body rose. There was a fluttering in his belly.

"Morrighan," he said.

She smiled, and his pulse surged. "You recognize me, despite my disguises."

His eyes narrowed at her, and he said with as much self-assurance as was at his disposal, "I remember you. From the battle. You were having a good old time on your faerie knoll, waiting to watch us all die, dancing around and whatnot. You're Mór Ríogain, Morrighu, Mórrigna, Morgana, Morgan La Fey, Lady of the Lake, Phantom Queen, goddess of war—I know who you are."

Morrighan heaved a great sigh, and the sight of her breasts rising and falling in the dappled sunlight held his attention. She stood and approached him. The earthy scent of her filled his head as she passed. His hand twitched to touch her, but only one finger brushed her shimmering gown. It felt as light as a breeze. She went to a grassy slope below a huge oak, then sat on it and set her feet wide. The fabric of the gown draped between her smooth thighs, and his attention was now fixed there.

His pulse thudded in his ears. With a husky voice in a tight throat he said, "I've asked this before: What do you want from me?" At that moment, he thought he might be willing to give a lot to lie with her. Months of celibacy were crowding in on him, turning rational thought to mush. Cutting a deal with the goddess of war seemed doable.

Leaning forward, knees pressed wider by her elbows, she said, "I want the greatest gift a man can give a woman. I want yourself. Here." She lifted the hem of her gown and drew the entire drape of fabric over her head, leaving it all beneath and behind her. Naked and unutterably beautiful, she leaned against her knee and held out her other hand to him to draw him near.

His blood sang. He couldn't help but go to her and take her hand in his. Nevertheless, he made himself say, "Why? Why me?"

She reached for his belt buckle and pulled it open. Free of the only thing that held it up, his kilt slipped from him and dropped to the ground, leaving him in a knee-length sark. He drew that sark over his head and let it fall behind him in a heap of linen.

Morrighan pulled him to her so he knelt, took his face between her hands, and kissed his mouth. He responded, opening his mouth to her. His body thudded for her. His skin tingled. His pulse hammered in his groin. His skull itched. As wrong as he knew this was, he also knew the pain of stopping would be monstrous. Stopping wasn't an option. He leaned over her. Her hand ran up his back, then down his belly, and he prepared to mount her.

S omething slapped his face. *"Dylan!"* The slap came again. *"Och, Dylan!"*

He awoke. Sinann hovered over him, barely visible in the glow of coals in the hearth. The children were still peacefully asleep, undisturbed, Sìle a limp rag doll in his arms. He groaned.

The faerie hissed, angry, "Dylan, I think ye need to be telling me what that dream was."

Horrible pain. He eased Sìle back down next to her brother and slipped from the bed to put another peat on the fire. When it caught, he took his kilt from the floor and drew it around him, huddling on the stool. The ache cramped his muscles, his blood racing but warming nothing. "What did I do? Did I say anything?"

"Nae. 'Twas but yer pounding heart that gave ye away, and it was racing to kill ye if it went much longer. I thought ye might be dying even then." Sinann came to squat next to him by the hearth. "What was it, lad? It dinnae sound good, yer heart thudding so."

"Morrighan."

She nodded, a light of understanding in her eyes. " 'Tis lucky I stopped ye, then."

Dylan groaned. "One more minute, Tink. I couldn't have had just one more minute?" Ten would have been better, but in another minute the faerie might not have been able to wake him up. "It was just a dream. No big deal." Except for the ache that now felt like a vise grip had clamped onto his very favorite bits of anatomy.

"That one wants something from ye. Something you wouldnae give up merely for the asking."

"Like what?" The pain was easing now, and he was more able to think straight. He massaged a knot of muscle over his left knee. "What could she possibly want from me?"

The faerie crossed her arms and raised her chin. "Well, now, I've been telling ye for years how important ye are. I asked the sword to bring me a hero the like of the great Cuchulain, and it reached into the future for you. Perhaps the Morrighan wishes the same destruction for you as for him."

A shiver took him, and he pulled the kilt tighter. Still he felt cold, and so put a fresh peat on the fire. "He was a warrior and died in battle. She's the goddess of war. Sounds like business as usual to me. Besides, Tink, I'm not Cuchulain. He was an arrogant prig, and his father was a god." At thought of his own father, the drunken batterer, he rolled his eyes. "Trust me on this one, I can't claim divine paternity. What does she want from me?"

Sinann shrugged her thin shoulders. "The Morrighan surely wants what she always wants. Like a *baobhan sidhe*, she is."

Dylan frowned, puzzled. "Faerie witch?"

Sinann leaned in and provided the English in a voice filled with disgust: "*Succubus*. I'll wager what I interrupted was a nearly successful attempt at seducing ye, and dinnae lie to me, for I can see ye doubled over like ye were kicked there." She waved an accusing finger at his groin.

He blinked, started to deny, but looked away and said instead, "It was only a dream. It wasn't real."

"*Och,* and I thought I'd taught ye something of the Craft! Look at the marks on yer arm from the first dream she sent ye; then tell me ye werenae just about to leave something real of yerself behind with her."

Dylan made a face, shook his head, and started to reply, but the faerie interrupted, waving her palms back and forth in dismissal. "Nae, the seed isnae the whole of what she would be after. But with it, she might *get* what she truly wants. Whatever that may be, I cannae say."

That plunged Dylan deep into thought. He rolled up his right sleeve and fingered the fang marks left by Morrighan when, in a dream, she'd attacked him in the form of a wolf. It had happened shortly before losing his sword near Perth. He'd awakened then with a bleeding bite mark on his arm, and now the small, white dots of scar were dimly visible by the firelight.

Another thought struck him, and his heart skipped with hope. "Tink, what about the dream of Cait? Could that be just as real? Is it Cait herself coming to me in the mornings?"

A shadow fell across Sinann's face. "I cannae say, lad. I wouldnae expect it. More often than not, a dream is naught but a dream."

He crossed his arms on his knees and rested his head on them, staring into the fire and longing for his dream of Cait to be more than that.

Daghda awoke to a long, loud string of foul language. He blinked sleepily at Morrighan and waited for her to be finished. She flounced about the place, naked, stamping her feet and wailing curses to the surrounding roots of her protector trees. The fire rose and fell with her voice, and Daghda started with alarm once when he thought it would set fire to an outcrop of exposed root overhead.

"Take care, ye shrill beast, or ye'll kill the tree and we'll be marked by its dead branches." Even if she didn't kill it, he'd have to appease the tree spirit for the offense.

She turned on him. "He was mine! I had him in my hands! That *each-uisge* Sinann let him escape!"

The leader of the ancient *Tuatha De Danann* lay back and stretched, unconcerned with Morrighan's distress. *"Och,"* he groaned theatrically, and his voice dripped sarcasm, "poor, poor Morrighan. The little granddaughter of the sea god slipped him from yer clutches? She, whose powers are nearly gone? A shameful, shameful thing, that. Were I you, I'd hide my head from the *Sidhe* for a century or so."

Daghda was certain he did not care a whit for her problem. "What, may I ask, is the terrible concern for this Matheson lad? I'm beginning to feel a wee bit slighted in yer attentions." An understatement. He wished for Dylan Matheson to disappear from the face of the earth.

He sat up and leaned over the hearth to pick at the remains of that evening's meal, which lay on a wooden platter by the stone. His voice took on an even sharper edge as he said, "Sure, if he gives ye much more trouble, I'll be required to put my sword through him just to have yer attention again."

Morrighan swooped down on him and shoved him against the pillows and skins. "Never dare to touch him! He's worth ten of yourself!"

Anger rose, and he encouraged her to get off him by twisting her wrist. "I'm a god! *An Daghda Mór, Eochaid Ollathair!* Who is this mortal that I should even take notice of him, let alone suffer him to be at ye like a dog?"

She yanked her wrist from his grasp and shoved him back onto the cushions by the shoulders. The mischief in her eyes made him curious and no longer angry. She was up to something, and sometimes that could be fun. "Nae who he is, but where he's from. He knows things 'twill happen."

Daghda frowned, scornful. "A seer?"

She shook her head and grinned as she smoothed the hair away from his eyes. "Nae a seer. A *knower*. He doesnae see the future; that lad is *from* the future."

CHAPTER 7

A t sunrise, Dylan woke the kids to take them home. He dressed them, then patiently made the trip down the spiral stairs of the tower, which Sìle insisted on descending under her own steam. It was slow going, one step at a time, Sìle letting herself down backward. But if he picked her up before she was finished, she would scream until he put her down. She didn't allow him to pick her up until they were all at the bottom; then she held up her arms for him. He chuckled. "Just like your mother," he murmured as he hauled her onto his hip and tucked her inside his plaid for the walk to the high glen.

There was work to be done at home, and more of it today than usual, since he'd been unable to make it back the night before to spin wool before bed. Spinning wool was women's work, and that made the job a mite tricky. He wouldn't be caught dead doing it where anyone could see, but it had to be done, and Sarah hadn't the time to do it for him.

He could have simply traded the raw wool to others in the village, but it would go far too cheaply that way. In his opinion, there was no reason why he shouldn't spend his evenings alone increasing the value of his property, so long as he kept to himself while he did it. He would get more for his fleeces then, trading the thread for costlier items, and keeping some of the thread for knitting stockings. Malcolm had taught him to knit, which, weirdly enough, was not necessarily women's work in this place. It kept a man's hands busy and productive during long winter nights by the fire and long summer days watching sheep graze.

Crossing the drawbridge from the castle to the mainland, he let Ciaran run ahead. It was a cold, cloudy day, but the air was crisp. Ice crunched under Dylan's boots between patches of loose snow, and little Sìle's nose was turning pink in the cold wind that blew her hair around her face. Ciaran gave a shout and ran off to join Eóin and Gregor, who were coming from the village and headed toward the track that led past the bog toward the high glen. He hurried along after them, little legs scurrying, shouting for them to let him catch up.

The shrieking of Ranald, who was perched in the gatehouse and pointing at Sinann as she flew along over Dylan's head, followed them across the bridge. Dylan turned and put a finger to his lips, so the young man quieted.

Dylan turned to see, up ahead in the village, Sarah talking to Tormod in front of Nana Pettigrew's house. Her cloak was wrapped tightly around her shoulders, and her was head tilted oddly—as if she were trying to avoid speaking directly to the blacksmith. Tormod was tall, like most of the Mathesons, but in his ageing he'd become somewhat hunched over. His long nose made him look like a vulture, and with the accompanying gray salted into his light brown beard brought Dylan to mind of Dickens' Fagin. Funny, he'd never seen Tormod like that before.

Dylan adjusted Sìle's weight on his hip and cradled her in his arm. Grasping the black wool of her father's coat in one tight fist, she pressed her face to his side. Against the cold, he wrapped her snugly in the plaid flung over his shoulder as he slowed among a stand of pine trees to watch Sarah and Tormod.

He tried not to stare but couldn't help the curiosity. The blacksmith had long been enamored of Sarah, and now appeared to be wooing her again. None too subtly nor successfully, either, for he was touching her arm and trying to take her hand in public. Both being single, it wasn't exactly improper, but it bordered on unseemly because it was plain Sarah didn't want her hand held by Tormod.

It was equally plain the blacksmith didn't mind being forward, even brazen, with a widowed kitchen maid, for she was obviously uncomfortable in the face of his persistence. She was declining those attentions as gracefully as Dylan had ever seen a woman cut a man dead, but Tormod just wasn't getting it. Whenever she tried to step away from him, he followed. Then she would stop walking so he wouldn't simply follow her to where she was going. Which, this time of day, would be Dylan's house.

Dylan slowed more, to stopping, and pretended to adjust Sìle's weight on his hip again and his plaid around her shoulders. He discreetly watched the two, wondering if Sarah might finally give in and accept the attention. For years he'd wished Tormod would win her over and make her happy, thereby alleviating his own guilt. But she'd never gone with the blacksmith, unhappy in her hopeless adoration. The guilt, knowing Sinann had made the love spell on his behalf, had been a constant in Dylan's life since his arrival in this century, and even now Tormod's failure was difficult to watch.

But, instead of going his own way home, Dylan's mouth opened of its own accord and he called out, "Sarah!"

She turned, relieved, and her face lit up to see him. She took a few steps away from Tormod. The blacksmith's face darkened, and he stuffed his hands into his armpits, nodded greeting to Dylan, then said something in parting to Sarah. She hesitated and turned to throw him a displeased glance. Then she hurried over to join Dylan and Sìle on the path past the bog to the high glen.

"What did he say to you?" Dylan frowned, certain Tormod had thrown her an ugly parting shot.

The color was high in Sarah's cheeks, and Dylan wasn't sure whether it was because of the cold or pleasure that he'd rescued her. "Naught," she replied, and the color in her cheeks deepened. Dylan let it drop.

He didn't know why he'd called to her; to be sure, he wasn't certain it had been a wise thing to do. It had been an impulse. He couldn't help it. So now he was walking back to the house with Sarah.

There was a stretch of silence as they climbed the trail, then Sarah said, "Nana tells me they arrested Iain Mór and his brother last night but let them go straight away this morning. It seems the *Sassunaich* were after naught in particular, or else they're to see what the Laird will do now, whether he'll give away what they're after." Her voice was soft, hesitant.

Dylan thought she might be still embarrassed over the ruse they'd played the night before. He wasn't certain he wanted to bring it up, except he had to.

"Thank you for letting me into your room."

She looked away, but said, "*Och*, it wasnae a choice. If I'd let them hurt you, I could never have forgiven myself. In addition, I surely dinnae care what those animals think of my virtue."

Dylan couldn't reply, for he knew the treatment she would receive in the future from the soldiers would be affected by their new perception of her virtue. As a chaste widow, she'd been as respected by the English soldiers as was possible for a Scottish woman. But now, with her reputation tarnished, she might be a more likely target for abuse.

Or even rape. During the last rising, while he and most of the men of the clan had been away, one of the castle maids had died mysteriously. Nobody talked much of Seonag, but the little Dylan had heard suggested she'd been the subject of more than her share of attention from the Redcoats before her death by gunfire. Oblique comments among the clansmen made him wonder whether it might have been suicide. She was buried in the churchyard, which would have been impossible if she were known to have killed herself, but still there were suspicions that the pistol shot that had killed her might have been self-inflicted. Nobody seemed to agree on whether the gun had been found beside the body. Dylan didn't know what to think, but the most telling thing was that nobody had been accused of the murder.

As he and Sarah walked together to the high glen, there was a long silence. Dylan was favoring his left leg again. Not a limp but neither a steady stride. He hated the weakness. Too much of his life depended on being able-bodied, and the vulnerability was a danger to himself and the people around him. It would be good when summer came and the cold weather would ease up some. Then he would feel stronger.

Finally Sarah said, "It's good ye've kept the bairns, difficult though it must be for a man."

Dylan rankled at her sexism, but nodded. "I couldn't let them go to Una. Though she's good to them, I'd be set adrift. I couldn't bear it." He'd returned from the future to be a father to his son. Giving up Ciaran and Sile was unthinkable.

"Ye're a fine father." She looked too long into his eyes, and he had to look away.

Rattled in a way he'd never felt before and couldn't comprehend, he replied in a flat voice, "The children are all I have left of Cait." Even as the words left his mouth, he knew they were a mistake.

It was Sarah's turn to look away, and Dylan's heart clenched. Time. He needed more time. A lot more of it.

There was silence the rest of the way to the high glen.

At the house, Sarah went about her work and Dylan skipped his work-out to make some progress with his whiskey. Staff in hand, he headed out, following the burn into the forest.

He'd planted less barley in the last growing season than in other years and so would probably end up with only two casks of the *uisge beatha* this winter instead of the usual three. He wouldn't feel the lack for a while, though, until another three years from now when this winter's distilling would be ready to sell. Next year, when his first three barrels would be ready, it would be the first whiskey in Scotland to be aged in casks more than a few months before distribution in jugs and bottles.

The faint trail followed the burn, then at the fall circled around and down. There it ended at the pool formed by the waterfall. Carefully now, Dylan stepped into the brush and wended his way farther along the burn without leaving a trail. Instead of stepping on leaves, he nudged his foot under them and left them as they had been.

In another century or so the concept of aging alcoholic beverages would finally be applied to whiskey, and the law would then require Scotch whiskey to be aged at least three years, but these days the stuff was con-sumed raw like American moonshine. Dylan knew there was a better way. Besides being not as pleasant to drink, the raw whiskey was a health hazard. One man living in the glen was blind from it, and over the years a few had died. Dylan might even save a life or two by introducing this idea before its time.

Though it would be a challenge to single-handedly get Highland whis-key drinkers to sacrifice a bit of kick for flavor and safety, Dylan was counting on building a market for aged whiskey well in advance of the rest of the industry. He figured his knowledge of the future had to be good for something, and he knew keeping Glen Ciorram economically viable in newly capitalist and increasingly industrialized Scotland would be the best way to prevent the *Sassunaich* overrunning this glen during the next century or so. It was a risk, but worth a try.

Finally he crossed the burn and climbed to a ledge set under the overhang of a cliff. It was a small clearing, where Dylan had built a fire for his still. Within the cliff was a cave, where he'd stashed the casks while the whiskey aged. They were old sherry casks, cadged from Gracie at the castle. Three were marked 1717, three 1718, and only one so far had 1719 drawn on it with ashes. It was looking like only one more would join them this year.

He set his staff against the rock wall and went to work, rekindling the fire under the iron pot.

Most stills in Scotland, and all the stills in Ciorram, were illegal because of high English taxes, but Dylan wanted to go legit as soon as he could, if he could. With luck, the King's excise men wouldn't learn of the still and confiscate it before he could afford to pay the taxes on his output.

Unfortunately, he realized his newly found Catholicism wasn't going to help his business interests. But he'd been born a Methodist, which denomination wouldn't exist yet for many decades. He'd identified himself as Catholic for more than five years, and the clansmen had never known him to be anything else. Turning Protestant at this point would be viewed as abandoning his people, and rightly so. For the sake of the clan's future, he needed to find ways around the persecutory laws that didn't involve asking the entire glen to convert to a religion they believed in their hearts would condemn them to eternal damnation.

Dylan liked this spot. It was quiet here. Safe. Sometimes, if he concentrated, he could even recall the sense of security he'd taken for granted in the twentieth century. Situated so deep in the forest where there were no obvious trails, the place was not easily accessed by patrolling soldiers who hated to dismount their horses. The terrain was rocky, crags of granite in some places turning steep slopes into blank walls. Rock faces disguised the scant smoke from the fire that wasn't quite dispersed by overarching trees.

He enjoyed this work. Soaking the barley in sacks left in the burn, letting it germinate, malting it over the fire, fermenting the malt, was all peaceful, discreet activity. The clearing was deep in the heart of his lands, nestled in earth and stone and surrounded by oak and pine trees. Tending the still was a time of no interruption, when he could think and plan, but mostly it was a time when he felt the master of things around him. He had faith the things he accomplished here would eventually benefit himself and his loved ones. It was here he felt the rightness of the world.

Once a load of worts was in, fermenting, Dylan went back to the house for breakfast. Then, having eaten, he fed the kine and hauled water for them; shoveled out the byre, meanwhile catching a bucket of urine to be made into ammonia for cleaning and dying; cleared the hearthstone of ashes, which he saved for making soap; took up the muddy old reeds and bracken from the floor, which hadn't been changed in months, and replaced them with new; then hitched the garron to the cart again and went to work spreading manure over more of his fields.

As usual, the boring work allowed his mind to wander. Purposeful in his avoidance of the subjects of Cait and Sarah, he led his thoughts to his old life. He wondered how his mother was getting along. Or, rather, how she would get along centuries from now. He wondered whether she'd listened to him when he'd asked her to leave that sonofabitch who was his father. As hard as he tried, though, he couldn't imagine her walking away from the old man. She was too good a wife, too invested in keeping everything around her smooth and pretty. It had been decades that she put up with the battering. She was so skilled at hiding the truth, she most likely hid it from herself as well.

Sinann fluttered behind him. "Come to the *broch* with me."

Dylan was startled out of his reflections but declined to reply and continued to fork manure onto the ground.

"*Och,* he's amusing himself, dreaming of the goddess of war with all her lips spread wide."

He smiled. "No, but now that you mention it, I think I'll just tuck that image away for later."

Brightly, she said, "And meanwhile, you can come to the *broch* with me." She made a gesture in the direction of the tower, waving him on.

Again, he ignored the suggestion and said as if he hadn't heard it, "Sinann, you've heard me talk about my parents."

She settled onto the rails of the cart to attend. "Aye. Your da being too taken with the drink, and your mother struggling not to notice and being beaten for her trouble."

"Aye. In a nutshell." Dylan thought for a moment, then went on as he continued with his work, "I left her my property in my will, and even without that, she would have had the wherewithal to leave him. She'd inherited money from her parents. She knows I want her to get out of there. She won't be safe until she does. I'm afraid he's going to kill her one day."

The faerie nodded. " 'Tis not unheard of."

"I hate him, you know. I've hated him all my life." The pitchfork went into the cart full of manure as if it were his father.

She made a noise of disgust. "Ye cannae hate him."

"I can, too. I do. There was one time . . ." Dylan stopped and leaned on his pitchfork for a moment as the memory slammed into him sideways. It had been years since he'd thought of that day, and now it made him feel dirty to recall it.

He continued slowly, quietly, "There was this one time when I was . . . oh, I think I was four. I'm pretty sure I wasn't in school yet, but I was old enough to know right from wrong. One night Dad came home drunk. . . . Well, he always came home drunk. Or stoned, or whatever he was into back then. I was never really sure, but I think it was alcohol because Mom always seemed to have this attitude toward other drugs that she didn't have about scotch. Anyway, he was really out of it. But, you see, I was used to seeing him like that. I had no idea at the time why he was that way.

"So he comes in, and Mom is trying to get him fed. I was in the foyer, hiding because I was supposed to be in bed. But I heard him shouting, and I wanted to see what was going on, so I sneaked downstairs to watch. He used to scare the snot out of me." Dylan tilted his head, then shook it in wonder. "You know, I don't think I've ever seen my father that I wasn't either frightened or repulsed."

He shrugged. "Anyway, she's offering him dinner that's on the table, and he's bitching that it's probably cold. She's trying to assure him it's not. He tells her to shut up. She does. He goes into the dining room, and I'm peeking around the doorway and through the arch at the other side of the living room. He sits, takes one bite, and throws the dinner across the room. Me, I about crapped in my jammies. I thought I'd done something and he would come after me."

"Did he sometimes come after ye?"

One shoulder shrugged. He'd never said this out loud to anyone but Cody. "Yeah. He stopped when I started to get good at defending myself." He took a deep breath, looked around as if for eavesdroppers, and continued. "So then things got really weird. She comes back into the living room, 'cause she knows she's going to get it. And he comes after her. *Boom!* He hits her. Then he grabs her hair and hits her some more. She's crying . . . and . . . well, I'm just watching this." Dylan's chest tightened, but he continued, "And he just keeps hitting her. Pretty soon she's not even trying to talk, and then she drops to the floor. Then he started kicking her. Hard. And she wasn't making any sound. She just lay there. And he was still kicking her."

Sinann made a soft noise of disgust in the back of her throat.

"So then he finally stopped kicking her and came at me. I crammed myself into that little, narrow space between the wall and the bottom steps of the stairs in the foyer. 'Cause I knew I'd get clobbered if he caught me up that late. But it wasn't me he was after. He didn't even see me. He went into the office, threw some things around for a moment, then came back out with a revolver in his hand."

"And a 'revolver' would be . . . ?"

"Oh." He held up his fist with thumb and forefinger stuck out. "It's a pistol. It's got this barrel in it, full of bullet cartridges that turns as it fires, so it's called a revolver. It . . . you know, revolves. That way, it can fire more than one shot without reloading."

The faerie's eyes were wide. "A wondrous thing!"

Dylan shot her a cross look and said, "Yeah. Real fucking nifty. Dad went back into the living room again, and I peeked around the doorframe as he pressed the gun to my mom's head. I think my heart stopped, and I almost shouted at him. But I didn't. And then he pulled the trigger. The gun clicked. Empty chamber. He pulled the trigger again, it clicked again. Six times, and only then did he decide it was time to stop because the gun was empty. He threw it, and it broke a picture frame over the mantel. Glass went everywhere. Then he plopped down on the couch and passed out."

Sinann said softly, "And so yer father tried to kill yer mother?"

Dylan stood, poking the pitchfork into the frozen ground over and over, then shrugged. "I don't know whether or not he knew the gun was empty. What I did know was that *I* did not know. I mean, I thought my father was about to kill my mother, but I just stood there and watched. I didn't say anything. I just let him do it."

The faerie was frowning, her face screwed into a look of deep puzzlement. "And so . . . it's yer*self* who ye hate?"

"I just let him do it."

"*Och*, ye were but a wee lad. Nae older than Ciaran. And he was yer father. Nae matter what he might do, or have done, he was yer father and the authority of the house. At so young an age, ye couldnae have guessed he would do anything wrong."

"I hate him for what he did. For what he did to me."

She shook her head. "Ye cannae hate him."

"All my life I've wished to have had the courage to at least make myself known that night. I hate him for doing that to me. I hate him because he's a coward who hits women, who can't face the world unless he's blitzed out of his tree, and who did nothing but make people miserable and afraid of him for the whole thirty years I knew him."

"Not yer sire. Ye cannae hate him. Perhaps he cannae command respect, but hating him isnae necessary. 'Tis enough to disrespect him."

Dylan nodded. "Then I guess I disrespect the hell out of him. If I hadn't left when I did, I probably would have eventually disrespected him into a bloody pulp. I couldn't just stand by and watch him do that to her. Not anymore."

"And what's worrying you now is . . ."

He glanced up at her. She knew him too damn well. "What's worrying me now is that I left her unprotected. I'm afraid he'll hurt her—kill her for real." For a moment he flashed on a day he'd left Cait unprotected and shook his head to make the thought go away. "I want to know what's going to happen."

That brought a high, tinkling laugh from the faerie. "Oh, aye, now ye're in the same boat as the rest of us, not knowing the future!"

He shrugged. "I wish I could know she would be safe. I guess I won't know that until I've died."

"I would say so."

There was a long silence as he went back to throwing fertilizer, then he asked, "You figure she'll miss me?"

"She's yer mother. Of course she will."

There was another long silence, then he asked, "You figure she'll come looking for me?"

"I would, were ye my son."

"Maybe she'll find me."

"Ye'll be long dead by then."

Dylan stopped work, stunned by the realization he would be dead centuries before his mother would even be born. Then he looked straight into Sinann's eyes. "Maybe she'll find you instead." Hope rose.

The faerie shook her head, for his intent must have shown in his eyes. "I wouldnae risk sending her to ye. By sending your friend, Ciaran will have been saved, but I couldnae risk your mother. I havenae sufficient control. She could appear anywhere, and not necessarily in my own lifetime. Without either of us to look after her, she could be in more danger there than where she is." She shook her head. "Nae. 'Tis far too perilous."

Dylan sighed and fell deep into thought. "Yeah. Even if you managed to send her here, it wouldn't be good for her. I couldn't keep her safe. Or healthy." It clenched his heart to admit it, and he thrust the pitchfork hard into the cart.

Sinann wouldn't let him dwell on his mother. She fluttered into the air and said brightly, "Now put the pitchfork away and come with me. We're needing to learn what it is the Morrighan is after. You've enough power for it now, and should make the attempt while the moon is still full."

He shook his head. "Too much work to do. Give me a couple of days. I can do it then."

"It may be too late then." She made a noise in the back of her throat. "It may be too late now."

"No. There's too much work to do. I can't be farting around with Morrighan." He shoved the pitchfork into the cart, then went to the garron's head to lead him forward a few more yards. Then he walked to the back of the cart for another forkful.

"If I lighten the load?"

Dylan paused in midthrow, thought a moment, and looked around. "How much lighter?" He hated letting Sinann do his work for him, because it would bring comment from those who already thought he was in league with demons.

"Let me lead the garron for ye."

He looked at the little white horse and considered it. In years past, Cait had led the garron for him, making the job go smoothly and quickly as he followed along behind with the pitchfork. Ciaran would be big enough to accomplish it year after next, but this year was still too small to control the rambunctious animal. If Sinann did it, the garron would appear to be leading himself. But Dylan nodded.

"All right. If anyone gives me grief, though, I'll have to tell them I've trained my horse. I'll need you around to demonstrate that training if I'm confronted." Glancing around, he decided the risk wasn't high. Sarah and the children had gone to the castle, so the chances of being seen were slim.

"Aye, I'll be here." Sinann flew to the garron's head and lit on the ground. "Have I ever let ye down, lad?"

He frowned, and she quickly added, "When it truly mattered?"

With a grudging agreement, he let her lead the garron. The job went much more quickly with the horse and cart at a steady walk while he shoveled fertilizer from the back. The day's work was finished well before sunset. Dylan returned the garron and the cart and hung his tools on the byre wall where they belonged. Then he cleaned up in the burn, collected into a cloth sack the necessities for the mystical work ahead, and set out for the *broch*.

Sinann fluttered beside him on the way. "Nae the best time of day for this, while the sun wanes—"

"It's almost dusk; the only time better would be sunrise or midnight. I can pull it off. I just wish I had something of hers at hand." They were traversing the lower glen to the track that led to the *broch sidhe*. A tower known for the presence of faeries, it was avoided by most mortals and therefore the safest place for activities such as practicing the Craft. Dylan carried the old grain sack over his shoulder.

"She'd never let ye keep it, were ye to obtain such a thing."

Dylan knew that was so. His life would surely be forfeit for the Morrighan to regain possession of anything he might use against her.

The *broch* was immeasurably ancient. Even Sinann didn't know who had built it, and it was already old by the time of heroic Fearghas MacMhathain, the early Matheson ancestor who had died of battle wounds inflicted by a band of raiding Vikings. After vanquishing the enemy, Fearghas had made it to the *broch*, and as he died stained the ground inside it red with his blood. Today the ground was frozen, but Dylan knew, for he'd seen it, beneath the dead grass at his feet was earth as bright, arterial red as if Fearghas were still bleeding onto it.

The gray, moss-covered stones of the *broch* walls surrounded Dylan in antiquity, cutting him off from the concerns of his daily life and allowing him to focus on the job at hand. The gnarled oak tree rustled in the wind on the outside, but where the winter-bare branches had grown through a window to the inside of the *broch* the tree was still. Sinann flew to the stone steps at the wall, just under those branches.

"What say you? Skyclad or nae?" asked the faerie with a twinkle in her eye.

Dylan threw her a sideways glance. "I don't care to catch my death today, thank you. I'll be keeping my clothes on." He'd never had a cold in his life and sure didn't want one now, in this time before antibiotics, painkillers, and decongestant. He reached into the sack for the four candles he'd brought and placed them at the four compass points of the hearthstone in the center of the tower. Sinann lit them for him, for the sake of expediency.

He crossed himself and murmured a quick prayer for the blessing of the proceeding, feeling no conflict between his Christian religion and the use of natural power. In centuries past, Catholic priests had done no less, and the divining he was about to accomplish was no more a religious act to him than would be flipping on a light switch.

From the sack he produced a sprig of holly with red berries, and a sprig of mistletoe. He went to the oak to cut from it a twig. Then the sack yielded some small pieces of firewood, which he set in the middle of the hearthstone. Sinann obliged by lighting it for him. As it burned, sending a thin line of smoke into the still air, Dylan knelt before the hearth and held the three elements of his spell cupped inside his two hands.

Screwing his eyes shut, he concentrated his *maucht* and imagined the power flowing from him into the plants in his hands.

Sinann commented, hugging her knees as she sat on the steps, "It would have been far better, had ye fasted."

Dylan's concentration broke and he lowered his hands. "So, which is it, do you want to wait or not?"

She shook her head. "Proceed. The waning has begun."

"Fine. Then be quiet." He raised his cupped hands again and focused. The life energy flowed through him, and as he let it flow into the plants he thought of his goal to see Morrighan's purpose. His desire to know her intent went with the *maucht*. Soon the twigs felt warm in his hands, and he dropped them into the fire.

Still focusing on his goal, he rose and walked three times around the fire, deiseil. Clockwise, always, was the way to bring luck and power. Murmuring words of enchantment, he was able to say only some of them in the old tongue; the rest he said in modern Gaelic. Then he knelt at the edge of the hearth and leaned over the fire, taking whiffs of the smoke from the green woods. He let the scent fill his head, then further let it fill his body—his arms, torso, groin, legs—until he felt his skin filled with *maucht* as well as the spirits of the holly, oak, and mistletoe.

Slowly, laboriously, he formed a vision of Morrighan. Beautiful, black-haired, black-eyed war goddess. His skin prickled with goose bumps. His chest rose and fell with deep breaths. Around him the world dissolved and then returned.

He was in a burrow somewhere. Firelight flickered across tree roots. His head buzzed, and he was filled with a maddening itch. Desire. Blood and sex. Bathing in blood. Glorious death. Repulsed, he nevertheless probed further. He needed to know her mind. Needed to—

A shriek split the air.

Cold—sudden, ice cold—filled him where the plant spirits had been an instant before. Blinding pain tore his mind. A spasm shook him, and he fell back to collapse on the frozen ground. The cold of the winter-locked earth took him, and he shivered and shuddered. On and on it went, uncontrollably, until he lost consciousness.

He felt the cold long before he could feel anything else. The cold and the darkness filled him. Groaning, confused, and in pain, he opened his eyes onto darkness. Quivering from the cold, he pulled his plaid around himself and sat up. His fire was out, and all the candles had guttered. The interior of the *broch* was silver on gray under the full moon. He looked around.

"Sinann?"

No answer.

"Sinann, it didn't work." His voice was little more than a croak, and it hurt to speak. "She saw me coming, I guess. I got in but didn't find out anything."

Still no answer. He reached into the grain sack with a trembling hand, to find his Goddess Stone—a rock with a natural hole worn through the center. He looked through it like a monocle, but didn't find Sinann. *Huh.* If he couldn't see her with the stone, she must not be around. Maybe she went back to the house. He'd have to chew her out good for leaving him in the *broch* to freeze. Even his bones felt chilled. If he'd lain unconscious much longer after dark, he might have frozen to death. The ache in his left leg was so sharp now it made him wonder if it would even hold him up on the walk to the castle.

He sighed. "Blasted faerie." A gust of breeze touched him and sent a shiver through him, making him pull his plaid and his coat tighter. Struggling to his feet, knees shaking, he looked around again. "Sinann?" Just like her to take off. Probably embarrassed. He picked up his empty sack and rolled it into a wad, then headed off at a limp for the castle. It was going to be tricky to make it there past the soldiers, who would surely be patrolling heavily this soon after sunset, but it was too damn cold to wait long enough for the risk to pass. Gracie would need to make up the guest room again, for sneaking the kids home past the *Sassunaich* just wasn't a chance he cared to take with their safety.

*　　*　　*

"Evil! Evil man!"

Daghda watched Morrighan fume, then held her hand to keep her from doing damage to her belongings. She tried to yank away, and pulled, but he held her firm and drew her back down onto the bed beside him, where a moment before she'd been in deep, peaceful slumber.

"The cheek! The brazen gall of it!" She gulped air, her eyes wide and her lips drawn back in a snarl.

"Aye. 'Tis appalling." He was as angry as she, though it was not his habit to display it as she did.

Disgusting, it was—a mortal soul inside the Morrighan! There had been a time he would have destroyed with a gesture any man who would attempt such a thing. But his powers had gone long ago. Tonight, when he realized what was happening, he could only awaken her in time to prevent the mortal's spirit wending its way into her mind. She had been able to repulse the mortal and punish him. That cheeky Sinann, as well. This Matheson fellow was proving a nuisance, and the Daghda was quite ready to put an end to the impudent mortal's worthless life.

But at this moment he had his hands full with Morrighan's fury. She tried to rise, her eyes blazing and her hair flying. He pressed her down onto the bed next to him. She cried out, "She's taught him things mortals cannae know!" Her eyes were wide, and her chest heaved. Daghda watched it, and his attention wandered for a moment. Then he returned to the subject at hand.

"Sinann Eire."

"Aye. The granddaughter of Lir has given away secrets. Too many secrets."

Daghda frowned. "Mortals use the power. They always have."

Morrighan's voice took on an edge of derision, "But they cannae seek to learn the mind of the Sidhe. Her own powers are weak, so she teaches a mortal to do her bidding."

"*Och.*" The implications of that sent a shiver down Daghda's spine. To hear a cat laugh out loud would not have given him such pause. He said, assuring, "He'd never be as powerful as yourself. Or any of the *Tuatha De Danann.*"

"Nae. 'Tis true. But he shouldnae be this powerful at all. He kens far too much. He kens things I do not."

A chill of alarm skittered over Daghda's skin. Anger at Sinann reddened his vision. "You've killed the impudent sea faerie, I expect?"

She rolled toward him, and a smile crossed her face. She slithered on top of him and slipped between his knees. Leaning between his thighs and pressing herself to him, she said, "I've done far better, for killing is nae for me to do." She waved her hand in dismissal. "Let men in battle shed the blood; I urge them to it only. So Sinann willnae die. For the rest of her dear mortal's life, with her powers annulled by my spell, she'll do nae more than watch her precious Matheson of the future, unable to speak to him or be seen by him. She cannae communicate with him in any way. For all his life she'll be nae more than the air to him."

Daghda smiled and slipped his arms around her waist to press her close. "It's a cunning woman ye are."

CHAPTER 8

For two more days Dylan fertilized his fields; then, when that job was finished, he turned his attention to the distilling and spinning. He threshed and milled more oats to refill the sack from which Sarah made parritch and bannocks, cared for his kine and sheep, made repairs in the thatching on his house, and whittled a small wooden staff for Ciaran to use in his kung fu lessons.

Each morning after Dylan's workout, Ciaran would take a short bit of private instruction with his father, as well as joining the Sunday evening sessions in the castle bailey with the Ciorram men and boys. He was the littlest student, struggling hard to keep up, but he put a brave face on it. Sometimes Dylan couldn't help a smile of pride to watch his son spar fiercely, standing up to Gregor, who was nearly twice his size but not nearly as well disciplined.

On most days in the household of Dìlean Dubh, after supper there was a short lesson in reading and English, though it would be another three years before Ciaran would be old enough to attend school at the castle. Sìle, being a girl, would have her entire education at home, so there was little sense in waiting till Ciaran was seven before beginning to teach them to read and speak English.

Besides the Bible and the book of poetry Cait had brought to the marriage, Dylan now owned copies of Shakespeare's *Hamlet* and Sir Thomas Malory's *Le Morte D'Arthur*. In Dylan's day, far in the future, those stories would be much too violent for children. But in these times of public hangings, sword and pistol duels, and the constant threat of the English occupational force, such violence was commonly witnessed by children. Hiding it from them in literature would be at the very least pointless. Also, books were expensive and the options for printed fiction were limited. Dylan took what he could get and taught his children to read.

After the lesson, which was directed at Ciaran while two-year-old Sìle played nearby, Dylan would read to the kids until they became droopy-eyed, then put them to bed. The rest of the long winter evening, until sleep claimed himself as well, was spent at small tasks that could be done indoors by candlelight. Then he would wash in a bucket of water that had warmed to room temperature by the fire and crawl into bed. Always he hoped for a dreamless night.

During these weeks the Morrighan seemed to be letting him alone, and he wondered why. He knew her kind too well to think he would escape retribution for his intrusion. The waiting made him uneasy, and his discomfort increased with the arrival of the parish priest.

After months away from Ciorram, Father Turnbull made it to the glen. Because enforcement of the anti-Catholic laws was spotty in areas controlled by Catholic lairds, Mass could still be conducted in the ancient church across from the garrison, so long as the priest himself was not seen coming and going. But with the church in sight of the garrison, that was next to impossible. Even though Father Turnbull was more or less safe on the lands of Iain Mór Matheson of Ciorram, subterfuge and misdirection was required to get him to and from the glen. He was most vulnerable to arrest on leaving.

For all the danger risked by the clansmen on behalf of the priest, Dylan thought the man should have been a bit less nasty to the folks who protected him during his stay. However, over the years since his appointment to the parish, Turnbull had remained obstinately judgmental of everyone around him and fully out of touch with his flock. Seen more often than not wearing the insincere smile of a television evangelist, he stalked the glen in his black habit like an avenging scarecrow, telling folks what was wrong with their lives and doing it in incredibly bad Gaelic. Dylan had never understood why the priest had been unable to learn the language of his parishioners, except that Turnbull was a Lowlander and disdained the

Gaels as unsophisticated. His relationship with his parishioners was fraught with tension and distrust. Dylan figured, with this guy making the rounds of the few remaining congregations, Catholicism in Scotland was in danger from more than just the King of England.

When it was time for the priest to move on to his next stop, Dylan was tapped to escort him. Sitting with the other men by the hearth in the Great Hall on Monday night, Iain Mór informed him he was to take Father Turnbull on to Killilan in the morning.

Dylan said nothing, but merely nodded. The priest smiled at him, that tight, crinkly eyed smile that made Dylan want to imitate it so Turnbull would see how he was fooling nobody. But his own face remained impassive.

The priest said in English, though there were several non-English–speakers present, "I look forward to traveling with you, Dylan. It'll give us an opportunity to talk."

Dylan replied in English so the priest would understand. "I expect that means I should leave my invisible friends at home, then?" Not that Sinann was around these days, and he had not yet decided whether that was a good thing or a bad thing.

That brought a laugh from those in the vicinity who understood English, and there was a murmur of translation for those who didn't. Everyone in the glen knew Dylan was suspected of consorting with demons, for he was frequently caught talking to himself. He usually claimed to be praying when that happened, but Turnbull had never bought it. Dylan's trips to the *broch* and his reputation for nearly supernatural fighting skill didn't set well with the priest.

Turnbull said, "Indeed." He certainly knew it had been meant as a joke but refused to treat it as one.

With an impish grin akin to the expression his students in the twentieth century had once called his "cute teacher smile," he added, "Then, by all means, they'll stay home. Aye. Indeed they shall. No matter how they might protest, I'll tell them, 'No, you stay here, for the good Father doesn't care for your company, and your presence upsets him.' " Again, his listeners laughed. Turnbull's smile tightened.

At dawn the next morning, Dylan climbed into a borrowed fishing boat at the shore of the island on which the *Tigh* stood. All the boats of the village were along this bit of shore, for the water here was deep and rarely froze on this side of the island. He would have liked to jettison the net, which lay in a huge pile near the bow, but folks in red coats were watching, and he needed to appear the sincere fisherman. Several other men helped him load a huge basket covered with a ragged piece of linen, which they set next to the mast. About six inches of water sloshed around down there. If the leak turned out to be a bad one, Dylan expected he'd be bailing for most of the trip. A linen sack followed the basket and was tucked away in a dry spot near the stern.

The men shoved the boat off into the water, and Dylan unfurled the sail to pick up the wind. He guided the boat onto Loch Sgàthan and headed west. It would be a long, slow trip across the huge loch.

Not long after leaving the *Tigh,* the basket reverberated with a long, musical fart. Dylan found it difficult to keep his laughter silent, so he turned up his coat collar against the winter wind and *hee-heed* inside the black wool. Another blast of gas followed several minutes later. The air inside that basket was probably pretty nasty by now, and worsening as the morning wore on and more were let go.

It wasn't long before Turnbull's voice came from the basket. "Is it safe yet?"

"No." Besides that the boat was visible from a great distance on the loch, and they could be met anywhere along the shore by an alert patrol, Dylan wished to put off having the priest's company as long as possible. He sailed on, and Turnbull continued to break wind. Dylan amused himself by considering how much faster they would go if he could harness all that methane and continued to giggle into his coat.

Soon after, Turnbull's plaintive voice asked once again whether it might be safe.

It wasn't really, but Dylan didn't have the heart to keep him in the basket any longer. "All right, we're safe." They were nearly at the west end of the loch, so perhaps they wouldn't be spotted.

Turnbull rose from the basket, red of face and moving stiffly. The freezing wind blew his hair every which way. Dylan held the basket as he climbed out, for it wouldn't do for the priest to end up in the cold loch. Turnbull sat in the prow of the boat and pulled his coat around him as he watched the shore approach.

Finally, after a journey that took the better part of the morning, they ran against the edge of the ice lining the shore. Cracking and crunching, it broke around the hull of the boat until they came to shallow water and heavier ice. Then the boat would go no farther. Dylan stepped out at the bow and verified the ice was thick enough to stand on. Then he helped the priest and the sack containing his leather traveling case onto land. They began walking toward Killilan.

Dylan declined to chat much. The cold on the loch and the freezing water soaking his leggings had put a chill in his left leg, and he favored it. The pain wasn't much—just enough to keep the back of his mind aware of the weakness, and it made him less than cheery.

Though the sky was heavily overcast, Dylan stopped for a rest when the day seemed as high as it would get. His stomach had begun to growl, and he needed to be considerate of his charge. Though Turnbull was quite accustomed to travel by foot, he was still a man of the cloth and shouldn't be required to prove his physical stamina like other men. Dylan built a healthy fire to warm them and produced bannocks and cheese from his sporran. He gave half to the priest, and they ate. Chewing slowly, almost absently, Dylan stretched his left leg and held it near the fire to loosen it up. The musket ball scar caused muscle stiffness, and the shin bone Sinann had once broken brought the deep ache. Little wonder he was limping.

Turnbull swallowed and finally spoke. "Have you prayed about that leg?"

Dylan nearly groaned but kept his silence for the moment. Then he said, "Aye."

"You shouldn't be limping, then." His voice held a firmness of conviction usually found in the truly ignorant who don't even know they don't have all the answers.

There was no possible reply to that, so Dylan kept shut. But the priest wouldn't let it go.

"You should understand, my son, that physical weakness is an outer sign of spiritual weakness." Again, it was as if he were reading from a book without even seeing the man before him.

"The leg was broken." Dylan drew his leg back under him.

"I'm dead certain it's not angels you speak to when you think nobody hears. Perhaps, were you to leave them alone, your leg wouldn't be sore."

Dylan couldn't argue with that, for it happened to be true. Never mind that Sinann had broken his leg to keep him from doing something far more stupid than talking to faeries. So he said nothing and stared into the crackling fire.

There was a long silence, then Turnbull said, "You don't like me very much, do you?"

Dylan cut a sideways glance, wondering what sort of trap this was. Not only did he not like Turnbull as a person, he didn't trust him as a priest, either. However, he folded his hands together and said truthfully, "You're a man of God. You take risks in your work, which you do for the sake of other people. I respect that." He refrained from mentioning his lack of respect for the priest's overbearing way of going about that work.

After another moment of deep thought, Turnbull drew a long breath and intoned, "Most often when I am disliked, it is because of a lack of faith in the other person. Or else I'm talking to a Protestant, which amounts to the same thing." Dylan's ears warmed, and he wondered if he was about to be accused of Protestantism. But the priest continued, "In you, however, I see something else. There's something quite different about you, Dylan."

Dylan shrugged. "I was born in America." For the past five years, that had gone a long way toward explaining all sorts of ways in which he was different from the Mathesons of this century.

But the priest shook his head. "No. I can't say as that's it. You see, what puzzles me is that, even though you are a devout Catholic and you are faithful to the true religion, you . . ." He stammered for a moment, then gave up trying to explain what he meant. He said, "I don't know. It's as if, on the one hand you are not Christian and on another hand you embody all that is Christian."

That made Dylan blink. He looked over at Turnbull, his eyebrows raised.

"You see," continued the priest, "it's extremely difficult to explain."

"How am I not Christian?"

"It doesn't seem to upset you that people think you speak to demons."

Dylan snorted. "You're the only one who thinks that. At least, you're the only one who says it's demons, and I think you have your education in France to blame for that. If it doesn't upset me, it's because the accusation is untrue, and nothing you say, do, or think will make it true. My personal conversations are with nobody any more evil than yourself. If I seem to talk to thin air, it's because . . . well, it helps me sort out my thoughts." True. Talking to Sinann always seemed to help him work things out in his mind. Then, with a sudden urge to tweak the priest's pride, he said, "A bit like confession during times when there's no priest to be found."

Turnbull's mouth became a hard line with the corners turned down. "Well, I would feel better about your spiritual health if I didn't hear about the amount of time you spend in that tower, burning leaves." Again with the Continental attitude toward pagan thought, defining it as devil worship. Father Buchanan hadn't felt that way, for he'd been educated here in Scotland.

Dylan bit the inside corner of his mouth for a moment, then said, "Father, do you believe in faeries?"

The priest shook his head.

"Then why are you afraid of the tower? What could possibly happen there to concern you?"

"There are no faeries. Therefore, the creatures that inhabit the tower must be demons." A sudden breeze kicked up and blew Turnbull's hair every which way. Then it died as suddenly, leaving him to shake his hair away from his face.

"What makes you think there are creatures in the tower at all?"

"Why else would you go there to commune with the invisible?"

Dylan shrugged. "To meditate?" Sometimes. Sometimes in summer he went there to sleep in the sun, and once he'd gone there to make love. "I go there to meditate."

"About God?"

"Of course." Certainly he'd thought about God in the tower. He'd prayed there more than once.

"You would swear it to me? An oath? You go there only to meditate?"

Thinking fast, for oaths were a serious thing even to him and never to be taken lightly, he said, "I swear to you that I've never in my life had discourse with demons, save those wearing red coats and carrying muskets."

That made Turnbull smile, the first genuine grin Dylan had ever seen on him. He smiled back. Maybe the priest wasn't such an utter prig after all.

A sudden rustling in the winter-silent forest caught his attention. Dylan rose to a crouch and drew Brigid. He gestured to the priest to be still, then moved in the direction of the sound. Listening hard, a chill skittered up his spine, for he could now hear breathing. A lot of it. And off to the side was a faint hint of movement, as if several men were taking up position. But he couldn't see anyone in the thick woods. Slowly, hoping they couldn't see him yet either, he backed toward the fire and gestured for Turnbull to follow him away to the woods. The priest picked up the sack containing his satchel.

At that moment the woods came alive with red coats and muskets. Dragoons. *Speak of the devil.* "Run!" he yelled to the priest and dashed for the woods. He heard the thump of the sack with the luggage as Turnbull swung it and caught a Redcoat full in the face. Then Dylan realized the priest wasn't following. He glanced back.

Major Bedford was there, telling the men who had grabbed the priest to tie him to one of the horses. Dylan skidded to a stop. He couldn't leave Father Turnbull behind. But before he could take a step back toward the soldiers, the ground crumbled beneath his feet. The bracken beside him fell away, and he was suddenly floating, falling, tumbling, rolling with the dirt and bushes. Then the world went black.

When Dylan awoke, he immediately vomited onto the ground beside him. His head thudded with an ache beyond comprehension. Something was tangling his legs, and it seemed he was upside down. Vomit clung to his upper lip. He spat and tried to look around, but all he could see was a tangle of uprooted bushes. It was twilight, and he shivered with the cold. He'd been unconscious for an awful long time.

He moved to right himself and slid downward in loosened earth, past a large boulder. Finally he came to rest and was able to find his feet. He stood and looked around. Brigid was half buried in the dirt. He picked her up, wiped her off, and scabbarded her at his legging.

He hadn't fallen far. It would be an easy climb to where he'd been. His head ached and would do so for a long time, he was certain. Concussion was familiar to him, and he recognized the heaving gut. With a sigh, he began climbing.

The clearing above was empty. Bedford had taken Turnbull, probably back to the garrison, and most likely left Dylan for dead. From there the priest would be transferred to Fort William for trial then transportation to America. Dylan's heart sank at the thought of yet another prisoner in exile. With so many Scots being arrested and transported, these days even Dylan was beginning to think of travel to his birthplace as a fate comparable to death. He headed toward the spot on the loch where he'd left the boat.

As he approached the loch, he slowed and began to listen. Carefully, he crept forward, silent among the trees and bracken and invisible in the darkness. The boat sat just ahead, bathed in moonlight, tilted on the shore and the end of its furled sail flapping. Dylan listened.

Below the flapping sound and the crunching as the boat shifted against the ice, he heard whispering. Another few moments, and he was able to determine the direction from which the sound was coming. Off to his left, in the trees, they were. Two Redcoats waiting for him to return to his boat. Damn.

Carefully and silently, Dylan faded back into the woods to circle wide and make his way to Ciorram on foot, wondering whether he'd been recognized by Bedford. He figured not. If he'd been recognized, they would have come after him down the slope with their muskets, and he never would have regained consciousness.

Throughout the night as he went, the forest seemed to close in on him. The pine and oak pressed on the path, twigs clattering in the night wind and their branches groaning near and far. He could sense their disapproval he'd let the priest be taken.

Head aching, Dylan wasn't in a mood for it. "Shut up, trees."

They quieted.

The glen was stunned at news of Father Turnbull's arrest. Dylan found Iain in the Great Hall to tell him. Artair, perched on a trestle table nearby, when he heard uttered an indignant roar and leapt to his feet to approach across the Great Hall.

"Ye let them take the priest?!"

Dylan declined to reply. His own shame at his failure to protect the priest was acute enough. Except for the thudding of his head and the nausea in his gut, shame was all he could feel just then. He barely heard Artair's words. Iain asked for details. Dylan related what had happened, and the Laird listened with an impassive face. Once the full story was told, he merely nodded acknowledgment, then gestured to a gillie to come. Artair, meanwhile, muttered darkly about not wanting to stand too close to Dylan when the lightning would strike him dead. Iain hushed him and declared in a voice loud enough for all to hear that if Dylan hadn't saved Father Turnbull, he couldn't have been saved by anyone.

The lad was to carry a message to Killilan that Father Turnbull had been arrested. Then Iain took Dylan and Artair to the hearth, where Malcolm was warming his old bones, to discuss the matter. They talked so far into the night it seemed they were in danger of greeting the sunrise, for this was a serious matter. The clan wasn't going to like their priest being taken away.

However, the conference produced no better ideas than to petition the garrison for the priest's release. A message was sent to the Duke of Gordon, but it would most likely be fruitless. The priest had been taken, and the Protestant government wasn't inclined to reverse itself in these cases.

Petition was made for the priest's release, but as predicted, it went ignored. There was no recourse for a priest caught wearing his habit and carrying the accoutrements of his vocation. Off he went to Fort William.

Dylan was mortified.

CHAPTER 9

Once the excitement of the arrest had died down, the *Sassunaich* became restless, as they did every winter when there were fewer folks out and about to harass. The number of men of fighting age in Ciorram had taken a dip during the last uprising, and the unprotected women were terrified of the bored soldiers. They kept to their houses so strictly that even a curfew and its promise of transgressors to chase down was little distraction for the dragoons. The English took to harassing poor, retarded Ranald whenever he showed himself outside the castle.

At first they limited themselves to verbal abuse to confuse and frighten him. Ranald was easily confused, and though not easily frightened, whenever he did succumb to fear he reacted in strange ways deeply entertaining to the bullies in red coats. He sometimes shouted at them; other times he danced around in a circle with his arms wrapped about his head. Sometimes he would simply lie on the ground and weep from the terror.

It didn't take long for the soldiers to invent a game to play. Similar to polo, the object was to slap the young man on the behind with the flat of a saber. The slaps made him cry out in pain and frequently drew blood. Even retarded Ranald quickly learned that the sound of a saber being drawn meant trouble.

Though the Mathesons struggled to protect their handicapped cousin by keeping him indoors, he took it as incarceration and often escaped. The soldiers loved their game, not tolerating intervention, and once the swords were drawn, there was no rescuing Ranald until the Redcoats tired of harassing him.

Ciorram continued to live beneath the fear as winter wore on. A baby boy was born in the village, and there was much joy made of the survival of both mother and infant. Soon more women came up expecting, and the hopeful talk in the glen was for the future of the clan. Tormod's sixteen-year-old son and another Matheson boy the same age acquired brides—one a MacLeod and the other a MacGregor—and were handfasted against the eventual arrival of a priest if a replacement for Father Turnbull could ever be found. New houses would be built for them once peat could be cut, and the tenancies in the glen adjusted to accommodate the new households.

Donnchadh Matheson, who was Tormod's apprentice and Ailis Hewitt's little brother, had his eye on a girl. But she was still very young, and he would probably not marry until his apprenticeship was finished.

It was to Tormod's great and public humiliation that he'd even needed an apprentice, his son having rejected training many years before. Blacksmithing was too much work, in the son's opinion, so when Donnchadh had been orphaned, Tormod had taken him in. The apprentice would more than likely stay in the household after marrying and find his niche as Ciorram's blacksmith when Tormod died or, if he was lucky, declined into retirement and then died.

Particularly this seemed to the clan as likely, since it didn't appear Tormod would marry again, so smitten with Sarah as he was. He would need to be cared for by Donnchadh's wife.

As spring approached, it seemed the love bug was in the air. Even Artair seemed bitten, a surprise to everyone in the glen.

His arrogance and promise of power had long attracted girls from all the nearby clans, but though he encouraged the attention, it often seemed he willingly sabotaged all possibilities of marriage. There had even been one recent overture from a MacDonell father, whose daughter was quite pretty, in the interest of discouraging further raids between the clans. But Artair's attitude had always been to sample at will but never buy. Negotiations had not gone well to begin with, and when it was discovered the wee lairdie had sampled far too early, the MacDonells withdrew. The girl's father had been so enraged, the Mathesons thought there might be a battle to be fought. Reparations had been demanded, which were denied by Iain. It was not long after that Dùghlas's kine had been taken.

The new hopeful, a MacGregor girl, came on a cold, snowy day in early March. Dylan was summoned to the castle to greet several of that clan who had arrived from the south for a talk with Iain Mór. He scrubbed and dressed to be presentable, then set out from the high glen just as a light snow began to fall.

The flakes were coming faster and larger as he entered Glen Ciorram by the bog trail and approached the village. He stuffed his hands into his coat pockets and tilted his head against the snowfall, so the flakes would land on his hair instead of his face. Coming in sight of the nearest fields, Dylan spotted some dragoons riding back and forth near Tormod's house. At first it seemed they were executing maneuvering exercises, a common enough sight on the empty winter fields, but then Dylan noticed the small figure standing on the ground in the midst of them. Screams drifted across the cold field, and Dylan groaned.

Taking off at a run, he knew Ranald was probably bleeding by now. No others in the village were in sight. Doors and shutters closed, they had all withdrawn from the shame of their fear. Dylan's anger was what kept him from hanging back until the dragoons were finished. He ran on, vaulting stone dikes that stood between himself and Ranald.

The screams grew louder as Ranald became more panicky. There were three cavalry soldiers taking turns slapping Ranald's behind, and the young man's sark was cut to pieces. Red stripes crisscrossed his skin, and a trickle ran down one leg. He was crying and shouting at the Redcoats, turning around and around in an attempt to keep the target away. But there were three of them, and no direction was safe.

Dylan shouted at the Redcoats to stop, and they were surprised into it. One of them laughed. Ranald ran to Dylan and threw skinny arms around his neck, still wailing, tears running down his face and neck. Saying nothing, Dylan picked up Ranald and turned to take him back to the castle.

One of the dragoons shouted, "I suppose we could use that other fellow for practice, then."

Dylan turned back around, and without thinking, he let his rage speak for him. "I'll kill every last one of you." He meant it.

A silence fell over the men as the Redcoats debated whether to punish him for that. Then one of the *Sassunaich* said, his tone bored and dissolute,

"Come along, fellows. This snow is too bothersome, and he's most likely nothing more than a drunkard. Let's return to our fire."

The others muttered agreement and let Dylan take Ranald away. The young man clung to Dylan, weeping into his coat, all the way into the castle. There Dylan found Iain Mór and several prominent Mathesons sitting with the contingent of five MacGregors around the fire, chatting happily of Jacobite activity and drinking ale served by a kitchen maid.

The room burst into an uproar at sight of Dylan's bleeding cargo. Maids were dispatched for wash water and rags. Dylan shook snow from his hair, then set Ranald on his feet and lifted the ragged ends of sark to examine the damage.

"Bring a needle and thread, too." One of the gashes was deep enough to require stitches. "And Gracie . . ." The head maid turned to listen. "Boil them before you bring them. It helps prevent infection."

She frowned. "How—"

"A boiled needle is cleaner than one that isn't."

"Begging yer pardon, but I dinnae keep a dirty—"

"Just, please, do it."

Gracie looked to Iain, who glanced at Dylan, then nodded to her. She shrugged and harrumphed, then hurried to do the bidding of her Laird.

Once Ranald was cleaned and sewn up by the maids, and Dylan had washed the blood from himself, Dylan joined the other men who then returned to their conversation by the fire.

He settled in, as angry as they about the *Sassunach* presence. As they brought him into the talk, he was intrigued by news the MacGregors carried of a rising instigated by three men in the service of the exiled King James VIII: Cardinal Alberoni, the Duke of Ormonde, and the Earl of Marischal. The rising was beginning, and the feeling around the fire was that it wasn't a moment too soon.

Seumas arrived to greet his kinsmen, and he and Dylan both listened with great amusement to a story of his cousin and Dylan's former employer, Rob Roy MacGregor.

"Rob took a band of men to raid cattle for the provisioning of Jacobites, ye see." The leader of the MacGregors, who Dylan knew as Iain Beag, told the story with much gesturing and chortling and shifting in his seat. He was missing several front teeth, which made understanding him an adventure in concentration as he spat and slurred his words. "In one such raid, during January 'twas, Rob's men overran a posse of men working for Montrose. One of the posse was killed in the fight, and now Montrose has put a reward on Rob's head of two hundred pounds."

Seumas laughed out loud, and Dylan agreed with a snicker. Both knowing Rob, they also knew the reward would go uncollected, no matter how highly sought it might be. Rob was too wily and slick for that. Dylan also knew from history that Montrose would never have satisfaction for the imaginary debt for which he'd already spent years persecuting MacGregor.

Said Iain Mór with a chuckle that shook his large frame, "Montrose will be glad he'll not have to add the reward money to the sum he willnae collect from Rob."

Seumas laughed again and added, "Not to mention the thousands of pounds' worth of cattle we lifted from Montrose's lands."

A general murmur of agreement rippled through the group. Artair's attention wandered, and Dylan's followed it to see what the wee lairdie might be up to. It was only then he noticed the young woman sitting nearby. Artair was glancing over at her, and she was blushing prettily in response. She was a *very* young woman, a lovely MacGregor daughter, petite and lively, with the whitest skin and the brightest red hair Dylan had ever seen. But not a freckle to be seen, so she was a sheltered girl. And so tiny! Iain Beag was her father, and she took after him. Unlike Robin Hood's merry man, he lived up to his name—Little John—and was as slight of build as she.

Artair, under her flattering gaze, puffed up like a peacock, his back straighter and his chest deeper than Dylan had ever seen it. His earnest struggle to keep the thread of conversation was apparent by his comments, but he fell behind as his attention strayed to the girl with the pale bosom and the rosy cheeks. His comments became increasingly unresponsive to the conversation. It made Dylan smile, and he nearly laughed out loud when Artair gave up on the talk, fell silent, and focused his attention on the girl.

The open stare and shifting in Artair's seat finally brought comment from Iain Beag. He said, "Young Artair, do ye recollect my daughter, Fiona?"

Without taking his eyes from the girl, Artair replied, "Aye, I do." Then he addressed her directly, "I've nae seen ye since ye were a wee lass." His voice had somehow taken on a depth and softness that Dylan had never heard in the young man before. He'd seen it in other boys smitten for the first time but never thought it would happen to Artair. Perhaps the little punk was growing up.

All that week, Fiona appeared wherever Artair happened to be. Never *with* him, exactly, but if Artair was in the room, it was a safe bet Fiona was nearby. Rumors drifted about that Iain Beag MacGregor had a good chance of marrying his daughter off to the heir presumptive of Ciorram, and nobody was surprised.

When Robin approached Dylan and in low voice asked what he thought of the prospect, Dylan replied with a grin, "I think their children are going to have very red hair." He figured Artair settling down could only be good for Ciorram. Perhaps a wife was what the kid needed to smooth off his rough edges.

During that Sunday's fight class, the red-haired beauty was gawking at the proud young man. As the men shed their kilts to spar in their knee-length sarks, Artair flexed his arms and tossed back his hair. Dylan was reminded of a twentieth-century pro wrestler and had to turn away to hide his smile, lest he be asked to explain his amusement. He focused on his own stretching.

These martial art lessons had been going on in the castle bailey for three years. In his dojo back home Dylan had also taught fencing, but there was little he could teach the men of this century about swords. Kung fu, on the other hand, was not yet well known in Scotland and was a useful skill for any fighting man. The Mathesons were a long way off from mastery of the style, but Dylan had recently learned that style was un-important if a skill gave an edge in defense of one's life. He taught the men to take what they could from the lessons to augment the skills they'd learned in their own culture.

These days, the men were developing into a coherent unit, almost resembling the trained soldiers of a modern army. The rigor of the formal exercises executed en masse, combined with the warrior ethic of Highland culture, was a thing to see. Ruddy-cheeked, aggressive Scottish men, some wearing kilts but most in sarks, trews, and leggings, performing smoothly and correctly their prescribed exercises, brought Dylan to mind of the renowned Highland regiments that would one day be the pride of the British Army. He noted it with very mixed feelings.

Fiona was bundled tight in her traveling cloak at the side of the bailey, near the animal pens outside the kitchen. Her eyes wide at the things being taught and her smile bright whenever Artair's eyes found her, it was obvious to Dylan she was as enamored of the wee lairdie as he was of her. Dylan, feeling generous that evening, let Artair dominate the class.

Artair's energy that night was high. Cheeks flushed with enthusiasm, he was out to show the girl what he could do. Dylan took him for a sparring partner. Big mistake. It might have been all right if he hadn't already decided to make Artair look good, but with a heart softened at the sight of love in bloom, Dylan was vulnerable.

The wee lairdie came at him fast, which was usual for him and expected, and Dylan fended him well. But when the exchange ended, just as he was about to commend the lad's speed, he was assaulted again and caught a fist-and-elbow combination in the face.

Without the slightest thought, Dylan responded with a series of punches before spinning at Artair with a back roundhouse kick, then another, then another, and when the lad was on the ground, Dylan hauled off for a snap kick to a kidney. Then again. He had chambered for a third before he was able to control himself and turn away.

It was shameful. Shouts rose from the other students. Dylan looked back to see Artair writhing on the ground in serious pain. Fiona cried out and ran to him where he lay helpless on the ground. Dylan turned and walked away, still aflame with a need to kill Artair. At a safe distance, he paced back and forth, dabbing at his bleeding nose and casting sideways glances at the student he'd just clobbered. He hated himself.

He didn't need to dismiss the class, for the bulk of the men had gathered around Artair and were carrying him into the Great Hall. Fiona followed, cooing over the poor, hurt boy. Robin and Seumas hung back, and Robin drifted over to Dylan.

"He's deserved it for a long time."

Dylan's soul cringed, though the anger persisted and its claws gripped him with blinding, searing pain. He had to take several deep breaths before he could say, "No. Not like that. I was trying to kill him. If I'd had a dirk drawn, I would have. He's just a student. I shouldn't have gone off like that."

"Dinnae fash—"

"Thanks, Robin." Dylan looked over at Ciaran, who had witnessed the entire disgraceful performance and was now regarding his father with wide eyes. "I appreciate the support. But now I've got to explain to my son why what I just did was a bad thing."

Robin said softly, "Oh. Aye."

Dylan went to his son and lifted him to sit on a mounting block by the stable door. Then he squatted on his heels to be eye to eye. "I wish I hadn't done that."

The boy blinked. "Why? You won."

"Aye, I sure did. I'm a better fighter than Artair. But that's the reason I give the lessons; I know more. Which is why I don't need to prove I'm a better fighter. I'm his teacher, not his competitor. He was wrong in hitting me when I wasn't expecting it, but I made a bigger mistake by hurting him so badly in return. I didn't need to do that. I could have just told him to stop. Or I could have returned the same punch he gave me. But I didn't need to injure him the way I did. I'm more skilled at this than he is. I should have had more restraint."

Ciaran was silent, frowning.

"Do you understand, son?"

"No, Da. He hurt you." The boy's cheeks were a splotchy red. "I think he wants to hurt you some more, and when I get big, I'm going to make him stop. If he hurts you when I get big, I'll be killing him."

Dylan took his son by the arm. "No. Don't say that. Never do things like that when you're angry. I was mad at Artair, and that's why I hurt him. If I'd waited until I'd calmed down, I wouldn't have hurt him so much."

Tears stood in Ciaran's eyes, and Dylan could tell he wasn't getting through. His son stared at his swollen lip, and Dylan self-consciously touched his tongue to it. Ciaran said, "He hurt my Da. He'd better not do it again."

"Think about what I said, Ciaran. I mean it. Now I'm going to go inside and apologize to Artair." He took his son's hand and they went into the Great Hall.

Artair was sitting up at one of the trestle tables, and Fiona was holding a wet rag to his face. Almost everyone else had gone about their business. Malcolm and Iain were playing chess near the hearth, and some maids were scrubbing tables, but it was apparent the evening was over.

Dylan lifted Ciaran to one of the benches so he could sit on the table, and said to Artair, "I apologize. I shouldn't have come at you like that."

Artair glared at him. "Why not?"

Now Dylan was stuck for a reply. It was true he was far more skilled at unarmed combat than Artair, but to point that out just then seemed crass. Instead, he said, "We were only sparring. It was wrong for me to attack you in anger because I was unable to deflect your punches." His tongue touched his swelling lip again, and he lied, "I know you would never have landed them if you'd thought I wasn't expecting it."

The glare on Artair's face softened, and he glanced at Fiona. The girl was smiling at him with a look that said she thought he was a hero. Artair's voice sounded more reasonable now as he said, "Aye. It was an accident. No hard feelings, then."

Dylan nodded, and they shook hands. Then Dylan collected Sìle to take the kids home. He wondered when Artair would get him back for this.

It didn't take long. Two nights later, the men dropped their kilts to play a football game in the pasture along the loch shore to the south of the village. Dressed in sarks, boots, and leggings, the Mathesons squared off against the MacGregors, with Artair, Marc Hewitt, and Seumas making up for short numbers on the MacGregor side. Dylan led the Mathesons, and at first it was a friendly rivalry.

The game was more or less the same as the soccer Dylan had played as a boy, but was just different enough for him to easily let go of thinking of it as soccer. The heavy leather ball had less bounce than the well-inflated rubber ones of his youth, and the play was much rougher. No sissy personal foul rules about interference or kicking the other players. Chasing the ball across the field, sometimes in tight packs, things got rough. In this glen, any game that didn't produce blood was not thought to have been well played.

So Dylan had become used to having his shin whacked playing football. Usually it was the right one because that was his dominant side, but whenever the left was hit he would bite his lip and carry on. No big deal.

That afternoon the MacGregors and the Mathesons abandoned niceties and tore after each other, chasing up and down the field with great joy and violence. Artair got Dylan a good one on his left shin. Pain jolted up his leg. Dylan stumbled a couple of steps, falling behind the ball, but recovered himself quickly and ran on to catch up. Each step was fresh pain, but he couldn't let it be seen by the other players. He refused to limp.

Attempting to reclaim the ball as he ran, Dylan reached out with his right to kick it away from Iain Beag, and as he did, Artair clobbered his left leg again, on which his weight rested.

Dylan grunted this time and nearly went down as his left leg folded, but he recovered with his right by letting the ball go. Iain Beag ran in for a goal.

The pause in the play allowed Dylan to stand with his weight on his right while the pain in his left subsided. The anger ripped through him, but he focused the red rage behind his eyes and decided the Mathesons were going to win the game. Gritting his teeth, he ran to rejoin the play. No way was he going to let Artair see him limping.

But the wee lairdie must have known the leg was weak, for at the very next opportunity he hauled off and whacked Dylan's left shin again. This time Dylan hit the ground, and though the leg felt broken this time, he rolled and scrambled to his feet. Each step was agony, but it spurred him on to play harder. He took the ball away from Artair, dribbled it back down the field, and scored. There was no limping as he walked away from the goal, though each step was a jolt clear to his hip.

Artair nailed him one more time, but when it galvanized Dylan and brought on another goal for the Mathesons, he seemed to give it up. The Mathesons won, though Artair certainly had his revenge for the sparring incident. The next day Dylan's leg was swollen to twice its size and didn't want to hold him up. He spent the day by his fire, whittling eating utensils from scrap wood, so there would be no limping. For the rest of the week, he walked on it as if there were no pain. Damned if he was going to let everyone see his weakness.

CHAPTER 10

More stories of Rob Roy's exploits were told by the Mac-Gregors, well enjoyed and passed along by the Ciorram Mathesons who felt vicarious vindication for their own struggles against the Redcoats and the Whigs. But, while news of the rising and the possibility of restoration of a Catholic monarch lifted the hearts of Catholic Glen Ciorram, it brought an irritation to the soldiers patrolling that area of the Highlands. Annoyance arrests increased. And though the men taken by the soldiers were usually released unharmed within a day or two, the increased arrests served to step up the fear among the Mathesons. For Dylan, whose hatred of Redcoats was deep and indelible, the sight of a red uniform now also brought a surge of dread and a cold sweat. He knew well how disastrous a capricious arrest could be for him if he were taken alone.

Near the end of the month he was leaving Nana Pettigrew's house. He'd had his spun wool woven and sewn into some clothing for his kids, giving extra wool for the labor, and had come to get the finished clothing. The winter was losing its grip on the village now, and though the weather couldn't be called warm, it was less uncomfortable than it had been. On the track in the middle of the village, he met Robin Innis, who was on his way to Nana's with a live chicken dangling by its feet.

Dylan figured he was looking to get laid, as Robin had no wife and wasn't keeping company with anyone. Nana was making a fair living, now that the Ciorram men had gotten over having to share with the Redcoats. They had acquiesced quickly when it became apparent there were no village lasses willing to step in to take her business.

Dylan greeted his friend. "Come to get your ashes hauled, aye, Robin?" Though he shuddered at the thought of anyone buying comfort from the village prostitute in these preantibiotic times when syphilis was as deadly as AIDS, he also knew it was useless to talk to anyone here of disease. To eighteenth-century Scots, the concept of disease caused by invisible creatures was as quantum particles and nuclear fusion were to himself. Folks here barely grasped the concept of communicable disease at all, let alone viruses and bacteria.

"Aye, Dylan," said Robin. "I suppose ye've come for a niggle as well, then."

Dylan shifted the weight of the bundle of clothing under his arm and said, "You know better than that, Rob." On the subject of his abstinence, Dylan let everyone think he was keeping himself chaste for religious reasons only. "I waited for Cait, and I can wait for the next wife, whoever she might be."

Robin's smile was wistful. "*Och*, lad. Ye're waiting for Cait even yet."

Dylan made a disparaging noise in his throat, but softly, and looked around at the village so Robin couldn't see in his eyes the truth of it.

Ranald, in nothing but a dirty sark and bare feet that were muddy to his knees, was up the track a short distance, squealing and trilling to himself as he chased around a lumbering beetle. Every so often he would poke at it with his finger, then shriek and laugh, and follow the bug some more. It made Dylan smile to watch, for it was good to see someone take such joy in something so small.

As he watched Ranald, he half-listened to Robin suggest he begin looking for a wife again, for the sake of the children, and a surge of annoyance took him. Not at Robin, but at sight of a pair of dragoons coming at a trot over the rise in the trail up the glen. "Crap," he muttered.

"Ranald!" He called out to the young man. "Ranald! Get inside!" He took some steps toward Ranald and waved him toward the nearest house, across from Nana's. "Get inside!"

Ranald only stood and stared at him, his back to the approaching dragoons. He laughed, shrill and delighted, and jumped up and down like a pogo stick. "The faerie!" he shouted, and he pointed over Dylan's head. "The faerie!"

Huh? Dylan looked behind him but saw nothing. A stray breeze fluffed his hair. He turned back. This was no time to puzzle over whatever strange things Ranald might think he saw. "Ranald! Go! Run!"

But the young man only squealed and jumped up and down. The game was on now, to see whether Ranald could get out of being captured and put indoors. Dylan's heart sank. He began to run toward him, dropping the bundle as he went.

A laughing shout went up among the approaching dragoons, and two sabers were pulled from scabbards. Metal rang. The lead dragoon kicked his horse to a gallop. The sword was held aloft, ready to swing.

"No! Ranald!" Dylan skidded to a stop on the dirt track. He was too far away to get there in time. "Jeez . . ."

The young man frowned and turned as he heard the horse behind him. A dismayed squeal erupted from him. The sword was set to whack him with the flat of the blade. He went to dodge but wasn't quick enough. The lead soldier caught him on the behind, leaving a slit in his sark and a red line on his dirty skin.

Ranald cried out from the pain and terror, and spun to face the second rider as the first one began to circle. The linen behind him drooped open, and a dribble of blood ran down his leg. He put his hands over his face. But as the second rider approached, Ranald suddenly gave a shout and bent to snatch a jagged rock from the ground. The second rider's saber came around and whacked the retarded man on the behind. Another thin red line appeared on a buttock.

Dylan and Robin stood in the middle of the track and watched, helpless to do anything against the dragoons, who carried muskets as well as swords.

Ranald shrieked again with pain, turned, and cocked his arm to hurl the rock at the second rider.

"Oh, God," said Robin. "Ranald . . ." He dropped the chicken, and it went hurrying and fluttering away.

The rock caught the dragoon's eye. He emitted a vile string of Anglo-Saxon vulgarisms as blood dribbled down his cheek. Ranald jumped up and down, squealing with laughter and pointing at the bleeding soldier. Dylan saw what was coming and took several steps toward Ranald. "No," he muttered to himself because he didn't dare shout it aloud. "No, don't."

"Right," said the first rider, who pointed to Ranald with his sword, eyes flashing with anger that was almost gleeful. "That's it." He kicked his horse to a gallop, sword cocked. Before the horrified eyes of Dylan and Robin, the first dragoon rode back down on the retarded man and cut his throat, nearly sweeping off his head. Blood gushed into the air and rained on soldier and horse. Ranald collapsed, his head plopped in the dirt at a weird angle. A pool of blood spread around him in surges. His heart pumped five times before finally quitting. The thin body jittered for a moment, then lay still.

Red fury took Dylan, and rational thought ceased. He made an inarticulate roar as he started toward the murdering Redcoat. Robin leapt on him and wrestled him to the ground in a bear hug. With his arms pinned to his sides, Dylan writhed with all his strength. He kicked and growled, but Robin held him down and climbed on top of him. Robin kept him from rising and killing the English soldier.

"Damn," said the dragoon who had just covered himself with blood. "Look at this mess." Then he peered at his bleeding comrade and said, "Let's get you back to the barracks, Henry."

Henry was still cursing every Scot north of the Highland Line and their entire ancestry to the time of the Picts, but kicked his horse to a gallop and followed his comrade back up the track toward the garrison.

Not until they were well out of sight did Robin let Dylan up from the ground. Dylan scrambled to his feet and took a couple of blind, angry swings at Robin, but his friend was also his student, and neither swing connected.

People who lived in the nearby houses were venturing out now to see what had happened. At sight of Ranald's body, women wept, men swore, and the children chattered in hushed, awed tones at the great, running amounts of blood still spreading and soaking into the ground.

Dylan turned to look. More Matheson blood staining the ground. He stared at it, heartsick, and wished to see English blood running as freely.

"I'm going to the garrison," he told Robin.

"No. Ye're not." His friend held him back by his arm. "They'll kill you as well, and with greater pleasure."

Dylan shook his head and continued staring at the body. "I can't let this just go. It's murder."

"It's the English. Leave it—"

"No!" Robin blinked at him, and he continued in a more restrained voice, "I'll talk to Bedford. Just talk."

Robin considered that. "Just talk?"

Dylan nodded.

"I'll go with ye."

Dylan thought about that for a moment, then nodded. The desire to kill every Redcoat in the garrison was still strong, and he realized he would need help to keep his temper.

He turned to Nana, who stood outside her door, staring at Ranald's body, and took Brigid from the legging scabbard. "Nana," he handed her the dirk, "take this. Keep it for me. And this." He reached into his sark for his *sgian dubh* and handed that over as well. "I'll be back for them in a while." She nodded and took the weapons. Robin's also.

Then Dylan asked for a needle, and she frowned. "I'll bring it back," he promised. "I just need a needle to take with me. A long one."

She went inside for a moment, then returned with a long, thin embroidery needle.

So Dylan and Robin both went unarmed to the garrison. "What do ye figure ye'll accomplish with this talk?" Robin asked.

"Dunno. But I can't just not do anything. I've got to try to get Bedford to realize what's happening here and that he's got to control his men."

Down the length of the glen they walked, through the dogleg past the church, and up the slope to where the thatched stone building stood, surrounded by outbuildings and enclosures for the horses. Since the appropriations of 1715, in this glen only the dragoons were in possession of horses large enough for riding.

A sentry at the gate to the fortification saw them approach and lifted his musket to aim it at them. Dylan halted and held up his hands, palms forward. Robin did likewise. "I want to talk to Bedford."

The soldier's voice took a belligerent tone, "Who is that, you say?"

Dylan sighed. "I would respectfully request a moment of Major Bedford's time, if he's agreeable. My name is Dylan Matheson, and this man here is Robin Innis. You can see we're both unarmed."

The man with the musket seemed to agree with the claim and nodded for the Scots to proceed through the gate.

It was a small enclosure, just large enough to house the men who patrolled and enforced English law and Whig interests in the vicinity. Fort

William was several days' walk south and west of Ciorram. Even with the military buildup of the past few years, the Queen Anne Garrison was still a tiny outpost in comparison.

As Dylan and Robin walked toward the barracks, a thin, well-dressed Lowlander emerged from the building and paused for a moment to adjust his wig, which was slipping a bit on his head and taking his hat with it. He shoved it straight, then went on. Dylan hesitated a moment, puzzled that the man looked familiar, then put his gaze on the ground and kept going as if he'd seen nothing. But what he'd seen stunned him to his soles, for it was Felix, Connor Ramsay's former clerk.

In Edinburgh, while Dylan had been employed as Ramsay's body-guard, Felix's loyalties had always been suspect. Dylan had never been certain who had betrayed him to the Crown at Queensferry, nor could he be certain of who had sent robbers after Seumas and himself in Perth, or who had stolen the smuggler's letter from Ramsay's desk, but he had always suspected Felix. And now here was the little weasel, hanging around Major Bedford again and passing far too close to Dylan for comfort. Re-gardless of Dylan's pardon, Felix's presence was a danger.

Felix adjusted his wig again as he went toward the stable. Perhaps he was on his way out of Ciorram. Dylan hoped so. Anything that scoundrel had his hand in couldn't be good, and now Dylan wondered if Felix had taken Ramsay's place in Bedford's illicit business affairs. Smuggling and white slavery were the sources of funding that enabled the influence-rich but inheritance-poor Bedford to rise through the ranks of His Majesty's forces. Only God knew what else Felix and Bedford might have up their sleeves now that Ramsay was out of the way.

The Scots presented themselves to the sentry on watch outside the barracks and were directed around the side of the building to a private entrance. Offices had been added since Dylan's last visit to the garrison. As they approached the indicated door, Felix came from the stable, riding the Major's fractious horse with the white markings. He headed at a trot for the gate, leaving the garrison.

Good.

The sentry went inside to announce their presence. Bedford gave a curt invitation to enter, and Dylan and Robin did so. The room was large and airy, with a smooth wooden floor and enormous glass windows. Dylan couldn't help gawking, for it had been years since he'd seen this much glass in one room. Though the panes were small and rippled, blurring the view beyond recognition, they were numerous. The late afternoon sunshine warming the floor reminded him of the plate glass at the front of his dojo in Tennessee. A slight homesickness crept in on him.

Bedford was at his desk, looking industrious with quill in hand, the top buttons of his red tunic undone and his hat on a table behind him. One eyebrow raised at sight of Dylan, and he sat back in his chair.

"Dylan Dubh."

The Scots were not invited to sit, nor did Bedford stand. Mac-Corkindale was nowhere in evidence, which would be expected if Bedford had been meeting with Felix. Dylan set the needle in his left hand with the point at the base of his thumb and the eye beneath his middle finger. Then he ran the fingers of his other hand through his hair to get it off his face and came straight to the point.

"One of your men just killed one of our people for no reason." Dylan winced, hating the way that sounded. The worst of it was that he knew nothing would come of this. He was pissing up a rope to ask for vindication from this bigoted ass.

Bedford sighed and returned his attention to his paperwork, saying, "As I heard it, one of my soldiers was assaulted and sustained serious injury."

"Ranald had the mind of a child. He threw the rock because the soldiers hit him with their swords."

"So you admit the man who died had thrown a rock." The Major gave little attention to the matter, his voice distracted. His gaze was on the paperwork before him.

The red anger crept up Dylan's back, and his mind slipped away. With his middle finger he pressed the point of the needle into the mound at the base of his thumb. The pain cleared his head some, and he continued. "Child. He was a child. He had the mental capacity of a small boy."

Bedford finally looked up. "He was a full-grown man. Twenty-two years of age, if my information is correct. My own son is but ten years old and knows not to throw rocks at his betters." Dylan's stomach turned to learn Bedford had reproduced. The Major continued, "I can hardly accept a plea of ignorance in any case. Otherwise my men would be the targets of any man, woman, or child in this Godforsaken dale who wouldn't mind admitting to being an idiot. Your Ranald threw a rock and wounded one of my men. The soldiers defended themselves. The matter is closed."

The needle was pressed again. "I want both those soldiers punished

... *reprimanded*." Dylan hoped to take something back to the clan and thought he might get it by lowering his expectations. "I want them publicly reprimanded for hitting Ranald with their swords."

"They weren't hurting him."

Anger flared. "Like hell . . ." The needle went farther in, and the pain crept up his wrist. Dylan caught himself and said, "He was injured. Usually he was. They hit him with the flat of their swords but cut him nevertheless. He was hurt. Bleeding. And his sark was slit open. They were hurting him."

A sour look came over Bedford's face, and he twiddled the quill in his fingers. "You both may leave now. I'll not punish my men for the sake of any idiot, let alone a *Scottish* one."

Dylan leaned over the desk and pressed the needle even farther. Anger and pain roared in his head, sweat popped out on his forehead, and he took several deep breaths through his nose before speaking. "They were hurting him, and when he defended himself, they killed him. Ranald Matheson may have been mentally deficient, but he was also well loved in this glen. Even more than that, your men have made of him a symbol of the treatment we have received from you people during this occupation."

Bedford set his hands down on the desk and leaned against the back of his chair as if shocked at Dylan's words. "Don't be ridiculous. This is no occupation. We're not a foreign power." His tone was condescending, and he apparently believed he was telling Dylan an immutable fact he should have known already.

In went the needle, its eye now poking into Dylan's middle finger. Blood running down his palm dripped from his knuckle onto the floor. Sarcasm filled Dylan's voice as he turned Bedford's hatred to his own use. "*Och*, aye, it's true the English and the Scots are all the same and not a difference of race between us."

That brought a flush of embarrassment to the Major's face.

Dylan had a brief moment of victory, then continued, disgusted at Bedford's vulnerability of bigotry, "I'm telling you, Major Bedford, if you don't make an example of those two men, you will cause this glen to resist you. Clan Matheson will dig in their heels and give you trouble at every opportunity. Your men won't be safe unless you do this."

"Are you threatening me, Matheson?" The light in Bedford's eyes suggested he hoped Dylan would step out of line enough for an arrest.

Dylan backed off from the desk a step, raised his chin, and said, "No.

It's not a threat. But nobody, not Iain Mór nor myself—and especially not Artair—none of us will be able to stop the trouble once you've pissed off the clan enough for individuals to take matters into their own hands."

"How thoughtful of you to be so concerned about the welfare of my men."

"I don't give a damn about your men. I could swim in English blood as easily as in the loch. I don't wish to see my people rise against you, for they would die in greater numbers. I only want you to prevent more deaths."

Bedford finally stood. "If you wish to prevent deaths, then encourage your people to not throw rocks at armed dragoons." He looked at Robin, then back at Dylan, and said, "Now. Is that all?"

Dylan took a moment to overcome the urge to reach across the desk and yank Bedford over it by the front of his tunic. He pressed the needle hard into his thumb, until his finger and thumb touched. He said, his voice tight, "Aye."

"Then you may withdraw. I've work to do."

There was a long moment as Dylan debated arguing further, then he turned and left the room. Robin followed.

" 'Twas a brave effort, Dylan." There was nothing to say in reply, so Dylan kept silent as they made their way to the gate. But Robin continued, "Ye took a risk going in there."

"*We* took a risk."

Robin considered that for a moment, then nodded. "Aye. We did. Nobody will fault us for failing."

Dylan shook his head. "It wasn't complete failure. Colonel Klink in there is now on notice that the fun and games are over. Though there'll never be any public reprimand, he'll probably warn his men privately against capricious harassment. We might just have us a few weeks, or even months, of peace around here. Good job, Robin."

His friend grinned.

Outside the garrison gate, Dylan looked at his bloody palm and removed his impaled fingertip from the end of the needle. It had gone in about a quarter inch at the eye end. The rest of the needle was embedded in the base of his thumb. Robin looked, then looked away with a groan. Dylan tried to pull the needle from his hand, but the thin steel was slippery with blood. His fingers couldn't get a solid enough grip to get it out. "Crap," he muttered.

"Sarah," said Robin. Dylan looked up.

Sarah approached on the track from the village, and the men hurried to intercept her before she came too close to the gate and its armed guard.

"What are you doing here?"

"I came to see if you were all right. Were he to arrest the two of ye, none of us would hear of it for at least a day, if he bothered to tell us at all." She spotted the blood on his hand and took it into both of hers. "*Och*, what have ye done?"

Dylan tried to retrieve his hand, but she kept it. He said, "It's nothing. But I'm going to need to borrow Tormod's pliers to get it out."

Without another word, Sarah bent to take the needle between her teeth. With one yank, it was free. The pain was quick, then gone. She took the needle from her mouth, then wiped blood from her lip with her cloak before also wiping it from the needle.

Her tone was chiding. "I'm certain there was an excellent reason for you doing this. I'll return this needle to Nana for ye." She took care in clearing the eye of blood with her fingernail, as matter-of-fact as if she were cleaning rust from it.

Dylan was speechless. He held his finger to the base of his thumb to stop the bleeding, and with his other hand reached out to wipe a spot of blood from Sarah's cheek.

For a moment she looked like she might say something but then only turned to go. Finally, he said, "Thank you."

She turned back long enough to say, "Ye're welcome."

Robin opened his mouth to say something to Dylan as well, but closed it. Dylan was glad. He didn't want to hear again how he should marry Sarah, especially just then.

CHAPTER 11

At the beginning of April the weather warmed some, taking the edge off the winter. The glen continued to simmer in the anger over Ranald's death, folks muttering darkly that the *Sassunaich* would pay. Dragoon patrols increased, and tension grew, but Dylan had been right about the capricious harassment. The dragoons began to take a little less joy in harassing the locals, and ugly encounters became fewer.

Sarah continued to come and go from Dylan's house with her sons, remaining a large part of his world. He began to notice her presence bothered him less than it once had. The look in her eye seemed less out of place now. He wanted to ask Sinann whether she'd removed the love spell, but he knew better than that. Sinann's powers didn't include spell removal—not even her own spells—and she couldn't have removed it even if she'd wanted.

Besides, the faerie hadn't shown herself since that night at the tower. Repeated searches with the Goddess Stone told him she'd left entirely. It bugged him. After years of hanging around, she had her nerve to just up and disappear like that.

At lunch one day, the children had finished eating and were playing in the dooryard while Dylan ate inside at the table. Sarah was laundering a bucketful of stockings: items small enough to hang indoors for drying, and worn close enough to the skin to require frequent washing. A linen cord was strung across the room, secured to the rafters at either end, and the stockings were hung directly over the fire. She checked them frequently, lest the dried stockings should burn. Burnt wool was an unbearable stench, even in a house where cattle and goats were resident all winter.

He watched her move back and forth along the line. She was tall like Cait, but so was almost everyone else in the glen. Sarah had been born a Ross, and was a distant cousin of Cait's mother, who was a Sutherland. Her married name was Matheson, her late husband having been a less distant cousin of the Laird himself. Just about everyone in the glen could trace a connection to Iain, and therefore his daughter, so any similarities between Sarah and Cait were no more significant than those between any others of the clan. She was also thinner than Cait, though she had once been much heavier. Raising two sons as a widow, it was likely she had less to eat now than when he'd first met her. There had been a time when he'd thought thinness was attractive, but now he knew it to be a sign of poor diet or ill health.

Sarah did not have the blue eyes so common among the Mathesons; her eyes were dark brown and her hair chestnut. Though she was no longer plump, there were rosettes in her cheeks denoting a health that by itself made a woman attractive. They glowed beneath pale skin only slightly touched by smallpox scars. Her face did not deny her age—she was nearly the same age as himself and did not look younger—but neither did she look older than she was the way many women did. Dylan couldn't deny her beauty, which lay in her health, strength, and grace. His gaze lingered as he chewed thoughtfully on a nicely toasted bannock.

She caught him staring, and a smile touched her mouth. He glanced away, but on reflection decided he should be able to look if he wanted. It was his house, after all. He sat back and looked again, noticing the sway of her hips under the tightly laced bodice. A smile came to his own face as the blush in her cheeks crept down to her neck. Concentrating on her work, she wrung out a stocking, extra-specially drip-free, then stood to hang it on the line.

"Thank you for lunch," he said.

"*Och,*" was all she said, without so much as a glance toward him, and continued with the laundry.

He watched her for a moment longer, then put his coat back on and returned to work, humming Roy Orbison's "Pretty Woman" to himself as he went.

The whiskey yield for the winter was, as he'd calculated, only two casks. Next year probably wouldn't be any different, for he was sowing less barley because of the land he was now having to let lay fallow each season. Relentless plowing and sowing, year after year, would wear the soil until it would quit producing. Letting it grow weeds for one season out of three kept the soil vital. When he'd begun farming this glen, the entirety of the land had been fallow for two years previous, and so he'd been able to plow slope to slope the entire glen. But last season he began to rotate the fields. Until the whiskey would begin bringing income into the household and the oats became less vital for barter, there would have to be less barley sown.

Sinann still was away. Dylan began to wonder if she was angry with him and was punishing him. That thought made him chuckle to himself. Some punishment.

Sunday, April 9, would be Easter. Dylan, at least, knew it as Easter. Other Highlanders called it *càisg*, or if speaking English, *pasch*. It was the one festival that seemed most similar to the American tradition of Dylan's time, and he planned on an Easter egg hunt for his children that year. For days beforehand, Dylan saved the eggs from the yard hens, and on Saturday night Sarah dyed them for Eóin, Gregor, Ciaran, and Sìle to hunt. Egg coloring was one of the few traditions of this century that had made it to Dylan's generation intact, and so watching Sarah decorate the eggs brought a rare sense of nostalgia for his childhood.

She drew designs on the white shells with a willow twig dipped in melted candle wax, then boiled them in dye mixtures made from bracken, onion, and whin. When she cajoled Dylan to try his hand at a design, he resisted.

"Nah. I'm no artist. I couldn't draw a straight line." He leaned back in his chair at the table.

She made a soft noise in the back of her throat. "It's nae a straight line ye need. A straight line wouldnae be pretty. So see what sorts of curved lines ye might find for an egg."

The smile that had begun with the dyeing widened with embarrassment. "Nah . . ."

Sarah leaned across the table and graced him with a warm smile. "I cannae believe ye fear a wee crooked line. Not after the brave face ye put on after that football game with Artair doing his best to break yer leg."

Dylan's jaw must have dropped, stunned she'd noticed, for she leaned back in her chair as she dipped her twig into the melted wax and dabbed it on the egg in her hand. She shook her head and said, "Ye gave naught away that day. Yer face never betrayed yer sore leg. A lesser man would have at least favored it, as ye sometimes do when ye're truly cold or tired. But that day there was no sign of pain, and so I cannae understand what ye might fear from a colored egg." She handed him an egg. "Here. Make ones with the children's names on them, and see if Sìle can recognize hers."

He had no argument for that, and so reached for a willow twig. Nearly lying on the table, leaning with both arms to steady himself, he drew Sìle's name on it in big block letters. Then, just for fun, he turned it over and drew a smiley face like the ones that had been popular when he was in grammar school.

The egg came out pale green, with a very wobbly white smile. It was silly, but the amusement eased his soul. And it made Sarah giggle. For one shining moment he forgot the Redcoats and the coming uprising. Hope for peace rose, and his heart felt lighter than it had in months. He gazed fondly at his new green friend and wondered if everything might turn out all right after all.

Shortly before sunrise, he hid the eggs near the house.

With no priest in the parish, there was no possibility of Mass when the sun came up that day. But most of the households in the glen, including Dylan's, made do with a scripture reading or family prayer. Then, when Sarah and her sons arrived, the kids each took a basket to hunt eggs on the farm, and Dylan threatened sanctions against the boys if they didn't let Sìle find her share of the easy ones. Promises were made, and the boys ran off, with Sìle following at a leisurely toddle.

Checking out the grass by the burn, she found an egg right away. With a squeal of joy and pride, she ran to her father to show him the lavender-colored egg. He oohed over it with her for a moment, then instructed her to put it in her basket. She obeyed with enthusiasm, then, laughing in a high giggle, she ventured out to find more eggs.

Dylan and Sarah watched her go, and a smile crept across his face. "Reminds me of when I was a boy. We used to have a big hunt every year. The whole town would be there, and about a thousand kids would swarm all over the place, looking for eggs." They began walking slowly, following Sile to keep an eye on her.

"There were so many small children in your village?" Her voice was filled with the wonder of such a thing.

He blinked, surprised he'd slipped so stupidly. "Uh, really they came from all over. It was a big celebration, and everyone wanted to be there."

She nodded. "A gathering. I see."

"Yeah, like that."

"So good for that many to come so far every year."

He smiled. "Yeah, well, they were some serious egg-hunters."

That made her smile, too, and it was good to see.

As the weather continued to warm that month, new grass began to appear on the steep pastures surrounding Dylan's land and Glen Ciorram below. The Mathesons brought their kine from their byres. Bony from a long, northern winter with barely enough fodder to keep them alive, the small, black cattle had to be pulled and assisted onto the pasture. There they would stay until the lower pastures were grazed out, then in July they would be moved to the shielings to be watched over by the young folk. The grazing in the high shieling pastures was thin and wouldn't last long, but a couple of months would give the lower pastures time to recover for another grazing before winter.

An occasional sunny day allowed Dylan to pull the wooden shutters from the two windows in his house, but the nights were still cold enough to require putting them back at sunset.

Though the soldiers at the garrison had eased back on the capricious harassment, tension between them and the Mathesons still festered. Ranald's death had gone unanswered, and that didn't set well with the clansmen. At first the Scots held their anger, for they knew any attempt to secure retribution would be answered with more deadly force. But the more time passed, the more frustration grew, and the more muttered talk there was of the disgrace of letting the soldiers get away with the murder.

One day a dragoon was spotted returning from his patrol on foot, carrying his weapons and gear on the track at the north side of the glen. Word made the rounds someone had dug a hole along the trail through the wooded hills, then covered it with sod and dirt. The dragoon's horse had stepped in it and broken its leg, and the soldier had been forced to shoot the animal and walk back to the garrison.

None of the Mathesons admitted to digging the hole, but everyone knew it had been Artair. It was widely believed Tormod and Dùghlas had been accomplices. The stupid gesture disgusted Dylan, but he kept silent in the face of wide approval of the act from the rest of the clan. The soldiers were angry and touchier by the day, but the Matheson men were now able to hold their heads a bit higher. Dylan hoped the anger would be assuaged now.

The stakes were raised, though, when someone crept into the garrison one night and made off with the soldiers' stores of English wheat flour. Even Artair denied that feat, but his denial didn't wash when the dragoons came to arrest him, Iain Mór, Malcolm, and Dylan.

The Redcoats tossed all four of them into the holding cell at the garrison, then chained them each by an ankle to a long iron rail bolted to the floor. Old Malcolm was obviously in pain, having been shoved to the floor with the others. He leaned against the damp stone wall and shut his eyes.

"Took it a little too far this time, eh, Artair?" Dylan wished the *Sassunaich* would kill the wee lairdie and solve everyone's problems.

"Shut up." His eyes narrowed at Dylan, and he spoke as if struggling to hold his temper. "I dinnae steal anything."

Iain warned, "Quiet. The both of ye. The English dinnae need to hear aught we would say."

The four fell silent, and sat, glaring at each other, as they waited for questioning.

Dylan had been interrogated by the Major before and bore his worst scars from it. He couldn't help his heart thudding in his chest as he was unchained from the cell floor, his feet then both shackled, and taken to a room at the end of the barracks. The terror quite drove the anger from him, and the freedom from it was almost sweet relief.

There he was chained by his wrists to the stone wall and stood to face Bedford and MacCorkindale. The Private left the room. Though this room had once been Bedford's quarters, now the place was bare save for a wooden table at the opposite end. Bedford leaned against it, his arms crossed in front of him. Dylan glanced around the room for a whip and found it hung on a peg behind the door. He began to sweat. Bedford wouldn't hesitate to use that on him. Maybe he wouldn't try to kill this time, which was not within his prerogative as interrogator, but he was perfectly entitled to limited use for the purpose of extracting information. He would surely do so, with pleasure, if given an excuse.

MacCorkindale spoke, leaving Bedford to stare silently with cold, hooded eyes. "Right. Let's begin. Tell us what you know about the theft of garrison stores."

Dylan feigned relief. "Oh, is that all you guys want to know?" Unwilling to let on he was afraid, he took refuge in an insouciant persona borrowed from old TV cop shows. "We can wrap this up right away, then, because I don't know anything. The first I heard about the whole thing was when your goons busted into my house and hauled me away, and even then they weren't real chatty on the subject. They just snarled something about some old wheat flour. So you can let me go now, because I don't know anything."

"It was Artair. We're certain of it."

Dylan shook his head. "No, I don't think so. He would have bragged about this. But he doesn't know any more than I do. I mean, *wheat* flour. Who around here likes that stuff, anyway?"

"The glen is angry about the imbecile."

"You searched our homes. Did you find your flour? I expect not, or I wouldn't be here. Have you thought about questioning any of the MacDonells? The MacLeods? You're dead certain it was us? I mean, thievery . . . it's not a very Matheson thing to do. Certainly it's not something Artair would dream up."

Tormod would, but Artair wouldn't hold with becoming a sneak thief. If Artair were to steal flour, it would be to destroy it in an extremely visible manner. Like, maybe, he'd throw it all down the well and destroy two—

Oh, jeez. Dylan squeezed his eyes shut and bet the soldiers were about to find their flour, just as soon as someone let down the bucket into the well.

Bedford spoke up. "You're all thieves. The lot of you would filch food as soon as work for it. Stealing cattle is the favorite pastime of you Highlanders."

Dylan sighed and gazed at the floor. There was no explaining to a *Sassunach* the difference between reiving cattle and sneaking flour. He pulled on the chains that held his wrists to the wall, and lied, "Look, it wasn't Artair. Nor anyone else in this glen."

There was a knock on the door, and another private was bade to enter. He reported the discovery of all eight sacks of flour at the bottom of the garrison well. Dylan closed his eyes and mentally cursed Artair.

With both Bedford and MacCorkindale very angry now, the interrogation continued for another couple of hours. Dylan guessed it was a couple by the movement of the sun outside the barred windows. The questions went in circles, Bedford and MacCorkindale accusing and Dylan denying, until Bedford decided to order Dylan to be released from the shackles and returned to the cell.

The fear of flogging subsided, anger returned and for an hour after being chained in the cell again, he yanked furiously on the chain attaching his ankle to the iron pole. His vision reddened, he pulled blindly with both hands, though he knew he wouldn't come near loosening it. Only when his shoulder ached and his fingers showed red marks did he finally screw his eyes shut and collapse against the cell wall. He hated this place. He hated everything about it and everyone in it. The rage surged through him, and as he let it, he ignored the stares of the others in the cell.

Gradually he calmed, and there was plenty of time to think. The vile anger lurked in the back of his mind now, like an animal waiting to pounce, and he began to examine it, probing at it with the small part of his mind that was now clear. It seemed there were only certain times the rage gained control, and there were even times it wasn't in evidence at all. His kids could make it go away, he realized. Whenever he was around Ciaran and Sìle, there were no irrational urges. The children calmed him. Reasonable discussion didn't seem to set it off. But whenever his pride was bruised or if he were injured physically, the rage grabbed hold and wouldn't let go. When that happened, it was like a madness. Reality faded, colors became brighter in his vision, and the pain of being in its clutches urged him to actions he knew were wrong. He thought if he were ever to fail in his control, he might go over the edge of insanity and never return.

Now he began to wonder if this was what had caused his father to behave so horribly for so long. What if it were some kind of genetic disorder? Would he descend into habitual, random violence the way his father had? The thought made him shiver and shake his head to himself in denial. No way. He would never let himself be like that. Whatever control it took, he would never let himself become like his father.

For three days, the four men were held and questioned. Every few hours, day and night, one of them was hauled away to the interrogation room, to be returned and another one taken. Dylan persisted in his theory of the MacDonells, even under threat of the whip and even though he was dead certain Artair was the culprit. He wanted to be the one to clobber Artair when they got out of there.

The four were released on the third day. They were all hungry, dirty, exhausted, and their nerves were strained. Dylan was ashamed of his relief that the whip had not been used.

During his incarceration, two early lambs had been born in his flock. Being a mite too early, and with Dylan incapacitated, they both died the day he was released. But there was benefit to be had from them regardless. The ewes could now be milked, and the lamb hides were taken and cured. Dylan traded one of them to Nana Pettigrew for a dress for Sìle and a new sark for himself. His old sarks were both in sad shape, showing thin spots at elbows and shoulders and gaping holes at the beltline. A sark that couldn't hold items dropped inside for carrying was next to worthless as a garment, never mind how fair the weather.

Dylan returned home with the sark and changed into it. In his sitting room, he took his plaid from over his shoulder and wrapped it around his waist to keep it from dragging the floor as he changed, then pulled both his old sarks from under his belt then over his head. He threw the oldest one into the rag basket, put the next oldest one on a peg for grubby wear, then went into the bedroom with the water bucket to have a scrub before donning the new one.

It would be a pleasure to wear a new sark, for the thicker cloth was warmer. Whole clothes made him feel more whole himself, and even his scarred back enjoyed the crisp feel of new linen. He hung the sark on the wall peg, set the bucket on the small table, and picked up a rag to dunk it. He scrubbed his neck and behind his ears, and didn't pay much mind to the sound of Sarah returning to the house. More than likely, she'd forgotten something and come to take it with her to the castle.

Water dribbled onto his plaid as he washed his chest and under his arms. Idly he daydreamed of the hot showers of his old life. He would give a lot for indoor plumbing, were it attainable, but anymore, the closest he could come to a shower was to stand under the waterfall in the woods. Amazingly cold, such a shower was something to be attempted only during high summer after a long day of hard, hot work.

Then his mind segued into specific thoughts of hot showers with a certain hot girlfriend, and he closed his eyes to imagine. Ginny may have been a nitwit, but she had loved to play in the water, and the communal showers in his dojo had been very, very roomy. A smile touched his mouth as he reached behind to wash his back, an increasingly difficult task as he became older and less limber.

"Here, let me help ye."

Dylan jumped at Sarah's soft voice and she took the rag from his hand. He turned to her. "No, that's all right. I can do it myself." There had been a time when it would have mortified him for anyone at all to see the horrible scars on his back, and even though he'd come to terms with the mutilation, he still wasn't eager for anyone to gawk at him.

"Dylan, it's been half a year since a washrag has touched the middle of yer back. You need my help more than you need yer modesty. Shyness is for young lads who have never known a woman." He was taken aback, unsure of how to react. But the note of amusement in her voice put his pride on the line, for he couldn't bear for her to think he was timid. He acquiesced and turned to let her wash his back.

Her touch was light. Careful. His eyelids drooped at the pleasure as she scrubbed the spots he could never seem to reach properly. It felt good to have a woman's hand on him again, though he knew it would go no further than this. Bold as she may be, and pleasurable as it was to have his back scrubbed, he had no wish to take it further.

Then he heard her sniffle, and he looked around at her. "What's wrong?"

She continued rubbing his back with the rag, but hesitated a moment before saying, "Terrible pain." Her fingers brushed his skin from one shoulder to his waist opposite, following the longest whip mark.

He grunted, agreeing, then replied, "Don't let it bother you. It doesn't hurt anymore. I don't even think about it anymore." He reached for the towel on the table to dry himself, and Sarah stood back. The pain in her eyes told him she was feeling every stroke that had marked him. "No, really. It doesn't hurt. Not for a long time." He took the new sark from the peg and drew it over his head.

Sarah turned away and busied herself in the sitting room, gathering the cheese and butter she'd come for as he finished dressing in the bedroom. He tucked the sark into his kilt, under the wide belt, then lifted the kilt and reached under to pull the sark tail all the way through and down to his knees where it belonged. Then he arranged his plaid over his shoulder again and was properly dressed.

Dylan returned to work, and Sarah went on to the castle.

With the second lambskin, Dylan decided to make a pair of gloves. For whom, he wasn't sure. Working at his table by candlelight, in the back of his mind he had a vague idea of selling them to someone in the glen or sending them with Seumas on his next foray to Glen Dochart for trading there. But as he poked tiny holes with his awl for delicate stitches, he slowly began to realize he was making the gloves for Sarah. It was at once alarming and amusing.

"Tell me you didn't put a spell on me, Sinann," he said to the air and continued working. But of course Sinann was still AWOL and there was no reply. So he muttered to himself in falsetto imitation of the faerie, "*Och, do ye imagine I needed to put a spell on ye, as horny as ye are?*" He laughed at his own joke, then replied to himself, "Knock it off, Tink, it's not like that." Then again in the falsetto, "*Aye, ye're naught but a man. Ye cannae help yerself.*" Dylan sighed, and proceeded with the sewing, hoping he wasn't enchanted the way Sarah was. He'd have to ask the faerie when she returned.

When he finished the gloves, he gave them to Sarah at breakfast one morning. Coming in from his workout, he placed them beside her bowl, tied together with a red ribbon made into a bow. Sarah gaped at them as he picked up Sìle from his own seat at the other end of the table and sat down.

Eóin exclaimed in great excitement, and Ciaran stood on the bench to see.

Gregor said only, *"Och!"*

Sìle writhed in Dylan's arms until he let her down, and she ran to see.

"What's this?" said Eóin. "Are the two of ye going to marry?"

"We're not." It was out, sounding angry, before Dylan could edit himself, and he was sorry the instant it was.

Gregor said, "Good."

Eóin elbowed his brother. "Dinnae say that."

Sarah turned bright red and picked up her spoon again. Dylan amended in a light, joking voice he hoped didn't sound lame, "She hasn't asked me yet. You can't expect me to reply to such a question if I don't know the young lady's intention, can you? A man must maintain his dignity, after all."

The boys laughed, hard and loud. Sìle giggled, though she was too little to know what was so funny. Sarah even smiled a little at him, and fingered the red bow.

Dylan said to her, "They're in appreciation of all you've done for us, and a token of my high regard." That brought a real smile and a nod of understanding.

She picked them up and slipped the bow apart, then tried on the gloves. They fit snugly. Being leather, they would stretch and soon would be an exact match to her hands. Fleece to the inside, they would be warm and comfortable.

When breakfast was finished, it was time for work. Dylan rose from the table and went to put on his coat. Then he picked up a small bundle of chicken eggs he'd collected that morning, slipped them into his sark, and an ax head which he put into his coat pocket.

Sarah followed him to the door and laid a gloved hand on his arm. He turned, and at the too familiar look of adoration in her eyes he wondered if he'd made a mistake. He was feeding her obsession, and nothing good could come of that. Sinann would surely have told him so, had she been there, and she would have done it before he'd made the error. Dang, he was beginning to miss that faerie.

Sarah's voice was soft. "Thank you. It's very kind."

He wanted to reply that it had been nothing, but it hadn't been, and she would know it. Such gloves were far too costly in the Highlands to be shrugged off as nothing. He also realized he had meant something by it. Not marriage, to be sure, but something more than appreciation for a job well done. What he said was, "You're good to the children, Sarah. We care for you."

The light in her eyes changed, and he knew the question she would ask was whether he was speaking only on behalf of the children. He wasn't. In fact, he wasn't speaking at all for the children, but strictly for himself. Still, he couldn't explain. The words, if he'd said them, would have come out all wrong and would have been too entangled with disclaimers about what he still felt for Cait.

Rather than speak and end up with his foot in his mouth, he simply leaned down to kiss her lightly on the mouth. She did nothing. Said nothing, but just stood there looking like she couldn't move.

Then he hurried to adjust his plaid and get out the door before she could recover herself enough to say anything.

There was business to be done in Ciorram. Dylan needed a new ax blade, for his old one had cracked and was now unsafe to use. He would trade it in as scrap metal, along with the eggs, for a new one. As he walked, a misty rain began to fall—a "soft" day where outlines blurred in the distance, the sod beneath one's feet became springy, and the very air seemed thicker.

Tormod was in a surly mood when he arrived. Dylan pulled the ax blade from his pocket, but Tormod only grunted when Dylan showed him the crack. He was bent over his forge, under the thatched stone shelter near his house, stoking his fire. Once done, he picked up a piece of steel with his tongs and thrust it into the forge.

Dylan wiped his wet hair from his forehead and said, "I'll need a new one."

"Haven't got a new one. I'll have to repair the old one." He watched the steel, which appeared to be a future blade for a kitchen knife.

There was a long silence as Dylan boggled. Finally he said, "Repair a crack? In an ax?"

" 'Tis either that or use it as it is."

Dylan's voice filled with disdain. "I'd as likely kill someone with it when it lets go. How long before you can make me a new one?"

Tormod shrugged, then was silent. He poked the piece of steel in the fire. Dylan waited for a true reply, but there didn't seem to be one forthcoming. Something else was bugging the blacksmith, and Dylan figured he knew what it was.

Finally, he shifted his weight, looked around at the fields surrounding Tormod's house and shed, the mist floating between dikes and hedges, and said, "I can't tell her who to love, Tormod."

The blacksmith made a disgusted noise, straightened, and turned to look down his long nose at Dylan. "Marry someone, and she'll quit waiting for ye." Then he returned to his work.

Dylan sighed. "You know she won't. She didn't stop when I was married to Cait. Nothing I do is going to make her change her mind. She's a stubborn woman, Tormod, you know it. You'd think she was a Matheson by birth."

Unsmiling, Tormod poked the steel again and sulked, for he knew the truth of it as well as Dylan. He said, "Then ye should marry her. Make her happy if I cannae."

"Tormod, that's not a reason to—"

"*A Dhilein!*" The blacksmith's temper blew, and he waved his tongs at Dylan. "Ye're a friggin' dog in a friggin' manger, Dylan Dubh! She's around ye every day, mooning and a-sighing, and ye cannae even see her for the treasure she is! I see her when ye're near, and I would give my life for her to look at me the way she does you. It's killing me to see her a-pining like that. At least if ye married her, then I'd see her happy. At least there would be that."

"I can't—"

"Shame on you, Dylan." Tormod gave the piece of steel another shove with the tongs, then had to pull it out some, for he'd shoved it too far into the fire.

There was another very long silence, and Dylan looked out across the glen. Anger rose, so he kept his silence while it raged inside his head. Damn Tormod for telling him this! Damn everyone who presumed to tell him what to do! He turned away, the better to keep from fighting Tormod, and wandered a few steps in the yard.

Slowly he calmed. The rain dripped from his hair into his collar and from his beard down his chest. His head cooled. Deep breaths cleared his thoughts. Tormod took the glowing red steel from the fire, checked it with a clang of his hammer on the anvil, then put it back for a bit longer. Dylan turned back toward Tormod and addressed him from where he stood. "I'll take your recommendation under advisement." Damned if he would marry Sarah because Tormod said so, though. Then he hefted the cracked ax blade and said, "How long to get a new blade?"

Without looking up, Tormod said, "Next week. Leave the old one, and I'll need more eggs than what ye've brought." He pointed with his chin to the bulge in Dylan's sark. "That many again."

Dylan tossed his old ax blade into a wooden box of scrap metal, where it landed with a flat clank and fell into two pieces. He stared at it for a moment. *Huh.* Then he drew the eggs from his sark. "Aye. You'll have them." He knew he was being gouged, but let it go. It assuaged some of the guilt. He set the eggs into the box as well, on top of the blade pieces.

Tormod nodded, then pulled the red-hot steel from the forge and began pounding on it. Sparks flew to the sound of Tormod's hammer as Dylan returned home.

The next morning, the dawn was almost there, but not quite. Dylan was awakened by his wife's voice murmuring his name. "*A Dhilein.* Wake up."

He stirred, and a smile crept across his face. Her arms were around him, her body warm and soft beside him. He raised on one elbow and kissed her, probing some, and she giggled.

She said, "Ye've taken good care of the weans."

He nodded, wondering why she was telling him this. She took good care of them, too. She was the best mother they could ask for.

"Dylan, I wish ye to understand I still love you."

The pain swooped in as he awakened and remembered, but Cait didn't disappear this time. He was awake in the darkness, but could still feel her in his arms. The familiar scent of her hair filled his head, and his heart clenched. "Cait," he whispered. "I miss you. Every day, I miss you." He pressed his mouth to her forehead and said, his voice tight, "It hurts so much."

"I'm here, my husband," she murmured, "I'll never leave you. My heart is yours forever, nae matter what might happen." With that, she collapsed to nothingness.

Dylan slumped onto the mattress, cold and alone. He reached for the gold ring hung on the linen cord and held it in his fist.

CHAPTER 12

It took a couple of days for Barri to come to terms with living in Dylan's apartment. Living alone was an adjustment in itself, but it became insignificant next to the task of dealing with the memories. She sifted through his things, examined and mulled over his clothing, his dishes, the toiletries he'd left in the bathroom. It was all very disturbing.

Especially, the string of condoms in the nightstand drawer gave her a turn. At first she didn't realize what the little square packet was, and she picked it up. The others followed. She dropped it immediately when she felt of the circular item inside, but an image came, far too vivid, of her son using one. She shoved the drawer shut, left the room, and busied herself elsewhere. That night she slept on the sofa in the living room.

Sorting Dylan's belongings was closure, though. Gradually, over the following days, the pain eased, and she was able to feel less like she was waiting for him to come home. With acceptance came a desire to square things away. Putting his belongings in order would be the best way to honor him, she felt. On the third day she was finally able to start cleaning the dust, throwing out the old, nasty food in the cupboards and refrigerator, and boxing the clothing for the thrift store.

The books on Scotland would stay, for they seemed the possessions most dear to him, and she would keep the linens and towels for a while

. . . just because. The furniture—well, she wasn't sure yet what to do with that. None of it was very nice, and the sofa sagged horribly, but she didn't have it in her yet to redecorate. One step at a time.

The dusting went slowly, for there was so much of it. Window cleaner and furniture polish on a dust cloth did little more than leave great, black smears, so Barri filled a bucket with warm, soapy water and began scrubbing. The sharp smell of detergent filled the room, and she forced herself to stop feeling like she was washing away the last of Dylan. She concentrated on listening to the echoes of noises Ronnie was making downstairs, bare feet slapping the mats, as he warmed up for his afternoon classes.

She was at this when Cody hollered from the exercise floor below. "Mrs. Matheson?"

"Come on up, Cody," she replied, and continued cleaning.

The girl slowly climbed the steps to the balcony, holding her stomach as if it would fall to her feet if she let go. Barri knew it probably felt like it might, for she remembered well her own pregnancy. Cody's large purse hung on her elbow and banged her knees as she walked, and she was a mite red in the face from exertion.

Barri rose. "Come, sit down. I should have come downstairs instead."

"Nah." Cody waved away the suggestion. "Ronnie is down there; he's got a class in fifteen minutes. We'd be in the way. I'll just sit here." She eased herself onto the sofa and sighed. Barri knelt by the bucket again and went back to wiping down shelves. The TV, stereo, and other things she'd moved from the shelves sat on the floor, scattered about like an exploded electronics store.

Cody looked around at the mess, and Barri cringed that she should see it this way, but Cody didn't seem to care. She reached over the arm of the sofa to the end table for the stack of CDs that had been temporarily displaced. Browsing the handful, she read off the artist names. "Springsteen . . . Springsteen . . . Springsteen . . . Little Steven . . . Springsteen . . . Springsteen." She chuckled. "Gee, Dylan, obsessive much?"

Then she set the CDs back down, turned to Barri, and said, "How are you doing?"

Barri shrugged. "I'll be all right." She also looked around the room, at all that was left of Dylan. "It's strange, but in a way it's almost like I've stopped picking at the wound and am letting it heal. I've kept it open far too long." She paused for a moment, staring into the middle distance, then slowly said, "There is also that cleaning helps me not to think about Kenneth. It's kind of an old habit."

"Dylan wouldn't want you to be hurting so long. He wanted you to live here, and where he is he must finally be happy."

Barri had to smile at that, though for a moment her throat closed so she couldn't breathe. She repeatedly squeezed and dunked the sponge in her hand as if she were concentrating on the job. A cough loosened the tightness. Gradually, the pain eased, and she sighed. She dunked her sponge into the bucket, wrung it out, and returned to cleaning shelves. Voices echoed in the dojo downstairs. People were arriving for the class.

Cody said, "Are you sure you're all right?"

Barri nodded. "It's been two years. It's time."

"The reason I ask," Cody adjusted her seat, "is that I've found something on that highwayman, Black Dylan."

Still wiping, dunking, and wringing, then wiping again, Barri nodded. "You said that the other night. You'd found something. But you didn't say what, and I was beginning to wonder if you were just fooling." It was nice of Cody to try to get her mind off Dylan and Kenneth, but the old story told by Kenneth's father didn't hold much interest. It was ancient history, dead and gone.

But Cody's voice took on a gravity that caught her ear. "I found something that corroborates a story I've known to be true since before Dylan went to Scotland."

Barri smiled and continued wiping. "What do you mean? What story? Did Dylan find something out before he left?"

A dry smile crossed Cody's face. "Yeah, you could say that." She leaned forward as best she could and said, "Mrs. Matheson, before I tell you this, you need to know that I'm not crazy. And I will show you I'm not."

Barri stopped scrubbing, intrigued. *Crazy?* "All right." Feeling every groaning, crotchety joint from the waist down, she climbed to her feet from her knees, then stood for a moment as her joints settled back into place. She went to the bathroom for one of the blue towels and returned, wiping her hands dry. She sat on the other end of the couch, perched on the edge of the cushion to listen. "Go on." She couldn't imagine what Cody had found, but the girl sounded like she thought it was terribly important.

Cody sucked on her lower lip before speaking, as if screwing up the courage to say whatever it was. "Mrs. Matheson, I don't know how to say this, so I've got to say it straight out. And it's going to sound crazy—"

"But it won't be." Barri put on her most polite smile. She was a patient woman, but Cody's behavior had her awfully curious.

Cody nodded. "Mrs. Matheson, when Dylan went to Scotland, he went back in time."

"In time for what?"

"No." Cody's eyes screwed shut for a moment, then she opened them and looked at Barri. "He went backward. In time. Back to the eighteenth century."

The words made no sense. As if they were jumbled. Barri frowned, puzzled. "I beg your pardon?"

"You remember when he was at the Highland Games, and he was stabbed?" Barri blinked and nodded, unable to guess what this could have to do with Black Dylan. Cody took a deep breath and began talking very quickly. "Well, he wasn't stabbed at the Games. He was run through during a battle in 1715. He had been there for two years, then was returned to our time because he was hurt, then when he got better, he missed his son and the girl he was going to marry, and so he went back to Scotland to find the faerie and get her to send him back. In time. And she did."

They sounded like nonsense words. Faerie. Battle. Dylan's son. "His *son?*"

"He had two children, you see. I went there, too. The faerie sent me back a year and a half ago, to 1718, and I saw him. Them. He was married. Widowed, I mean. He had two children. I saw them."

Barri slumped and leaned against the cushions at the back of the couch. Poor Cody had surely snapped under the strain of her condition. "Oh, Cody . . ." Her heart sank as one more tragedy descended. "Cody, please don't—"

Cody leaned forward as far as she could, to reach for Barri's hand. "I tell you, I'm not crazy. Please, Mrs. Matheson. Please, just take a moment and allow yourself to believe. For just *one* moment. Please. Then, if you still find it impossible to contemplate, I'll shut up about it. We'll just pretend I never said this. Okay?"

One moment. Barri looked into Cody's face, wishing she could believe. To think that Dylan might have had a life, wife, children . . . it was so tempting. She took a deep breath, and though she didn't truly feel it, she said, "All right. I believe you. Tell me why I'm not crazy to believe."

Cody reached into her purse and brought out a book. It was one of those large picture books for coffee tables. On the cover was a painting of a horseman of eighteenth-century England, wearing ruffles and velvet, a black tricorn hat, a gold-hilted sword at his side, riding a galloping black steed. The title of the book was *The Highwayman Came Riding*. It was the sort of book that gave a light once-over to a subject, with lots of photos and drawings, which people put on coffee tables for guests to glance at. It was wide and heavy, with large, captioned photographs interspersed with amusing text. As Cody flipped through it, Barri saw photographs of portrait paintings from the eighteenth century, some pictures of spurs reportedly worn by actual highwaymen, and other museum pieces of the period.

"Look." Cody opened the book up flat and handed it to her.

The page presented bore a large photograph of a wanted poster. Torn, yellowed, and stained, some of the text on it was difficult to read. Above the text was a drawing of a young, dark-haired man with a cruel mouth. The text said, "Wanted for robbery: Dilan Mac Clay, who, with accomplices, by open violence did rob several men of their purses in the vicinities of Stirling and Callander. Standing six feet tall, and thin, black-haired and blue eyed." The caption dated the leaflet at 1715 and gave the archive as the National Library of Scotland.

Barri felt there must be something here she was missing, but couldn't see through to what it was. She kept her tone patient, trying to smile through her puzzlement. "All right. This is Black Dylan?"

"Yes. It's also our Dylan. Your son. Dylan Robert Matheson."

A weak laugh bubbled up, and she could only utter a soft, "No."

"It is. Look." Cody laid her hand over the lower half of the drawing, below the nose on the face. "It's him."

"No." Barri knew there was a confusion here, but wasn't certain whether she was the one misunderstanding. "He was a robber. My Dylan could never have done these things. That's not him." She leaned over the page and ran a finger over the list of accusations. "Robbing purses . . . open viol . . ."

Then she saw it, and a shiver ran up Barri's spine. She *could* see it. In spite of the poorly executed drawing done from memory, and ignoring the curled lip she knew was an invention of a terrified witness, she saw it was him. The straight, dark hair, as shaggy as it had been that day after his surgery, the level eyebrows, the slightly hooded eyes that were colorless in the drawing to denote blue. She laid a hand over her mouth and murmured, "Oh, my God."

Cody leaned forward, excited. "Do you understand? Do you believe now?"

"Oh my God. He didn't die in Scotland?"

Cody sagged back into the cushion and shook her head. "No, Mrs. Matheson. He *did* die in Scotland. But he didn't die when he was thirty. He was thirty-five when I saw him last, but he surely did die eventually. Probably about two hundred and fifty years ago."

That night, Barri stood on the balcony overlooking the dojo below, listening to the final class of the day being taught. Ronnie's voice echoed in the room, barely intelligible above, where she was, as the words bounced around like so many Ping-Pong balls. She didn't mind the noise. It was less lonely than the silence at other times of the day, and listening to the kids downstairs was almost like being a part of the world. Cody had gone hours before, leaving her to digest what had been said. The book lay on the coffee table, open to the drawing of the Scottish highwayman.

Barri turned to gaze at it. Could that truly be Dylan? Something in her was ready to believe, but surely it was nothing more than wishful thinking. Was she still just grieving for her son, or was there something recognizable in the drawing?

Looking closer, she sat on the sofa again. The mouth on the man in the drawing was absolutely not Dylan's. It was impossible to imagine a sneer like that on him. Ever. But when she covered the mouth with her hand, the eyes leapt out at her. The brow was his. Not only his, but his father's. Kenneth had the same eyes and forehead. She crossed her arms and hugged herself.

The name Dilan might be a coincidence. Or it might not. Possibly the highwayman in the drawing was the Matheson of the legend—Black Dylan. But to think this man was her son was to believe in the impossible.

On the other hand, laid next to the horror of accepting his murder at the age of thirty, believing in magic and time travel wasn't such a huge thing. She stared at the drawing for a long time, wishing to see Dylan in it. The more she stared, the more she realized there was no way to truly know.

Soon the class was over, and Ronnie straightened up before turning out the lights and locking the door to go home. Barri was left in the apartment, alone in the darkness. The living quarters, clean now, smelled of disinfectant mingled with steam from the showers downstairs. She put the bucket away in the kitchen and rinsed out the sponge before setting it by the sink faucet. It had been all day since she'd eaten, but she wasn't hungry. A shower would be nice. Yes, she would take a shower, then perhaps turn on the TV. It was too quiet in here.

Walking through the living room on her way to the bedroom, she instead drifted over to the shelves of books. Scotland's history was there: its wars, its kings, its culture. She reached out and took a book at random, opened it, and found herself reading about the conflict between Robert the Bruce and England's King Edward I. Dry facts and dates. Names of people she couldn't picture in her mind. The book held little interest. She glanced over at the book on the table, still open to the drawing of the highwayman, and a small bit of Scottish history fleshed out for her. That man had been somebody's son, whether or not he was hers.

There was a knock at the back door, and she went to answer it, still browsing the history of Robert the Bruce. Just as she reached for the doorknob, a hard pounding came that rattled the window in the door. Startled, she took a step back, then forward again to reach for the curtain over the window.

Kenneth stood on the stairway outside, his face angry under the stark porch light. He had the wild gleam in his eyes that she recognized as too much alcohol. Her heart leapt to her throat, and terror skittered up her back. She dropped the curtain, but he'd seen her and banged on the door again.

"Let me in, bitch!"

Oh, no. Barri held the book to her chest and backed away, into the living room. Her heart pounded in her ears. Kenneth shouted again and kicked the door. The glass rattled. He kicked it again, and broke the glass. It rained onto the linoleum floor with a musical tinkle.

"You're still my wife. I got rights!"

"Kenneth! Go away! Leave me alone!"

It was like trying to talk a freight train off its tracks. He reached through the broken pane to the knob and opened the door. His leather-soled shoes crunched across the scattered glass shards in the entry. His breathing was hard and heavy with habitual anger. Barri fled before him, down the stairs to the dojo, which was the only other exit from the building.

He rushed down on her and grabbed her by the hair just as she reached the stairs. She cried out. Her feet slipped from under her, and she toppled. Kenneth went with her, down the steps, trying to regain balance by grappling with the banister as it slipped past, but he failed and fell onto her. They both tumbled and rolled onto the dojo floor.

In the tangle, Kenneth's hands found her throat. She kicked and writhed. Spots swam before her eyes. The world distilled to one thing: get away from Kenneth. He knelt over her and pinned her neck with his weight. With all her strength, she kicked at him, again and again, until his hold loosened and he fell back against a rack of long sticks. The sticks fell on him, in a wooden mass clatter across the hardwood floor. Barri found her feet. Kenneth clambered to his feet and came at her again, but she snatched one of the sticks from the floor and stuck it into his gut.

Air *oofed* from him. He grabbed the stick, but she shoved him backward with it so he reeled and had to let go. But he was still between her and the door. She held the stick like a baseball bat, cocked over her shoulder. If she couldn't go through that door, she had to make him go through it.

"You can't do this to me, Barri." The fury in him made her quiver with fear, but she knew if she put the stick down, he would come at her again and possibly kill her this time. He continued, "You used to love me." His tone was offended, as if she'd denied him some sort of God-given right to be loved, no matter what he might do.

Grief for the time when she had loved him was like a sock in the stomach, and her throat tightened. "You used to deserve it."

His face reddened and his eyes darkened. He came at her again in a rage, his arms out to grab her. She swung the stick, and it broke against his head. He emitted an inarticulate howl and staggered sideways.

The stick was now much shorter, and the broken end had a jagged point. She held it like a prod now, threatening him with the point. "Get away. Get away now." It was unimaginable she might hurt him, and she wished feverishly he would just leave her alone.

The light in his eyes wavered. He seemed unsure whether to believe she might stab him with the stick. She pressed her lips together, trying to look like she meant what she said. An image of Dylan popped into her mind's eye, faced off against a sparring partner with the intense expression of a fighter. She frowned and her eyes narrowed, to imitate him. She took a step forward and brandished the stick.

That was when Kenneth backed off. She pressed it. "Go," she ordered, and made a poking motion with her weapon. He backed away toward the exit. The glass doors of the dojo rattled as he banged against the panic bars, and it took him several shoves before he managed to get them open.

Barri let him go and watched him climb into his car and leave. Then she flipped the lock pins on one door and threw the deadbolt on the other. Clearly she needed to talk to Ronnie about making sure this door was locked. She climbed to the apartment, her weapon still in hand, though Kenneth was gone. The back door was broken and hanging open.

Shaking took her, and she sank to the living room carpet to hug her knees, rocking back and forth, and wish for her life back.

CHAPTER 13

I t was in the third week of April that Dylan had a visit to his home from Niall MacCorkindale. At night, after the kids had gone to bed, he was sitting at his table, composing a letter to a marble merchant in Glasgow.

Italian marble was awfully expensive, and gravestones of any kind not common in these parts. Like the gold ring he'd given Cait on their wedding day, it would be thought of as a waste of money.

But the farm had come through the winter in fair shape, and the valuables Ramsay had been carrying the day he'd fought and lost to Dylan weren't needed for other things. Dylan had a letter of exchange for the gold and silver he'd taken from Ramsay and sold, amounting to enough to buy a plain piece of marble and have it engraved for Cait. Such a letter frequently passed through many hands during its life, for cash was scarce and goods sometimes difficult to transport. Seumas would deliver the letter to the engraver in Glasgow on his next foray to the city in late summer, then carry the carved stone to Ciorram. Cait's marker would be in the churchyard by fall.

As he wrote, a breeze ruffled his hair and the flame of the single candle in the middle of the table danced. A chill ran through him. He looked up to find where the draft was coming from, but saw nothing. The shutter was firmly in place, stuffed into the framed hole in the wall that functioned as a window. And the breeze died away in any case.

The door of Dylan's house opened, and he looked up with the pleasure and full expectation of receiving a kinsman for a visit. But then he stood, shocked to his soles, at sight of a uniformed Redcoat.

"Good evening," said MacCorkindale, a note of formality in his voice. "May I come sit a spell with ye?" There was some tension, as if he were none too certain he wouldn't be shot.

Dylan raised his chin and regarded his visitor. He knew that Mac-Corkindale knew he couldn't refuse the request. Besides being a representative of the occupying government and entitled to enter any dwelling at any time for any reason, the Lieutenant, having asked politely, was now a guest in Dylan's home.

Though Dylan had been raised a twentieth-century American, he now lived by the standards of his eighteenth-century clan. That meant not only was his theoretic right to privacy no longer a reality, but even his feelings on the matter were now secondary to his obligation to good manners. As a prominent member of the Ciorram Mathesons, his good standing depended on adherence to tradition. In addition, because he'd been born a colonial, ostensibly from Virginia, he had, and would always have, something to prove to his Scottish kinsmen.

A nod to the other chair, near the fire, gave the Redcoat to know he was invited to sit.

MacCorkindale removed his helmet and gloves and sat. Dylan returned to his chair at the table, sitting sideways to face the room and his guest. Dylan said, "I can't offer you ale, for there is none, and there is nothing left from supper but one bannock and some cold greens." He figured MacCorkindale would turn up his nose at the greens, for they were food for poor folk, and there were few in Scotland who liked them. Dylan was not the only one in the glen who did eat them, but he was the only man of his stature he knew who would admit to gathering greens from the woods and cress from the burns because he liked them. When Cait had been alive, he'd even talked her into growing a few cabbages, though she had been mortified to do it.

The Lieutenant shook his head. "Thank ye, no. I've come for talk only."

Dylan set his quill down next to the ink pot and wiped his stained fingers on a rag he kept handy while writing. "Talk? Of what?" He glanced at the door, wondering where the Redcoat's escort was. He hoped they weren't outside, poking their bayonets into the thatching. . . .

"I came alone." MacCorkindale answered the unasked question. Dylan leaned against the back of his chair, one arm draped over it. This was intriguing, at least. There was a pleasant but no-nonsense expression on the Lieutenant's round face. He continued, "I've heard things about you, Dylan Matheson, that make nae sense to me."

A wry smile curled one corner of Dylan's mouth. "Like what? That I talk to demons and that my mother was a seal?"

The Lieutenant smiled. "Aye. It's plain ye ken the wee folk. Ye're the only man in the glen who will go near the *broch*. It's a place even I willnae venture."

Dylan had to let go a broad smile at that. "How very wise, unless you're looking to have your red English coat stripped from you in pieces by the faeries." Sinann's powers as weak as they were, her most useful defense against the English Army was to pop buttons and seams on the occasional uniform. He glanced around the room, wishing once again for Sinann to come back.

"I wish to talk of your involvement with the Jacobites in the last attempt on the throne by James Stuart."

Dylan's back stiffened. "I was pardoned of that. The paper with the King's seal is in that cabinet behind you."

MacCorkindale glanced at the cabinet but only turned back and nodded, aware of the pardon. "Then you surely will stay out of the current unpleasantness."

"*Och.*" Dylan gripped the corner of his table with white knuckles as anger rose. "If you think I'm likely to volunteer my life for a lost cause, you're nuts."

"Ye detest the English and King George."

"I despise the English Army. Your red coat is turning my stomach even now." The red claws of rage climbed his back, and he held his temper by a thread. In an effort to control himself, he brought to mind his father. More than anything else, he didn't want to be like the old man. Slowly his vision cleared, and rational thought became easier.

"Nevertheless, though ye fought with the Jacobites, I'm told ye dinnae support the Pretender."

Dylan blinked, surprised. "Does the Crown give a damn how I felt when I fought? All you people cared about was my whereabouts during the uprising. Besides, lots of men fought in that rising because they were told to by their lairds. They were obligated, regardless of their personal feelings."

MacCorkindale nodded. "But you were not one of them."

"No, I was dodging the law because I'd been unjustly accused of writing rude letters about the Queen. Even if I'd thought George was the Second Coming and wanted to join his army, I was forced onto the Jacobite side."

He pointed a finger at the Redcoat. "Which, incidentally, do not assume I support George. Fact is, I think the whole conflict is really fucking stupid." Though the American Constitution was nearly sixty years in the future, and separation of Church and state only a faint hope in some radical hearts, he had to say this because he believed it deep down. "I think going to war over whether the King should be Catholic or Protestant is—"

"Some would call that a betrayal of the one true religion."

Dylan's eyes narrowed. MacCorkindale was starting to puzzle him to the point of frustration. "You're a Catholic. I've seen you cross yourself. Does it bother you that the king you defend is not only a Protestant, but an active persecutor of Catholics?"

MacCorkindale nodded. "Aye, it does."

Both men went still, as if listening for eavesdroppers. What the Lieutenant had just said flirted with the boundaries of treason, a stunning thing to hear from an officer in His Majesty's service. Even MacCorkindale paled a little, as if surprised he'd blurted it.

Dylan then said softly and slowly, "Then allow me to conjecture here. It bothers you because it means you're an outsider among your fellow officers, regardless of whether or not they know you're Catholic. It bothers you because there are laws that make it difficult for Catholics to do business outside the clan, and because we have to go through legal contortions to bequeath our property to our heirs. It bothers you because if you need or want a sacrament, you are obligated by law to arrest any priest who might minister to you."

The Lieutenant nodded.

"Then you tell me. Why do you defend the King? I mean, besides that he pays a wage that is better than starvation."

MacCorkindale straightened and said forthrightly, "Because I took an oath to defend the Crown, and George is the rightful, lawful ruler."

"If he is, it's only by virtue of the treason of King William, who took the throne from James II and then said, 'Oh, by the way, from now on all British monarchs are going to be Protestants like me.' "

That brought a chuckle from MacCorkindale. "You ken, it isnae so simple."

Some of the tension left Dylan, to hear laughter from the Redcoat, and he leaned against the back of his chair again. "I know it's not. If it were simple, you'd be the Catholic Jacobite and I'd be the King's man who knows a lost cause when he sees one. If it were truly simple, Charles would have kept his head, James would have kept his throne, there'd be a whole lot more MacDonalds left than there are, and I wouldn't be sitting here, trying to answer impossible questions." He leaned forward in his chair and lowered his voice. "Just why *are* you here, Niall? I don't imagine it's to apologize for your men killing a poor, defenseless fool who never hurt anyone."

The Lieutenant flushed. He replied, "I'm wondering if it might be possible you deserve the pardon the King so generously bestowed."

Dylan blinked, surprised, and sat up. "What's that supposed to mean?"

"If ye were never a Jacobite in yer heart—"

"Which, as Bedford so rightly pointed out the day he flogged me into a wad of bloody meat for the sake of information he hoped to obtain, matters not in the . . ." A shadow crossed MacCorkindale's face, and Dylan suddenly knew what this was about. "Information. You're hoping I've got information I'm willing to blurt." He squeezed his eyes shut and gripped the table until his hand trembled. "No." Nothing more would come. Nothing more dared come.

"Then why—"

"*No!*" Dylan stood. "You want to know what I support? I support whatever will keep my clan fed and in one piece," his teeth clenched, "and my kinsmen *not* beheaded on a whim. I support the lives and happiness of the people in this glen. I support my Laird, because I've pledged to support him, and my place in the clan requires me to do my duty to him. And to them."

MacCorkindale stood also, to be eye to eye. "Ye've pledged to support the King, as well. When you took the oath on receiving yer pardon."

Dylan opened his mouth to reply that he'd taken no oath, then shut it. *He'd not been required to take any oath.* Bedford had handed him the paper bearing George's seal, but had never asked for the oath. Because there had been assassins waiting outside to murder Dylan and take his land grant, Bedford must not have considered the oath necessary. Perhaps he'd forgotten. Dylan blinked, his mind scrambling for a reply, then said, "I've broken no laws. I've lived up to the terms of my pardon." A lie, but he reminded himself this was a Redcoat he was talking to, and he owed no honesty to the English Army and had made no oath of allegiance to King George. He had, however, pledged loyalty to Iain Mór.

"Are ye certain ye've nae broken any laws?"

"I am." Dylan was certain of nothing, especially his legal standing on most things, but appearing vulnerable now would be a deadly mistake. He told the lie without the least hesitation or guilt.

"Were I to search the property, would I find aught amiss?" The Redcoat was eyeing him carefully, in search of a false moment.

"No." His mind flashed to the whiskey still and casks hidden in the woods, but he kept a blank face.

"Good." MacCorkindale put on his helmet and adjusted the strap. His mouth was a firm line, and knots of muscle stood out on his jaw. "I'll leave you to your lawful occasions, then. And as a loyal subject of King George, I expect to hear from you if at any time you come across information regarding the current unrest."

Dylan bit his lips together, and the buzzing in his brain was nearly unbearable. His better sense told him to shut up, but his mouth paid no attention. "I said, MacCorkindale, you'll get no information from me." His fists clenched at his sides, and all he wanted just then was to throttle MacCorkindale and watch his eyes bug out. Instead, he said, his voice a low growl, "King George will get what he's owed, and nothing more. Get out of my house."

The Lieutenant pulled on his gloves. "Aye. Good night." He then ducked out the door, maintaining the dignity of having concluded his business.

Dylan sat at his table and ran his fingers through his hair over and over to calm himself.

His gaze landed on something shiny on the floor by the hearth. He went to look, and picked it up from among the reeds near the other chair. It was a button from a Redcoat uniform, which must have popped off while MacCorkindale had been sitting there.

Dylan looked around the room but didn't see Sinann. *Huh.*

* * *

Daghda had a rather large lamb shank in his hands and was gnawing the last of the meat from it. Sitting on a tree root and leaning back against the earth wall behind him, he wiped a dribble of grease from his chin onto his tunic.

Morrighan sat among her tools and herbs, surrounded by candles and absorbed in her plans for that mortal, Matheson. Daghda had thought she would be done with all that, but she still wanted to know the future. Daghda didn't see the point. The future would happen in any case, with or without her interference. But she was enjoying the diversion, so who was he to tell her to stop? A smile put a curve on her pretty mouth, and he liked that.

The air over the table warmed, and he looked up. An intruder? He glanced over at Morrighan. Did she bring him? But, no, she was absorbed in her work with the mortar and pestle, not even noticing the disturbance. Daghda dropped the bone to the floor, wiped his hand and his chin on his tunic, and reached for his sword. With a single zing of metal on metal, he drew it and had the intruder at its point just as he became a presence.

He was a she. The white sea-faerie, Sinann. Her eyes went wide at sight of the sword at her throat, and she jerked back. "What is it ye want?" Daghda demanded. Uninvited, she should have died right then. But now he was curious, and knew Morrighan had an interest in making this one suffer. He poked her breast bone and repeated himself.

"I want ye both to leave the poor mortal alone." The whites of her eyes showed just a little too largely, betraying her fear in spite of her brave chin and solid stance atop the table. She drew large breaths, just a little too desperately to fool him.

Morrighan said from across the room, "Put the sword down, Daghda. Let her make her case."

He frowned. "Ye're wanting to listen to the *each-uisge*?"

Morrighan shrugged, so Daghda put the sword away and returned to his seat. The sea faerie said, "I want ye to leave Dylan alone."

"You mean, leave yerself alone."

"I told him to use the Craft to know yer purpose. 'Tis my fault he did it."

"And you are suffering for it. As he will suffer for it. He's nae a child, Sinann. Even less a child than yerself, measuring by conduct. He was aware of the import of his actions. He wielded the power, and he bears the blame. Surely ye taught him that much. He understood what he was about."

"He's suffered enough."

That brought a laugh from the red faerie. "He's suffered because he's without the guidance of his tamed *sidhe*? Such a value ye put on yer own company!"

Sinann leapt into the air and hovered, an unwise move. Daghda was one of the few who knew of Morrighan's jealousy of those with wings. Even from here, he could see the evil light in her eyes as she watched the sea faerie's wings flutter.

Sinann said, "Dylan has a purpose. Ye dinnae understand the thing ye're interfering with. 'Tis greater than the lot of us."

Morrighan stood, angry now, and approached Sinann. "There is nothing greater than the *Sidhe*. We once ruled the earth."

"But we dinnae any longer. It's time we accepted we're nae the most powerful beings in the world. We're nae longer the important ones."

Daghda's eyes went wide with alarm, for he could see the Morrighan was about to lose her temper. It was a short fuse on that one, and a powerful charge when it would blow. He opened his mouth to warn the white faerie, but not quickly enough. Morrighan hauled back her hand and threw it toward Sinann, sending a bolt of power enough to slam the little faerie against the wall of the lair. Sinann dropped to the floor, limp and unmoving.

He stood and leaned over to peer at her.

"Did I kill her?" Morrighan didn't sound as if she cared one way or the other.

"Nae. There's still breathing. Barely, but she's alive."

"Och," was Morrighan's only comment. She returned to her work.

After a few moments, Sinann stirred and sat up. Daghda went to her and knelt. Morrighan ignored them both as he spoke to the white faerie. "Go. I willnae kill ye now, but next time I will. Dinnae return. And dinnae try to return to yer mortal. Accept that he's lost to ye. Yer Dylan may as well be dead. Give up."

A light entered Sinann's eye, and she stood to face him with as much anger as he'd ever seen in the Morrighan. She fairly vibrated with the rage, and her voice trembled as she told him, "I think not, laddie." In a twinkling, she leapt, and flew across the room to the burrow.

"No!" Daghda ran after. The Morrighan cried out, but without wings they were both hopelessly slow.

Down the narrow, earthen tunnel they raced, through chambers they passed. At each chamber they found the impudent white bitch rummaging through their belongings. *"You!"* He leapt at her, but she flew away as lightly as a hummingbird, off and down another burrow. She laughed at each near miss, and that drove him to greater speed.

But then there was a cry of triumph ahead. He caught up to her in Morrighan's sanctum. Just as the two of them rushed into the room, there was a glimpse of the sea faerie standing by an opened chest of baubles.

Her eyes went wide as she turned and saw them, then she snapped her fingers and was gone.

"Get her!" Morrighan was furious. She spun, looking around the room as if Sinann could still be there.

"Where? Can *you* follow her?"

There was no reply, which meant "No."

Daghda went to the chest, which overflowed with jewelry. Gold necklaces of precious stones—rubies, sapphires, diamonds—bracelets and armbands, torques of silver and gold, all poured out the top of the wooden box bound in iron. He ran his fingers into the tangle. "What did she get? Is anything missing?"

Morrighan came to look, and poked around in the priceless jumble. "I dinnae think she did. Had she time, she would have taken it all. You must have frightened her away quick enough." She rummaged through the jewels some more, then said, "No. I see nothing missing."

That was a relief. Daghda wouldn't care to hear the wailing if any of the gold or silver had gone missing.

The day after MacCorkindale's visit, most of the Ciorram livestock was taken by the garrison. The kine had been grazing for a few weeks on the pastures and had put on a fair amount of weight. It was too early to sell any of the animals at market, for they wouldn't bring a good price, but some of the weaker animals could now be slaughtered for fresh meat.

Certain flocks of the Ciorram sheep, having grazed throughout the winter as Dylan's had, were less thin than most in the Highlands were at this time of year. The shearing would be soon, and once that was done, a few animals would become mutton for the sake of stewpots that had gone meatless for longer than was thought good for health. The arrival of

Easter put an end to Lent, when meat was not eaten, so there had been eggs, but most years it was well past Easter that the first fresh meat was slaughtered.

So the Ciorram men were more than dismayed when a detail of Red-coats rode into the castle bailey. The Laird was called out to meet them, and Iain came from the Great Hall with Artair. Curious and concerned, Dylan drifted over from the kitchen yard where he'd been trading some goat cheese for a sack of onions. The Sergeant of the dragoons dismounted, with a corporal to his right, and presented an order graced with Bedford's seal.

Iain read the paper and grunted. He reddened with anger. "Says here ye're to collect every head of kine in Matheson households, and half the sheep." Then he muttered to himself in Gaelic, "I expect we should round up half the rats in the glen so they can eat hearty, then?" That brought a laugh from the other clansmen.

There had never before been an appropriation involving this many animals. It had a sense of unreality about it. Iain passed the order to Dylan, who scanned it and handed it off to Artair. Dylan boggled. This couldn't be right. Even Bedford couldn't be this cruel.

Robin Innis and Marc Hewitt, standing at the top of the stairs to the barracks over the stable, were the only other Scots in sight, for there were few brave enough to stick their noses into business involving dragoons. The bailey was still.

Artair, still reading, began to curse the English, vehemently and with random invective. The soldiers gazed at him, unmoved, for they were accustomed to Gaelic mutterings they didn't understand. Gaelic was never taken seriously, heard by the Redcoats only as primitive gibberish. Their job was to appropriate the animals, nothing more. Artair handed the order back to Iain, who shoved it back at the Sergeant. The Redcoat was a young man, pale and pink-cheeked, but with a stillness beyond his apparent years.

"Tell Bedford to go to hell," Iain said.

The soldier declined to accept the paper. "I have my orders, sir."

"That paper says households with but one sheep are to give it over. Ye intend to leave the poorest of the glen destitute? Without even a ewe for milk?"

The young Redcoat's voice brightened. "You do understand there will be silver given in exchange for the livestock." His tone suggested he thought money would allay the resistance of the Scots to give up their animals. It also betrayed his belief the Laird might be too illiterate to understand the exchange that had been carefully detailed in Bedford's order. Dylan's jaw clenched, and he looked away, for he knew most Mathesons in the glen—indeed, most Scots throughout the country—to be better educated than the average Englishman.

"I said, tell him to go to hell. He'll have our property over my dead body." His nostrils flared as the seriousness of the situation sank in. The Redcoats really did intend to let the clan starve.

The Sergeant blinked but showed no other reaction. "I'm afraid my orders are to accomplish that very thing, if necessary. Further resistance will result in your arrest, I assure you, sir."

"I cannae give—"

"Corporal, aim!" The Sergeant's next in command raised his musket to aim at Iain. The muzzle was at point-blank against the Laird's head.

The Scotsmen tensed. Artair said nothing. There was a long moment of silence.

Then the Sergeant said with the bland understatement perfected by the English to an art, "I assume we've a meeting of the minds, then. You have the order. I anticipate receiving the livestock by noon tomorrow. My men and I will bivouac outside your gate until this is accomplished."

He addressed his corporal in a lowered voice, "Stand down." The dragoon obeyed.

Iain said flatly, "I've tenants who are a day's walk from here."

The Sergeant considered that for a moment, then said, "Right. Day after tomorrow, then. Good day." With that, he and his men left the bailey.

Iain lost no time in complying, declaring there was no point in delay that would accomplish nothing more than irritating the soldiers. He did, however, direct the castle guard to help the farmers shear their sheep before turning them over. Little as it was, as much wool as could be taken in one day would stay with the Mathesons. The animals of the glen and surrounding hillsides were gathered that day, and messengers sent to the outlying farms.

On Dylan's farm the following day, Sarah came to see what was going on as Dylan and Coinneach divided his flock with the help of the dogs. They carefully examined each animal to determine which would stay and which would go to feed the soldiers. No sense in sending the stronger ones. Quickly, they sheared the ones that would not be staying, a hurried and sloppy job that was better than nothing.

It was very late when finally the sheep were culled and sheared. Coinneach, Doirinn, and Fionn barely had time to take the sheared sheep and all of Dylan's kine on to the castle before dark. With a heavy heart, Dylan watched them go as he shut the enclosure gate. Sarah approached and watched with him.

His gut knotted with concern for his carefully bred flock. He'd worked hard to properly cross-breed the few Cheviots with his Highland sheep, and now it seemed his remaining flock would be slaughtered to keep the clan alive. By summer there wouldn't be a single living sheep in the glen. Anger rose. The horrible helplessness in the grip of the *Sassunaich* felt crippling. Like failure in a conflict that would never be over and could never be surrendered. There was no hope except to endure.

Sarah said, "The clan will survive it. The English cannae overcome us. They never could."

He looked at her as a strange feeling stole over him that she'd read his mind. He opened his mouth to speak, but hesitated. Would she understand? She was a Scot, but she was also a woman. She expected protection from the men of the clan and was not to blame if that protection failed. He was going to keep silent, but now she looked at him expectantly. He had to say something. So he said, "I'm sorry."

A puzzled light came into her eyes. "For what?"

One shoulder shrugged, and he gazed off over the remaining sheep, looking scarce in the enclosure. "You shouldn't have to be afraid." Then he glanced at her to see if she understood.

She didn't; he could see it on her face, and she told him as much. "I dinnae ken what you mean." A light blush darkened her cheeks as well, and now he needed to explain himself.

His weight shifted. "Well, I guess I wish I could just chase away the Redcoats and tell them never to come bother us again." That made her chuckle, and he smiled, relieved. He continued, "It's my duty. I haven't done it."

There was a long silence, and he began to wish he'd kept shut. But instead of letting it go like he should have, he tried to explain further, "I should have been there for Cait."

Sarah began to speak, hesitated, then said, "Aye. Cait."

"I feel responsible."

Sarah nodded. Dylan didn't know what he'd expected, but was disappointed. Perhaps he'd hoped she would assure him Cait's death hadn't been his fault, that he had no shortcomings for which to feel guilty. Now, with the clan's livestock on its way to feed the English occupiers, the sense of ineffectuality was sharp.

"We'll need to do something. We can't live on what they've left us." His voice sounded lame in his ears.

"I'm certain whatever Iain Mór decides to do will be the best thing."

With that, she turned and went into the house. Dylan sighed as he watched her go, wishing he knew what to say to her, or what he wanted her to say to him. Further, on a level way down deep, he wondered why he gave a damn.

He took a step toward the house but stopped short, startled, as something dropped past his nose and landed at his feet. Bending to look, he poked his fingers around in the grass and found something hard. A ring.

"Huh." A glance at the sky told him nothing about where it had come from. It sure couldn't have come from a plane flying by overhead. A glance around revealed no lurking persons who could have thrown it. Besides, the trajectory of the thing had been straight down. As if it had been simply dropped.

He examined the ring for clues, turning this way and that his finger where it rested on the tip. It was a small ring of silver, graced with three small opals. The metal had been worked in a design of geometric Celtic knot. For a moment he stared hard at it, unable to tell where the loops began or ended.

Opals made him nervous. There was an urge to throw the ring away, for the stone could be unlucky for some people. But he couldn't bring himself to just toss the valuable piece. He slipped it into his sporran, along with his Goddess Stone and money purse, and told himself he'd sell it as soon as possible.

Then he looked up at the sky again, but saw nothing but clouds.

CHAPTER 14

"**B**edford is under the impression we can eat shillings." Artair sat next to his brother before the hearth in the Great Hall. It was a well-attended *céilidh* that Sunday, after the animals had been turned over to the garrison. The men of the glen filled the room to discuss what was to be done to feed the clan. The women at the other end of the room pretended to talk amongst themselves but fell silent often. They listened in on the men talk, desperate to know what lay ahead for them all.

The Crown had paid winter prices for the cattle and sheep—a paltry amount because the animals were not yet fattened on the pastures. But the amount of money mattered not at all, for it was only money. During spring in the Highlands, food simply wasn't available for sale. Even bartering would be difficult until summer. The sheep and kine had been irreplaceable, and the English Army might as well have paid in rocks for all the value the silver had for the Highlanders.

Dylan said, "Have they done this to the MacDonells or the MacLeods? The Mackenzies? Sutherland?"

"Nae. It's ourselves only that's supporting this garrison." A murmur of indignant agreement rippled through the cluster of men, and Artair continued, " 'Tis nae from need, 'tis but to starve us."

Colin said, " 'Tis punishment for the sacks of wheat and their poor wee well."

Dùghlas said, "They bought the cattle when they were too thin to require a good price, and now graze them on our pastures." Even Dùghlas was hurt by the appropriation, though he'd lost all his cattle to the MacDonells that winter. For him, now, there was no hope of recovering his loss until the rest of the clan recovered before him.

Iain Mór was silent, one elbow propped on the arm of his chair, listening carefully to the opinions of the men around him. He busied himself, tamping tobacco into his wooden pipe with one large thumb.

Artair said, "We cannae live on a few sheep. Without meat, our children and old folk will die of disease. Our men will weaken. The women will miscarry their bairns." Three women in Ciorram were expecting to deliver that summer and had already gone far too long without meat.

Dylan didn't know what Bedford was up to, but Artair was right. Cattle were the basis of the economy, and everything hinged on the number of calves born in the spring that survived and grew to a good weight. It determined the number of animals to be sold off or slaughtered by the following winter. They'd been left with no animals and not enough money to replenish the herd when stock eventually could be bought. Numbers would be low next year. It might take years after that for them to recover. There would be little meat slaughtered and none sold in Ciorram this year, and not much the following year or the year after.

In addition, there would be no milk or butter, and precious little wool for clothing. No leather for shoes, belts, and gloves. The clan had gone from comfortable to subsistence living in one day.

It was also true this action must be punitive. There was no reason to appropriate so much stock at once, so early in the year. Bedford wanted to hurt the Mathesons.

"Artair is right," Dylan said. That brought a shocked silence, for nobody expected him to ever utter those words. He continued, "We've got to replenish our herds somehow."

Artair grabbed the moment, filled with Dylan's unexpected support. "We'll raise a *creach* on the *Sassunach* herd."

A strong murmur of agreement ran through the gathered men, and Artair basked in it, leaning back in his chair and nodding. Iain remained silent, puffing on his pipe and sending tendrils of smoke into the air.

Then Dylan said, "No. We'll reive the MacDonells."

Artair flushed and leaned forward to insist. " 'Tis our own kine the soldiers have taken. We've a right—"

"We'd be stupid to take from the soldiers. Also, that's exactly what Bedford wants. He'd love to catch us with their herd."

" 'Tis *our* herd."

Dylan pounded a fist on his knee. " 'Tis *not* our herd! We sold it to them, and they have the bill of sale. You can see it any way you like, but the Crown is going to call the kine theirs, and there's nothing you can do about it. Our only chance of having enough—"

"We've reived the *Sassunach* herd before."

Dylan leaned forward, directly into Artair's face. "And your father died for it! Not to mention the *creach* failed. Is that what you're wanting? To get Iain Mór killed?" He sat back and peered at Artair through narrowed eyes. "I bet you'd like that. I bet you're just aching to see him get cut down by those dragoons."

Artair cut a glance toward Iain, who sat in his chair, calmly drawing on his dead pipe but looking at Artair as if waiting for a reply. None was forthcoming.

Dylan continued, "We should raid the MacDonells. They've got it coming in any case. They stole Dùghlas's kine."

"They've nae abundance on their pastures this spring." Iain's voice was even, but pointed. He held a candle to his tobacco, trying to relight it.

"More than we have. I think the MacDonells should be made to do their share of supporting our local law enforcement agency." Dylan glanced around at the other men. "Aye?"

Iain thought for a moment, sat up in his chair, then nodded. "Aye." Artair glowered at Dylan from beneath pale eyebrows, then was further discomfited when Iain continued, "Dylan, you'll take some men and lead them into MacDonell lands."

"Iain! I should lead them!" Artair's voice had a whining quality that made even Dylan wince for him.

Iain glared at Artair and leaned forward in his seat, pointing at him with the stem of his pipe. "For one thing, laddie, I'll send whoever I've a mind to send, and ye'll have nae say in the matter so long as I'm alive to have the say myself. Furthermore, Dylan learned his skills under Rob Roy MacGregor. He's the best man among us to lead a *creach*. Ye'll learn from him and be glad for it!"

Artair fell silent and sat back in his chair, staring at Dylan from under sullen eyebrows. Dylan didn't give a damn. He was going to lead the men safely to MacDonell lands and back, so the clan would not starve.

The party of ten Matheson men left the glen under cover of darkness. Following an unlikely route out, toward Glen Affric, Dylan expected to mitigate the chance of detection by the garrison. He had his men circle wide before heading north.

Artair was an annoyance from the first. Bedding down at daylight in heather between outcrops of rock, Dylan could hear him muttering under his breath to Tormod and Dùghlas, loud enough to hear but not clear enough to catch more than a few words of what was said. The wee lairdie was talking against him, trying to discredit him. Efforts to get a rise among the men against Dylan had always failed before, but these days Artair had the support of Tormod and Dùghlas. They muttered along with Artair, also wrapped in their plaids among the heather.

Dylan knew he couldn't expect support from the blacksmith again until the question of Sarah was resolved. Perhaps not even then. Tormod was, after all, a Matheson and as stubborn as the rest of them. As for Dùghlas, he and Artair were the same age and were longtime friends. He would most likely become Artair's *fear-còmhnaidh* on his succession to the laird-ship. Coinneach generally followed his brother's lead, and though his youth limited his influence, he also tended to side with Artair and strengthen his numbers. They formed the core of Artair's backing within the clan and would be Dylan's greatest enemies were he to succeed to the lairdship while Artair was still alive.

Colin Matheson, who was an older tenant, and Marc Hewitt waffled in their support the way some clans waited until the last moment to decide which ruler to support during an uprising. They would most likely keep a low profile until the question was settled.

That left, on this *creach*, Robin, Seumas, and Keith who were unflagging friends of Dylan. But since Robin was an Innis, Seumas a MacGregor, and Keith a Campbell, they carried little weight with the rest of the clan. Though they'd all pledged their loyalty to Iain Mór, only Robin could trace lineage to the Ciorram Mathesons and that through the female line. Dylan knew it would be unwise to press any unimportant issues with Artair on this trip, for he would lose. His only wish just then was to make it back home with enough cattle to keep the clan fed.

Ready for sleep, he crossed himself and whispered the prayer that in recent months had become his habit before events that would test him: "Dear God, please give me the strength to do what I must, to never shrink from my obligations. Help me to conduct myself with honor at all times. Please keep my children safe. Above all, let me be reunited with my beloved Cait. Amen." With that, he pulled his plaid tight around himself and slept.

It was with great care the Matheson reivers approached their goal, the MacDonell pastures. In order to avoid occupied houses, they followed a narrow track through a crevice above where the kine would be. It wound around and zigzagged downward. The closer they came, the more care they took in their silence.

Near the pasture, Dylan's ears perked and pulse surged as he recognized the distant clanging of steel below. Damn, he wished that faerie were here! The one thing his invisible ally was best at was reconnaissance. Nothing for it, though, but to send one of the men and hope he wouldn't be seen. He led the group on as far as he dared, turned to halt them, then gestured for them to gather on him and listen up. "Quickly, Artair, slip into the pasture and tell me what you find. If it's what I think it is, we've got to act fast." Artair hurried onward, and the rest of the men crouched among boulders to wait. Dylan himself climbed one of those boulders to see what he could see. The pasture below was dotted with huge outcrops of granite, cattle milling about as large, shifting shadows.

Artair returned in a very short time, panting from the run and from excitement. "There's a battle up ahead—I can hear their voices. I recognize Donnchadh an Sealgair MacLeod. The MacLeods are after the same cattle we are. The herd is large. It must be every head the MacDonells possess!"

Dylan frowned at that. The MacLeods had a long-standing hatred for the MacDonells in these parts and wouldn't hesitate to take off with enough cattle to starve the clan. It seemed they were even now trying to kill as many MacDonells as possible before taking the *spréidhe*. He said, "It's a large herd. They're scattered from the fighting. Wandering around."

"Let's join the MacLeods. Fight the MacDonells." Artair's suggestion was met with a general agreement, for the Mathesons had no love for the MacDonells either. Several dirks came out.

"No!" A blinding ache billowed in Dylan's head, and his only wish just then was to put Brigid through Artair's throat. He squeezed his eyes shut and said, "No. We have a chance to take the *spréidhe* and beat it out of here before anyone realizes any are gone. If we help the MacLeods, afterward we'll have to fight them for the cattle, too." He took deep breaths as the ache faded and he could see again. "Do what I tell you, Artair, or I'll kill you here and throw your body over the back of a cow for the ride home."

That brought a general snicker, even from Tormod.

Artair snorted, angry. "Coward!"

In a flash Dylan reached out and with one knuckle whapped Artair's Adam's apple, hard. The wee lairdie collapsed to his knees, holding his throat in agony. Dylan said, "Cut it out. I'm not in the mood to take your crap. Just do what I say, we'll all get home in one piece with the *spréidhe*, and then you can tell Iain how mean I was to you. How's that?"

Artair was unable to reply. He coughed and gagged.

"I'll take that as a 'Yes, sir, that's fine with me, sir.' " Dylan turned to the other men and said, "All right. Follow me. We'll find the herd and cut out as many head as we can while the MacLeods and MacDonells are fighting each other and paying no attention to the kine. Come."

Artair climbed to his feet, and the men followed. With stealth and speed, the Mathesons descended to the pasture. Now shouting could be heard over the clashing swords. Most of the fighting was going on at the edge of the pasture to the left, and the cattle were shying away from it, moving to the Mathesons' right. In the moonlight could be seen dozens of dark shapes of agitated kine, shifting and lowing in confusion. It was a confusion that worked well to cover the approach of the Mathesons.

"If you get turned around in the dark, look for Artair against the sky." There was a quarter moon tonight, with no cloud cover, and that would work both for them and against them. It would light their way, but would also reveal them to others. Dylan then gestured off to the right, and Robin led Seumas, Keith, and Colin in that direction. Dylan pointed to Dùghlas, Coinneach, Tormod, and Marc and gestured straight ahead. They went. Then Dylan waved to Artair to climb the rocky hill above. It was less risky than to let him loose down among the kine and the fighting. "Climb high for a good vantage point. Give us a hoot of an owl if we need to break it off. Otherwise, make certain you can be seen against the sky." Artair nodded and reluctantly went.

Dylan went into the moonlit pasture below, where the shadows of men and cattle moved across a silvery grassland. The surrounding rocks and trees were black, featureless shadows, and Dylan looked to the sky and the descending moon to the west. As he'd expected, Artair was silhouetted against the sky. But hopefully he would not be noticed by the struggling MacDonells and MacLeods. He would give the Mathesons a bearing to locate in the darkness the narrow track on which they'd entered.

The work was difficult, to cut cattle from a spooked herd without raising the attention of the fighting men nearby. But they had to work quickly, lest either the MacLeods or the MacDonells win their struggle and discover a third party interested in the kine. Dylan and his men, with efficiency born of generations of herders, cut a manageable number of beasts from the MacDonell herd and moved them toward the track through the rocks. More would have been better, for they'd lost a lot of cattle to the soldiers. But this number would get them through the summer and keep the clan from having to slaughter all its sheep.

While he worked, Dylan kept an ear out for the fighting between the MacDonells and the MacLeods. Swords clanged, and there was much shouting and confusion. As long as there was plenty of noise, Dylan felt comfortable.

The cattle came in two clusters. First Robin's group, then Dùghlas's. In single file now, the *spréidhe* made their way between boulders and up the rocky trail. Artair met them there, excited to see the ease with which they'd slipped away. "More," he said. "There are dozens more down there. We can take a lot more than this."

"We're not going to be greedy," said Dylan.

Artair made a guttural sound of disgust. "This isn't enough to replace all the *Sassunaich* took."

"It's enough to keep the clan from going hungry. Leave it, and let's go!"

Artair turned to Tormod and Dùghlas. "Come with me, we're going to get more." He hurried down the trail toward the herd. The two men hesitated a moment, glanced at Dylan, but then followed.

"Artair!" Dylan hissed. He muttered to Robin to take charge of the cattle, then followed Artair and his mutineers. Shouting after them was a bad idea, so he had to catch up with Artair to convince him to return. The easy thing would have been to leave them be and let the MacDonells and MacLeods dispatch them, but Dylan couldn't do that. In the first place, he needed all his men to herd the cattle back to Ciorram. In the second place, he was responsible for them and couldn't just leave them behind, no matter how big a pain in the ass they were.

Just as he caught up with them, at the bottom of the trail, the sounds of fighting diminished. One of the MacLeods let go a shout of victory as some shadows scurried away from the cattle. Artair stopped on the track.

Dylan caught up, and grabbed Artair by the coat collar. "Listen, you little shit, get back to the cattle. Now." Shadows of men moved across the pasture, fanning out to herd the scattered animals that remained. Dylan hurried to say, "They're done fighting. They'll be coming after their spoils now. Let's go."

Artair uttered a curse and bumped into Dylan in his hurry to get away from the pasture. Tormod and Dùghlas followed. Dylan brought up the rear, hoping they hadn't been seen and looking back to see whether they were followed.

He took his men and cattle toward MacLeod territory for a distance, then on a wide expanse of solid rock made a turn toward Glen Ciorram. The unshod cattle would make almost no mark on the stone. Also, there was little risk of being tracked to Ciorram, for the MacDonell survivors of the fight were sure to identify the reivers as MacLeods. They stopped briefly to sleep at dawn.

A few hours later, the Mathesons rose and continued on. They made their way quickly up the rocky track toward Ciorram with the twenty head they'd managed to lift. It wasn't the largest *creach* Dylan had ever accomplished, but it was enough.

Dylan walked at the head of the herd, on the lookout now for soldiers. Though Bedford may have assumed the Mathesons would try to raid the garrison, Dylan didn't figure him to be dense enough to consider it the only possible reaction from the clan. Bedford had to know there would be a *creach*, and would have his men alert for one.

Sure enough, at about noon Dylan spotted a rustling tree in the distance ahead. He halted his men and found a vantage point to look. It was a surprise to see the tree was not very close, and was much taller than he'd thought. It shook and danced in the distance like an invisible tornado had just touched down on it. Dylan frowned, wondering what on earth could be shaking that tree.

However, he didn't care to see it up close and find out. Instead, he returned to his men and ordered them back around to follow another route. It would add a few miles to the trip, but they would end up in the high glen. There, the cattle could then be hidden in the forest downstream from the waterfall. Some would be slaughtered, and some presented as having been bought. Those would be pastured for fattening.

As the men and cattle retreated, Dylan gazed back at the dancing tree and again wished Sinann were there to tell him what was going on. Where had she gone? She'd never stayed away this long before. Heck, usually he had to fight her to get her to leave him alone. He tried to remember when was the last time he'd seen her. Months ago, it seemed. In February, when . . .

Oh, no. He realized the last time he'd seen Sinann was when the spell directed at Morrighan backfired. Dylan's mind flew with horrifying possibilities.

The mood among the men for the rest of the trip back was of celebration. They were safe home and the *spréidhe* hidden in good time. They made jokes and talked with light hearts as they walked. And nobody, not even Artair, was muttering dark things about Dylan anymore.

A celebratory *céilidh* gathered at the castle when they arrived. Joy at their safe return, and for the cattle that would keep them in better comfort than the English would have liked, shone on the faces of the women and children. The sense of well-being in the Great Hall moved the worries about Sinann to the back of Dylan's mind, and he smiled to himself. Listening to the stories, most of which he'd heard before but always loved to hear again, there was a rightness about it that made his soul settle just a little more comfortably into his life. Problems faded and weakened. The world brightened a little. He glanced around the room to where the women had clustered, and for a brief moment found himself searching for Cait.

He looked away and chided himself. It wouldn't hurt so much if he could just quit expecting to see her. Rationally, he knew he needed to move on. But, too deeply, he couldn't accept she was gone. Sometimes, like now when he wanted most to avoid the pain of remembering, a deeper, colder fear arose that he might forget her entirely. He couldn't let that happen. Too much of himself would be gone if she were forgotten.

After a while, he looked over at the women again just to prove to himself he could do it without expecting Cait to be there. His gaze fell on Sarah. She was whispering to Ailis Hewitt, her smile warm and her eyes filled with bright joy. It warmed his heart, and he couldn't help but smile.

Then he shifted uncomfortably in his seat and returned his attention to the bard. In that moment, smiling at Sarah, he'd *wanted* to forget Cait. He went cold, and he stuffed his hands into his armpits. No. He'd never forget. Ever.

CHAPTER 15

Barri called the police, and Kenneth was arrested again. But he was out on bail the following day. Once more her lawyer obtained a restraining order for her, but she knew it would do no good if Kenneth got to drinking again and decided to teach her another lesson. Now she feared to leave the dojo. She had a workman come to nail a sheet of plywood over the hole in her back door and install a deadbolt lock. At trial Kenneth was fined, but did no more jail time for the assault. Now every knock on the door sent her heart into her mouth. Each trip to the grocery store was a tense, white-knuckle nightmare.

The divorce went through, with much ugliness from Kenneth. Though he never returned to the dojo, he phoned often. He accused her of having a lover, shouting it over the phone in a drunken slobber and with as much crude language as he could utilize. As she listened, something inside her told her to hang up, but something stronger in her insisted that would be more rude than she was willing to become. Tolerating his behavior was better than lowering herself to it.

So she listened until she could make an excuse to tell him good-bye, then she did. Each day she dreaded encountering him in public, for he had no shame in creating a scene. She found herself avoiding certain of her friends to avoid Kenneth, and slowly was able to sort out which relationships would remain hers and which would be given over to him. Her life dwindled even more than it had when Dylan died.

Over the next few months Barri thought hard about what Cody had said. She spent long hours looking at the drawing and longer hours sitting in Dylan's rowboat on the lake, thinking.

Drifting, going nowhere but bobbing on the water, she thought about who she was. It was a bit of a shock to discover she wasn't certain. She'd never lived alone before, and until now had never thought she could. Even during the years she'd spent traveling with Kenneth, she'd been dependent on him. She'd grown her hair long and ironed it straight because that was how everyone else wore theirs. She'd held opinions because they had been popular, and later had changed herself to accommodate Kenneth's career. She'd spent so much energy constructing the outside of herself that she no longer knew what was on the inside. Now, alone so much of the time, she was forced to pick through her life to decide what was real and what wasn't.

Raising Dylan had truly been a part of her, she was sure of that. It was impossible to imagine not having been his mother. The house was not her. She didn't miss that old, oversized place. She didn't miss the struggle to keep Kenneth pacified. Only now did she realize what a consumption of time and effort it had been to live with him, for now, without him, she was left with great stretches of time with nothing to do.

She wondered if she might get a job. Part-time, anyway, so there would be a reason to leave the dojo from time to time. Or perhaps volunteer work. There must be someone here in town in need of an extra pair of hands.

It was an exciting thought. A smile came to her face as she pictured herself being hired and making herself useful. Yes, that seemed like a plan. Her heart beat faster at the thought of finding out what she might be able to do. Scary, but exciting. She unshipped the oars on the boat and let them plop into the water, got her bearings on the dojo, and set a course for the shore.

I t was simple enough to find a part-time clerical position at the hospital. They put her in a pink jacket, and she manned the administration desk in the emergency room for four hours five days a week. For the first time in her life, she had somewhere to go and felt good about it. The world around her began to make sense again. She made new friends and discovered there were other people in the world who could understand her predicament and who didn't judge her.

Cindy, for instance, was a few years older than Barri and had been through two divorces. Her three children were grown and moved away, and now she lived with her third husband. The husband was on disability, and Cindy supported them both as a nurse.

Rail thin and somewhat horse-faced, Cindy wore scrubs loose enough to billow and float as she walked. Her hair was short and steel gray, so frizzy she used a hair pick on it instead of a comb. Though the trials of her life had been etched on her face in deep lines and fine wrinkles, she also sported crow's feet at her eyes that indicated she bore them all with humor. Her presence was therapy, and over the weeks Barri felt her own problems loosen and fall away.

One day Cindy was hanging around the desk during a quiet spell, drinking coffee from the pot they kept on the counter behind. Barri preferred tea, and sipped hers carefully while it cooled some. Cindy wore deep purple scrubs and the biggest, cushiest pair of sneakers Barri had ever seen, and leaned against the counter as she shot the breeze and blew across the top of her very hot, very strong coffee.

Dr. Nathan Bartleby walked past at a fair clip, his nose deep in someone's chart. Barri couldn't help but watch him go, but when she turned back to Cindy, she also had to blush at the look on the nurse's face.

"He's a cutie, all right." Cindy sounded like she might bust out laughing any second.

Barri sipped her tea. "He's very young."

"Nuh uh. Forty-seven. That's not too young. Not in my book, anyway. He can hang his stethoscope on my headboard any old day." She waggled her eyebrows and made Barri nearly choke on her tea.

"Cindy!" Though her ears turned red, she was nevertheless amused. "You're married!"

"I am?" She smacked her forehead as if she'd forgotten. "Well, dang! I guess I'll just have to let you have him, then. And here I was, all set to run away with that fine-looking man. You just spoiled all my fun!"

That made Barri giggle, and she glanced in the direction Dr. Bartleby had taken, though he was long gone. Cindy was saying now, "I'll tell you what, Barri, when a woman gets to be our age, and looking as well put together as you do, she can date a man five years younger, and nobody would even know, let alone care. He's divorced, three kids, two grandkids, and he looks good enough to . . . well, you know. I say go for it."

Barri shook her head. "I don't know. I'm afraid it would look silly."

"Hey, never mind how it looks. Just think of how it would *feel*." A comic look of rapture lit her face.

Another giggle passed between them, and Barri flushed to realize she was now seeing Dr. Bartleby in a whole new light. It had been years since she'd thought of anyone but Kenneth that way, and lately not even Kenneth.

They both looked up as a man came through the automatic doors across the room. Cold sweat broke out, and Barri set her cup down on the counter. *Speak of the devil.* She stood, and Cindy quit leaning on the counter, a puzzled frown on her face.

"Kenneth, the restraining order—"

"Fuck the restraining order. I wanna talk to my wife."

"I'm not your wife anymore." She tried to keep her voice level. Reasonable. If she could stay even, maybe he wouldn't raise his voice too much. Maybe she could get him out of here before there was a scene. Panic rose. If he lost her this job, he would continue doing it. Anything she would ever try to do, he would ruin. She would never be safe.

He said, "So you're working now. In a hospital." Looking around at the waiting room, he said, "Killed anyone yet?"

She closed her eyes, then opened them and said, "Kenneth, leave."

"I can't believe they pay you. Fucking incompetent. Put you in front of a computer, they might as well have a chimpanzee back there."

Cindy said, "Barri, let me get security."

Barri nodded, then addressed Kenneth. "If you don't leave immediately, there will be an off-duty cop here in about thirty seconds to arrest you. This will be your third arrest. You've violated the restraining order, and I will have you put in jail for a year."

"Fuck—"

"I mean it, Kenneth. Leave. Now." Her fingers were slippery on the desktop, but she kept her voice calm and looked him in the eye.

Kenneth paused for a moment, looking into her eyes, as if registering something that surprised him. Then he grinned and said, "Aw, come on, Barri. I was just joking." He shrugged. "Just kidding around."

This was a familiar tack with him, but it usually took him hours to come around to this. More often than not, it only happened after he'd done damage. Her first impulse was to do what she always did, and reconcile, but she held firm this time. "I know you were just kidding, but I'm not. Leave now."

He stared at her for a long moment. Barri noticed people were gathering at the doors, ready to come help but waiting first to see if help was needed. Kenneth blinked at her, then looked around at all the waiting people. Finally he stuffed his hands into his pockets and turned to leave.

Barri sank into her chair, shaking, as folks in varicolored scrubs gathered around. They asked if she was all right, and she nodded. Cindy arrived with the guard on duty, who then went out to the parking lot to make certain Kenneth had left the premises. Several coworkers patted her back and assured her she had done the right thing, but she felt mortified. Everyone there had seen the shame of her life. Kenneth had invaded the one place she felt safe and needed, and had called her incompetent. No matter how well she knew it was untrue, something inside her wondered if Kenneth might be right. Further, that traitor inside her wondered whether the people around her thought the same thing.

When she was able to look up to know who had seen the shameful display, her heart sank to find Dr. Bartleby standing across the room, watching. The lighthearted joy she'd felt earlier now crumbled.

Her shift was over at five o'clock. Several hours had passed since Kenneth had left, so she declined the security escort to the parking lot. She knew Kenneth well enough to figure he was passed out at home by now or in a bar somewhere working on being passed out. There was no knowing how he spent his day now that she wasn't at home for him to berate, but he couldn't have changed much just because she was no longer around.

When she arrived at her car, though, she wished she'd brought the cop with her. The green SUV was standing on four rims, the flattened tires beneath them four black, rubber puddles. The sidewalls had been so badly slashed there were slivers of rubber lying on the pavement. Barri groaned and looked around for Kenneth. He probably wasn't still there, coward that he was, but she wouldn't have put it past him to stick around and see her reaction to this adolescent idiocy.

Dr. Bartleby was there, approaching with his hands in his jacket pockets and a quizzical look on his face. Barri wanted to crawl into a hole until he would pass, and hoped he wouldn't notice the four flat tires. But he already had, and stopped for a closer look.

There was a look of sympathy on his face when he said, "Your husband?" He hurried to correct himself, "I mean, your ex-husband?"

She nodded and stared at the rear tire in hopes he would simply pass by and leave her to her embarrassment.

But she wasn't that lucky. He said, "Do you belong to an auto club?"

She shook her head, embarrassed even further. Kenneth had handled all that, and she'd not thought about those sorts of details.

Dr. Bartleby took his cell phone from his jacket pocket, then consulted a card in his wallet to dial.

Barri protested. "You don't need to do that. I'll just call—" He held up a palm to silence her, then spoke. A few quick sentences to request a tow truck, then he flipped the phone closed and restored it to his pocket. She said, "I'll be all right now. Thank you. It was very kind."

He looked around as if for the tow truck that wouldn't be there for a while yet, and said, "Bad enough you'll have to buy four new tires; you shouldn't get stuck with the roadside assistance charge. You don't mind my company while waiting, do you?" There was confidence in his manner but no arrogance. And she was relieved he hadn't mentioned the possibility of Kenneth returning to harass her while she waited by herself in this parking lot.

"Thank you," she replied, and said, "Would you care to sit down?" She unlocked the front passenger door and opened it for him, then went around to the driver's side to sit.

With the key in the ignition, she rolled down the two front windows for air. Summer was almost upon them, and it wouldn't be dark for a while yet, but the air was brisk. The heat trapped in the car, which had sat in the sun all day, dissipated on the breeze, but the seat beneath her was warm and comfortable. There was a long silence.

Finally, she said, "I really appreciate this. It's very kind of you."

Dr. Bartleby shrugged. "It's nothing." Then he glanced over at her and for the first time his smooth exterior slipped. "I mean, it's not *nothing*. That is, it's not a real inconvenience. I have no plans for this evening, and I'm glad for the chance to save a damsel in distress. It should boost my ego a bit, and then I can go home feeling all warm and fuzzy afterward."

Barri peered at him sideways, uncertain whether to take him seriously. The grin on his face told her he was joking, and she chuckled as she relaxed a little. "You get off on being a hero?"

His smile widened. "Of course. I often cruise parking lots in hopes of finding women in need of my cell phone. My auto club is beginning to wonder why my car is always breaking down."

That brought a laugh. Another silence settled, and it strung out as they watched cars come and go in the gas station next door. Then he said, "I admire the way you stood up to your ex today. I think most women would have retreated to the staff lounge, or the ladies' room, or something. You just stood there and told him what was what. That took nerve."

"I'm a nervy broad, then?"

He hurried to assure her otherwise, that she'd misunderstood, and she hurried to respond that she'd been kidding. He said, "Oh." Then he chuckled. "Yes. Kidding."

There was another long silence, while Barri mentally cursed her idiotic mouth. But then he said, "Would you care for some dinner one night this week?"

Barri's jaw dropped, but she closed it in a hurry. "A date?"

He smiled, shrugged, and looked around at the landscape. "Yeah. We could go into Nashville. It would be nice."

She couldn't help but smile. "Yes," she said, "I'd like that."

"Oh, good. Then slashing your tires was worth the trouble." When she frowned at that, he hurried to say, "Kidding. I was kidding."

Barri smiled, and her heart fluttered to be going out on a date. She'd almost forgotten what one of those might be like.

In the apartment that night, a tapping noise woke her up. The moonlight washed across the bed as she looked around to see where that insistent noise was coming from. It came again, and she realized there was somebody at the back door, tapping on the plywood. She slipped from the bed and drew on her robe. The floor was cold on her feet, but she didn't bother looking for her slippers.

Cautious these days, she refrained from turning on a light as she went to answer the door. Instead, she went to the kitchen window and observed her visitor from darkness. Her heart leapt to see it was a police officer, his face lit by the halogen lamps on the Main Street causeway. In uniform, with his notebook, he was looking at the kitchen window but didn't seem able to see her.

News of Dylan? Had they found a body?

She shook her head. It was the middle of the night. Dylan had been gone for over two years, anything concerning him would certainly wait till morning. She shook her head, annoyed with herself. Thinking this way never helped. All it ever did was make her jittery and weepy. She took a deep breath, tightened the robe around her waist, and went to see what was the matter that would bring the police to her door so late.

The cop came to attention when she opened up. He was young, and had a blond crew cut that in the streetlights made a pale halo around his head. "I'm looking for a Dylan Matheson?" He read from a business card on his clipboard.

A shiver ran through her. "I'm sorry, he isn't here. Dylan died quite a while ago." A brief wonder flickered across her mind that she was apologizing for Dylan's death.

A disappointed look crossed the officer's face, but he persisted. "So Dylan Matheson did live here? I saw the name on the window out front . . ."

"Dylan was my son. He lived here until recently. I live here now." She began to wonder what the purpose of this was. It was cold here in the open doorway, and she was sleepy. If he had no information about Dylan, which he certainly couldn't if he didn't even know her son was dead, she wished to return to bed.

But the officer read from a notebook. "Do you know a Kenneth Matheson?"

Again, she nodded and frowned. "We were married. Now we're divorced." Good God, was he serving papers? Now? A great weariness swept over her.

He shifted his weight. "I'm afraid I have some bad news for you, ma'am." He shrugged and said in a sotto voce afterthought, "Or maybe not so bad, depending."

"I'm sorry, I don't understand." The struggle to remain polite was wearing on her. In a moment she was liable to say something testy.

The officer took a deep breath and continued, "You see, Kenneth Matheson died in a car wreck this evening. There is no one at his home address. We found a business card in his wallet, belonging to Dylan Matheson, who we took to be a relative, so we thought there might be someone here who could help us find the next of kin. I expect that would be you."

"He has a sister. She lives up on the ridge." Having said that, she then wondered why Kenneth still had that card. She'd given it to him back when Dylan had first opened the dojo, but Kenneth had shown no interest in either the card, the dojo, nor Dylan himself for years.

Her next thought was to realize what the young man had said. She blinked at him, wondering if she'd misheard. "He's dead?" It couldn't be true. With Kenneth gone, there was nobody left in her life. "Kenneth's dead?" Kenneth couldn't be dead. There had always been Kenneth in the world. He couldn't just die.

"Yes, ma'am. He ran his car into a light pole out on the bypass earlier this evening. He died immediately."

Barri sighed. "He'd been drinking."

"Yes, ma'am, he had been. Quite a bit, apparently. His blood alcohol level indicated he may have passed out at the wheel."

She considered that for a moment, for the information wasn't easily realized. Nothing seemed to sink in. So she waited until it did before moving on. "Nobody else was hurt?"

"No, ma'am."

She nodded. "Thank God for that." There was another long moment, while the officer waited, then she said, "Is there anything I need to do tonight? Does he need to be identified?"

"No, ma'am, not tonight. I'm just here to notify you and let you know where he is. You or Mr. Matheson's sister can contact the hospital in the morning." The officer gave her his own calling card, bade her good night, and left down the rickety back stairs. Barri closed the door behind him.

In the darkness of the back entry, she waited to cry, but there was nothing. The memories wouldn't come, nor any emotion. Exhaustion swept in on her, and all she wanted was to go to bed. Perhaps if she slept, in the morning she might know how to feel about this. She returned to the bedroom and slipped back under the covers.

However, she never did know. Kenneth's sister and her sons came from up on the ridge to help bury Kenneth and receive his property. Barri stood at the periphery of things, though she'd been married to him for several decades. She didn't wish involvement. She was terrified everyone around her would see she hadn't loved Kenneth in a long time. With all the grace at her command, she moved through the process and found herself praised for her stoic demeanor.

*   *   *

It wasn't long after Kenneth's funeral that Cody delivered her baby. Joy lifted Barri's heart as she read the note handed to her when she arrived at work. She manned the desk for four hours, impatient to be free, but when her shift was over, she stopped at the gift shop for a helium balloon before hurrying on upstairs.

"Hello?" Barri wasn't certain she had the right room, and so tapped on the door with a fingernail as she entered. The balloon bobbed behind her, and she tugged on it to free it from the doorframe.

Raymond was there, seated at the foot of the bed. He looked up and stood to draw back the privacy curtain. "Barri is here," he murmured to Cody.

The new mother was wan but smiling. "Seven hours," she told Barri. "It took *seven hours*. Next time I want drugs. Lots and lots of drugs. Knock me out." She snapped her fingers to indicate just how quickly she would like to be knocked out.

Barri tied the balloon to the tray table, then sat on the foot of the bed as Cody moved the baby blanket to uncover the nursing child. It brought an odd, shifting feeling; a flood of memories of Dylan and longing for the grandchildren she would never have. But her smile was genuine, and she was truthful as she said, "He's going to look like Raymond."

Cody giggled. "All babies look like Winston Churchill or Mahatma Gandhi. He's a Gandhi."

Raymond said, a wide smile on his face and his voice bubbling with pride, "Then after he gets bigger he'll look like me." Barri had never seen him this excited. Emotion didn't seem to come easily to Raymond, and so his movements were jerky. Nervous. He appeared as if a poke in the wrong place might cause him to burst. But with nothing of consequence to accomplish, he sat in a plastic chair and tried to look casual. The goofy smile on his face stayed.

Cody said, "We're naming him Dylan. I hope that's all right with you."

"Oh!" Another welter of mixed feelings swarmed over Barri, and she covered her mouth with a hand. A smile came, with a deep flush, and she said, "Oh, that's lovely. Thank you."

Raymond laughed. "Never mind that every alphabetized list he'll be on for the rest of his life will show him as 'Marshall, Dylan.' "

That sent Barri into a fit of giggles that, though embarrassing, felt good. She rocked back and forth with the amusement. Tears tried to steal into her eyes, but she blinked them back and sighed.

The door opened, and Nathan poked his head into the room. "Yes, there you are. The date for the symphony is the twelfth."

Barri did a mental check of her calendar, which admittedly was not crowded, then nodded. "Yes. I can make it."

He smiled. "Good. Five o'clock, then. We'll have dinner."

"It sounds delightful."

Nathan nodded, then waved a hand of greeting to Cody and Raymond before ducking out.

Cody's eyes were wide. "Oh, we're dating a doctor now!"

Barri smiled, feeling as perky as she ever had. "Yes, I am. Nathan is so sweet. I've never met anyone like him before."

"Well, there wasn't much for him to live up to, was there?"

"No," Barri sighed and shook her head, "I'm afraid there wasn't."

Raymond looked at his watch and grunted. "I've got to go. There's this meeting—"

"It's all right. You've got your phone with you. I can call if I need to. Do you have time to go home and take a shower first?"

Raymond nodded and rose to give his wife a quick kiss, then kissed his son's fuzzy head. "I'll be back as soon as I can."

"Get some sleep tonight. It'll be your last chance for the next few months."

He laughed and hurried from the room.

Cody sighed as she watched him leave, and said, "He's changing. The baby has already made a big difference with him." She looked at Barri and continued conspiratorially, "I like it." Then she seemed to notice her friend's appearance and said, "Oh, you changed your hair! It looks great!"

Barri touched the curls around her face and shrugged. "I stopped straightening it and just let it go now. I'm afraid it might look too young for me."

"No, it's perfect. You know, I don't think Dylan ever knew you had curly hair. It was always so . . . well, smooth. He always . . ." She hesitated, then stammered a bit, and finally decided to finish the sentence. "Dylan said once it looked like a football helmet."

That brought a laugh, a surprisingly hearty one that rose from deep inside. "He said that?"

Cody shrugged. "Well, we were still in high school then. But I'll tell you what, you look better than I've ever seen you. Have you lost some weight?"

Barri shook her head and chuckled.

"Well, you've sure changed. Working here at the hospital and all, it's like you glow. Dylan would be flat surprised to see you now. He would be so pleased to see you happy finally."

The laughter stumbled to a halt, and Barri sighed. "I suppose he would."

There was a long silence, then she said, "Cody, you said you went to the past and saw him there. Is it the truth? You aren't just saying that?" Her voice was low. She couldn't believe she was actually asking this, and would be mortified to be overheard.

Cody eagerly nodded. "Yes. You believe me, then? You understand who he was?"

There was a hesitation, then Barri whispered, "I want to believe. Tell me more about what you saw. What is he like now? I mean, was. Then." So long ago. It was difficult to grasp.

Cody thought for a moment, then said carefully, "He matured a lot. I saw him after he'd been there four or five years, I think. At the time, he was a widower with two kids. His wife had just been murdered that morning."

Barri crossed her arms and hugged herself, horrified. "Oh. Poor Dylan . . ."

"Well, so there was a funeral and all. Everyone was so nice. Those people were very strange, but they were nice. He told them I was his cousin, so they treated me like I was one of them. It was . . ." she shrugged, ". . . *odd*. I'd never been accepted like that by strangers before."

"What was it like to live there? How did he live?" Her arms stayed across her chest. She wasn't certain whether she really wanted to hear this but couldn't pass up any information about Dylan, no matter how difficult it might be to take.

Cody made a face and waved her hand before her nose as if there were a bad smell. "It was awful. Everything was dirty. Everything smelled. The cow barn was a room inside the house. And the sheep were in a pen out back. The house was made out of dirt, I think. Something really hard, anyway, but not wood or bricks. There were things growing all over the walls and thatching. Vines and flowers and stuff. It had a thatched roof.

I'd never realized before how thick thatching was, but they put about a *ton* of straw up there. I guess that's how it keeps out the rain. Anyway, there were dirt floors covered with straw, and kids playing in it."

"How could he stand to live like that?"

Cody shrugged. "He didn't seem to mind. I don't think he thought much about it at all."

Barri said, "There was no running water."

"He got used to carrying buckets, I guess. Though he did mention he missed indoor plumbing, it didn't seem to be a big deal to him."

"No cars."

"No roads, and lots of time to get there. Nobody ever was in a hurry to get anywhere, near as I could tell. Nobody owned a watch, or even a clock that I could see, and they kept track of time by looking at the sun. I don't think anyone knew, or cared, how long a minute was."

"There was no refrigeration. Didn't the food make him sick?"

"They slaughter the meat as it's needed." Her face went dreamy as a memory occurred to her and she reached a hand toward Barri. "Oh, you haven't lived until you've had beef roasted the same day it was killed." Barri made a face, but Cody insisted. "No, really. I mean, it was pretty bland and not particularly abundant, but everything just . . . well, it all tasted more like food. Everything was what it was, and nothing tasted like preservatives or filler or coloring. It's very weird, but even after only a couple of days I got to where I even liked the little bits of ash or burnt spots on the bread. It was like barbeque every day."

"But what about lice and fleas? There were no insecticides."

Cody laughed and adjusted the weight of her son on her arm. "Well, I hardly ever use pesticides on my hair. They groomed themselves just like us." A frown crossed her face and she said, "Well, a little like us. There were some people there who didn't take care of themselves so well. But most of the folks I saw were just as careful as we are. They had combs with these really fine teeth." She held the tips of her fingers and thumb very close to indicate a tiny fraction of an inch. "*Very* small, to get the nits out. And they used soap. They made it out of ashes, I think. Well-groomed people didn't have parasites, just like here. Things were less convenient, but Dylan said he didn't think convenience was as important as the people he lived with."

That struck Barri hard. "He went back to be with a lot of strangers?"

Cody reached out a hand again to reassure, but Barri ignored it. "I mean . . . I'm sure he didn't mean you. He didn't leave to get away from you. But think about it, Mrs. Matheson. You're his mother; he couldn't stay with you forever. He never had gotten along with his father. He had friends here, but no other family except some cousins. No wife, no children—he didn't even have a girlfriend when he left. Back there, he had not just a wife and kids, but a whole extended family he was close to."

After a bit of thinking, Cody continued, "You know, I think he was happy *because* he fit in. I mean, Dylan was always pretty sure of what he wanted, you know?"

Barri nodded. One thing she knew for a certainty about her son was that nothing could sway him once he'd set his mind to something.

Cody continued, "I think he'd decided he was going to be a part of that clan. He went back for his son, and for his wife, but I think he also went back because it was where he belonged. They respected him. I could tell a lot of the people there looked up to him."

"They did?" A flutter of pride stirred in Barri.

Cody nodded. "He was happy, Mrs. Matheson. Even when his wife died, he knew he still belonged there. He believed he was there for a reason."

With a bit of a start, Barri realized she had come to accept the fact that her son truly had gone to live in eighteenth-century Scotland. And as she thought it over, she realized her heart was now lighter because of it. He'd gone to *live*. Perhaps even to have a full life.

Then her heart beat faster as she realized something else. Cody had seen him; the faerie had sent her to where Dylan was. There was a way to find Dylan, and Barri wanted to try it.

CHAPTER 16

Dylan could tell he was dreaming. The quality of consciousness was too sharp. Too selective. The grass on which he sat too green. He also knew that everything around him was nevertheless real. The rocks below and the ocean beyond were utterly factual. He knew if he fell from this cliff he would not only die in his bed, but his body would be discovered the next morning, broken and bloody.

So he sat, waiting. The wind lifted his hair from his face and filled his head with the salty tang of the sea. The loose front of his sark billowed, and his plaid slipped from his shoulder to drape over his hand on the ground beside him. Birds flocked nearby, raucous and busy, flashing white and gray against the crystalline blue sky. On an outcrop of rock on the shore below, a herd of seals basked in the sun. In all his life he'd never lived near the sea, until he came to Scotland. Now, though he was much closer than before, he was also still a day's travel from it, and visits to it now were more seldom and less pleasant.

Looking out to the wide, flat horizon, the vastness of the ocean put him in awe, the way a night sky made other men feel small in the expanses of space. There was so much life out there: the unknowable depths, the landscape beneath that wouldn't be explored for centuries and even in his own time couldn't be fully grasped. It made him realize just how much of the world he didn't understand and would never understand.

Still he waited.

In time, a pair of hands caressed his shoulders from behind. He didn't need to turn around to know who was there.

"Morrighan."

She knelt behind him, one thigh to either side of him, and pressed herself to his back as her arms came around to his chest. He held her wrists to stop her exploring inside his sark. "You recognize me, then?" she murmured near his ear.

"This has your touch." He grinned as she nuzzled his cheek, "So to speak." She drew back the collar of his sark to take the skin of his neck between her teeth, and he said, "What is it you want?"

"I want you." The low sound of her husky voice in his ear sent a quiver through him.

"And after you've had me?" The desire rose in him, surging and receding, then surging again as Morrighan pressed herself to him in soft rhythm, her lips caressing his ear. He remembered Sinann's warning, but the little white faerie seemed distant now. Unimportant. Turning to face Morrighan, speaking slowly, as if to make himself more clear, "What . . . do . . . you . . ." he continued turning and leaned into her until she lay on the ground and he was on all fours above her, kneeling between her thighs, ". . . want?"

"I've had my eye on ye since that day on Sheriffmuir." Her bare leg rose from the red velvet cloak she wore and stroked his side. "Ye fought well. A magnificent warrior, brave and strong."

"Uh-huh." Her thighs were parted below him. It wouldn't take much. Just to open her cloak and lift his kilt. He could feel the heat from her, and the fire in her black eyes begged him to do it. His throat was nearly closed with the effort of control, but he said, "Why me? What's the deal?"

"Such a question from the famous Dilean Dubh nan Chlaidheimh." Her fingers pressed the back of his neck. "Black Dylan of the Sword is what they call ye, aye? So let's have a look at it." Her other hand reached for his kilt.

Quickly he intercepted her hand, but then drew aside the gold-embroidered edges of her cloak and stroked her naked belly. She smiled and bit her bloodred lower lip. Her hips rocked toward him. "Tell me," he said, and kissed her. He spread her thighs with his knees and continued running his hand over her. "Tell me what it is you desire." He kneaded the taut muscles of her thigh and pressed it against his hip.

Her breaths were heavy. Panting. Her breasts rose and fell beneath him, and he took one into his mouth. The need to pull aside the wool cloth of the kilt separating them was exquisite pain, piercing body and soul. His pulse thudded in two places, a split second apart, and his skin flushed. But he said again, "Tell me. I require it." His hand found the moist center of her. Her back arched as he stroked her oh, so lightly. Her hips sought him, but he kept his touch light. Always near, but never where she wanted it most. "Tell me."

She moaned as she said, "I wish you to tell me. I would know the circumstances of the uprising. Spaniards have landed in Scotland, and they're now garrisoned at Eilean Donan. Three hundred or so, and a number of Highlanders. I would ken what you remember."

Alarm made his pounding blood run cold, and he shivered. *She knew.* She must have seen him return to the battlefield from the future in a new sark and healed body. His fingers went deeper, to make her gasp. "You want to know the outcome before it happens?"

Her hand reached for the hem of his kilt, but he fended her with his elbow and continued stroking her. His desire for her waned, and though he ached, it was receding rapidly. However, he continued gently to feed her longing and repeated, "You want to know the future?"

Raised on one elbow, she held his shoulders with her other arm and pressed her mouth to his. She sucked on his lip, then gasped as she said, "Please. I must . . ."

He took that as a "yes." He growled, "Where's Sinann?"

Morrighan made an animal sound, half anger and half pain. "Where ye cannae find her. She's being punished." *Sinann was still alive.* Sweet joy. Sinann was alive somewhere. But Morrighan continued, "Ye'll nae see that one again."

"Bring her back."

"I willnae." She went for his kilt again.

"Then never mind," he said, woke himself, and sat up in bed.

A deep groan rumbled in Dylan's chest. He shivered in the darkness, his groin a horrendous ache. Ignoring the cold, he slipped from under the covers and went to the small wooden table near his bed. There, he dunked his sticky hand into the wash bucket. He washed her from him, even to rinsing out his mouth. Though he might have saved the trace of her on a cloth to use against her in a spell, he was much better off to wash her away. The Morrighan was far too powerful, and such a spell might backfire worse than the last one had.

As he dried, he shivered in the darkness, so he pulled the blanket from his bed and drew it around himself. The night was dead still, nowhere near dawn, but Dylan knew going back to sleep wasn't possible. It wasn't even certain he could sit still for long, he was so edgy. His skin felt prickly, and there was a burning in every muscle of his body. He went to the sitting room and rekindled the banked fire. Huddled inside the blanket from his bed, he sat on a low stool by the hearth and thought of what had just happened. The Morrighan wanted to know the future. Why?

It didn't matter why. She was the goddess of war, and had no business knowing the future. Nobody should know the future, as far as Dylan was concerned. Even he knew too much, and was certain only that nobody of this time should know those things. Part of him feared the possibility of a powerful faerie being able to change what he knew must be.

Then he thought of Sinann. What had Morrighan done with the little sea faerie? "Sinann?"

No answer. The faerie wasn't around. Now he knew he'd have to pay hell to get her back. He pulled the blanket around himself more tightly and sat, deep in thought.

"Dinnae fear. You're stronger than she. 'Twas silly of her to make the attempt on ye, for ye love another and willnae have the goddess."

Dylan's heart leapt. It was Cait's voice. Unmistakably. He looked around the dim room but couldn't see her. Most of the house was in darkness, and the tiny fire beside him threw no light into the corners of the room. He ventured, hoping to flush her out, "I love you."

"And you love Sarah." It wasn't an accusation. Her tone was of assurance.

Then he saw her, and his spirit soared. He missed her so much! Sitting in her accustomed chair by the fire, but her hands empty of carding, spinning, or sewing, she looked across at him.

He stood, leaving his blanket on the floor behind him, and went to her. In his nightshirt, he knelt before her and took her hand in both of his. "Cait, no."

She smiled. "*Och,* aye. I can see it in ye. And it makes me happy my bairns will have a good mother."

Frowning, puzzled, he shook his head. "No."

" 'Tis a blessing. Ye must remarry."

"I could never forget you." His gaze drank her in, memorizing, filling himself with the sight of her.

Now she laughed, a bright, sunny chuckle that was music to him. "Of course not. Neither will ye love her as ye loved me. For she and I are nae the same woman. But ye must marry, for the sake of Ciaran and Sìle. Also, Eóin and Gregor have been far too long without a father. You would be a good father to them. Eóin has looked up to you since ye first came. Then there is that ye must marry for yer own sake."

He looked into her face, struggling to understand. But he still shook his head. "Things are all right the way they are. I don't want to marry again."

Her eyes darkened. "And why not?"

"I don't love her."

She smiled again and lit up his soul. "Ye do, too," she said in her *you're being silly again* voice. She brushed a lock of hair from his eyes and pressed her palm against his cheek. "Ye care for her a great deal. Ye said it yerself."

"I wouldn't die for her."

"*Och,* the Jacobites ye'll die for, but nae Sarah?"

He had to smile. "It's not the same thing."

" 'Tis. Sarah is a kinswoman, and it's the clan ye fought for. The children. The children are our destiny. Ye must make certain my future willnae die. *Our* future. It matters not the least how ye love her, but ye must love her because she is of the clan. You must marry her because ye need her. And she loves ye so. I couldnae have left ye in better hands."

Dylan squeezed his eyes shut and his heart clenched. "I can't love her the same way in return."

Cait's voice went low and soft. "If ye would love her half as well as ye do me, she would be a passing fortunate wife. Open yer heart, my husband."

"So someone can put another knife in it?" He looked up at her, surprised at what he'd just said. Fear of losing Sarah the way he'd lost Cait had never before crossed his mind, but now he realized it had colored all his thoughts of her. He didn't want to be that vulnerable again.

"Aye. Ye cannae be afraid. Not if ye're to save the clan, as Sinann says."

Another smile touched the corners of his mouth, and he bent to kiss the hand he held in her lap. Her other hand pressed his cheek until his head rested on her knee. She smoothed his hair away from his forehead and stroked his beard so gently he thought he might drop off to sleep. He'd never been happier than when lying with her in his arms. He said, "You weren't supposed to die. We were supposed to grow old together."

"Aye."

"Stay with me."

She whispered, "I willnae come to you again, my husband. I must move onward, and so must you."

He raised his head and opened his mouth to protest, but before he could, she was gone. His hands rested on the seat of the chair in front of him.

Horribly cold, he slumped to sit on the floor and rested his head in his arms on the chair seat, there to shiver beside the dying fire.

CHAPTER 17

Shortly before Beltane, the shearing of the remaining sheep was in progress when a messenger came from the castle for Dylan. "Come straight away," gasped the gillie, who was the teenaged son of one of the kitchen maids. "Iain Mór wishes your attention." The boy then ran off without waiting for a reply, leaving Dylan standing in the middle of the sheep pen with a half-shorn ewe between his knees and a pair of clippers in his hand. Dylan would go at the Laird's bidding, it was certain, and the boy didn't need to verify.

He sighed, but didn't delay in cleaning up. He covered the cut fleeces against the rain he smelled in the air, then returned the triangular-bladed shears to their hook on his byre wall. Since this sounded like a formal audience and he didn't wish to appear underdressed, he repleated his kilt, wore his sporran, and went armed with his dirks. Then he headed down the track to the castle.

A while later he arrived in the Great Hall and looked around for Iain but didn't see him. The gillie, who was now occupied in stacking wood by the large hearth, called out his name and pointed toward the corridor that led to the North Tower. Iain's office. Dylan went, and found the meeting to be not only formal but also very small. Iain sat behind his desk. Malcolm was ensconced in the arrow loop behind and to the right, one foot braced against the stone and his staff at his side. Artair stood by the tapestry, his arms crossed over his chest and his expression verging on a scowl.

As Dylan shut the door behind him, the Laird said, "Sit, the both of ye."

Artair moved to an ornate, upholstered chair of French origin facing the desk, and Dylan took the one next to it. As he sat, he glanced at the tapestry behind the chairs. A chill skittered through him as he noticed the likeness of Sinann in it was looking straight at him. A look of terror had widened her eyes, and her lips were moving. But he couldn't make out what she was trying to say, and couldn't let on in front of Iain the nature of the tapestry's enchantment. He had to sit, facing Iain, and forced himself to push Sinann to the back of his mind. She was surely in great trouble, but there was nothing he could do about it for the moment.

Dylan focused on Iain, wondering what was so all-fired important to have taken him away from his shearing.

Iain came straight to the point. "The rising is going badly."

Dylan resisted the sudden, ridiculous impulse to say, "Duh." Instead, he nodded and said, "Very few of the clans have declared for the Jacobites. They're waiting for the Spanish fleet to land in England." He took a deep breath, shifted in his seat, and risked his next sentence, "Which may never happen."

Iain shook his head, and Dylan's heart sank. "Nae. They'll land. Spain needs a victory over George. They'll come, sure enough. Three hundred Spaniards are already garrisoned in Eilean Donan with the MacGregors, MacDonalds, and the others who have declared. The rest of the Spanish fleet will come, sure enough."

Artair gripped the arms of his chair with great excitement and leaned forward. "Are we to join them, then?"

Iain nodded. "Aye. I've decided. We've forty-three men of fighting age in the glen to offer. I'll be taking them—"

"Let me lead the men." Dylan had to do it. Whatever it took to keep the onus of treason away from the Ciorram lairdship when the rising would fail, he had to do it. He swallowed hard his anger at having been volunteered to die in Glen Shiel, a rage fed by the knowledge his death would be for nothing, and volunteered to take Iain's place of leadership in the battle.

But Artair didn't see it as sacrifice. He leapt to his feet and nearly knocked over the chair behind him. "Like hell, you'll lead." His face reddened, angry enough to fight Dylan right there in the office.

Dylan reached for Brigid, but he stayed his hand. By now he recognized the irrational rage in him, so he went still and held his breath this time until it would pass.

Iain said, "Nae, Artair. Leave him. He'll nae be leading the men."

The young man returned to his seat, perched uneasily to leap from it at Dylan's very next misstep.

Dylan blinked away the altered perception and turned to his Laird as he recovered himself. "But, Iain, if you declare the clan and lead the men, and the rising fails, regardless of whether you live or not, your lands would be confiscated. The entire clan would be displaced. The men would be transported, or worse. If I go, and am captured or killed, it's no more than my own foolishness that I was there to begin with. And the same to be said about any of the Matheson men with me."

Iain's brow crumpled. "Foolishness, is it?"

"If I lead, you can pass it off to the Redcoats as that. If you go, there will be no hope." Dylan added hastily, but not quickly enough, "If the rising fails."

Artair sneered and tossed his hair from his face. "Ye're already convinced of it. I dinnae think I care to follow such a man."

Dylan squeezed his eyes shut, wishing he could tell them why he knew it would fail. Beneath that, he also wished he could throttle Artair and watch his eyes bug out. His fingernails dug into his palms as he refrained from doing so. He said, his voice tight, "A good commander plans for more than one contingency. If we win, then James takes the throne and we live. But if by some disastrous happening we don't prevail, we can't throw away the lives of everyone in the glen." *Especially Ciaran and Sile.*

He looked to Malcolm for support and found the old man dozing in the alcove, his forehead leaned against his staff. No help there. But Dylan pressed. "You have a chance to lie low and not attract the ire of the Crown."

Iain's face reddened, and Dylan knew he'd taken his argument too far. The Laird's voice held an ugly edge of disgust. "Ye forget, lad. We attract the ire of the Crown by our religion, and they would see us all dead regardless of whether we fight. There is nae choice but to fight the laws meant to destroy the one true faith. They've got our priest, and now we've no one to administer the sacraments. If I dinnae stand, as Laird of this glen, against the arrests of our priests, they will be after the lay folk as well, and be transporting the lot of us to America simply for the act of crossing ourselves. If we join the rising, they might kill us with guns and swords, but if we dinnae fight, we'll die by their hatred. Slowly, but we'll die nonetheless."

Dylan was silenced, knowing there was enough truth to this to make an argument a waste of breath. Never mind that King James II had been as intolerant of Protestants as William and the more recent monarchs had been of Catholics, in this time and place it came down to survival. Justice had nothing to do with any of it; they had to fight to stay alive.

Iain shook his head. "We cannae even do business in Glasgow or Edinburgh without assistance from outsiders." Seumas MacGregor was their Protestant go-between these days. His background as an outlaw made him less than particular about his business contacts, and thereby he helped the Ciorram Mathesons circumvent the hatred of Protestants who had money and influence.

Iain took a deep breath and continued in a voice that shook with anger, "Many Mathesons died in the rising four years ago. Before that, the *Sassunaich* killed my father and any other of us who stood up to them. We cannae let them continue to kill us."

Dylan opened his mouth for a reply, but Iain overrode him. "However, ye make a good point about contingencies. Artair will lead them in my place."

Dylan insisted, "I have battle experience."

Iain sat back and crossed his arms over his chest. "Aye. And that is why you shall be his *fear-còmhnaidh*. Stand at his right hand, and give him the benefit of yer knowledge."

A groan rose in Dylan's throat, but he swallowed it. The thing was done, and there was nothing but to accept the Laird's directive. Dylan sat up in his chair, rigid, and nodded. "Aye."

A smug look settled on Artair, and he leaned back in his chair. Iain proceeded to lay out the plan for getting the men out of Ciorram without alerting the *Sassunaich*.

Dylan fumed as he listened, an intense wish burning in his gut that Sinann were there. He glanced back at the tapestry, but it was now still. Where was she? What had Morrighan done with her? How could he find her again? He thought about sneaking into Iain's office later to try communicating with the image in the tapestry.

The plan was for the forty Ciorram men, plus Dylan and Artair, to slip out of the glen from under the noses of the few Redcoats left in the garrison. Over the next three days, men would go hunting and not return. Some would climb into fishing boats to land at a remote part of the loch and double back. Others would disappear from their houses in the middle of the night. Those Mathesons remaining—the women, children, and men too old or infirm to fight—would carry on as if nothing had changed, and if anyone asked where the men were, each would be accounted for by a story. The longer the better, for the *Sassunaich* had no patience for the shaggy dog ramblings of the Ciorram Mathesons.

Dylan hurried to finish his shearing and bundle the fleeces for storage. He tried not to think about what would happen to his home if he didn't make it through the battle in Glen Shiel, but images came of his orphaned children anyway. The best he could hope for then would be that his children would be raised and educated by the Laird and the land kept for Ciaran until he reached his majority.

But if things went badly enough, especially with the Ciorram heir presumptive leading the men, Iain could still be taken as a traitor and the entire glen, along with Dylan's land if his participation became known to the Crown, would be confiscated and sold or awarded to another clan. The Ciorram Mathesons would be homeless and defenseless. Everything Dylan loved would be destroyed or in danger. God knew what would happen to his children then.

Two days after the meeting, Dylan was at the castle to leave his children with the Laird. Una would care for them while he was away, and so he delivered them to the Great Hall. This place was getting to be a second home to the kids. Not good. Their home was with him in the high glen, not in the castle with their grandparents. But there was nothing he could do about this. Even if Cait were still alive, he'd want them all here at the castle while he was gone, and the dogs, as well. Doirinn and Fionn were in the bailey now, sniffing tails with the Laird's dogs.

Dylan lifted each of the kids to sit on a trestle table, then leaned down with his hands on his knees to talk eye to eye. "You be good for your Grandmother and Granddaddy, you hear?"

They nodded. "Aye," said Ciaran. Sìle's eyes were wide. Dylan was pretty sure she didn't know what was going on, but she probably understood he was going away for a longer time than usual. Ciaran thought it was for a hunting trip. "When can I go, Da?"

"Not until you're big enough to draw a bow and hit a target." Though guns were sometimes used for hunting, powder and shot were expensive, and their single-shot nature made them still less preferred than the bow and the sword. It was no fun being attacked by a wounded buck or boar while holding a discharged flintlock.

"When ye come back with a big buck, will ye make me a dirk from the horn?"

"You're too little yet for a dirk. Grow up some more, and I'll make you a fine dirk with a blade from Toledo." That mollified his son, who smiled at the prospect of one day having his very own dirk of fine steel. Dylan wished he could promise to bring back something for them, but if he made it back at all, it wouldn't be with anything he would want to present to his children.

He felt like the worst sort of liar, telling them this crap. But, liar or not, it was better they should think he was stalking deer than to know he was going to be shot at by Redcoats. He kissed them both, then set them back on the floor and let them run and play with the other children.

Most of the castle was gathering for supper. Dylan noticed Iain Mór near the hearth, drawing on a tankard. That meant the office would be empty. Good.

Quickly and discreetly, he slipped into the hallway and made his way to the North Tower. He saw nobody, and he figured they must all be either eating or serving. There wasn't much time, but perhaps he could slip into Iain's office and try to communicate with Sinann. If, by chance, she happened to be gazing through the tapestry at that moment.

The curved hallway of the tower was dark, but a sliver of light came from Iain's office. The door was ajar. Dylan frowned but hoped it was Malcolm there. Malcolm might leave him alone with the tapestry, for the old man trusted him more than anyone ever had in his life. He stepped to the door and gave it a shove.

Through the doorway he could see the tapestry on the far side of the round room. Sinann was observing the room through it, all right, for the image was leaping, its wings flapping and arms waving to catch his attention. But there was no voice to what she was saying. He pushed the door open farther and stepped into the room.

Artair was there, sitting at Iain's desk and flipping through a ledger page by page. He was looking for something. The young man looked up and paled. Dylan figured he'd caught the wee lairdie searching for the property transfer papers. Why he would want them was impossible to guess, since it was plain Iain still favored Artair for his successor. Otherwise, Dylan would be leading the men to the rising.

Dylan glanced at the tapestry again, and Sinann stood with her hands on her hips and a disgusted look on her face. Then he turned to Artair and said, "Looking for something?"

"There is . . ." It was plain the wheels were cranking fast behind Artair's eyes, manufacturing a lie. "There . . . I'm looking for the records of the sale of, um, the kine to the garrison."

Sheesh. At least he could have come up with something that actually involved the book on the desk. Dylan pointed to the shelves behind the chair and said with an edge to his voice that meant he wasn't fooled, "You'll be wanting this year's ledger, then. That there book's a mite aged to be of interest to you." If Artair thought Iain had left those papers where they'd seen them, he must be crazy *and* stupid.

Artair made a pretense of realizing he was looking at the wrong book, said *"Och"* for the sake of form, then returned the book to the shelf. He turned to Dylan and said, "Is there something you're needing, then?"

Dylan glanced at the tapestry. Sinann had a hand to her mouth as if she were shouting, and he could see her mouth the words, "Help me!" He wanted desperately to kick Artair out of the office to spend some private time playing charades with the faerie, but knew Artair wouldn't leave him there alone. The wee lairdie would assume Dylan was looking for the same papers himself. Never mind that they were most likely in Malcolm's possession by now.

Dylan said, "No. Gracie was just wondering why you weren't at supper. In fact, the entire castle was commenting on it."

Artair paled, and his eyes darkened. "I suppose I should go eat, then. Make everyone happy."

"Aye. You should." Dylan held the door open to let Artair pass, and hesitated as he glanced once again at the tapestry. Sinann was still pleading for him to help her, but he had no choice other than to follow Artair from the room and close the door.

In the Great Hall, Artair sat down to his supper and carefully watched Dylan head for the bailey doors. It wouldn't be a good idea to return to the office.

A high, loud squeal came from the other end of the room, and Dylan recognized his daughter's favorite noise. Then she shouted, "Da! *Daaaaa!*" He turned, stunned.

Sìle came running, down the row of tables. "Da!" He knelt as she reached him. "Da!" Then she grabbed his face with both hands, placed a huge, gleeful, smacking smooch next to his nose, giggled, then ran away back to her supper. Folks nearby laughed and grinned to watch her.

He stood and watched her go, wanting anything but to be leaving just then. She climbed back onto her bench and addressed her bowl again. His heart both ached and soared, so that he wanted to laugh and cry at once. Staring across the room, he couldn't move and could hardly breathe.

But finally Dylan forced himself to leave, having just heard his daughter's first word.

By the time he reached the high glen, the moonless night had fallen. He paused to retrieve the rapier, cavalry saber, and broadsword from inside the roof thatching of his house. They had been hidden deep inside, far enough in to mitigate the dampness that would damage the blades. He'd kept them as clean as possible in hiding and had wrapped them in oil cloth, but when he took a close look at the blades inside the house, he found some small spots of rust here and there. He hated to see a good weapon deteriorate and wished he could put them all in display cases, behind glass, there to be admired rather than used. But instead he sat at his table to sharpen and polish them so they would kill more efficiently.

He would carry the broadsword to battle himself, preferring the familiar blade he'd carried for more than two years. The other two weapons would go to Robin and Dùghlas, for neither of them had possessed swords of their own since the confiscations of 1716. Those who had been able to hide their weapons would carry swords, but the few who owned only dirks would also carry into battle pitchforks and other farm tools sharp or heavy enough to cut or pierce flesh.

Dylan was at this work, running his whetstone along the blade edge of the broadsword, when Sarah came. Alarm rose. Sarah would never come here after dark without a good reason. She ducked through the door as she announced herself, then shut it behind her, her arm pressed to her stomach. It appeared she was holding something large under her cloak.

He stood, sword in hand. "Sarah. Are the children all right?"

She nodded. "It's something else has brought me here."

He relaxed and set the sword on the table. "Then, it's a pleasant surprise to see you." He was puzzled, nevertheless. It wasn't her habit to just drop in like this.

She smiled and nodded again. "I've something for you." She opened her cloak and produced a targe—a shield of wood, covered in leather and dotted in a pattern of large, iron studs. The leather was darkened with age, and the front of it was adorned with a number of deep slashes; this targe had seen action. Sarah ran her fingers over the knobs of hammered iron that made concentric circles around a short center spike. "Eóin brought this to me one day, having stolen it from the garrison."

Dylan's eyes went wide with surprise. "He did what?"

"Oh, I chastised him severely. I told him stealing an old targe was not worth him being arrested, but if he wanted to give me my death of fright he should continue doing it at every opportunity." She hefted the targe. "Now, on reflection, I'm thinking that if this shield might protect you from harm, it may give some value to the risk he took."

She held it up for him to see. "It'll never be missed, is my guess. By all accounts, Major Bedford has a sizable collection of old Scottish weaponry hidden away in crates there. God knows what he intends to do with it all. More than likely he's sending it home to London."

Dylan figured Bedford was making off with all in Scotland that was not nailed down. "He's got a son there, he says."

Sarah nodded. "Daniel Junior. Lives in a great, towering manor the Major built for his wife and named after himself. The wife is a poor, delicate thing and cannae live in Scotland away from her father's circle of rich friends. The cold weather would be her undoing, ye ken." Her voice dripped with sarcasm and disdain for delicate English women.

"You know a lot about Bedford's personal life."

"*Och,* the entire glen has kent it since he was but a lieutenant newly assigned here. On his arrival he complained about it enough for it to be the laughingstock of everyone hereabouts." She held out the targe. "Well, the wean isnae getting this."

Dylan accepted it. "Thank you." She drew her cloak around herself, readying to leave. On impulse, he said, "Won't you sit a spell?"

She opened her mouth to decline, starting to shake her head, but hesitated. He set the targe on the floor against a table leg, and waited for her reply. He understood the feelings tugging at her. It was uncertain why he'd asked her to stay, but it was certain he didn't care to be alone just then, his last night in the glen. Possibly his last ever at home. He said, "Your company tonight would be a blessing."

She smiled, appearing glad for the encouragement. With a nod, she lifted her cloak from her shoulders. Dylan came to take it for her and hung it on a peg by the door, then indicated the chair by the fire for her. Another peat went on the fire, and he brought his chair from the table so he could sit near. A fleeting chill stole across him as he remembered the many nights sitting there with Cait, but he shook it off. "You won't mind if I finish my work while we visit, aye?"

She shook her head. "Of course not. It wouldnae do for you to face the English with a dull sword."

A smile curled his mouth as he picked up his broadsword, whetstone, and polishing cloth. Then he sat in the second chair to work.

At first, conversation was light. They spoke of poetry, a subject that didn't seem to have ever come up between them before. Oddly, this had the tentative feel of a first date, even though they'd known each other for years. Statements were couched gently, each hesitant for fear of touching a sore spot. Now he realized his attempts to speak personally before had failed because there were too many small things about each other they didn't know. Though there was a history of friendship and kinship, tonight it was plain they were testing new ground carefully, avoiding any possible unpleasantness. So they chatted about literature, a whole new level for them.

Dylan's few books, aside from the Bible, were by English authors, but it turned out Sarah's passion was for the Greek epics. Dylan had read some Homer in college but remembered little beyond the basic story lines. Now he listened to Sarah recite her favorite passages of the *Iliad*, her voice expressive of her involvement in the lives of Achilles and Hector and all the gods. Even though she'd once been married to a cousin of the Laird, Dylan had only ever known Sarah as a castle servant, and so was surprised to learn she was so well educated. As she spoke, she began to relax. Her voice warmed.

Sarah had never been relaxed around him before, he realized. Ever. He'd never seen her smile like this nor heard her speak with such animation. For the first time since he'd met her, Sarah's eyes lit up with something besides hopeless adoration.

His work finished, he set the swords in their scabbards on the table and returned to his chair. The fire waned, and he refreshed it. They went on talking. The candle on the table was very low when the conversation turned to his impending departure. Neither wished for him to go, but both knew it was inevitable.

His voice tightened. "Sarah . . . if I die, I want you to tell the children—"

"Ye willnae die." The terror in her was so sudden and powerful, he felt it himself, like a wound.

Shaken, he blinked. But he insisted, "But if it happens, tell them I love them."

"Of course ye do. And of course I would, were ye to die. But ye will not."

He nodded. "All right. Then I won't." He grinned, and joked, "Just for you, I'll stay alive."

She blushed at that. He put a hand over hers on her knee and opened his mouth to assure her it had been in jest, but then he changed his mind. It hadn't been entirely in jest. Like many jokes, it had been an attempt at telling a truth without taking responsibility for the telling. He decided to own up.

"You're not to be embarrassed, but it's true I will try very hard to come home. I'll want to see you again, as well as the children."

Tears glistened in her eyes. She said, her voice so low as to be little more than a whisper, "I've waited so long to hear ye say that. So long for ye to want to say it—that you would wish to see me."

There was no reply to that, except, "I never meant to hurt you."

She nodded. Her mouth opened for a reply, but nothing came out. He couldn't think of anything more to say, either, so he leaned over and kissed her.

It was as if she melted in his mouth. Her lips so soft, and the tear that ran from her eye so salty. She laid a hand aside his face to keep him there, and he was happy enough to stay. The candle guttered on the table behind him, and as the room dimmed, the many aches of the world also dimmed. He slipped an arm around her waist, and she slid forward on her chair to wrap her arms around his neck.

It was a long kiss. Dylan wished it would go on and on, partly because he enjoyed it and partly because he wasn't sure how it would end or what would come next.

But Sarah stood and drew him by the hand from his chair. In the bare seconds it took to rise, his mind flew to decide whether to follow where she would go. She would surely be mortified if he didn't, but also could be hurt even more deeply later on if he acquiesced now but not later. In the last second she kissed him. Again he wished for it to go on, and that decided him. It would be good to take a chance on the future.

He slipped his arms around her and held her close. His heart beat faster, and he realized he very much wanted to be with her tonight. With each passing moment, he wanted it more.

When she pulled away from him and drew him after, she tugged at her kerchief and let her hair cascade over her shoulders. It was astonishing how long her hair was, for he'd never seen her without the *corrachd trichearnach*. It was only by the small lock that showed at the front he had known its color. Now he thrust his fingers into it and let it flow over his hand in waves. He followed her from the dim sitting room to the deep darkness of the bedroom.

Dylan's bedroom was little different from any others of the peat houses in the glen and certainly not large enough in which to lose one's way. When they reached the bed, Sarah turned to kiss him again and began to unbutton his sark.

Even in near total darkness, there was no mistaking Sarah for Cait. Her hands on his clothing, pressed to his chest, moved over him with a reverence unlike anything he'd ever before experienced. At once more intense yet less dramatic than the deep passion he'd had with Cait, Sarah's touch was certainly more loving than any he'd known before his wife. She unbuckled his belt, and he unwound his kilt from his body to set it on Sìle's empty bunk, then she slipped her arms around his neck. Her sweet kiss touched a well of affection in him he'd thought closed. He responded by pulling her to him, and let the well open.

Dylan tried not to kid himself; this wasn't a joining of soul mates. But neither was it the casual sort of lust he'd had for girlfriends in the twentieth century. In his youth, when sex had been nothing more than recreation, breathless excitement was all anyone had ever asked of him or given in return. But this was not breathless in the least. Rather, it was a warmth and a comfort that touched him in places he'd lately been trying to forget he had. It made his head swim with longing. He tugged on her laces to loosen her dress.

In the darkness, undressing provided a delightful excuse for exploration. Feeling around for laces and buttons, and freeing Sarah of impediments, Dylan learned her newly bared skin. And she his. Goose bumps rose in the night air. He ran his fingers into her hair again and enjoyed the feel of its thick waves.

Having set aside his belt, kilt, and sark, Sarah knelt before him to remove his boots and leggings. Her fingers fluttered along the inside of his thigh toward the sheepskin covering his shin. As she freed his legs from covering, her lips pressed there above his knee. It tickled and made him smile.

Then he helped her to stand, and she reached for his shoulders to steady herself. Skin on skin, her soft breasts brushed the length of his body. He drew her to him and kissed her, savoring the delicious softness of her in his arms. So yielding. So warm. She shivered under his hands.

He picked her up to lay her on the bed and slipped in beside her, under the blankets. It was warm there. Sarah's light touch roamed over him with a sense of excitement he didn't need to see in her eyes. She'd been married before, as had he. But how he compared to Alasdair was a concern that passed quickly, for it was plain she wasn't thinking about her dead husband. For the present, he put his mind from Cait. This was Sarah beside him, whose body and desires were different from Cait's.

"Lie back," he whispered, though there was nobody within a mile to hear them.

She hesitated, but acquiesced as he pressed her onto her back against the mattress. He leaned on one elbow beside her and slipped an arm under her near thigh to lift her leg over his hip. He joined with her. Slowly and gently, he moved and adjusted until he lay beside her yet inside her.

She sighed in the darkness and reached down to draw his knee up between her thighs and against her belly. He pressed harder against her as he moved. Lying entirely on his side now, he touched his lips to her shoulder, slipped his arm around her waist, and held her. Sarah put her arm behind his neck and down his back, where her fingernails scratched an itch along his spine he hadn't known he had. Her breast against his face was a softness rare in his life. She drew him farther in by his knee, and whispered, "Ye're a man of surprises, Dylan."

He chuckled, his hips moving in gentle, comfortable rhythm.

She continued, barely uttering the words in his ear, "I cannae tell which legs are mine and which are yours. I've never felt such a thing before." He curled up around her, surrounding her with his arms and legs, and picked up his rhythm. Able to keep this position indefinitely, without the least fatigue, he settled in to enjoy her. Moving all the while, he kissed her mouth, her breast, he ran his hand over every part of her, and explored the soft part of her that made her gasp and her back arch.

She reached for his hand, but hesitated, then reached again only to touch his wrist lightly. Little sounds like half words were uttered in the darkness.

"Am I hurting you?"

She managed, "*Och*, no."

So he persisted, though she gasped again. Her hips began to move, and the sounds coming from her became more frequent and less articulate.

A high moan escaped her as he kept on, and she began to whisper his name under her breath. She loved him, she said, and he knew it was true. Even at this moment, when she quivered under his hand and his head swam with delight for her body, that fact made a difference to him. He decided it was a very good thing. All extraneous things fell away from his thoughts, and now all he knew was how wonderful it was to be here with the lovely Sarah, and how he wished it could last forever.

He tried to make it last, but now it was his turn to shudder and gasp. His face against her breast, he trembled, pressing himself into her hard. She took his knee again and held it to her belly like she would never let him go.

Lying next to her, he stayed where he was as long as he could. The warmth of her entered him there, seeming to diffuse throughout his body. She said, breathless, "I never thought I could do that. I'd heard tell of the ecstasy, but thought it was nae for me."

"Do . . . what, *that*? You're joking." She murmured she had not been joking. He kissed her, and tried to imagine how dull life must have been for her with Alasdair. He held her, listening as her breathing steadied. Eventually, he untangled himself and dozed with his head on her shoulder.

Soon he would have to leave the bed, though. It would be time to leave the house. Time to fight for the Jacobites again. This time perhaps to die.

Sarah was asleep when he finally rose. It was several hours before dawn, and he would need all of them to get to the rendezvous before daylight. He debated waking her, but didn't figure he should risk a delay. It wouldn't take much to talk him into another hour or so in bed, and being late for the battle would do his reputation no good at all.

He dressed, then went to the sitting room to arm himself. He lit a fresh candle and set it in the holder on the table, pressed onto the remains of the previous one. The *sgian dubh* was strapped under his left arm. Brigid went into the scabbard strapped to his legging, and the broadsword went onto the baldric, which he then slung across his chest, the sword to hang at his side. The other two swords he tied again into the oilcloth bundle.

As he worked, his mind began to focus on the days to come. Death was more than just possible, and he made efforts to inure himself from the fear. Carefully, he discarded emotional thoughts. He calmed himself as he put his gear in order.

With his sporran on his belt, he filled a ration bag of oatmeal and put that in it. Also in the sporran were the Goddess Stone and his drawstring purse containing the few shillings which were all the cash he had remaining after ordering Cait's headstone. He reached into the cabinet for the oilcloth packet containing his pardon for the last uprising, but changed his mind and put it back with the rest of his legal papers. It was his habit to never travel anywhere without his proof of pardon, but where he was going it would do him no good. Worse than doing him no good, it would serve to identify his body, should he be killed and the English find him. Better for the children if his body were to go unidentified and his participation in this doomed attempt on the throne to never be proven.

Dylan then tied the sword bundle to the targe and made a loop in the rope. He was almost ready. His pulse picked up as dread sneaked in on him. He fought it back. He'd seen battle before and knew it to be nothing other than ugly, dirty, and terrifying. Furthermore, unlike his compatriots, he had the awful knowledge his side would lose. There would be no glory of any kind from this battle, ever, even if he survived it.

Before leaving, he stopped by the fire and pulled from his sark the crucifix hung around his neck. Cait's wedding ring hung with it. He held them both in his fist as he went to one knee and crossed himself. Then, with the cross and gold ring held in both tight fists and pressed to his forehead, he prayed in a low voice, "Dear God, please give me the strength to do what I must, to never shrink from my obligations. Help me to conduct myself with honor at all times. Please keep my children safe. Above all, let me be reunited with my beloved Cait. Amen."

Then he let the ring and the crucifix drop back into his sark, and stood, turning to reach for his coat on its peg by the door. At the bedroom door, Sarah's dark eyes stared at him from a face far too pale in the dimness. Her hair draped over her bare shoulders, she appeared terribly vulnerable. Intimate in a way he'd never seen her before. She seemed violated. His heart sank.

She said, "It was silly of me."

"Sarah—"

"Nae." She shook her head. Quickly, she closed the wattle bedroom door.

Damn. His heart steeled against the future, it wasn't in him to go in to comfort her. There wasn't time. Nor was he inclined to examine his feelings just then, let alone attempt to explain them to her. If he didn't leave now, he might miss the rendezvous. Worse, he might be caught by the dawn too close to the glen and have to explain himself and his weapons to a *Sassunach* patrol.

Without a word, he drew on his coat, arranged his plaid over it, and secured it with a plain steel brooch, slung the targe and swords across his back, then likewise he slung a waterskin hung from a leather thong, and left the dimness of the house for the darkness of the forested mountains.

CHAPTER 18

Dylan reached the rendezvous at dawn. All the fighting men of Ciorram had made it there and were camped in a narrow ravine where the cover was thick and the smoke from their fires dispersed in high trees. The men were scattered up the ravine, in groups of five or six around several small fires. The shade was deep, and the groups were a small presence in the forest. The better to go unseen by the *Sassunaich*. As Dylan looked around at the lounging men, some talking, some sleeping, others preparing their weapons, he saw how each man anticipated this fight in which it was certain many of them would die.

Many of the younger men, such as young Coinneach, who had not been old enough to fight in 1715, were flushed with excitement. Only a few were jittery or pale, staring deep into the middle distance. Of the older men who had survived the last rising, and the much older men who had also fought at Killiecrankie as teenagers, most were silent and calm.

As Dylan passed, greeting his kinsmen as he went, he heard one man telling a story of the 1689 rising, to a tense, rapt audience. He stopped to listen for a spell. It was, of course, about the battle of Killiecrankie, which had been the last palpable victory for the Jacobite cause. It would remain so for another twenty-six years, until Prestonpans, which would begin the rising of 1745 with a royal butt-kicking of King George's men. So, for now, Killiecrankie was the popular story in these parts. But when the narrative came to a description of a Redcoat cut nearly in half by a claymore, Dylan moved on. As much as he hated the English Army, he was not entertained by battle stories. Sheriffmuir was still too vivid and terrible a memory.

Though Dylan couldn't read minds and know how the men had come to terms with what lay ahead, he knew each of them surely had. Just as he had. As with the no-mind discipline of his Eastern studies, he put from his thoughts the complex fears and what-ifs. Having nearly died once in battle, he knew worrying did no good. Thinking too much about what might happen was a waste of energy. By letting go of the future, his mind was free to think only of the moment at hand, and he knew that focus might just save his life when the time came.

A fight broke out between two of the young men farther up the ravine, and Dylan headed that direction to deal with it. Several of the older men beat him to it, though, pulling the teenagers from each other and telling them to bloody well knock it off and save it for the English. Dylan let things calm down and looked around for Artair.

The wee lairdie was at a fire near the center of the gathering, encamped between some boulders and surrounded by a few of his closest friends. Dùghlas was there, and Tormod, along with a few others. The inner circle sat on parts of the surrounding rock and small logs while the arrogant young man with a thin, reddish beard spoke of how the Jacobites, being strong men brave and true, were certain to defeat however many debauched, weakling southerners the English Army might set against them. He looked up when Dylan approached.

Tired, hungry, and not the least moved one way or another by Artair's enthusiasm, Dylan presented himself, threw an insouciant American military salute, and announced, "I'm here." Then he turned to survey the forty men gathered and found Robin and Seumas asleep near each other in a right comfortable-looking hollow of dead leaves. "I'll be over there until we move out."

Artair's habitual sneering tone rose. "Dinnae get too comfortable, Dylan Dubh. The men are eager to leave."

Dylan turned back, and his eyes narrowed. It probably was more like Artair was eager to leave, never mind the men. Dylan shifted his weight and glanced around at the gathered Mathesons, some of whom were asleep and hadn't been there much longer than he had. Even Artair couldn't have been there more than a couple of hours. The sharp rage that had hold of Dylan of late flushed his face, and he took deep breaths to calm himself and present a cavalier air.

He shrugged. "Nah, I expect there's plenty of time to sleep, seeing as how only an idiot would march this many heavily and illegally armed men in broad daylight toward an uprising in progress. Unless, of course, he wanted to waste good men in a pointless skirmish with English patrols. But that wouldn't be you, I'm sure, for it wouldn't set well at all with the Laird for all his fighting men to be killed or captured before even joining the rebels."

There was a long, tense silence. Artair flushed and glanced around at the men by the fire, then said, "Be sure ye're awake and have eaten by sunset, for we'll be marching to Eilean Donan then."

"Aye. I will."

Dylan then went over to that nice leafy spot. He set his gear on the ground, sat, and took a handful of oatmeal from the sporran. With water from the skin, he made a stiff paste of *drammach*, which he then ate with his fingers.

Seumas opened his eyes and said groggily, "I've spent a more enjoyable Beltane."

Dylan chuckled, then fell silent at thought of a certain Beltane festival five years before. It was the first night he'd spent with Cait, after she'd jumped the fire in a fertility rite that was older than memory. The image was sweet, a pleasant one to entertain himself as he dropped off to sleep. He said, "Aye," then brushed off his hands, pulled his plaid around himself, and curled up in the leaves. He closed his eyes to sleep till sunset, when Beltane would begin.

But Robin leaned up on his elbow and said in a low whisper, "Dylan Dubh, there's something we feel ye must understand."

The tension in the whisper caught Dylan's attention. He grunted to indicate he was listening.

"Seumas and I . . . we were talking, and some of the other men . . . we think ye should be aware that there are men who are here only because you are here. There are many of us who would not follow Artair but will follow you."

Dylan raised his head to read Robin's face. Then Seumas's. They both wore expressions of dead earnest. This development was a surprise. Though Dylan had known there were men who would prefer to follow him, he'd had no idea any were adamant enough to refuse the leadership of Artair. And he'd had no idea they were "many." He whispered in reply, "Artair is the authority here. He's appointed by the Laird—"

"He cannae hold the men. Not more than half, in any case."

Half. That sharp a division in loyalty could mean trouble. He said, "Who?"

Robin named twenty-three men, including himself, Seumas, Keith Campbell, and Marc Hewitt.

"How strongly do you all feel about this?" Allowing a schism between those loyal to him and those remaining loyal to Artair would involve Mathesons killing each other. That was absolutely the last thing Dylan wanted. Far from saving the clan, it would destroy them more completely than anything the English could accomplish. Now he knew why Iain Mór had forced Artair to take him as second-in-command. Iain must have known Artair couldn't hold all the men.

Seumas shrugged. "Ye could take them if ye wanted. Robin and I both will follow you to hell if that's where ye care to lead. The rest would be glad enough to join us, for they ken Artair cares naught for his men but only for himself and his own glory."

Robin added, "We've all seen the sort of laird ye would be. We've seen the respect for yer men and the cool head ye keep. I saw ye in the football game when Artair was trying to lame ye. I could see he nearly broke yer leg, but there wasnae a single sign of pain to be found on yer face. More than half the men here are yours. If Artair were to become laird, he would be hard put to keep the clan."

Dylan's first impulse was to tell them both they were nuts to even think this way, but he needed to respect the gift of loyalty that had just been pledged to him. He nodded and said, "Good. It's good to have men such as yourselves behind me. But where I will lead you right now is to follow Artair. We can't let the clan be split. We must face the *Sassunaich* together. Until that job is finished, we must abide by the wishes of Iain Mór, who is our Laird, and his wish is for us to follow Artair."

"But he'll have us all destroyed."

"Robin, you've pledged your loyalty, and now I need your trust. Believe that I can . . . *influence* Artair. Trust that I won't let him do anything stupid." There were chuckles from both Robin and Seumas. Dylan had to smile, too. "Okay, I won't let him do anything *really* stupid."

The other men nodded, then settled back down to sleep. Dylan ad-

justed himself in the leaves and lay back, but now the images that moved
through his head as he dropped off were less entertaining than the ones
he'd enjoyed before.

It was not ordinarily a long trail to Eilean Donan, but when avoiding
detection by alert English forces, the trip took far more than the usual day.
Bearing west through the Killilan forest, the Mathesons cut short of the
village and doubled back to make the ford near Camas-luinie.

As Dylan walked, he plundered his memory for what he'd once read
about the coming battle. Foremost in his mind was that it would be a
humiliating defeat, even more so than Sheriffmuir. The main Spanish invasion of England would fail—had already failed—because of bad
weather. Unsupported, the Jacobites would lose what little will they had
to fight and would scatter. The English Army would take Glen Shiel and
capture the three hundred Spanish troops that had landed at Stornoway
and were now garrisoned at Eilean Donan. Then, for the next twenty-five
years, the Jacobites would be held in check.

But that wasn't all he'd read, he was sure. There had to be more. Why
had the Jacobites cut and run? What had triggered the rout? Dylan wished
Sinann were here. Talking things out with her had always helped him to
think. If she were here for him to tell the story out loud, he might remember more of it.

He looked at the surrounding trees and opened his senses to them.
Now that he knew how to hear them, he listened. But none of them seemed
to be Sinann. Her voice wasn't there. Where was she? What had she been
trying to tell him in Iain's office? He had to figure out a way to get her
back, but sure didn't know how he was going to do it.

Once the Matheson contingent had crossed the ford, the rest of the
trek was through the lowest points of ravines that zigzagged between
mountains toward Loch Duich. By not crossing directly over peaks, the
Matheson forces avoided the risk of being seen on anyone's horizon. Finally
they came down from the mountains under cover of trees lining a burn,
to the loch shore. They followed that shore to the castle on the loch.

Like the *Tigh a' Mhadaidh Bhàin*, Eilean Donan was built on an island.
But unlike the *Tigh* it commanded three important waterways from the
sea. Perched at the juncture of three lochs—Loch Duich, Loch Alsh, and
Loch Long—it was reached by a stone causeway from the eastern shore.
The approach by land was steep and narrow.

Several hundred Highlanders were encamped along the shore near the causeway, some at the base of the castle walls on the island. With a gillie ahead, bearing the Matheson standard, the forty men were allowed to move through the troops and approach the castle at the portcullis. They were greeted by a young man who had the look of the MacDonalds about him, though he wore no plant badge to identify himself.

His gaze skimmed the front ranks of Mathesons, then settled, and he stepped toward Dylan. " 'Tis a wee bit late, ye are," the young man said to the one he apparently took for the leader. There was an edge to his voice, despite the look of relief on his face. "But we're happy to see ye nonetheless." He gestured toward the shore. "Ye'll need to take yer men—"

"They're *my* men." Artair stepped between Dylan and the lad, who blinked and reddened at his error. "I'm Artair Matheson of Glen Ciorram, and 'tis I who have brought these forty-one men. This man here is my *fear-còmhnaidh*, Dylan Dubh Matheson." The young man's look at Artair was dubious, but he nodded greeting to Dylan and apologized to Artair, introducing himself as Coll MacDonald.

MacDonald gestured to the encampment again. "Ye're welcome to find space on the shore amongst the clansmen. We've but twelve hundred or so men, including the Spaniards. We've powder and shot for them as have got guns, but we've nae muskets to spare. So it would be good, were ye to have brought yer own guns." His voice betrayed him as hopeful for more muskets to have come support the cause.

Artair nodded. "We've a few." Then he turned to Dylan. "Take the men and see they're settled."

"Aye." Dylan turned to the men and issued an order to head back across to the mainland. Artair was escorted by the MacDonald lad through the portcullis, most likely for introductions to those in command. Dylan knew the commander of these forces to be William Murray, the Marquis of Tullibardine.

Dylan took his men around the gathered MacKenzies, Camerons, Murrays, MacGregors, and lesser factions of other clans. They moved to occupy a burnside near a small wooded area, along relatively level ground. Young Coinneach was given charge of a few other young men and sent for wood or peat for fires, then Dylan and several others set about lighting what was at hand. Once a nice little blaze was going, Dylan requested to be brought the standard of the Ciorram Laird.

When it came, he folded it carefully and smoothed it. This was the flag of his ancestors, by which they had been identified in armor. It represented identity as a Matheson. Reverently, he set it on the flame. There was some muttering, but carefully and thoroughly he burned it, making sure nothing recognizable was left of the flag that, if captured, would have given away the Ciorram presence in the uprising. He was certain he didn't have to explain this to the men. Nobody would have brought items that would identify their bodies. They all knew the importance of anonymity in defeat, and trusted their stories to be told in victory.

Once the men were resting, some of them wrapped in their plaids by their fires and snoring, Dylan rose to take a look around. A nudge to Robin with his boot, and his friend rose, gathered his plaid, arranged it around his shoulder, and tucked it into his belt to join him.

They skirted the encampments and walked across the causeway to the castle portcullis. The small bailey inside was surrounded on three sides by stone curtain wall, and the fourth side by a large tower. Some men in uniforms of the Spanish Army sat or lounged near a few fires built here and there on the stone pavement. Their assured demeanor reminded Dylan he was the only man in the castle who knew the Spanish invasion in the south had already failed.

In the far corner of the bailey was the entrance to the smaller building on the quay. It was many-storied, the bottom floor lower than the large tower, at the level of the loch below. A Spanish guard of two men stood by the large doors Dylan took to be the entrance to the Great Hall. The traffic to and from that building was thin, limited to men of status. That was where he needed to be.

The Spanish guard blocked their way with muskets as Dylan and Robin attempted entry to the Great Hall. *"Nombre?"*

Dylan sighed and struggled to recall his one semester of high school Spanish. He couldn't remember what *nombre* meant, but it was plain they needed to identify themselves. He said, *"Me llamo Dylan Dubh."* No sense in giving his full real name, even though the Spaniard wasn't likely to even remember it. He added, *"Yo quiero Artair Matheson."* Fresh out of Spanish vocabulary now, he slipped into English since the Spaniard was more likely to know English than Gaelic, "I'm his assistant." He dug deeper into his school memories and unearthed, *"Yo ayudar."*

The light of understanding came to the Spaniard's eyes, and said with a passable pronunciation, *"fear-còmhnaidh?"*

Dylan blinked, surprised. *"Tha,"* he replied. "I mean, *Sí.* Yes."

The words that followed came too fast for Dylan to decipher more than the nodding and, *"Sí."* Dylan and Robin went past the guard. They hung their swords on pegs in the foyer, alongside rows of magnificent, exquisitely crafted and expensive weapons belonging to the important men inside. Gold and silver glittered by torchlight, and one of the sword hilts was studded with gemstones. It looked French to Dylan, but these days anything ornate seemed French. His eye lingered longingly on the display of weaponry as he and Robin then passed into the Great Hall.

There were far fewer kilted men in this room than among the soldiers bivouacked on the shore. Most of the men in conference around tables and in groups of chairs wore breeches, velvet coats, and powdered wigs, with only the occasional clan leader in kilted plaid. Dylan searched among them for Artair's green coat and light, reddish hair, and spotted the wee lairdie across the room. He started toward him.

"Mac a'Chlaidheimh!" The voice was familiar, and Dylan turned, searching. It was his former employer, Rob Roy MacGregor, who had nicknamed him Son of the Sword, a name Dylan hadn't used since his pardon. The voice came again, definitely Rob. *"Dilean Dubh nan Chlaidheimh!"*

Dylan turned toward the voice, a greeting on his lips, but it died at sight of the dark red hair and beetling eyebrows of Rob, whose expression was not welcoming. His eyes narrowed.

"Rob."

Never one to mince words, MacGregor came at Dylan and went straight to the point, his finger jabbing the air. "So it's deserters they're recruiting now." He was several inches shorter than Dylan but stood up to him as if much taller.

Red claws of anger sank into Dylan's back, and rage crept along it to flush his ears. He knew Rob referred to the battle at Sheriffmuir, where they last had parted ways. "Deserters? We were left by our fearless leader to die." He leaned into Rob's accusing finger as his voice rose. "We were the ones who were deserted. In any case, it's not like you did any actual fighting. Timed it just right, it would appear." Having had this argument before with Mar, repeating himself angered him more.

"The battle wasnae over." MacGregor's face also reddened.

"Did you happen to tell Mar that while you were sneaking him out of the country? Mar quit the field, leaving us in shreds. You bet your ass, the battle was over." Dylan's fists clenched, and all he could think of was how lovely it would be to punch out this overbearing short shit. He shook his head to clear it. Years ago, he'd respected MacGregor as a strong leader and a fair employer, but today he suddenly wanted nothing but to kill him. "The rising was over, and all that was left was to get Mar safely away."

Men were gathering, gawking at the argument. MacGregor's eyes glinted with anger. "A job left to me."

Dylan said through clenched teeth, "God forbid you should have to actually accomplish something."

"More than was accomplished on the battlefield."

"That's it." Dylan lost control and reached for Brigid. MacGregor responded by drawing his own dirk at his belt.

"*Och*, Have ye gone mad, man?"

The onlookers pressed back to form a circle around the fighters. Dylan made a quick swipe, and MacGregor dodged. Another swipe, which was parried, and suddenly Dylan was on the defensive. He made a circular parry, stepped in, and with his left shoved MacGregor so he stumbled against another man. Growling, MacGregor turned to attack again. His long arms more than made up for his lack of height, for the extra reach was accompanied by blinding speed.

Rage blinded as well. Dylan's heart thudded and his breaths came heavily as he did his level best to kill MacGregor. But though he knew he was at a disadvantage with his anger, and tried to clear his head, for the first time in his life he was completely unable to bring the emotion under control. He attacked MacGregor with no thought of what the response would be, and got a slash across the back of his hand for his trouble.

"*Fuck!*" Metallic pain shot up his arm, and he switched Brigid to his left.

"Stand down, man. I dinnae wish to kill ye."

Dylan paid no attention to the offer of peace. He flung dripping blood from his hand into MacGregor's eyes and attacked again. MacGregor parried, ignoring the red spatters on his face. It was impossible to reach the little man where it would count. Dylan swore and attacked once more. MacGregor fended him and circled again. Teeth clenched and body tense, Dylan realized he wasn't going to win this one.

Flaming rage licked his spine, but in the dim, far reaches of consciousness the thought came that not only would he not be able to kill Mac-Gregor, he didn't truly want to. Besides, the older outlaw would go a long way to avoid killing Dylan. He had the skill to toy with an opponent indefinitely and might do nothing more than slash him until he was tired of bleeding. Another even more dim part of him knew the fight had been pointless to begin with. He was behaving like an idiot.

"I said, stand down!" Rob sounded impatient with this foolishness.

Anger surged again, and Dylan's arm trembled to attack, but he backed off, raised both hands, and held still. For a long moment, he forced himself to stand perfectly still. Finally he was able to make his mouth say, "Amity, then."

MacGregor nodded. "It's King George we've come to fight, nae each other."

Dylan also nodded, and found himself calming. He was able now to return Brigid to her scabbard without rage clenching his body.

This had to end. He couldn't live his life a slave to the anger, and had to do something about it now. For a brief moment he summoned his *maucht* to banish the force inside him that had gained control. He filled himself with calm, and made the evil drain through his feet and through the stone floor into the earth.

The tension in the room eased as Dylan and Rob Roy shook hands.

A messenger hurried into the room, calling for the Marquis of Tullibardine. A bewigged gentleman near the hearth announced his presence and received a dispatch. The room stood quietly as he read it, going even more still as Tullibardine's face paled. Finally, he folded the letter wrapped in oilcloth and cleared his throat. He looked around the room and appeared to be weighing the pros and cons of revealing the contents of the message.

Finally he said, "Gentlemen, I'm afraid we are in serious straits. The invasion of London has failed."

A dark murmur of alarm riffled through the room.

CHAPTER 19

The men in the room broke into a roar of anger and alarm. Clan leaders pressed toward Tullibardine for more information and further orders. Artair approached Dylan and said, "Return to the men and wait."

"Aye." Dylan and Robin returned to the men to await Artair and orders.

Those orders, when Artair came in the evening, were for the Jacobite forces to make their way toward the MacKenzie Earl of Seaforth's lands in Gairloch to facilitate the escape of the commanders—Seaforth, Tullibardine, and Campbell of Glendaruel—who had been exiled in 1716 and would be executed if captured. The Hanoverian forces that had gathered were, by all accounts, still in Inverness. It was expected the way would be clear and the retreat calm and orderly.

But Dylan knew better. He couldn't remember what would go wrong, but he did know the Jacobites would end up entrenched near the Shiel Bridge, in the opposite direction of Seaforth's lands. There they would make their stand, and fail.

The clansmen retired to sleep the night and move out in the morning.

It was dawn when the first explosion on the loch brought the Highlanders to their feet. Dylan, sleeping by the cook fire he shared with his friends, jolted awake. In an instant he leapt to his feet and hurried up the slope, throwing his plaid over his shoulder and tossing his hair from his eyes as he went, looking for a vantage point to see what was happening. There, what he saw made his blood run cold. Three English warships stood on the loch, surrounding castle Eilean Donan from the water side. As he watched, a puff of smoke rose from the side of one ship, followed by a low report. A chunk of wall on the castle crumbled. Men on the island were scrambling and shouting. The castle answered, smoke rising from the crenelated battlement, and some rigging collapsed on one of the ships.

A low hum came from Dylan's right, and an explosion in the midst of the Jacobite troops near the shore sent earth and pieces of men flying and clansmen scrambling. Dylan flattened himself on the hillside, then looked to find two more English ships on Loch Long. *Crap.* Now he knew how the Jacobites were going to end up at the Shiel Bridge. Their escape to the north was blocked.

Some of the men, including Mathesons, rose with their muskets. Artair, also on the hill for vantage, shouted for muskets to ready.

Dylan ran to speak privately with him, for it would not do to contradict his commander publicly, "Artair, no! Wait till they land!"

"Fire!"

Several of the men fired, but not all. The older men knew what Dylan did and did not obey the command. But Artair shouted to them again to fire, and so they finally did. Dylan shook his head, disgusted. Fat lot of good that had done, shooting valuable ammunition so it would plop into the loch just short of its target. Maybe there were bruised English sailors hit by spent musket balls, but nothing more, and probably not even an eye had been put out.

The castle still returned fire with its cannon, but at the same time, Dylan saw, most of the garrison was evacuating with horses, supply wagons, and cannon. Jacobite leaders, clan leaders, and Spanish troops flooded from the portcullis, leaving only enough men to fire a few cannon in a rearguard action.

Artair shouted, "Gather on me, men!" Good, he was going to get them out of there. Dylan followed Artair to join the other clans as they moved south along the shore of Loch Duich toward the Shiel Bridge.

The Jacobite leaders tried to make it an organized retreat, and for the most part succeeded. As soon as they were out of musket range of the castle, the English landed and swarmed over it. Dylan looked back at the ruined castle and saw red-coated English marines scurrying this way and that like bugs, through the portcullis and along the battlement. Revulsion filled him, and he looked away.

While the English forces were busy with the few Spanish left garrisoned there, the Jacobites and the bulk of the Spaniards were given respite to flee. They did so.

But when they came to the Shiel Bridge at the head of the loch, Tullibardine didn't stop them. Instead, they continued to march up the glen. Puzzled, Dylan had an odd feeling he might be wrong about the coming battle. Surely he couldn't have been so wrong in what he remembered. The Jacobites were supposed to stop here to fight. The battle would take place a month from now, he was certain, for he remembered the date: June 10, 1719. Today was the fifth of May.

For the first time since coming to this century, Dylan was unsure of the inevitability of history. Now he wondered what was going to happen during the next month, and whether something might already have happened to change what he knew.

As they marched eastward, it appeared the commander was seeking a route to friendly lands, whatever friendly lands there might be anymore. It was a long, painful trek through Glen Shiel. Men wounded by the English cannon were carried along by their kinsmen. Some died quickly and were placed under cairns, but others would perish slowly from gangrene or infection. Not one sound came from the dying men, and few came from those who were still whole.

It was good and dark by the time they stopped to rest, ate *drammach*, then rolled into their kilts to sleep on the ground.

Scouts the next morning reported the English weren't following. Artair, who was privy to Tullibardine's war council that morning, reported it was thought the Hanoverian forces assumed the Jacobites had already dispersed. There was no pursuit. It had been decided to hang on, he said, and rest and regroup by Loch Cluanie in hopes of reviving support from the clans.

Dylan squeezed his eyes shut as his heart sank.

Two days later found them encamped on farmland near the head of the loch. The newly dead were buried and mourned. Fresh meat was shot or bought from farms nearby, and the men rested by fires. Even as Artair's reports from Tullibardine waxed hopeful, the general feeling of hopelessness increased among the thousand Jacobite troops. Talk in the councils was of hanging on until more clans would come to fight alongside them, but the waiting men had had enough and wanted to go home.

Over the next weeks, fights broke out among the clansmen as tensions increased. Old grievances rose to become problems between certain of the MacGregors and MacKenzies. Arguments became fistfights, which sometimes became knife fights, and it was all the clan leaders could do to keep their men whole for the next effort against the real enemy.

Whenever possible, Dylan avoided Artair, who preferred the company of Tullibardine in any case. The wee lairdie also spent time socializing with Iain Beag MacGregor, who was part of Rob Roy's contingent. Both the MacGregors and the Mathesons had been placed under the MacKenzie Laird, which put them in proximity with each other. Dylan often heard Iain Beag declare himself ready to rout the English and put an end to foreign occupation. Since Artair had an eye toward marrying MacGregor's daughter, it was plain Artair would keep the Mathesons with Tullibardine to the bitter end. And Dylan figured it would be a very bitter end.

Rather than let the Mathesons simmer in their boredom and uncertainty, Dylan frequently wandered among them. He would chat with Keith Rómach about his new family, or listen to Coinneach and Dùghlas talk about fighting Redcoats. He told them what it had been like to fight mounted cavalry, and they discussed tactics well into the night.

Summer was coming, and the men felt the need to go home to take care of their farms and families. Dylan's thoughts frequently turned to Glen Ciorram and his land, his children . . . and Sarah.

One evening Dylan was returning to the fire he shared with Seumas and Robin, and a piper among the Camerons started up. It was a set of small pipes, playing the *ceòl beag* for the benefit of a cluster who entertained themselves dancing. For now, the large pipes were put away and the loud fighting music that fired the blood saved for another day.

Someone else had a drum and began a lively tattoo that seemed to reach into Dylan's soul and yank. He paused for a moment, listening, and felt a primal stirring in him. For that moment, it was as if he could feel in himself not just the future centuries but all the millennia past. All of history lived in him.

Then the moment passed. He sighed and continued to his fire.

He found Seumas staring into the crackling flames with a distant look he recognized. "Thinking about your wife again, Seumas?"

His friend nodded. "Aye. We were married but a month, yet I long for her even now."

Dylan settled near the fire and drew his plaid around himself against the night. "I hear you, my friend."

"A body would think after so long a time . . ."

"No." Dylan shook his head. "You won't forget her."

Robin approached and stretched out on the ground within the circle of light thrown by the fire. He plucked a long blade of grass that had escaped the trampling of soldiers, and stuck it between his teeth. "Forget who?"

"My wife."

Robin nodded, having heard the story of how Seumas's wife had been killed by Redcoats in 1715. "You can take refuge in that she died protecting you from capture."

Seumas made a disgusted noise. "It doesnae make me feel better to know I am the reason she was killed. It tears at me most days."

"But some days it doesn't?" Dylan was intrigued now, for there was always guilt for him if he went an entire day without remembering Cait.

Seumas shrugged. "Many days it doesnae. Sometimes I find it's been a week or so since I last thought of her. It causes a fright, for were her ghost ever to realize it, she'd be a-haunting me for a certainty. But 'tis nae good to dwell on it, either. I cannae swim in my sorrows so often as to make me a dark cloud over everyone around me. Not like yourself, Dylan Dubh."

Dylan and Robin both laughed, but a shiver ran up Dylan's spine as he remembered the visit from his own wife's ghost. He sighed and leaned back on one elbow. "I know I won't be forgetting Cait any time soon."

Robin said, "None of us will."

Seumas agreed with a grunt.

"She was a fine lady, that one." There was a catch in Robin's voice that attracted Dylan's attention, so he sat up. He lowered his chin, leaned forward, and peered deep into Robin's face. The sorrow was all over the man, and it gave Dylan the creeps.

He said carefully, watching every slight movement of Robin's face, "Aye, she was the best wife any man could ask for, and a body so warm and sweet . . ."

Robin looked away, his eyes focused on the ground before him. As Dylan and Seumas watched, his eyes glistened with tears.

Seumas's voice was low. Quiet. "True, she touched many a heart."

Dylan said to Robin, "A long time ago you said you had your eye on a woman, but I never learned who she might be."

Robin sat up. "And you would never have. Ever." His voice was thick. He kept his eyes on the grass blade he split asunder in his fingers. "I swear I never touched her, Dylan. She never kent how I felt. I would never have done either of you that way. You're my friend, Dylan Dubh, and I owe ye my life. But I cannae help how I feel."

A flurry of anger and amusement rose, and Dylan didn't know whether to laugh, feel sorry for Robin's bad luck, or punch him out for daring to imagine he could love Cait. The pipes and drums skirled and thudded in the distance. Finally, he said, "*Och.* I expect there was more than just yourself mooning over her from a distance."

Robin appeared relieved. "You arenae angry, then?"

Dylan shrugged. "I believe you that you never touched her. To think otherwise would be an affront to her memory. She was a good and true woman."

Seumas laughed. "Also, a man would have to wish for death, to cross *Dilean Dubh nan Chlaidheimh* in that way."

A chuckle came from Robin, but none from Dylan.

There was a stretch of silence, then Dylan said, "Caring for Cait as you did—"

Robin lifted his chin to object, but Dylan silenced him with a raised finger. "*Caring for Cait as you did,* what would you say if I told you another woman has recently caught my eye?"

"Sarah," said Seumas, nodding.

"It would be a disgrace to her memory." Robin's face flushed, and his eyebrows met.

Seumas grimaced. "It wouldnae!"

"Seumas, she was a goddess. She deserves better than—"

"He deserves better than the loneliness!"

"She's been dead not even a year!"

"But Sarah is there for him now. A man shouldnae sleep alone when there's a willing and bonnie woman begging to share his bed and keep his home. And that Sarah is going to waste. God knows she willnae have anyone else; she might as well have Dylan. He should marry her, and good health and happiness to them both."

Robin fell silent. Dylan looked in turn at each of his friends and said, "You guys have given this a lot of thought."

Seumas laughed. " 'Twas a long, uneventful winter."

A smile touched Dylan's mouth. Deep in thought, he said, "But there is no replacing Cait." There was a murmur of agreement from Robin, but Seumas opened his mouth to say something. Dylan cut him off. "I mean, Seumas, you know how some women, even though they're very pretty, don't have a lot going on upstairs?" He tapped his forehead and the others chuckled and nodded. "It's like, all the lights are on . . . I mean, all the candles are lit but nobody's home. Know what I mean?"

Robin and Seumas both laughed and nodded. No man wanted a wife who couldn't think for herself. It was too much work for a man to run a farm *and* a household.

"But with Cait . . . she was like . . ." he tapped his head with all ten fingers at once, ". . . all the candles were lit, and there was a *party* going on." An image of Cait filled his mind—her smile, her bright eyes. His heart warmed, and he fell silent, thinking of Cait.

But Seumas said, his voice low and soft, "And with Sarah, all her candles are lit and there's a good woman at home. Waiting for ye."

Dylan looked at Seumas but didn't really see him. He was thinking hard about Sarah, now. He realized there truly was a good woman at home, waiting for him, and that he could love her.

Later, after they'd all rolled into their plaids for sleep, Dylan was still thinking hard about her. Remembering that silver and opal ring he'd found, he reached into his sporran. It was a fine piece of work. He imagined it on Sarah's hand and found he liked the idea. Sarah's birthday was in October. Opal was her birth stone, and would be lucky for her. Though the gold ring was Cait's, and would always be hers, this ring just might do for Sarah.

Though he tried to tell himself it was just as well she should go off and make Tormod happy, he now found he couldn't accept that. In fact, the more he thought about it, the more he realized he couldn't let it happen. Looking across the field to where the blacksmith sat by one of the Matheson fires, Dylan couldn't imagine them together. Tormod was too old, he felt. There was too much gray in his beard. Sarah couldn't love anyone that old. She couldn't want a husband that smelled like coal, carbon, and oil all the time. Surely she couldn't. She belonged in the high glen with his kids. And himself. Dylan realized if he didn't have Sarah to go home to, it wouldn't be the home he'd hoped for.

The next night, wishing to clean up before eating, Dylan found Tormod alone by the river, sitting on a boulder over the water and staring into it. He paused, unseen, and considered moving upstream to avoid conversation. Tormod was still, staring into the water.

But Dylan decided avoidance would be silly, as well as impossible to maintain. He went to the water's edge and squatted by it to wash his hands.

"Evening, Tormod."

The blacksmith grunted, then returned to his thoughts.

Dylan shook off his hands and was about to return to his fire when Tormod said, "I mean to marry her, Dylan Dubh."

Dylan's urge was to ignore him, but he knew this had to be dealt with. He turned back and said, "Have you asked her?"

There was a dark silence. Tormod finally said, "She willnae answer me."

That shocked Dylan to his toes. He'd been confident she would have given Tormod a flat "no." But no reply meant she was hedging her bet. She would marry Tormod once she'd given up on himself.

The prospect was abhorrent. At that moment, Dylan realized he'd been thinking of Sarah as his. The thought of her with another man pissed him off enough to do whatever it might take to keep it from happening. He said, "There's something you should know, Tormod." Dylan tried to tell himself he was doing a kindness, but on a deeper, less honorable level, he knew he was making certain Tormod wouldn't succeed with Sarah. "The last night before I left the glen, Sarah came to me." Tormod turned to peer at Dylan with growing alarm. "She came to my bed."

"Ye lie."

"I'm sorry, Tormod. But you needed to know."

The blacksmith stood and stepped off the rock onto the river bank. "It cannae be true. She wouldnae give herself away so easily to a man who doesnae love her."

"Tormod, you've got to let—"

"No! She dinnae come to you. She would never have! It was you! You seduced her!"

"I didn't."

"*Och!* Ye must have. If ye took her, it was against her will! Sarah is a good woman; she would never have done it. She's nae fornicator! It's a good woman ye've ruined!" He came at Dylan, who backed away a few steps. No more than a few, for he wouldn't care to appear a retreating coward.

"I haven't ruined her. I want—"

"Do ye think someone else will marry her now? Ye're wanting to lay another bastard off on an unsuspecting husband, then!"

Whoa. Dylan's fist balled up at his side, but he didn't strike. "You take that back." His teeth clenched and his ears warmed. "My son is no bastard, and no man raises my children but me."

"Tell that to Connor Ramsay, then. Ye're a chamberer! A fornicating seducer, with no more principle than a dog sniffing the backside of a bitch!"

Rage bent Dylan's mind, but in an effort to turn Tormod's wrath he said, "I mean to marry her."

That didn't have the expected result. Instead of standing down and accepting Dylan's honorable intentions, Tormod's eyes lit with feverish desperation. With no argument left, he hauled off and swung at Dylan, who deflected and stood his ground.

"Tormod—"

Another swing. Dylan deflected and backed away.

"Hey!" Dylan didn't want this. "She's made her decision, Tormod." Never mind that the last time he'd seen her she appeared to have given up on him. "Sarah came to me, I—"

Tormod feinted, then swung from the other side and caught Dylan's chin. He went to one knee, head buzzing.

"That's it." Dylan was done fooling around. With a roar he rose and attacked.

Tormod deflected and backed, but Dylan pressed. The blacksmith was slower than his teacher and so got the worst of the exchange as many swings landed. Dylan beat him back to the water, where Tormod teetered on the rock at the edge. Dylan considered for a second letting him alone, but Tormod's words about Ciaran stuck in his mind. He stepped in, punched Tormod in the belly, then an elbow in the face sent him over the side and into the water.

Tormod came up, sputtering, at the water's edge.

Dylan stood over him, meaning to not let him out if he persisted in his badmouthing. "Are you finished?"

The blacksmith glared at him.

"I'm going to marry Sarah. It's what she wants—it's what the whole bloody glen wants. Now it's what I want. You're to cease and desist in your advances. You're to treat her with respect from here on in. You will give up any thought of marrying her, or even being too familiar with her. Also, I require an apology for everything you just said to me here."

Tormod continued to glare up at him, water dripping from his hair and beard. His nostrils flared, and his face reddened in spite of the cold water.

"I'm waiting, Tormod."

Finally, Tormod said, "I'm sorry I called you a seducer."

"And . . . ?"

"I'm sorry I called Ciaran a bastard."

"All right, then." Dylan reached down to help Tormod out of the water. They returned to the camp together, in silence.

That night as Dylan lay by the fire he realized the anger of the encounter with Tormod was waning normally now. There had been no claws in his back during the fight. There was nothing gripping him or coloring his vision this time. Nothing but normal, righteous, yet manageable anger. He'd rid himself of the evil, and it was cool relief.

Wrapped in his plaid, he indulged in warm thoughts of home as he drifted to sleep.

H e was chained to a pillar—the same pillar on which he'd once been flogged nearly to death—his arms shackled overhead. Straw covered the floor, and torches in sconces lit the narrow room that stank of urine, old blood, and terror. Dylan yanked hard on the shackles, which rattled against the iron loop in the pillar behind him.

Fort William. He was back at Fort William, and it wasn't just a dream. He was chained with his back to the pillar, his clothes cut from him and scattered on the floor, and his back wasn't bleeding. At Fort William his back had been flogged bloody, then they'd turned him to face his torturer. Now he was faced out, but his back wasn't bleeding. This wasn't a memory. This was Morrighan screwing with him again. Time to wake up. He didn't want any part of this.

But the dream remained. He tried to awaken himself again, but failed. Again he tried, but he was in deep this time. Cold sweat broke out and real fear swept in. He yanked on the shackles, and they rattled against the iron loop embedded in the pillar.

A red-clad figure moved to stand before him, and he was not surprised to find it wasn't Bedford this time. "Morrighan." He'd almost forgotten about her in the confrontation with the English Navy.

The dark faerie stood before him, her eyes alight at the sight of him. His wrists were secured above and behind his head, and he was clad in leggings and boots only. Her gaze roamed over his body, taking in every detail.

His eyes narrowed, and his voice lowered to an ominous growl. "Let me go."

"Why should I?" A smile curled the corners of her mouth.

"I'm not going to give you what you want. You might as well give it up."

She chuckled, a strange, throaty sound. "And why do you think this here isnae exactly what I want?" She reached out to touch him with one red fingernail, and the flesh of his belly twitched.

He threw a snap kick, but she dodged and danced away, laughing as she went.

"Let me *go!*" He yanked on the chains again, and the shackles bit his wrists.

She circled behind the pillar, then came close to reach around and run her fingernails along his sides. He writhed, wishing for a shot at her, but she was out of his reach. Great gasps heaved in his chest, and he growled in fury.

"Ye shook me off," she said, a petulant tone in her voice.

"Shook what?" He wasn't in a mood for this crap.

"The enchantment. Ye shook me off. I happen to be the most powerful of the *Sidhe*, the goddess of war, and my spell—my very best spell of bloodlust—was as naught to you. Ye're nae a good laddie to be that way to a goddess." She pinched his nipple, and he squirmed.

"Bloodlust . . ." He knew what she meant. The red, overpowering anger. It hadn't been himself weakening, nor had it been a hereditary personality defect. It had been her enchantment bringing the blinding rage. "Why bloodlust?"

She shrugged. "Why not? A man with a taste for rage is, after all, a man after my own heart. And I'd hoped for ye to be after more of my parts than just that. I sent the sword to ye. I should think a bit of gratitude would have been in order, returning yer weapon to ye like that. I dinnae ken why ye resist. It would have been a magnificent coupling."

He declined to reply. He only gripped the chain with white knuckles and waited for her to get to the point of this exercise.

She continued, "Give me what I wish. Tell me who will prevail in the rising. Tell me why. Tell me of wars to come, and who will win them. Talk to me of who will die and who will garner power from those deaths."

Dylan bit his lips together. The slightest word from him on that subject might give something away. Power from death? The war goddess was far too powerful already. He stared at the floor, where his sark lay in tatters.

"I expect, since ye've taken up arms with the Jacobites, they must be the ones to win." There was a pause, then she said, "But then, ye fought on the losing side at Sheriffmuir."

"Why do you think I know this stuff?"

"Ye're from the future, are ye not? That sea horse Sinann brought ye here from centuries yet to be. She also sent ye away from the battlefield before my eyes and ye returned healed an instant later." She reached around and ran a finger along his battle scar. "Ye journeyed to a time when they can put right that which must otherwise have killed ye. It was a long visit ye had as well, though you appeared to be gone no more than a moment, for yer hair was longer on return and yer sark was all white and new. Not to mention yer new boots, which you yet wear, the like of which I've never before seen." She gestured to his boots, now tattered.

She came around front to peer at him, careful to stand beyond the reach of those quick and dangerous feet. "I've heard tell of magic that could send folk backward through time. When I saw ye come back from yer visit, I tried it myself."

"You failed." Of course she had. Sinann herself wasn't sure how she'd accomplished the trick. All she knew for sure was that each arrival through time had been tied to a moment of strong magic. Moments she couldn't control, because she herself was subject to the passage of time.

God forbid Morrighan should ever learn to move forward or backward in time at will. The havoc to be caused by the goddess of war was boggling. Destruction was her identity. Though he believed history couldn't be changed, and she might even be fated to bring about the astonishingly bloody wars and genocides of the next three centuries, he didn't care to have them on his own conscience.

"Aye, I failed. And so I turn to you. As a man who has seen this day from a vantage I can but imagine, I ask you what is to happen in this rising."

"No."

"I beg yer pardon?"

"I'm not telling."

"Then ye do have knowledge."

"I'll tell you nothing. Now, let me go. You might as well let me go, 'cause you're getting nothing from me."

A fire lit her eyes, and they glittered in the flickering torchlight. "I believe I have the means to convince ye." She snapped her fingers, and a whip appeared in her hands.

Dylan swallowed a groan. His fingers went slippery on the chain at his wrists. Extreme pain is mercifully soon forgotten, but often it doesn't take much to bring the memory into sharp focus. The agony of having the skin flayed from his back returned, and he yanked on his shackles. "No."

She shook out the whip, and he raised one knee and turned his hip toward her to shield his genitals. *Not there. Please, not there.*

"Tell me. Who prevails, and how?"

"No." He shook his head, struggling to stave off panic. He knew he couldn't hold out this time. What was at stake was too vague . . . too impersonal. If she flogged him, he would tell. He would spill his guts, then have to watch the results. His eternal soul would know, for the next three centuries, what he had done.

"Sinann," he muttered. "Help me, Sinann." *Oh, God, send the faerie. Please send someone. God help me.*

Morrighan hauled back with the whip, her eyes glittering with pleasure. The leather came forward. Dylan shouted, *"Sinann!"*

As the tip of the weapon snapped against his skin and the pain shocked him, Sinann's voice came to him. "Awaken!"

He awoke, shaking, and found himself wrapped in his plaid by the cooking fire in Glen Shiel. Pain warmed his belly, and he reached into his sark. His hand emerged bloody, smeared by a thin, shallow cut across his abdomen.

Then he looked around. "Sinann?" The others were still asleep, so he must not have shouted aloud in his sleep. He whispered, "Sinann, are you here?"

A breeze from nowhere ruffled his hair.

"Is that you?"

Another seemingly random breeze blew into his face and buffeted him all about. He chuckled and waved it away. "Okay, okay, Tink. I get it. Now I've got to figure out how to get you back."

CHAPTER 20

What was needed was a time and a private place in which to attempt communication with Sinann. Sitting in the midst of several hundred clansmen, throwing herbs on the fire and conversing with the breeze wasn't at all a good idea. For several nights he slept lightly, counting on Sinann to wake him if Morrighan tried any more fancy stuff. Then finally Dylan was able to slip away unnoticed in the middle of the night to try contacting the white faerie. He headed in a direction he hoped would take him to a place of privacy, climbing into the hills.

As he walked, an insistent puff of breeze on his right cheek caused him to veer left. A whiff on the left then sent him to the right. He guessed Sinann was guiding him. At least, he hoped she was. Soon he came to a place that was far enough from the encampment and its sentries for comfort. Now he ran a risk of being arrested for desertion, but figured he would make it back to camp undetected by sunrise.

The spot in the hills was more than just a clearing. It was a level area amid three large rocks, the entirety also surrounded by dense and gnarled Scotch pine and oak. Dylan built a small fire in the area under the leafy canopy, where the smoke would be dispersed and unseen by the encampment down the slope.

It was mild weather, gearing up for summer. At the edge of the clearing, Dylan lifted the baldric from his shoulder and laid his sword to the side. Then at the fireside he performed some basic focusing techniques, circling it three times *deiseil*, then knelt before it with Brigid between his hands. *"A null e, a nall e, slàinte!"*

It took several minutes of intense concentration. Every shred of himself he committed to finding Sinann. Then, immersed in the focus, he spoke slowly, "Sinann Eire, maiden of the *Tuatha De Danann*, granddaughter of the sea god, Lir, ancient guardian of Clan MacMhathain, speak to me." He set the point of the dirk into the ground between his knees and focused.

There was a long silence, then he repeated. More silence.

Frustration grew. He gripped Brigid's silver hilt and growled, *"Sinann!"*

Her voice then came. Dim, as if far away, but wavering in and out, it was distinctly Sinann. "It's about bloody time ye caught on, ye sumph!"

Yeah, that was Sinann, all right.

"What did Morrighan do to you?"

" 'Tis a spell." Her voice was more distinct now, as Dylan focused. "Ye must force her to remove it. If ye dinnae, I'll be drifting with neither body nor voice in the mortal world for eternity. Nae death for me, even when my time comes."

A smile curled the corner of Dylan's mouth, and he muttered under his breath, "No death for Sinann . . . can't have that."

"*Och*, it's a laugh riot ye are." Sinann fluttered the hair around his face. "Never mind the wit. Ye must conjure the Morrighan."

A shudder ran through him. The last thing he wanted was to bring that faerie bitch here. "There's got to be another way."

"There is none. Ye must conjure her."

"I've never done a conjure before." He'd never wanted to, either. It was bad enough trying to invade the Morrighan's mind; just about anything could happen by requesting her physical presence.

"Ye ken the spell, for I taught it to ye. Use the ring."

"The what?"

"The opal ring I gave ye. The one ye put in yer sporran. It's stolen from the Morrighan's treasure, and she doesnae ken I have it. Use the ring, for it belongs to her."

Dylan nearly lost his concentration in his surprise as Sinann continued,

"Whether ye can accomplish it or not, is to be seen. 'Tis the only way. Ye must do it to save me." With that, Sinann fell silent. Dylan could feel her depart, leaving a vacancy in his awareness where she'd been. It gave him the creeps, as if she'd died.

He shook his head to clear it. Taking deep breaths, he stood. With his feet set apart, he shook out his joints to release himself from the *maucht* he'd used. It flowed through him, then down through his feet into the ground. Gradually his breathing steadied. Once he felt fully grounded once again, he returned Brigid to her scabbard, put more wood on the fire, wrapped himself in his plaid, and lay down near the flame to rest and ready himself for the other task.

It hardly seemed like sleep at all before he was awakened by the buffeting yet localized breeze that was Sinann. Groggy, he waved her away and sat up. The forest was silent and dark, the fire having died to coals. Midnight, he was sure, as calculated by midpoint between sunset and dawn. This was the most auspicious time of the night to proceed with his work.

He arranged his plaid and ran his fingers through his hair, then drew Brigid to cut some leaves from a nearby oak. After rebuilding the fire so it blazed brightly, he tossed on the green leaves to produce a heavy smoke. Then he took the ring from his sporran and slipped it onto the tip of his index finger. He repeated the focusing techniques he'd done earlier, ending with Brigid's blade in the smoke this time instead of in the ground.

Focusing his *maucht* once more, he said under his breath, "Blade of silver, blade of the moon, hear my wish. Bring to me the Morrighan, goddess of war. Cut the fabric of distance and obstacle, and bring to me the Morrighan, goddess of war." Then he slipped the ring from his finger and placed it on the tip of his dirk within the rising smoke.

As he spoke, the smoke touching the silver metal and opal stones of the ring began to take shape. Quickly, he repeated the spell, and the smoke thickened. The green leaves in the fire threw more and more smoke, which soon took on the form of a woman.

She wailed as she whirled and leapt to the side of the fire to avoid falling into it. "You mortal!" she cried, with as much disgust in her voice as Dylan had ever in his life heard. "Insolence! Outrage! How *dare* you call me to your fire!" She spun on him, her diaphanous red dress flowing around her. "Dylan Matheson, send me back!" Her black eyes flashed red in the firelight.

"Release Sinann Eire. Let her back into the world." He stood ready for whatever she might attempt, Brigid in hand.

"I'll not."

"You will." He stepped toward her. "You'll release her, or I'll find a way to do the same to you."

She retreated before him, and for the first time a glimmer of respect came into her eyes. "Ye wouldnae. Ye couldnae."

"I certainly can." He scabbarded Brigid and reached for the faerie's wrist. "And, boy, wouldn't I." She snatched away from him, and he grabbed the wrist with his other hand, like capturing a snake by guessing which way it will dodge. She writhed in his grasp, surprisingly strong for a woman her size, but he supposed her strength was just right for a war goddess. "You're afraid of me. I know you're afraid. That's why you only came to me disguised, or in my dreams. I know the powers of the *Sidhe* are waning, and you're just lucky yours haven't faded as badly as Sinann's."

She said, "War is yet a strong force among men."

Teeth clenched, he turned her wrist until he saw pain, and leaned into her face. "But your own powers are fading. The more powerful I get, the more I run a chance of being able to send you where you've sent Sinann. So bring her back, or . . ."

"Unhand her, Matheson." It was a man's voice.

Dylan turned, still gripping Morrighan's wrist, to find a male faerie. He blinked in surprise, never having seen a masculine *sidhe* before.

"Kill him!" shouted Morrighan to the newcomer. "Daghda! Kill the impudent mortal!"

Daghda drew the cross-hilt broadsword he wore at his side, and it glowed, flashing bright in the firelight. He wore a belted tunic of the same shimmering cloth Sinann and Morrighan wore, but brown, and he was barefoot like every other faerie Dylan had seen. His dark hair was shaggy and his beard unkempt, but his eyes flashed with intelligence, and the pointed ears poking through his hair marked him as *Tuatha De Danann*. He was therefore not to be underestimated. "I said, unhand the woman." The tip of his sword made little circles in the air.

Dylan's sword was still in its scabbard, on the ground near Daghda's feet. Dylan let go of Morrighan and drew Brigid, circling away from his sword in hopes it had gone unnoticed. Daghda turned with him, sword at ready. Morrighan stayed where she was and squatted on her heels to watch.

Her eyes lit up, and her skin flushed with the prospect of blood, and it didn't seem to matter whose it would be. Her arms rested atop her knees, and her chin on her arms. Dylan divided his attention as much as he dared, to be sure she stayed put, though she didn't seem inclined to help her boyfriend.

"Do ye ken who I am, laddie?" A smile curled Daghda's mouth.

"No." Warm satisfaction filled Dylan's gut at the bald shock on Daghda's face. The tips of his pointed ears turned red. Dylan's lip twitched as he tried not to smile. Faerie ego was so fragile, and he knew so well where the soft spots were.

But then Daghda's expression closed, and his eyes narrowed again. "Prepare to learn it, then." He attacked.

Dylan yielded, allowing Daghda to advance on him, then sidestepped around until he and Daghda had reversed positions. A quick, judicious retreat, and he was standing over his sword. He transferred Brigid to his left hand, then stepped on the scabbard of the broadsword and snatched the weapon from it with his right. He turned to face his opponent. The whip mark on his belly ached and itched under his belt. As he moved, his sark stuck to his skin.

Daghda threw an irritated glance at Morrighan. She gazed back with only a bland stare, as if to say it was his own fault for not noticing the sword on the ground. It appeared she wouldn't take responsibility for warning him of his mistakes. Daghda cursed in the old tongue and returned his attention to Dylan.

Dylan said, "You're her boyfriend?" in a tone that cast doubt.

Daghda declined the bait and made a foray, which Dylan parried neatly and stood his ground. The faerie backed off and shook hair from his eyes.

Dylan's experience with faeries having been limited only to Sinann, who was a tiny, winged sea faerie, and Morrighan, who was the size of an average woman of slight build, he was somewhat surprised at Daghda's size. About the same height as himself, Daghda was the largest of the *Tuatha De Danann* Dylan had ever seen, and muscular. His faerie quickness with his weapon gave him an edge Dylan hoped wouldn't be his own undoing.

He began twirling his sword in a series of mulinettes to either side, swaying back and forth like a cobra. Daghda's expression didn't change. The faerie merely waited, cool and unmoved.

Huh. Dylan was running out of ways to send his opponent into dis-

array. Finally, he lowered his sword to stand flat-footed, deceptively balanced, appearing unbalanced, his head tilted to the side.

It worked. Daghda rushed to attack, and Dylan barely moved to parry
with Brigid, and attacked with his sword. Caught overbalanced, Daghda
was forced to parry with his left arm. He grabbed the blade and tried to
disarm Dylan, but the mortal kept a grip on his hilt and yanked. The blade
slipped from Daghda's hand as from a scabbard, slicing his palm and forearm to white bone. Dylan then parried Daghda's sword with Brigid again
before backing away, *en garde*.

The faerie uttered no sound, but came again. Dylan parried and gave
more ground, circling, but the Daghda was weakening. Blood dripped
steadily from his fingertips, and pain showed in a white rim around his
mouth.

Dylan said, his voice filled with condescending pity, "Give it up, old
guy. You ain't got it in you no more."

New fire lit Daghda's eyes, and he roared as he came at Dylan. Satisfied he'd finally made the faerie lose his temper, Dylan circled and backed
as he parried. Backed up near a tree, he dodged an attack instead of
parrying, and Daghda's broadsword embedded in the hard oak.

Dylan dropped his own sword, shoved Daghda away from his imprisoned weapon, and grabbed the faerie by the throat. Brigid's point dimpled
the pale skin just over the collarbone, where an artery surged.

"Release Sinann."

Morrighan shouted, "No!" She ran toward Dylan's abandoned sword.

Dylan shouted, "I'll kill him!"

She stopped cold before reaching the weapon. The struggle to decide
could be seen in her eyes. Daghda's eyes were hooded, expressionless, as
he waited.

Brigid drew a drop of blood, which trickled down Daghda's neck into
his tunic. Dylan insisted, "I said, release Sinann!"

Morrighan opened her mouth to reply, and Daghda said, "Do it, Morrighan. Release the *each-uisge*. Ye dinnae need her. Nor him."

Morrighan lifted her chin and said to Dylan, "Surely ye dinnae think
the Daghda is mortal . . ."

"Shut up!" Daghda's voice took on an edge of desperation, and white
fear finally showed around his eyes. "He's nae stupid! Do ye think he's
nae aware that most of the *Tuatha De Danann* have died? Do ye think

he'd let me go without at least cutting my throat from curiosity?" He stood gasping for a moment, then muttered as if to himself, "Stupid bitch!"

Dylan said under his breath, "Glad she's not my girlfriend."

Daghda made a throaty sound of disgust.

The Morrighan's face flushed with rage. It was plain in her eyes Daghda would hear about this for a long time after they got home. But it was now equally plain she wasn't going to let Dylan kill her lover. Morrighan waved her hand, and Sinann appeared.

The little white faerie gave a couple of happy leaps and stared at her now-visible hands with a look of shining joy.

Dylan shoved Daghda across the clearing to Morrighan, where the faerie stood with his bleeding arm pressed against his tunic. The shimmering fabric soaked up blood amazingly fast, and the dark stain ran down the front to drip onto the ground. Assuming he wouldn't bleed to death, the faerie would heal normally, since healing was not in the faerie repertoire of magic. But he probably wouldn't die. Not this century, at least. Not unless he crossed Dylan again. Dylan yanked the faerie sword from the tree and threw it to him. Daghda caught it neatly with his good hand.

Morrighan raised her hand high. "I should turn ye into a horse and ride ye home."

Sinann raised her hand just as high, and warned, "And it would be an ape riding him. Stay yer hand, or ye'll find it without opposing thumb."

Morrighan threw the tiny faerie an evil look seething with frustration, and Sinann continued, "Tend to yer man and dinnae mess with us again." The dark faerie waved her hand, and in an instant, she and Daghda were gone.

Sinann leapt into the air, flew to Dylan, and hugged him hard, her arms and legs wrapped completely around him. He reeled, then recovered his balance as she cried, "I kent you could do it! *Och*, ye're truly Cuchulain! I kent it!" She squeezed all the air from Dylan in her joy.

Chuckling, he pried her loose so he could breathe, and she hovered in the air before him, her face lit up in the widest smile he'd ever seen on her. He tilted his head at her and grinned. *"Don't mess with us?"*

She laughed, a high, tinkling giggle, and said, "I've been around ye too long, laddie. I've begun to talk like ye."

That brought a laugh. "Uh-huh." The sky was beginning to lighten now, just discernible from the dark trees all around. Looking around for his weapons, he spotted the silver opal ring, which had dropped to the ground and lay, shining, by the fire. He picked it up to examine it.

"This is Morrighan's?"

"Aye. I braved the goddess in her lair. It was—"

"I was going to give this to Sarah, but maybe I shouldn't." He turned it, admiring it and wishing it had been anyone else's.

"Indeed, no, ye should. Ye should marry her at the first opportunity, if she'll have ye. Opals are good luck for them as are born in October. Bad luck for everyone else, but for Sarah . . . I mean, ye ken ye need help in this now." Dylan frowned, wondering what she meant by that, but she continued, "It would make a fine, lucky wedding ring, once ye've consecrated it to yer own use." She flew to the edge of the clearing and plucked a handful of something. "Wolfclaw! Just the thing!" Then she flew to the fire and tossed it on. The green herb began to smoke. "Do it."

He shrugged. "I don't know, Sinann."

"Aye, do it now. Go ahead. 'Twill be all right." She waved him on toward the fire.

With a sigh, and the weightless feeling of stepping off a cliff, he knelt by the fire and held the ring in the rising smoke.

"Here is the ring I would give my wife. A ring with no beginning and no end, the circle of life and the circle of endless love." Then he focused on the metal and stone and saw all the impurities and bad energy leaving it, carried up with the smoke. All associations with the goddess of war were gone. Finished, he held it in his palm and stared at it. It was brighter now. Even prettier than before.

" 'Tis nae longer belonging to the Morrighan."

Dylan looked to the sky and realized he needed to make it back to camp before he was missed. He slipped the ring into his sporran, then scabbarded his sword and returned the baldric to his shoulder, and began the walk back to the Jacobite encampment.

All the way, Sinann chewed him out thoroughly for not finding her sooner, but he just nodded, and a smile touched his mouth. He was glad to have her back anyway.

The camp was in an uproar. Men who should have been still sleeping were milling around, talking excitedly. The alarm was palpable. Dylan found Robin.

"What's happened?"

"Ye dinnae hear?"

"I was in the woods to relieve myself."

"A scout returned with intelligence of troop movements south of here. General Wightman's English troops are on their way down the glen. They ken we're here, and they're coming after us."

CHAPTER 21

The order came to break camp and move back down Glen Shiel. Once again the Jacobites were heading for the Shiel Bridge, and the inevitability of history reasserted itself in Dylan's mind.

Now he was faced with a decision. He knew they would never escape as an intact army. The Jacobite Army, with its horses, cannon, and outlawed leaders, had no escape. But the individual men were not trapped. Most of the soldiers had homes to go to, and those with homes had a chance of making it back to their families. He knew if the Matheson contingent stayed with Tullibardine, many of them would die, and they would die for nothing. From where he stood, knowing what he did, he felt the right thing to do would be to take the Mathesons home to Ciorram, and save lives.

But he wasn't in command, Artair was. The wee lairdie was unlikely to let his men scatter in the face of English fire, no matter how hopeless the prospects. Artair was out for a chance to fight, to show his ability to lead in battle, and would never allow retreat until he'd had a taste of blood.

Furthermore, the men themselves would not desert until they were shown the hopelessness of the situation. To leave without first being released by their commander would be desertion. The men of the cause were bound by honor and principle, more so than their English counterparts, who were bound more by law and cash. As much as Dylan knew, there was nothing he could show. He would be deemed a madman and a coward, even a witch, if he encouraged desertion based on an unknowable future.

Dylan's whip gash was healing and itched madly as he walked, though he'd wrapped a length of linen around his waist for a bandage. Every once in a while he curled his fingers around his belt to scratch behind it.

Careful to keep a distance from the others while talking with Sinann, he whispered to her, "I've got to talk the men into deserting. I know I can save half of them—maybe the rest will follow."

She shook her head vigorously. "Nae, ye cannae. They'd never respect ye after, even were they to heed ye. They'd remember ye forever after as the man who convinced them to betray Scotland and their King."

Dylan looked over at Artair. "He won't let them go. Neither will Tullibardine. Not until men have died. And I'm the only one who knows for sure the attempt will fail. Many of them suspect it, but they don't know it like I do."

"Are ye certain of it? Is it a certainty they willnae succeed?"

"You've seen the truth. No matter what I do, history doesn't change. I've never been able to change anything." His heart clenched with memory. "I couldn't even save Cait. I would have died in her place if I could have. But I had no say in the matter."

"And what if ye went to Tullibardine to convince him of the folly of his final stand?"

"He'd have me in irons." Dylan considered that a moment, then added, "Or he'd shoot me on the spot. He couldn't let me loose among the men to say those things to them. They're already unhappy; he'd be afraid of a general desertion, and he would be right."

"But ye say the men will stay until they're released."

Dylan sighed. "Yes, that's true. Most of them, anyway."

"So what will ye do?"

"I'll keep my mouth shut and try to keep myself and my men alive until Tullibardine finally decides to release us."

Sinann nodded. "Aye, 'tis the only honorable choice, as well."

As much as he hated to, Dylan had to agree.

The march to the Shiel Bridge took two days, with the Redcoats close behind. Glen Shiel narrowed at its western end, to form a tight ravine just above Loch Duich, and there Tullibardine split his army into three groups.

Lord George Murray, who was Tullibardine's brother and second-in-command, took his men to the south side of the ravine. The Earl Marischal of Scotland entrenched himself with the Spaniards on the north bank and a bit to the west of Murray. The Mathesons and the MacGregors, under MacKenzie, took position on a mountainside above and to the Earl Marischal's left. The three groups in array were in a daunting position to repulse the English. Dylan saw why Tullibardine thought they had a chance. It seemed impregnable.

They waited. It was June 10, the day of the battle. Only Dylan knew how soon the fighting would start, for everyone else seemed to expect the English to catch up with them the following day. But Dylan knew the Redcoats couldn't be that far behind.

He was impatient for it to begin, just to get it over with. As much as he knew about the history about to be made, there was no way for him to know whether this was the day he would die. He was eager to have the question settled so he could stop thinking about it. While the men around him rested, speaking in low voices and readying their weapons, Dylan sat in the heather, thinking and gnawing on a piece of bread left in his sporran from the morning's ration. The love tap from Morrighan on his belly still itched. He concentrated on ignoring it but failed, and dug under his belt again with his fingers.

Sinann, sitting on a rock beside him, said conversationally, "So ye finally succumbed to Sarah's charms, then?"

It took him a moment to reorient himself enough to figure out the faerie meant that night in his bedroom. He gave her a sharp look and whispered, "You didn't watch. Tell me you didn't."

"Not even had I wanted to, for it was dark as a Redcoat's black heart in that room."

Dylan grunted, hoping she'd drop the subject. But no such luck.

A note of irony crept into the faerie's voice. "I did notice the warmth of her good-bye. It's a lucky thing she was unarmed, or ye might very well have ended up dead in your doorway."

Dylan grunted again. "She wasn't that upset. I'll talk to her when I get back. Straighten her out on the subject of Cait."

"Are ye certain Sarah will be there when ye return?"

Now he frowned. "Not be there? Sarah? Of course she'll be there. You put a spell on her. She's got to be there."

The faerie shook her head. "The only reason she hasnae shaken off the spell before now is that she hasnae wanted to. Ye recall how well ye were able to rid yerself of the enchantment of the Morrighan. Think how much easier it must be for Sarah to be free of my own paltry spell should she wish it. Now ye've had carnal knowledge of the woman. Ye've hurt her badly—"

"I have not. She overheard a prayer. Big deal."

"I heard the prayer, as well. Sounded to me as if ye were praying for death to take ye away from Sarah to be once again with the woman ye love."

Dylan opened his mouth for a retort but closed it to think instead. He did want to be rejoined with Cait, but only when it was time. Thinking back over what he'd said that night, he realized Sarah couldn't have known that.

Sinann continued, "Climbing out of bed with one woman and then praying for death to take ye to another . . . I'd call it, at the very least, impolitic."

Dylan tried to think of something he'd said that would have indicated to Sarah he cared for her, but there was nothing. Nothing explicit, in any case, in so many words. Those words had not come easily to him. There was nothing to say in response to Sinann—no defense—so he lowered his chin to his knee and twirled a stem of heather between his fingers.

The faerie leaned close and said into his ear, "I expect ye'll need to live through this battle in order to convince her she was mistaken in thinking ye took advantage of her."

He looked at her and sighed. "I don't want to talk about this anymore." The time for fighting was approaching, and he needed to prepare.

"All I said was—"

"*Tink!*" Dylan squeezed his eyes shut. His pulse was picking up, and he needed to calm himself. She quieted, and he began to focus. He let go of the future. Mentally, he said good-bye to his children. One by one, he left behind everything that mattered to him and freed himself to face what was ahead. Soon the world was distilled to nothing but himself and this day in which men would die violently.

It was early afternoon when the resting Jacobites spotted English troops making their way up the gorge. A charge of excitement ran through the dug-in clansmen, and they stood to ready for action. Dylan slipped his arm through the loops on the back of his targe and waited with his kinsmen on the north hill. Coinneach, to his left, was jittery, shifting his weight over and over almost as if running in place as he watched the enemy approach. One young MacGregor, who had a running mouth, repeated ad nauseam his plan to personally do away with every Englishman in sight, until he got poked in the arm and told to shut up.

Dylan hefted his targe, feeling the weight on his arm. He'd never used a shield before and wasn't sure he liked not having a hand free for Brigid. But today the battle would be lost. Winning the day wasn't a possibility, and his best hope was to stay alive. He was content to honor Sarah's wish for his protection and do his best to make it home to her.

Wightman's red-clad troops approached on both sides of the river below: clansmen loyal to George, Dutch mercenaries, dismounted dragoons, grenadiers, and regulars. The Jacobites watched, rapt. Many of them prayed out loud. Some of them cursed the English. Most were dead silent.

Dylan crossed himself as he repeated once more his prayer for strength. "Dear God, please give me the strength to do what I must, to never shrink from my obligations. Help me to conduct myself with honor at all times. Please keep my children safe. Above all, let me one day be reunited with my beloved Cait . . ." He glanced sideways at Sinann and added, ". . . when it is my turn to die. Bless Sarah and give her strength. Amen."

As soon as they were in position, the 1,600 Hanoverians opened fire with mortars on the southern hill. The explosions were thuds Dylan could sense in the air, but it was all very matter-of-fact. He watched with a weird sense of detachment, as if he didn't know he would soon be within range of the other English guns. As if this were happening to someone else. He'd done this before, and had come very close to death. His heart thudded in his chest like the artillery. He took deep, even breaths and readied himself, sword in hand.

Voices and muskets roared. The Redcoats on the north side fired, then both factions charged, bristling with bayonets and swords. The Jacobites responded with a charge of their own. Dylan descended with his kinsmen the heather-covered hill, targe up and broadsword cocked, roaring at full voice. The forces clashed with the deafening ring of steel on steel. Dylan engaged a Redcoat, hitting hard. Having the advantage of higher ground, he blocked hard with the targe, then shifted to throw a side-thrust kick to the astonished Redcoat. The soldier went tumbling, taking those behind with him. Dylan ran down to finish off two men with quick slashes to throat and abdomen. They both lay, caught on the mounds of heather, choking and writhing.

Immediately forgetting the dying *Sassunaich*, Dylan then turned to block with his targe a hit by another Redcoat and found himself struggling for an advantage. Grace wasn't even possible as bludgeoning and force became the best way to knock each other off balance on the steep hill. Dylan hit with his targe and slashed with his sword, clobbering anything solid red that came within sight.

When the English retreated to regroup, the Jacobites likewise regrouped to maintain the higher ground. The artillery continued to fire. Men were blown to bits by mortar explosions, and fires blossomed in the heather all around. The heat of them singed the men, and the stench of burnt flesh, blood, and hair made breathing a chore. The English charged. Again and again they attempted the hill, taking more Jacobites with each assault.

Then the clansmen near Dylan began to flee up the hill. He gave way with them, unwilling to be caught alone by the advancing English. Retreat was more difficult than assault, for it meant leaving one's back vulnerable to attack. The targe gave him just enough rear guard for him to keep up with the Jacobites without taking a sword in his back in the process.

At the top of the hill, he now saw the MacKenzies were carrying their wounded Laird to the rear. The Redcoats renewed their attack, and now Dylan once more found himself on the failing flank of the Jacobite Army. The Spaniards under the Earl Marischal followed the retreat up the mountain. The battle was over. The mountain was left to the forces of King George.

Night fell, and the tattered Jacobite Army took themselves out of immediate reach of the English. The chase would resume in the morning, but for now, in the darkness, there would be no more fighting. The Mathesons gathered on Artair, carrying Coinneach, Dùghlas, and Seumas, who had been wounded, and settled into a quick encampment under an oak tree above a burn. A small fire was lit so the wounded could be attended to.

Young Coinneach had a bad leg wound and was already nearly bled out. Two men pressed linen rags to it, but the bleeding wasn't stopping or even slowing. Coinneach was unconscious and wouldn't last more than a few minutes longer. They all knew it.

Dùghlas was slashed across the belly, but might survive if he were lucky enough his peritoneum weren't breached. He called to Coinneach, but there was no reply. Dùghlas's own bleeding was bad enough, and he lay near the fire on his plaid, helpless in the face of his brother's certain death. Tears made runnels in the dirt and blood on his face and soaked into his beard.

Seumas leaned against the moss-covered oak, breathing heavily and rapidly through his nose as he struggled with the pain of his wound. His left hand was gone. A linen rag had been tied tightly around the stump, but it was soaked through with blood that dripped onto his kilt. He was expected to bleed to death like Coinneach.

Dylan knelt by him to unwrap the wound, and found the artery still surging. *Crap.* He didn't know anything about this stuff, but it was obvious Seumas wouldn't make it if something wasn't done quickly. He took Seumas's soaked bandage and tied it as a tourniquet around his forearm as tight as he could. The bleeding slowed but didn't stop. Dylan knew he couldn't just leave it like that. Cutting off the blood entirely would give him gangrene. Dylan then reached under his kilt for the hem of his sark and ripped it, then pulled a thread from it.

"Someone got some whiskey? I need whiskey right now."

An unidentified voice made a crack about Dylan not being able to stand the sight of blood.

"Not to drink." Nobody was moving to comply. Dylan's voice took on a hard, angry edge. "I mean it! Get me some whiskey now!" A small skin was handed to him, and he splashed the linen thread and his fingers with some from it. "Now get me a brand from the fire and bring it so I can see." Robin brought a flaming stick and held it. Dylan pressed Seumas's arm against the oak, over the man's head, and indicated Tormod and Keith Rómach to hold it there. "Okay, Seumas," he said, "this is going to hurt."

A smile curled the corners of Seumas's mouth. "I wouldnae have guessed it."

Quickly, Dylan dug into the wound. It was an oddly slanted cut, with a ragged flap of skin that had once been the back of Seumas's hand. The two bones of Seumas's forearm slipped around in the wet mess, and the twitchy muscles jerked them back and forth. It was hard to find the end of even the largest blood vessel, but finally Dylan was able to isolate it and tie a knot around the end. The worst of the bleeding stopped. Just to be certain it would stay, he tied another knot. Then he splashed the entire stump end with more whiskey from the skin.

Seumas's breaths came in short, quick snorts through his nose, and he paled almost to passing out. But not a word passed his lips.

Colin brought his sword. "Here, to seal the wound." The end of it glowed red, having been heated in the fire.

"Right." Cauterization. Dylan had heard of it but had never seen it done. Again the men took Seumas's stump and held it against the trunk of the tree. Quickly, before the heat would leave the sword, Dylan applied the blade to the still-bleeding wound.

Seumas's arm jerked and his body trembled, but he made no sound. Once again Dylan applied the blade, and Seumas passed out.

"Seumas!" Dylan handed off the sword and shook his friend. "Seumas, stick with us." Dylan gave his face a light slap, and the wounded man groaned. Seumas was nearly blue with shock, and clammy. "It's done now, Seumas." A piece of linen was handed up to wrap around the stump, and Dylan tied it tightly to stanch the last of the bleeding.

"Lay him on his back, and someone hold his arm up. Make sure the stump is higher than his body, and pointed up. His head should be down." Basic first aid picked up God knew where when he was a kid was wandering into his memory, but that was all he knew. It was all the help he could give Seumas, who would now die or not die, according to his fate.

Dylan looked around at the men. "Someone . . . Tormod." Tormod grunted. "Keep an eye on the bleeding. Every little while, loosen the tourniquet—this bit of linen here—for a while, then tie it again. As tight as you can. Once the bleeding has stopped completely, you can leave it off." Tormod nodded acknowledgment, and Dylan stepped away to do . . . something.

Unsure where he thought he was headed, he stopped and looked around. He looked down at his hands, covered with Seumas's blood, then at his coat and kilt which were covered with the blood of many others. He went to the burn. Once again he needed to clean other men's blood from his hands and face.

It was then Dylan discovered the sleeve of his coat had a hole. It was soaked through with his own blood, and his left arm was stiffening and aching. He slipped his arm from its coat sleeve, and a tenderly conducted investigation revealed a stab wound in his shoulder. The blade, whatever blade it had been, for he didn't remember receiving the wound, had pierced him completely through the outer flesh of his arm. The bleeding had stopped, so he drew his coat back on and slung his plaid over the shoulder where it belonged, then got on with his business.

He went around to the men to determine their losses, and learned eight

Mathesons had died that day, their bodies left behind on the battlefield. Marc Hewitt was one of them. Dylan's heart clenched as he thought of Ailis and their two young sons.

Artair came from a council with Tullibardine and announced, "We'll face the English again in the morning."

Dylan blinked. "You're joking. This is a joke, right?"

"Nae. We've damaged them. We retain the high ground, and tomorrow we will repulse them. The clans will hear of the victory and come to support us."

Dylan, angry now, looked up the hill toward Tullibardine as he reverted to English and muttered, "Is he freaking nuts?" Artair frowned, but Dylan walked away from him and headed for Tullibardine. The wee lairdie followed.

"And what do ye think ye're up to?"

"Bug off, Artair."

Artair had been insulted by Dylan enough to recognize a slight when he heard one, even in twenty-first-century American English slang. Anger rose in his voice. "Ye dinnae speak for the Mathesons."

"No, but I speak for common sense. It's time someone finally told Tullibardine the uprising is over."

Sinann, flying behind, said, inaudible to Artair, "But ye said history cannae be changed. If ye dinnae convince Tullibardine to end it, will he nae end it regardless?"

Dylan stopped and stared at Sinann. She was right.

Artair, oblivious to the faerie, said, "Mind yer place. Ye could end up in the gatehouse once we've returned home."

Ignoring the wee lairdie, Dylan said to the invisible faerie, "But what if I'm supposed to convince him?"

As one, both Artair and Sinann said, " 'Tis nae yer place."

Sinann glared at Artair for a moment, then continued, "And what then, should ye happen to be wrong and ye *can* change history? Was it nae yer fear of telling the Morrighan of the future that she might make changes ye dinnae like?"

Dylan addressed the ground as he spoke to Sinann. "The Morrighan has powers I don't."

Artair blinked, then said, "I expect she has. Nevertheless—"

"I can't just let Tullibardine send these men straight into the teeth of the English Army tomorrow."

Said Sinann, "If he does, then he will have not followed yer history. If history can be altered, then perhaps the lads have a chance at winning."

Artair was railing something similar, for different reasons, but Dylan paid no attention. He looked around at the demoralized clansmen slumped on the ground by fires here and there, and sighed. It was plain there was no fight left in them. Nobody believed anymore the uncommitted clans would rise with them. Nobody believed there was still a chance to prevail. The only prospects before them were death or imprisonment. There was no spirit here anymore with which to carry victory.

He made his decision and walked away from Artair and Sinann toward Tullibardine, up the hill, to the spot the Jacobite leader had chosen to observe the nearby hillsides by moonlight. Tullibardine was in darkness under trees like his soldiers, surrounded by his velvet-clad buddies in breeches and wigs. He was subdued and looking very much the worse for wear, but talking in low tones of hope and recouping. He looked up as Dylan approached.

Dylan came straight to the point. "My lord, with all due respect, I ask you to think again before sending these men into a battle they all know they can't win."

Tullibardine, his wig shining dirty white in the moon overhead, looked up from his friends. He thought a moment before climbing to his feet. "This is impudence." Dylan could hear the fear in his voice, that Dylan's assertion might be true. "Be careful what you say, lest it be treason. Who are you?"

Dylan made a slight bow, a gesture of obeisance calculated to convince the Marquis to take him seriously. He said, "My name is Dylan Matheson, my lord. I mean no rudeness, but I march with the men. I hear them talking. The only thing that keeps them from scurrying in all directions is the pledge they made to their lairds and to you."

Tullibardine said, "Aye." So far, Dylan had said nothing that wasn't well known by all present.

Dylan continued, "But they haven't the heart for further battle. They're outnumbered and outgunned. They've taken a terrible beating today, in both body and mind. There isn't time to recover before the English will attack again. Our men, brave as they are, have nonetheless lost their faith in success. Loyal as they are, they no longer have their best to give you." Dylan stopped there, hoping Tullibardine would himself make the inference that, as a wise commander, he couldn't want to send unwilling men to certain death.

He seemed to. Tullibardine was still, a featureless figure in the darkness. He said, a note of wishing in his voice, "Is it possible you yourself are the only one whose will is gone?"

Dylan raised his chin, offended. "I'm still here, as they are, and will stay until released from obligation. I fought and was wounded at Sheriffmuir, and did not come here expecting a picnic. I'm confident I speak for more men than just myself. But I assure you, if you order me back into battle, I will go. Though I know it would be the end of all of us." He nodded toward the men of Tullibardine's tattered army. "As they also know it."

Slowly, the shadow that was Tullibardine seemed to shrink, as if all the air had been let out of him, leaving a shell empty of hope. He looked around at his associates and said, his voice desolate, "Well, then, George," he addressed his brother, "I was certain you were mistaken in your assessment, but now I suppose you may have been correct. The men have no fight left in them. The weight of the advice convinces me it's time to release the men."

Relief washed all through Dylan. He—Artair, rather—could take the Mathesons back to Glen Ciorram.

Tullibardine gave the order out to the entire Jacobite contingent to disperse and make their way to their homes as best they could. The men went immediately, under cover of darkness.

The Mathesons moved as quickly as possible, carrying Coinneach and Dùghlas with them. The route was harsh, over trackless mountains, and exhaustion forced them to stop at dawn. They were not far from Glen Ciorram but also not close enough to push on without rest. Artair called a halt.

While the other men wolfed handfuls of *drammach*, for none of them had eaten since before the battle, Dylan walked among them to make sure no wounds had gone septic. Young Coinneach had died during the night, bringing the death count to nine. Dùghlas, his belly wrapped tightly with bloodied linen, sat in silence over the body of his little brother.

Dylan crouched on his heels beside them and looked into the pale, blood-smeared face of the teenage boy. Coinneach was nearly beardless, only a few stray hairs grown in on his chin. The pit of Dylan's stomach hardened with grief. That Coinneach, Marc, and the others had died for nothing was almost unbearable.

Artair's voice came from behind. "We could have avenged the lad's death, had you not convinced Tullibardine the cause was lost."

Dylan stood and turned to face him, exhausted and in no mood for this argument. "Bite me, Artair."

" 'Twas a cowardly thing."

"It was the only recourse. Murray agreed, as well. There was nothing to be gained by more fighting except yet more death."

"Your place wasnae to tell Tullibardine what to do."

"Somebody had to tell him the men weren't strong enough to keep fighting." That brought a murmur of irritation from the men themselves, and Dylan bit his tongue for his error.

Artair drew his dirk. "I think 'tis time for you to leave the clan."

"Don't be stupid." Dylan pulled Brigid but stood casually, in hopes of avoiding bloodshed that nobody needed. "I'm going home to my children." Because of his wound, he was unable to lift his left arm to the side and didn't care for the disadvantage.

"Defend yerself, or I'll kill ye where ye stand."

With a sigh, Dylan raised his dirk. "Don't do this, Artair."

The young heir attacked, aiming at Dylan's belly. Dylan neatly parried, then gave a quick snap kick to the gut.

The wee lairdie held his stomach and uttered a groan. Dylan transferred Brigid to his left, though it was his bad side. Artair rushed him carelessly for his perceived advantage. Dylan sidestepped, grabbed his collar, and helped him headfirst into a tree. Artair's dirk dropped with a thud. Dylan kicked it away, gave Artair another shove against the heavy oak, then hauled him back and turned him around before shoving him back against it again. This time he grabbed wool coat, holding Artair there, and set Brigid's point against the young man's solar plexus. With the knife blade pointed up, the hilt braced against his own belly, it would take just the slightest shove to put the dirk into Artair's heart.

"Dinnae kill me!" Artair stood on tiptoe, trying to get away from the knife point.

"I'm not going to kill you. We've got enough honorable dead and wounded to carry without having to haul your worthless carcass back home." Relief washed across Artair's face, but Dylan kept Brigid where she was as he continued, "You're going to live to be laird, Artair, but know this: you will never be a good one. You will never be respected by your clan, you will never be honored by your men, you will never have success in battle, *until* you learn to take responsibility for the welfare of your people. So long as you hold your own interests above those of the clan, you will be a worthless piece of shit, forgotten by God and everyone else who matters. Your father never taught you that, your brother couldn't teach you, and so now I'm telling you, and you'd better fucking listen. If you want the Mathesons of Ciorram to prosper, you will learn to hold their interests before yours. It's that simple."

He released Artair and helped him regain his balance. Then he scabbarded Brigid and went to find a place to sleep. Robin clapped him on the back as he went. They each curled up in some heather near where Seumas lay, and the rest of the men settled in for a couple hours' rest. Artair went to sulk with Tormod and Dùghlas, but Dylan noticed no mutterings from that quarter as he dropped off to sleep.

At about noon, they arose for the last leg to Glen Ciorram. Artair was silent and sullen the rest of the way.

CHAPTER 22

In August, Barri phoned Cody.

"I think I need to go to Scotland."

There was a silence on the other end, and Barri could hear the baby Dylan babbling cheerfully in the background. Then Cody said, "What are you hoping to find?"

That was difficult to answer. Barri had thought long and hard about why she wanted to go. She believed in the faerie now. More than anything, she wanted Cody's story to be true. But, though she'd read all of the historical material she could find, there was only one other corroborating reference to be found. One sentence, in an obscure recounting of the days of Bonnie Prince Charlie, referred to a Ciaran Robert Matheson at the battle of Culloden, the final Jacobite attempt, in 1746. Nothing more about Black Dylan or Dilean Dubh.

On one level, she simply wanted to find out more about Dylan's life, and thought she might be able to do that by gaining access to local archives in Ciorram. But on a deeper level she was reluctant to admit, she hoped to find the faerie herself. Somewhere in the back of her mind lurked the dim hope of seeing Dylan again.

But she said, "I want to find out more."

"You think there's more to be learned by going there?"

"There's got to be more information there than here."

"What if you don't like what you find out?" Again there was silence, and Cody elaborated. "I mean, he was thirty-five in 1718. What if that's where the story ends? Do you want to know everything?"

That was easy to answer. "Yes. I do. I want to know everything." She wanted to *be* there. "I need to know whatever can be learned."

Cody sighed. "There might be nothing to learn. He had children; even if there are descendants there, you might still learn nothing more about Dylan than the story his grandfather told."

Barri had to agree but also felt she had to go. There was another long silence, then Cody said slowly, "You're planning on coming back, aren't you?" Then she muttered to herself, "Jeez, I can't believe I'm having this conversation again."

This was even more difficult to answer. The silence strung out as she struggled for words, until Cody finally spoke.

"Nathan will be disappointed if you just disappear. No, scratch disappointed. He'd be hurt."

Barri had to laugh at the thought of anyone missing her. "Surely he would get over it."

"Well, yeah, eventually. But you should remember there are people here who care about you."

Again Barri was at a loss for words. She thanked Cody, but still knew if there was a chance to see Dylan again, she would take it.

The flight was to Glasgow, where Barri rented a car to drive into the Highlands. It would have been far easier to ride a train, had the rails gone anywhere near Glen Ciorram. As it was, the closest she could have come by train would have been Fort William, where a rental car would have been hard to come by, leaving an inconvenient walk of several days to the village of Ciorram.

The drive was long but hardly boring. The mountains were breathtakingly beautiful everywhere she looked. It was almost a shame to have to keep her eyes on the road. Summer flowers scattered brilliant color over the hillsides, and the mountains themselves were dusted all over with purple heather. The little rental car buzzed past brown crags and through deep forests as she zigged and zagged her way along the highways, then the narrow mountain roads, to the place Dylan's trail in this world had ended—the tower where Scottish authorities had reported finding his blood-covered rental car.

It was nearly sunset when she arrived at the tower, just outside of Glen Ciorram. She should have gone on to the hotel, but couldn't wait till morning for this. Dusk was barely gathering as she looked around at the stone walls and perfectly groomed grass inside the tower. A large piece of stone sat in the middle of the area, looking as if it had just fallen from the tower walls. Tough, black fungus grew all through the grass, giving it a brindled sort of look. She stood in the middle of the tower, her heart pounding, both hopeful and fearful.

"Hello?" Barri turned in place, searching. Cody had told her the faerie's name, and now Barri struggled to remember it. "Sinann?" Was she pronouncing it correctly? Would the creature come if her name were pronounced wrong? "Hello, are you there?" Barri waited for a reply, but there was nothing.

The branches of the ancient oak tree overhead rustled in the breeze, but there was no Sinann. Barri began to feel like a fool, doubly disappointed for her failure and having come so very far for it. She sighed. "Little faerie? Will you come to me?" Again there was a breeze, but no little person. Tears stung her eyes, but she blinked them back. Bad enough to *be* a fool, she wouldn't look like one.

A glimpse of something white caught the corner of her vision, and she turned to look. But there was nothing white there. No faerie nor anything else. Barri looked all around again, but there was nothing resembling a faerie nor a person of any kind. She sat on the large piece of stone in the middle of the grassy area, knowing she should move on but unable to give up yet.

It was quiet here. No sound but the leaves in the trees and the occasional car passing on the road to Ciorram below. It smelled of earth and grass and, for a moment, of smoke. In that moment, she thought she saw Dylan kneeling before a smoking fire at the tower center, wearing a kilt and a black coat. His eyes were closed, and his lips were moving. He was dropping something into the fire. Some candles burned nearby.

But when she blinked, he was gone. It had been nothing more than her imagination. A lightheaded sense of insanity made the earth feel uncertain beneath her feet. Her pulse was tripping along at a quick, weak rate.

She looked around, but found nothing burning, and the smell was now gone.

Another glimpse of white caught her eye, but again there was nothing.

She said aloud, "You're not going to show yourself, are you? You know why I'm here—you know who I am."

There was no reply but silence.

The sky was turning sunset colors now. It was getting too cold out here to stand around and hope for a faerie that wouldn't come. Now she wondered if Cody's whole story was to be questioned. She was tired and confused.

Maybe the faerie hadn't even existed. Perhaps the story about Dylan had been invented just to soothe her. She cringed, wishing Cody were there to explain things. But the book with the drawing surely hadn't been an invention. The book was real. She didn't know what to think.

There was nothing left but to return to the car and see what she could find in Ciorram. But as she pulled onto the one-lane road, she thought of Nathan. At least he wouldn't be hurt, and perhaps that was somewhat worth her own disappointment.

Her heart was sore, but as she drove she couldn't help but feel it ease at the beauty around her. It was simple to understand why Dylan had been so fascinated by this place. The landscape was thick with human history, dotted with old buildings and rounded cairns, meandering stone walls, and pastures ridged with ancient patterns of plowing.

Glen Ciorram seemed at the end of the earth, it was so isolated. Barri drove past a Catholic church of gray stone, nestled in a ravine. As she drove onward, the ravine opened onto lush, rolling pastures cast in dying orange light. Low stone walls crisscrossed the landscape dominated by steep granite mountains to the left and high wooded ones to the right. The single-lane road meandered down the middle of the glen, until a few tract houses alerted her she was approaching the village.

Almost immediately she found herself circling a roundabout, uncertain which way to go from there. A couple of turns around it, however, enabled her to spot the way up Bog Road, where she'd been told she would find the hotel where she'd reserved a room.

The Ciorram Hotel was of modern architecture but was nevertheless old and run down. Barri's room was small, the plumbing rickety, and the window beside the bed declined to close all the way. Its saving grace was a grand view of Loch Sgàthan. Outside the obstinate window the mirrorlike surface of the lake seemed to go on forever, and behind some warehouses across the way part of the castle that sat directly above the water could be seen. A few large, white birds drifted near the island, and her heart skipped a beat to realize they were swans. Never in her life had she seen a live swan. A smile touched her mouth, and she found herself awash with the wondrous beauty of it.

Tomorrow she would accomplish something, she was certain. If she wasn't going to be magically transported to the eighteenth century by a compliant faerie, one thing she wanted to do while she was here was talk to the town historian, a gentleman named Ewan MacDonell. Cody had told her about some photocopies he'd sent her of birth and death records, so there might be a chance of gaining access to marriage records as well. Cody hadn't found Dylan's death record, and they both hoped he'd lived past the dates her photocopies covered. If she accomplished nothing else, she wanted to know how long Dylan had lived.

After showering, Barri lay down on the narrow but very soft bed and slept. Throughout the night, she dreamed of Dylan. Strange images came, of Dylan in a kilt with a sword at his side. As many times as he'd attended those festivals in Tennessee while dressed in period garb, she'd seen him dressed like that before. But in these dreams he was dirty, sometimes bloodied. There was a hard look to him, as he'd been after his surgery but never before. They were just images, these dreams. Like a slide show, but so real she thought she could reach out and touch him. But she didn't dare, lest they prove too fragile and the image would shatter.

This was her little boy as he'd become, she realized, for these images couldn't be a dream. She barely recognized him; this didn't come from her imagination. He'd grown to be not just a man but a hardened man. Things had happened to him she couldn't bear to contemplate, let alone conjure in her mind. She couldn't know what had made him this way. She wondered if he had remained the man she'd raised. She wondered if he'd so completely let go of his origins as to have forgotten her. The thought was too much to bear.

In the morning she awoke to a pervasive ache. It seemed too much effort to get out of the bed and move around. This town was where Dylan had died. She'd traveled five thousand miles to a place where nobody knew her and couldn't know her son, but she still felt he was here, in one form or another. Getting out of bed might mean finding him, and she was suddenly uncertain whether she wanted to know what there was to learn.

A deep breath cleared her head somewhat, and she decided there was nothing for it but to get on with it. She rose, dressed, breakfasted downstairs in the empty dining room, then went walking through the village in search of the historian who had written to Cody.

She found MacDonell's office, a tiny storefront on a side street not far from the roundabout, but it was closed. A handwritten placard indicated he was on holiday. A frown creased Barri's brow. Knowing that "holiday" was British for "vacation," she wondered whether he would be back before she was due to leave Scotland.

But for now there was nothing for it but to move on, and she looked around. The town was small, but seemed to be thriving in a quiet sort of way. A grammar school boasted a playground filled with children, and the presence of more than one pub suggested business was good. American fast food didn't seem to have made it this far into the countryside, but there was a fish and chips take-away shop near the roundabout and a Chinese restaurant a block away. Next to one of the pubs was a good-sized grocery store called MacGregor's, and up on the hillside, above the town, was a massive stone distillery.

A cold finger touched Barri's back, for single-malt scotch had been Kenneth's drink of choice once she'd convinced him to stop smoking pot. She tried to recall whether he'd ever bought the Glenciorram whiskey but couldn't remember. There'd been lots of Glenfiddich and Glenlivet, though, she was certain of that.

The warmth of the day and the walking had brought on a thirst, and not for scotch, so she stopped in at one of the pubs for a soft drink. It was a dark, close sort of place, with whitewashed walls covered with dusty landscape prints in heavy frames and highly polished dark wooden tables and chairs.

Some men stood in a cluster near the end of the bar, speaking in low but jovial voices. The young man behind the bar was busy wiping things and refilling glasses for the men with a dark brew that might have been ale. Barri wouldn't have known ale from root beer by looking at it, but the stuff was dark, and this was Scotland, so she assumed it was ale.

She sat on one of the stools and requested a diet cola. It was served from a can, in a glass with no ice. For a moment she peered at the drink, debating whether to inquire after ice, but then decided she was here to investigate, so why not begin finding things out now. The thing to do now was to see if there might be a reason for serving room-temperature sodas with no ice. She took a sip, and held out the glass to regard it as she tasted.

Not bad. She supposed "room temperature" in these parts could be a mite cooler than in the U.S. The soda also didn't seem as fizzy as what she was accustomed to. In the U.S., a room-temperature soda would taste entirely of carbonation, go down fizzy, and result in hiccups. But here, it tasted smooth. Not bad at all. She sipped it again.

The men at the other end of the bar were still talking, but she couldn't understand what they were saying. Even though she hadn't had any trouble understanding the folks at the hotel, she now realized they may have spoken slowly for her sake. Now she was hearing slang and one-word sentences that baffled her.

They were all older men, probably retired to be hanging out in a pub this time of day. One wore a tweed jacket and slacks, his hair a gray fringe over his ears. The others wore jeans, T-shirts, and fleece jackets—one yellow and the other pale blue. They were somewhat younger than the man in tweed, but not by much. They glanced in Barri's direction, and she averted her eyes to not be caught staring.

But then she wondered why she was avoiding contact. She was here to ask questions, and just because Mr. MacDonell wasn't around, she didn't need to hide from everyone else. Five thousand miles from home, it wasn't going to hurt her reputation to have a chat with men she didn't know. She returned her attention to the cluster of locals and said, "Excuse me, I wonder if I might ask you all some questions."

They turned, seeming surprised but also curious and eager for a diversion. The man in the blue fleece said, "What is it ye've a mind to ask?"

Barri took a deep breath, for nervousness struck, and her chest suddenly felt bound in iron. "My name is Barri Matheson. I was hoping to do a little genealogical research while I'm here, but the fellow who keeps the records—"

"Oh, aye, Ewan. He'll be gone the fortnight. Left yesterday for Antwerp. I dinnae suppose ye'll be staying that long."

Disappointment landed. "No. Only about four days."

The one in the yellow fleece moved toward her down the bar and said, "Ye're born a Matheson, then?"

She shook her head. "It's my husband's name. It's his family I've come to research."

There was a surprised silence from the men, then Yellow Fleece said, "*Och,* I was certain I saw some Matheson in ye. My mother was a Matheson, ye see, and . . ." He cut himself off and shrugged. "Well, I suppose I am mistaken."

Barri headed off the impending awkward silence. "Failing getting a look at the church records, I wonder if there might be another source of history here. The library, perhaps?"

All three men waved away the thought of finding anything useful in books. The one in tweed said, "Ye're talking to the one man in the entire glen who would truly be of use to ye, madame. If it's stories of Mathesons ye wish, I have them all right up here." Smiling wide with grayed and crooked teeth, he tapped his forehead with a wrinkled finger colored with brown spots and seemed tickled to have found an audience. "All my life I've collected and retold the stories, which ye'll never find in any book. Come." He gestured to a table by a window as he moved toward it. "Come sit with us, and I'll tell ye all I know of yer husband's clan."

Barri brought her diet cola and sat with the three, who introduced themselves. The man in the yellow fleece gave his name as Duncan MacGregor, the one in blue was Alastair Innis, and the man in tweed was Fearghas Matheson.

Barri had a vague feeling of needing to be somewhere else, as if she were playing hooky. But when she tried to think of where that might be, she realized there was nowhere else. This was what she'd come for. She settled in by the window to listen to the man in tweed.

Ale in hand, he started off with a ghost story about a white dog, for which the castle on the lake had been named. Apparently the dog, after having been killed in battle by the neighboring MacDonell clan, avenged his master's death by killing the entire war party on its way back to MacDonell lands. Fearghas's voice rose and fell with the intensity of the events in the story. Each character had his own voice, and the ghost dog was described in such vivid detail, Barri felt she could see the large, shaggy white hound at the castle gatehouse, blood dripping from its maw.

The storyteller then segued into an even older tale about a Matheson ancestor who single-handedly defended Glen Ciorram against Vikings, and when he died of his wounds, his blood stained the ground permanently red.

"Permanently?"

All three men nodded. "Aye," said Fearghas. "Inside the *broch*. I've seen it. The ground there is red as blood, and the roots of the grass as well. 'Tis a thing to see." The other men murmured agreement.

"You've all seen the red ground?"

They nodded, and Barri wondered if they were putting on a show for the tourist, until Duncan said in all sincerity, "I've seen the white dog, as well. 'Tis a bad omen. I was driving across the bridge to the castle one day when I was a young man, there to make a delivery, and saw the dog at the gatehouse. I came to a quick stop, I assure you. The beast turned three times widdershins, then settled onto the drive to lick its bloody chops. The very next day, my car was stolen."

"You're serious?"

"Dead serious." And there was not a hint of smirk on his face or a light of amusement in his eyes to indicate otherwise. As she looked at Duncan's mouth, it struck her the full lower lip reminded her of Dylan's. She blinked and shook off the thought as imagination. There were six billion people on the planet; the chances of someone in Scotland having a full lower lip like Dylan's were excellent.

Fearghas waved to the barkeep for another ale, and fresh drinks were brought all around. The storyteller continued with more magic concerning the *Broch Sidhe*, which he explained meant "faerie tower" in Gaelic.

Barri's attention perked at mention of the faerie. Apparently Sinann had been a busy little *sidhe* down through the centuries, for there were many stories of her helping the Mathesons. She'd brought rain during drought, had guided various Matheson lairds through wartime, and had once made a gift to the castle of an enchanted tapestry.

"How do you know it's enchanted?"

"It appeared magically one night, hung in the Laird's study. Woven into it is the likeness of Donnchadh Matheson, who was Laird at the time, which was the turn of the eighteenth century."

"What does it do, that it's enchanted?"

Fearghas shrugged. "I dinnae ken. Nobody alive does, I expect. Only the faerie herself."

Barri nodded and sipped her soda. The stories were starting to wander into less credible territory, so she steered them away from faeries and in the direction of Black Dylan. She said, "I have a name of a very distant cousin I would like to learn about. It's a story told to my father-in-law by an RAF officer named James Matheson."

Fearghas said, "Which war?"

She blinked. "Pardon?"

"In which war did your father-in-law encounter him? We've at least three James Mathesons from Ciorram who were and are in the Royal Air Force. Young Jimmy from the high glen up the Bog Road is currently serving, his father recently retired, and James Dilean Matheson flew during the last World War."

A flush of heat came when she heard the name. "James Dilean . . ."

"Oh, aye, a close cousin of my father, ye ken," said Fearghas with obvious pride in that fact. "Ye say yer father-in-law met him in the war?"

Barri nodded. "He told a story about an ancestor of his. A highwayman who worked for Rob Roy MacGregor, named Black Dylan."

A roar of enthusiasm took the table, the three men apparently pleased to learn the legend had traveled all the way to America. Fearghas said, "Oh, aye! *Dilean Dubh*! Black-haired Dylan!"

"Black-*haired* Dylan?" Barri had always thought the name referred to the highwayman's personality, and now she smiled.

Fearghas nodded. "Nearly so, in any case. Dark of skin, as well, according to the tale. I dinnae suppose cousin Jamie told of Black Dylan being a selkie?" The blank look on Barri's face must have given away her utter cluelessness, for he went on. "I wouldn't have thought so. Not to an American. When ye go about talking of people being seals, the outlanders tend to go all google-eyed on ye."

"Seals?"

"One story in the legend of Black Dylan is that he came from over the sea. He was the son of Roderick Matheson, who was the brother of Donnchadh, whose likeness was made in the tapestry." Barrie's pulse surged, for she knew Roderick was the name of Kenneth's—and Dylan's—earliest American Matheson ancestor. Fearghas continued, "One day Roderick went with the herds to Edinburgh, disappeared, and was never heard from again."

Barrie knew, through Dylan's interest in his Scottish ancestry, that Roderick had been transported to Virginia for a killing committed in Edinburgh. "Sixteen sixty-six," she said, without realizing she was speaking aloud.

The table went silent. Fearghas said, "Aye." He stared at her for a moment. Duncan looked like he was going to say something, then stopped himself. Fearghas then coughed and continued, "But years later, his son returned to Ciorram. Black of hair, he was, and dark-skinned. Tannedlike, I expect. But blue-eyed like his father. He told everyone he'd gotten his black hair from his mother, and that was when they knew he was a selkie. Roderick had been taken by the seal people, and married a selkie wife who bore him a son. When the son returned to his father's people, the lad took human form. And a braw man he was."

The note of pride in Fearghas's voice again caught Barri's attention. "You're a direct descendant of Black Dylan Matheson."

A wide grin crossed his face. "Aye. You could see, were my hair nae so gray these days, I was born with the dark hair."

"And the blue eyes."

Duncan snorted, "The entire glen's got the blue eyes."

"They do not." Fearghas said to Barri, "It's true, though, Ciorram is a small place, and a goodly percentage of those born here can trace relationship to any Matheson ancestor they care to. But some of us can trace it more directly than others." He threw Duncan a look.

"Sort of like the Kevin Bacon game," said Barri. That brought blank looks, so she shook her head. "Never mind."

Fearghas continued, "If it's Dilean Dubh ye're wanting to research, Ewan MacDonell isnae the fellow ye're needing to see."

Duncan agreed. "*Och,* he knows nothing beyond what his family did at Culloden. Which was precious little, but he thinks it was a flaming big deal."

Alastair, who had been mostly silent during the storytelling, said, "*Och,* what can ye expect from a man who spends his holidays in Belgium?" That brought a roar of laughter from the other two, which left Barri blank.

Once the amusement died down, Fearghas nodded. "The fellow ye need to see is the current Laird of *Tigh a' Mhadaidh Bhàin.*" He gestured out the window at a brown road sign with the name of the castle on it in Gaelic and English. An arrow pointed in the direction of the roundabout in the center of town. "Jamie's son. Iain Robert Matheson is his name."

CHAPTER 23

Dylan listened carefully to the silence among the men on the trek to Glen Ciorram. They all grieved for their fallen friends, and almost as deep was the pain for the lost cause itself. As much as they wanted to see their homes again, returning in defeat was a bitter thing. There was no honor in fleeing a battlefield, no matter how hopeless the cause.

Almost to Ciorram, in the shielings above and south of the peat bog, the men split up in order to reenter the glen without attracting the attention of the garrisoned soldiers. Artair took a group and traversed below the bog, headed straight for the castle, others detached themselves to head toward the western end of the loch where boats awaited, and Dylan took a party of men up toward his land.

They carried Coinneach's body with them to the high glen and would ready him for burial before splitting up to go to their homes. Nobody had yet figured out how to bury him in the churchyard, which stood within sight of the garrison, without alerting the *Sassunaich* to their participation in the battle.

Dylan's house was, of course, silent. The children were in the care of their grandparents, the dogs were at the castle with Iain's, and only Eóin would have had business on the farm during the past month, to feed the chickens, collect eggs, and pasture the hoofed livestock. The sheep were not in the enclosure, but rather would be in the pastures this time of day. A couple of hens pecked around the outside of the stone dike of the sheep enclosure, and Ginny grazed in the dooryard with her kid. It was strange to see the house with no smoke coming from the chimney hole. There was no wife there to keep the fire burning. No Cait, but also no Sarah. Once again, he found himself missing her and hoped to make amends.

After laying Coinneach on Dylan's table inside the house, Colin and some others went on down the high glen to the shortcut that would take them to the east end of Glen Ciorram, headed for Marc Hewitt's house to break the terrible news to his widow. Women from the village would come later to clean Coinneach's body and sew him into a shroud. Robin and Seumas went to wash the dried blood from themselves in the burn. Dylan, during a moment alone in the house as he used the chamber pot, directed Sinann to fly to the castle and assure him the children were safe. Then Dylan hid the swords in the thatching of his roof and also went to scrub.

Though Seumas's tourniquet was no longer necessary and had been discarded hours before, the bandage covering the stump was soaked through and stiff with blood. Dylan reached over and unwrapped the linen, cleaned the wound, and checked for infection. Though Dylan's knowledge of twentieth-century medicine extended mostly to the fact that it was more effective than eighteenth-century medicine, which made him nearly as worthless a caretaker as everyone else in this time, he was at least somewhat knowledgeable of ways of warding off infection. He noted there were no red streaks on Seumas's arm, and no pus. Once the wound was cleaned of dirt and old blood, Dylan lightly bandaged the arm with clean linen rags from a basket Cait had kept for such things. Though the worst bleeding had stopped, there was still pink seepage through the cloth. Dylan would find someone to sew together the ends of skin at the wrist.

As Dylan was tying the new bandage, Sinann popped into view, breathless.

"Come! Hurry!" Dylan gave her a hard look, and she replied to the unasked question. "I cannae find the children. The village is gone! It's terrible! Come quickly!"

Dylan felt the blood drain from his face but kept an impassive demeanor. He ordered Robin to follow him, and Seumas to stay with Coinneach. Dylan picked up his bear-head staff from inside his door and headed for the castle, telling Robin nothing but that he had business there. He struggled to appear calm as they went down the trail to Ciorram. Neither of them spoke, for Robin knew when to keep quiet around Dylan.

What they found as they emerged onto the glen stopped them both dead.

Several houses in the village center had been fired, burned to the ground, and only Nana Pettigrew's stood unharmed amid scattered piles of ashes. Some outlying houses were visible, but many of those had been burned as well. There were no cattle in sight, and very few sheep, though the shielings were empty of livestock and the herds wouldn't have been moved to the high pastures for another month in any case. It was plain a disaster of some sort—a *creach* that had gone far beyond the parameters of tradition—had befallen the Mathesons.

Robin finally spoke, his voice soft with awe. "Dear God in heaven, what was done here?" The two men broke into a run toward the castle.

As they hurried across the drawbridge, a cluster of people emerged from the castle gatehouse. They were women, wailing and carrying on, and moving in a group before a party of Redcoats with muskets at ready. Dylan and Robin stopped at the middle of the bridge. The soldiers held a man in custody, prodding him along with bayonets. It was Artair.

Dylan and Robin were spotted by the soldiers, who brought muskets to bear on them as well. The Scots were faced with two choices: surrender, or bolt and become fugitives. Dylan raised his hands. Robin took the cue and raised his also, as a dragoon came to take the staff and their dirks and shove them toward the island side of the drawbridge where Artair was held. The women and old men were all talking at once, each more desperate than the next to be heard. The children wailed. Artair was uncharacteristically quiet.

"What is going on?" Dylan forced his voice to be calm but loud enough to cut through the clamor. He wondered what had happened to the men who had returned with Artair. None of those who had fought at Glen Shiel were present, and Dylan hoped they would stay away. He looked around for Bedford, for this stank of him, but the Major was nowhere in sight.

MacCorkindale was in charge. He obliged Dylan with an angry reply. "You men are under arrest for making treasonous war against His Majesty, King George."

A fresh wail rose from the crowd, and they surged forward. Some of the dragoons turned muskets on the women and children. "Wait!" cried Dylan. He held his arms out for the crowd to stand back. They hushed and obeyed. The dragoons stood down.

Dylan's mind flew to know what to do. The arrest was not a surprise, but it also didn't explain the destroyed village. The piles of ashes were cold. The destruction was days old. He said, still calmly, "Where is Iain? He'll tell you there were no men sent to the rising."

The Lieutenant said, "The Laird is dead."

That shocked Dylan to the soles of his feet. *Dead?* He looked to Artair, but the young man was pale and silent. Dylan had never seen him like this.

MacCorkindale said, "A week ago. In a raid."

Artair didn't kill him, then. Good.

The Redcoat continued, his voice heavy with regret as well as recrimination, "Because Iain Mór sent men to fight against the Crown, as evidenced by the sword Artair carries, the entirety of Ciorram will be forfeit." Dylan boggled at the leap of logic just taken, but had known of men who were executed on less evidence. MacCorkindale motioned to his men that the prisoners should be taken away, and the soldiers began to shove them toward the horses across the bridge.

Dylan and Artair both shouted, "No!"

MacCorkindale halted the men and looked to Dylan and Artair each in turn. "A traitorous clan deserves eviction and exile."

Dylan said, "I'm the one—"

But Artair whirled and sucker-punched him. Dylan staggered into Robin, who caught him. Stars flashed in his vision and buzzed in his head, and for a moment it was an effort to stay conscious.

Dragoons grabbed both Artair and Dylan, but Artair rushed to say, "I'm the one who took the men, not him. Against the wishes of my brother, it was. I was the one carrying the sword, after all." He stared hard at Dylan in admonishment to shut up and listen. "I was armed when I was arrested. It's plain I've broken the law. Neither of these men were with us."

Dylan held a hand to his bleeding mouth, and hushed as he listened. What was the punk up to? As Iain's heir, his arrest would put the land straight into *Sassunach* hands! Then Artair said something Dylan had never dreamed could come from Artair.

"I'm nae the new Laird. I was never Iain's heir. The land was made over to Dylan when he married Cait. He had nothing to do with this. Neither Iain Mór nor Dylan Dubh approved of my adventure. I took the men. Nine of them, all dead in battle. It was me. Only me." The lad seemed deflated, but his eyes glittered with desperation that MacCorkindale believe him. Then he looked at Dylan and continued, "I couldnae bear the dishonor of letting other men take punishment for my actions. I couldnae then look my kinsmen in the eye."

Dylan was stunned. Artair was abdicating, on the chance of keeping the rest of Ciorram's men from being arrested. He'd been the only one caught with a sword, and so it was unlikely MacCorkindale would believe he'd not participated in the uprising. Since he was going to be arrested in any case, he was making himself the scapegoat, taking the consequence for everyone who had gone to Glen Shiel. He was denying the lairdship in order to protect the clan lands.

The Lieutenant peered at Artair, then at Dylan. MacCorkindale wasn't stupid, and was far from supportive of the cause, but also Dylan knew he was more likely than Bedford to give the benefit of any doubt if he thought it would keep the peace. He said to Artair, "You're nae the new Laird?"

Artair shook his head, his eyes to the ground. His ruddy cheeks flushed a bright red, and Dylan could tell what it took for him to do this. Artair stuffed his shaking hands into his armpits, tightly, as if hugging himself.

MacCorkindale turned to Dylan. "Is it true?"

Dylan slowly nodded and added, "Iain named me heir and signed the land over to me. He expressed a desire that his grandson would one day succeed me."

The light of understanding went on in MacCorkindale's eyes, and he nodded. That made sense.

And it wasn't exactly a lie. If it weren't for Dylan's marriage to Cait, making his son Iain's grandson, there would have been no question but that Iain's brother would have been preferred over his cousin. But MacCorkindale didn't need to know there was another paper naming Artair, so long as there was one naming Dylan.

But MacCorkindale then asked Dylan, "And where have you been these past weeks?"

Dylan gave the prepared lie, "I was in Glasgow, ordering my wife's gravestone."

"Took an uncommon long time, aye?"

Dylan nodded and let his voice take on a conversational tone, "Aye, it did. There was some trouble with the source for the marble. Transport costs were a mite high."

The Lieutenant frowned. "*Och*. Marble for a grave marker? A wee bit extravagant, don't ye think?"

Dylan lifted his chin, offended. "I loved my wife very much."

That brought a silence from MacCorkindale. He cleared his throat, gazed around at the gathered Mathesons, and announced, "I'm letting these men go, except for Artair Matheson." A murmur made its way through the crowd, and relief washed over Dylan. Artair was silent and still.

MacCorkindale continued, "However, I will arrest without hesitation any man who is later proven to have taken part in the disturbance." The Lieutenant must have known his threat was a weak one. Though there was a chance someone among the Hanoverians may have recognized someone among the Mathesons who had not died on the hill in Glen Shiel, it was unlikely, and it was a certainty nobody among the Jacobites would give testimony. It was easy enough for MacCorkindale to accept that Artair had taken only the nine who had not returned.

But the Lieutenant made clear his position on what had just happened as he shouted to the gathered clan. "Ken it well, all of you: the Crown cannae abide lawlessness. Any attempt to rescue this man will be met with the full wrath of His Majesty. You've a great deal of work ahead to rebuild your homes; I suggest ye get to it and never mind the cause anymore."

The speech was met with a dark silence. Even Dylan, who agreed with the sentiment, resented hearing the words from a man wearing the livery of the English Army, Scottish though he might be. MacCorkindale turned to mount his horse. The dirks and staff were returned to Dylan and Robin, but Artair's sword was retained, and they tied his hands together with a long rope. The soldiers also mounted. Artair was taken down the glen toward the garrison, walking at the end of that rope.

The entire clan watched him go, as they lost yet another kinsman to the English. Dylan looked down the glen at the departing figure of Artair and understood just how fickle was the fate that determined which Scots remained Scots and which were transported away to become Americans.

Finally, Robin said, "Ye're the Laird now, Dylan."

The realization struck Dylan breathless. *Laird.* Dylan Robert Matheson of Ciorram. There was a hysterical giggle from Sinann nearby, but he ignored her. This wasn't a time for laughter. Not by a long shot.

Neither was it the time to dwell on things he couldn't control. He looked around at the crowd and began to move through them toward the castle. *His* castle. Everyone began to talk at once, asking about food and what to do about their houses and kine. Everyone in the glen had lost a great deal in the raid they'd suffered. Over them all, he shouted, "Where are my children?"

Nobody could say. Nana offered that she'd seen them playing in the bailey earlier in the day, but that was all.

"Where's Sarah?"

"*Och*, Sarah was taken by the raiders," said Nana.

Dylan stopped cold and turned. "What?"

"She's not been seen since they came."

This wasn't making any sense. He called for Malcolm and hurried through the bailey as quickly as the crowd would let him. Robin followed close behind. Dylan shouted, "Malcolm! Is he still alive?" The women affirmed he was, so Dylan called again. *"Malcolm!"* Where was the old man? Too many things to do at once. Too many people were talking, vying for his attention, looking to him to solve everything.

Apparently, half the clan had been camped in and around the castle since the raid. Cook fires dotted the bailey, and little mounds of salvaged belongings were here and there. The sharp smell of burnt cloth and leather permeated everything.

Then men began to appear. The five who had returned with Artair came out of hiding. Tormod, among them, demanded to know what had happened to Artair, and one of the women began to explain as Dylan headed into the Great Hall.

He stopped in the middle of the room, closed his eyes for a moment, and focused. The clan. The clan came first. Though his first urge was to tear the castle apart in search of his kids, there were hundreds of people crowding into the room behind him who needed their own lives addressed. He turned to face his people.

More men arrived. Ailis began to ask after Marc, but went ignored as the men struggled to grasp what had happened to the village and to Artair.

Then, in the midst of it, Tormod drew his sword and shouted, "No!

Dylan Dubh is *nae* the rightful heir! I shallnae follow him!" Several other swords were drawn.

Women screamed and cleared away from the center of the room, hauling with them any child within reach. Tormod and others loyal to Artair faced off against men who had pledged to Dylan.

Dylan muttered, "Stick a fork in me, Sinann, 'cause I'm done." Fed to the teeth, Dylan stepped in between the two groups, drew Brigid and shouted, "I'll tell you what, Tormod. Let's fight this out—you and me, one-on-one. If you think you can kill me, be my guest. Then you can go get yourselves killed rescuing Artair, and I won't be in a position to give a damn one way or the other. My men will follow you if you win." He turned and addressed Robin and the rest. "Right, men? You'll pledge your loyalty to Tormod if he can kill me, right?"

The fifteen or so of Dylan's men lowered their weapons, many with amusement twitching at the corners of their mouths. They nodded and agreed to the terms.

Dylan turned back to Tormod. "See? So, let's fight. You kill me, you're in charge, and you go get Artair. I kill you, I'm the Laird. Sound good?"

Tormod's face was drawn and white. He looked to Dùghlas and Colin, but everyone in the room knew there would be no fight. It was well known Dylan would take no more than a second or two to kill Tormod. In the entire clan, there was nobody to challenge Dylan.

He lowered Brigid and said to the room, "Listen up, everyone! Artair sacrificed himself to save the clan, and I won't take that away from him by leading our few men straight into the teeth of a garrison filled with soldiers who are at this very moment sharpening their swords in expectation of our arrival."

Then he turned to Tormod, and anger put an edge on his voice. "You want to commit suicide, Tormod, I'll load you a pistol and let you have at it. But I've had enough defeat in the name of a lost cause for one week, thank you, and there is more pressing business at hand now. Our women and children need food, and they need homes. Sarah's been kidnapped." That caught the blacksmith's attention, and he lowered his sword, completely stunned. The men beside him followed suit to listen, and Dylan continued. "Our enemies today are the raiders who stole from us. To get Sarah back, I'll need every man who can carry a sword. Think twice, Tormod, about killing Mathesons today."

After a long silence, the remaining drawn swords were sheathed. Dylan looked around the room and said, "All right, then. Let's get to work on what's important." He turned away.

The men nodded in agreement.

But then Dylan turned back, touched Brigid to Tormod's solar plexus and added casually but in a hardened voice that would brook no disrespect, "And Tormod . . . try something like that again, and be assured I will have you hung. The only reason you're not headed for the guardhouse right now is that I need your sword to help rescue Sarah. I expect you're the second most motivated soul here to do it."

Tormod paled and nodded, knowing he was getting off lightly for inciting treason. He also knew Dylan absolutely would have him executed at the next sign of insurrection. "Aye, sir."

Dylan turned to his most loyal man. "Robin, lad. Take what's left of the castle guard. Find out how many households were burned out, and begin cutting peats for new houses." Robin hurried to comply, and most of those assembled went with him for the sake of having their homes rebuilt.

To Eóin he said, "Go find Ciaran and Sìle." The boy took off, running.

Dylan then turned to Nana. "Coinneach lies on the table in my house. Tend to him. And understand I expect a fair price for the winding sheet." Young Ena, in the midst of the crowd, cried out in dismay and began elbowing her way from the crowd, in tears. They all watched her go, silent.

Nana then said, "Linen is at a premium now, sir."

Dylan was firm. "I mean it. The price will be reasonable." Dùghlas would pay the burial costs, but Dylan was taking a special interest as Laird. "The boy died honorably."

Nana also hurried to comply, but paused when he added, "And don't be bleeding Seumas. He's lost quite enough of it already. And boil the thread and needle before you sew him up." A look crossed Nana's face, and he added, tired of having to explain this, "Don't argue, just do it."

She nodded and hurried away.

Ailis asked again where Marc was, fearful now that it was apparent there had been many deaths. When she was told in a low voice by one of the men her husband had been one of those deaths, she sat down hard on a stool. Dylan then announced the names of the others who would not be returning, and widows began to wail. Some hurried from the room, and others sat on benches to weep, consoled by other women. The men stared at each other, the two factions still wary and none of them comfortable witnessing the outburst of emotion.

Dylan addressed Gracie in a low voice. "How are the castle stores? How much was lost in the raid?" As he spoke, he removed his coat, slipped the buttons on his sark, and peeled the filthy linen from his back to examine the wound on his arm. The women nearby made an alarmed clucking, and one of them scurried away to the kitchen. A moment later, she was back with a steaming bowl and some towels.

Gracie thought a moment, then replied, "There's not a head of kine in the glen, for they were all pastured together and were easily herded off. Some sheep were left, being scattered about, and the flock of Cheviots on yer own land was untouched. But a good many sheep were taken, and many of those left behind were killed. From spite, I expect. Only the farthest outlying farms were spared any livestock."

The kitchen maid dabbed at the dried blood covering his upper arm, gradually finding her way to the wound itself. The flesh around it was revealed to be swollen and purple. The old blood smell was beginning to turn rank, and it curdled his stomach. The maid dipped one end of a towel into the water to dab some more.

Dylan continued questioning Gracie as the maid tended to him. "Was it the MacDonells?"

Everyone in the room shook their heads, and a murmur in the negative riffled throughout. Gracie said, " 'Twas the English."

Dylan frowned and sat on a trestle table to listen. The maid moved with him for a better position beside him to work.

"Soldiers?" That made no sense.

"Nae. 'Twas a band of English thieves. Some Lowland Scots, but many English. They came on horses, with guns and swords."

"And you could tell they weren't Highlanders in breeches because . . ."

"Because they were a-shouting to each other and sounding for all the world like dukes and earls on the hunt. And they rode horses. Fancy big Thoroughbreds, and they ran us down like quarry."

Dylan didn't figure there were any actual dukes or earls in the party, for he knew that to his kinsmen any English accent sounded ruling class. He asked, "How many men?"

She shrugged. "Fifty, perhaps. Maybe less. I dinnae think to count them."

"Where were the garrison soldiers at the time?"

She shrugged again. "Not here, for a certainty."

"Bedford was gone?" Dylan knew the Major hadn't been sent to Inverness when the forces had gathered against the Jacobites. Bedford's men had not been at Glen Shiel, or they would not have arrived back in Ciorram so soon to arrest Artair.

Gracie nodded. "The day before, the entire garrison had gone. On patrol, we figured. We dinnae ken where. It was a pleasure to see them go, and we never thought for a moment we could wish for them back. But with all the men gone . . ." She fell silent and her face reddened.

Una, who sat on a nearby bench, spoke up. Everyone fell silent, turned, and listened. "Were it not for the tyranny of the English, the men wouldnae have been away fighting their army, and we wouldnae have wished for the protection of that army from English raiders. Our own men would have been here." Her voice was low, but carrying. Dylan looked over at her and saw deep pain.

His voice softened, "How did Iain die?"

"My husband was the only man of fighting age left in the glen. He defended his lands and his people. He wounded but one of the raiders, and they killed him. They also killed Dùghlas's wife, and Keith Rómach's as well, as they defended their property and children."

Dylan blanched. It was beginning to look like the English would win, with so many Mathesons dead in so short a time. If the raid happened a week ago, the dead were already buried in the churchyard. Coinneach would join them sometime that night. Dylan ran his fingers into his hair and leaned his elbow on his knee for a long moment.

He then sat up and looked around at the faces of the clan. He took a deep breath and straightened, drew his sark back on, then his coat, and readjusted his plaid. "Well. Everyone tend to your business as you can. There's plowing to be done and children to look after. Peats will be cut for new houses, and food will be obtained. But first, we'll find these men and make them pay." He addressed Tormod directly. "We're going to find Sarah. Alive."

The reaction from the folks gathered around let him know this was the only thing he could have said that would have eased their minds.

Nothing but revenge against the raiders would have saved their honor and their sense of security.

The door from the corridor opened, and Dylan looked. "Malcolm!" The clansmen hushed and turned to look as well. Malcolm entered the Great Hall. Moving slowly with the help of his staff, for the condition that would surely kill him one day appeared to cause him great pain, he approached Dylan across the stone floor. Kinsmen parted to let him through.

Dylan stood, his pulse picking up. In Malcolm's hand, its baldric hanging from the scabbard, was the silver-hilted sword of King James.

Standing before Dylan, Malcolm straightened as best he could, looked him in the eye, and said, "Dylan Dubh, this sword was given to yer great-great grandfather, for service to His Majesty, King James I and VI." His papery voice faded a bit, and he cleared his throat to continue at a stronger volume for the room to hear. "For a century it has been handed down with the lairdship of the Ciorram Mathesons. Our clan has suffered terribly under the yoke of oppression. Many are dead, and more will die this winter for lack of food. We now look to you for the leadership the murdering English have brutally taken from us." He held out the sword for Dylan to take.

The intricate, swirling work of the swept-design hilt shone pale. Moon-like. Dylan had never in his life even touched such a fine weapon. When he'd first seen this sword, five years before, he'd coveted it only for its beauty. He'd thought only as a hobbyist, admiring a piece he'd thought would have been a nice thing to have.

But now, after all he'd gone through with his kinsmen, he understood fully the responsibility this sword symbolized. He was Laird. He controlled everything and everyone within Glen Ciorram. By *Sassunach* law he owned the land. By clan law, and according to the inherited jurisdiction still recognized by the Crown, he was empowered to judge and pass sentence on local lawbreakers. Every soul in the glen now looked to him to solve their problems and their squabbles, and to guide their future amid increasingly hostile national politics.

Furthermore, immediate concerns were pressing. The next few weeks, even the next few days, might spell the life or death of his people over the following twelve months. Livestock and seed corn needed to be found and bought, finagled or reived if the clan was to survive another winter.

Sinann said, as she had said repeatedly for more than five years, "Ye must save yer people, Dylan."

He looked at her, and finally knew she was right.

CHAPTER 24

Dylan received the broadsword reverently. He lifted the baldric over his shoulder so the scabbard hung at his side, then lightly touched the pommel. He shook Malcolm's hand and thanked him.

The remaining clansmen and women began to disperse, some coming to congratulate him and others merely slapping him heartily on the back as they passed. In general, the feeling seemed to be of relief. The clan had a new leader and all would be set right again. Dylan turned his mind to issues closer to his heart.

He whispered to Sinann, "Where are the children?"

She shrugged.

"If Nana saw them this morning, they weren't taken or killed by the raiders." He headed for the corridor leading to the towers, and Sinann kept pace, running, then fluttering in the air.

"Are ye certain Sarah is yet alive?"

Dylan stopped cold in his tracks, feeling like all the air had been punched from him. His voice low and strained, he said, "She must be. She has to be. It would be . . ."

"Now, I'll just rest here a moment," said Malcolm once the room had emptied. He eased himself carefully onto a nearby bench and leaned on his staff. "I'll just wait here whilst you go find yer son and daughter. And I'll give ye a hint, which may shorten the search a bit: as the soldiers were crossing the drawbridge a while ago, when they found Artair, I saw the weans run into the stable. But never did the searching *Sassunaich* flush them out."

Dylan grinned as he realized what had happened. "Thanks." He spun on his heel and ran from the Great Hall through the bailey entry.

Across the bailey, he burst into the stable. "Ciaran! Sìle! Hey!"

The kids appeared from thin air, sitting on the rickety table at the end of the room. "Da!" Ciaran had the talisman in his hand and his other arm around Sìle. He scrambled from the table and ran to his father, while Sìle tried to climb down by herself. Too short for her legs to reach the floor, and unable to see how far to drop, she dangled and wailed. Dylan took Ciaran into one arm and went to rescue her. He scooped her into his other arm and hoisted her around to his chest. Sìle buried her face in his coat and began to cry as he sat on the table with them both.

Ciaran's words tumbled over themselves. "Da! The English came! We came in here, and Sìle wanted to hide under the straw, but I said no, because when folks tell stories, they all tell how the English when they search for people poke their swords and bayonets in the straw, and we got on the table, and when they came in they put their swords in the straw like in the stories, but they never poked the air over the table, and so they dinnae find us!"

Dylan hugged Ciaran. "Good lad. It's a smart son I've got."

Sìle was heaving great, shaking sobs. Dylan sat Ciaran on the table next to him, then enveloped Sìle in his arms so she could burrow into his plaid and coat where it was safe. He murmured, "It's all right, wee one. The bad men have gone." Over and over, he assured her the *Sassunaich* were gone, but refrained from claiming they wouldn't be back. For he knew they would return eventually. Patiently, he let her cry it all out. Ciaran muttered about what a baby Sìle was, but Dylan shushed him.

When Sìle's crying wound down to a snuffle, he rose, still holding her inside his plaid. He helped Ciaran down from the table and took the children across the bailey. In the Great Hall, he sent Gracie for some food, since he hadn't eaten with the men earlier and was now feeling the hunger of nearly twenty-four hours without food. He sat himself and the children at one of the trestle tables to wait. Sìle was recovering now, and he dried her red eyes with the sleeve of his sark. He got her to play some peek-a-boo, and she began to brighten.

Robin arrived, sat across the table from Dylan, and gave a comprehensive report on the status of burned homes in the glen. Most of the damage, it seemed, had been done to the houses closest to the castle, but a few outlying places to the east had been hit. Even a couple of tenants half a day's walk from the village were now homeless. Trying to rebuild all the houses at once would leave the glen short of fuel for the winter, so the cutting of peats would have to move at a slower pace unless they dug from another bog. There were no others nearby of that size, but there was a small one farther up the loch shore and closer to the shielings. If it proved inadequate to the task, they would have to either delay rebuilding or go into debt to surrounding clans for building materials.

Dylan thanked him for the information and told him to continue cutting as much peat as could be taken. Robin hurried to obey, and Dylan then turned his attention to the next issue submitted by a waiting Matheson.

Dùghlas asked when they would bury poor Coinneach.

"Full dark," was Dylan's decision. Everyone with an immediate interest in the funeral should turn out in the bailey to accompany the body to the churchyard, and nobody else. No sense in attracting the attention of the garrison across the way. Coinneach would be given respectful burial on holy ground, but in utter silence. There was no priest to provide the formalities in any case, so it mattered little what might be said or not said over the corpse. Dùghlas went to organize the funeral.

A bowl of stewed mutton and a wooden plate stacked with bannocks came, a surfeit of food Dylan shared with the children. Ciaran asked, "Why is everyone asking you all these things, father?"

Dylan swallowed hard, and thought for a moment of how to approach this. He finally said, "Do you know what happened to your grandfather?"

Ciaran nodded. "He died in battle with the raiders. I saw it. They cut him with a sword, and he fell down." The boy's voice had an edge, as if he were struggling to sound brave and matter-of-fact, like a grown man, about having witnessed the bloody death of his grandfather.

Dylan said, "Right. So, since he is no longer able to be Laird, someone else has to be."

Ciaran nodded, and said, "Artair."

"No, Artair can't be next." Dylan sighed. "The English got him, too.

They won't kill him, but will most likely send him to America. That means I've got to be the Laird since I'm the next closest male relative." Sile fussed for the last of his bannock, even though there was another on the plate, and he gave it to her. She banged her heels against his shin as she chewed on the oat bread.

The little boy's mouth opened as if he would say something, but nothing came out, and his eyes flashed with one fleeting emotion after another. Finally, he said in a voice that was very, very small, "They'll kill you, too."

Dylan shook his head. "No, they will not. I'll be the kind of laird the English won't want to kill." At least, he hoped the Ciorram Mathesons would allow him to lead them into a less contentious relationship with the English occupiers. Further, he hoped he could stave off the assault on their religion at the same time. It was a dodgy proposition, religious conflicts being what they were, and there was an excellent chance he would fail on all counts.

Ciaran said, "Even after you kill the raiders for taking Sarah?"

Dylan frowned. "What do you know about Sarah and the raiders?"

"They scooped her up, right off her feet. When they killed Grandfather, Grandmother ran to get him. The one who killed Grandfather was going to kill her, too, but Sarah stopped him. She took a big stick and hit him right across the back with it. Like this." He demonstrated with an imaginary stick like swinging a baseball bat. "He turned his horse, and she ran off, but he caught up to her and picked her up. She was across the front of his saddle, kicking and all, and he rode away with her."

"She was alive when you saw her?"

Ciaran nodded. "They rode away with her, just like that. I thought it was Major Bedford, but it was just his horse instead."

Dylan frowned. "The Major's horse? Are you sure?"

"Aye. The big, wild one with the white markings. He was a-prancing, and a-pawing the air like a puppy."

"But it wasn't the Major himself?"

Ciaran shook his head. "Nae. He's got light hair. This fellow had none at all."

Dylan fell silent as he finished his supper. After eating, he let the children visit with Gracie in the kitchen while he went to Iain's office.

His office.

He closed the door behind him, then turned to survey the room. *Deep breath. Let it out slowly.* He ran all his fingers through his hair.

The arrow loops were closed tight, leaving only slivers of bright orange sunset to stretch across the stone floor. He lit candles—there were many on candelabra about the room—then he laid some peats on the low fire in the hearth. Across the room the large desk beckoned, and the red-upholstered chair behind it. They were his now also, but he wasn't ready for that.

But there was a folded paper on it. He picked it up and opened it. The paper was heavy and stiff in his fingers, freighted with importance in a time when paper was expensive and writing skills hard to come by. It was the deed transfer signing Ciorram over to himself, dated five years before. Dylan wondered whether Iain had actually written this so long ago or if he'd simply backdated it. No matter. It would save the clan from eviction, regardless. Malcolm had surely destroyed the other paper before bringing him the sword.

Dylan then opened the secret passage to hang the King's sword where it wouldn't be found in the event of another search. Exhausted, he slumped into a chair by the hearth to think.

So many killed, wounded, and taken prisoner in the past week! Coinneach, Marc, Iain, seven other men, and the wives of Dùghlas and Keith. Dùghlas himself. Seumas. Artair. Sarah. Dylan ran his fingers into his hair and leaned on his elbow. Until now Dylan had not had time to think of the losses, but here, in the silence, they crowded him; each one appalling in itself and the full impact of the sum overwhelming.

He began to tremble. As his eyes closed, a single tear fell over his cheek and into his beard. Too many Mathesons gone. Already the clan was diminishing. More than ever, he despised the English.

To the tapestry, he said, "Sinann, I've got to go find her."

The faerie popped into sight. "Of course, ye do. Ye cannae let a kinswoman be taken by the enemy, nae matter who the enemy and nae matter who the woman. The clan wouldnae respect ye, were ye to stay at home."

Dylan nodded, for he understood his duty. "But," he said, "I would go after her if she weren't Alasdair's widow and Eóin and Gregor's mother."

Her voice softened. "Ye truly care for her, then?"

A disgusted noise rasped in the back of his throat. "Of course, I do. I always did."

"As a kinswoman."

He shrugged. "Yeah. Even when Cait and I were together, I respected her for a kind woman and a good mother."

"But now . . ."

His heart clenched, and he no longer wanted to dig through his feelings. It was like poking a dead, smelly animal. So he said, "I couldn't save Cait, but maybe there's a chance to save Sarah. I want her back. Bedford's got her, I want her back."

"It would seem he does have her. He or someone allied with him who now rides the horse."

Then Dylan remembered and sat up in the chair. "*Felix*. That weasel! Last time I saw that horse, Felix was riding it."

"But Felix isnae bald."

"He wears a . . ." Dylan blinked with the realization. "He wears a wig that won't stay straight. He's got no hair under there." His blood sang with excitement. "It was Felix. He's got her. But where did he take her?"

The faerie shrugged. "I surely cannae say. Even more, I cannae say what he and Bedford might want with her."

That threw Dylan into deep thought. What *could* Bedford want with Sarah? She was just an unattached woman, not particularly significant politically, and her clan not able to pay ransom even if that were a common thing to ask for the return of folks who were not rich. As far as Bedford might know, Sarah was nothing more than a kitchen maid nobody would miss.

Dylan blinked. *Someone nobody would miss.* "The white slaver," he muttered.

Sinann's attention perked. "The good ship *Spirit*?"

"Aye. You remember in Edinburgh when we saw those people taken away, and Bedford said it was to Singapore. Where you said they don't think of whites as people. He and Ramsay were in partnership; Bedford obtained the warm, insignificant bodies, and Ramsay transported them. Robin and I saw Felix at the garrison. I'll bet he's taken over where Ramsay left off."

"But you never learned where Bedford was keeping the prisoners. Surely he isnae so bold as to hold them in the Tolbooth for the *Spirit*'s arrival."

Dylan shook his head. "It wasn't at the docks, either, or Seumas would have found them." He stood, ready to charge into the night after Sarah, but with no idea what direction to go. "They've got a week's head start on us. Sinann, what if she's already on the ship, headed for—"

There was a knock on the door.

He turned to answer. "Aye?"

A young voice came from the other side. Eóin. "Dylan Dubh, Coinneach in his winding sheet is in the bailey now. The party is gathered to take him to the churchyard."

"All right. I'll be along in a moment." Dylan stood and ran his fingers through his hair as he collected himself, then went to do his duty as laird to the honored dead.

It was a furtive funeral, accomplished in utter silence by the gray light of the quarter moon and attended only by Dylan, Coinneach's immediate family consisting of Dùghlas and two sisters, Ena, and Robin and Tormod who helped Dylan and Dùghlas carry the corpse. As soon as the grave was filled in, the burial party left, each headed straight home without a word. One more grave among those who had died the week before would go unnoticed by the garrison.

Making his way back to the castle, Dylan thought hard, trying to figure out where Bedford could be holding Sarah. He knew it had to be near Edinburgh, for several years ago he'd witnessed a surreptitious departure of the slaver's prisoners from the docks there. But even though he'd put Seumas on the alert at the time to find the holding facility, none had been found in the area. The place where Sarah was imprisoned could be anywhere.

It was midnight or so by the time he and Sinann climbed the West Tower to the guest room. Ciaran and Sìle had been put to bed. He crept soundlessly in, closed the door behind him, and stood for a moment by the bed, candle in hand, to watch his children sleep. They were angels. So much like himself, yet with the promise of becoming so much more than himself. So much better.

He needed to sleep also, but knew that if he got into the bed he would accomplish nothing more than waking up the kids. Sleep would elude him. So he put the candlestick on the wash stand and sat on the short stool by the fire to feed it another peat. Sinann appeared at his side, cross-legged on the floor.

"Rest, laddie," she whispered.

Dylan shook his head. "I can't. I've got to figure out how to find Sarah. If I go blundering about the countryside near Edinburgh, I'll never find her. They'll kill her or take her away if they catch wind I'm looking. There's got to be another way."

Staring at the fire, an idea began to form. He said slowly, "Sinann . . . Ramsay knew where the place is."

"Of course, he did."

"Wherever he is, his soul must still know. There's a spell—"

"No! Ye're nae strong enough." Sinann fluttered into the air, alarmed.

Dylan shushed her, though the children couldn't hear her. "I have to be. I've got to find her."

"But a spirit from the other side . . .'tis different from conjuring a living soul. You never can tell what might happen when you breach the divide. To control it takes a power ye cannae imagine."

Dylan looked up at her. "I have to try."

"No."

"Yes. I must."

She landed on her feet and straightened, a victorious look in her eye as if she were about to deliver the fatal blow to the argument. "Ye have naught of Ramsay's with which to cast the spell. For this ye must have something that was his, and you've spent the gold ye took off the body, and burnt the clothes."

"I have his sword. That rapier."

Sinann shook her head. "Nae. 'Tis nae longer his. 'Twas used in battle by Robin. He's killed with it."

Dylan frowned. Then his hand went to the front of his sark. Where had those teeth gone? When was the last time he'd seen them? "The teeth. Ramsay's teeth. Where are they?"

"Did ye nae throw them in the loch?"

He shook his head. "No. I was going to, but never did. Something happened . . ." Then he remembered. "They fell out of my sark when I came in here to sleep that night. They landed on the floor. I don't remember putting them back in my sark the next morning."

Sinann made a disgusted noise. "Ye *lost* them? Ye lost relics of the man who killed yer wife? Shame on you!"

Dylan muttered reluctant agreement, for it had, indeed, been careless. Relics could be powerful things in the wrong hands, and having Ramsay's teeth just lying around for anyone to find might have led to terrible things. He picked up the candle from the washstand to search. The bundle wasn't on top of any of the furniture, so he opened the armoire and began looking in drawers. "Nothing. They're not in here. The chambermaids would have put them somewhere in the room if they'd been found."

"Do ye think one of the maids could have taken them?"

Dylan shook his head. "Don't even think it. They've got to be here somewhere." His voice drifted off as he ran out of places to look inside the armoire, wash stand, and trunk. He looked around, thinking hard. "They were on the floor. They couldn't have just walked away by themselves."

"Ye should hope they dinnae leave by Ramsay's ghost!"

He threw her a dark glance and went to the stool by the hearth where he'd dropped his clothes that night. There was nothing on the floor. He searched the area around the hearth. It had been months since he'd lost those teeth—they could be anywhere. He looked beside the armoire and the wash stand. Nothing. Then he knelt by the bed to look under it.

Over the years of living in this low-tech century, he'd gradually lost his longing for most conveniences from the future. He'd grown accustomed to walking everywhere he went and warming himself by an open fire, among other things. But now he wished for a flashlight. The candle in his hand wasn't much use for lighting up dark, cramped spaces, and he disliked putting it under the bed, lest he set the mattress on fire. But as he peered into the flickering shadows it seemed there was a light-colored wad near the wall at the head of the bed. He set the candle on the floor and slipped underneath to feel around among the dust bunnies.

His hand found the small linen bundle filled with Ramsay's teeth. "I've got it. I've got the teeth."

Sinann made a worried hum and fidgeted as he backed out from under the bed. "Dinnae try the spell. Ye cannae take the risk, lad. Ye haven't the strength."

"You taught me." He stood and picked up the candle from the floor as he hefted the rattling bundle and shook a cobweb from his hair. "I was the novice of the granddaughter of the sea god Lir, remember? No longer novice. I'm powerful enough to make even the Morrighan nervous."

"Ye dinnae often notice the Morrighan raising the dead, do ye?"

A shiver raced up Dylan's spine. He said, "No. But I don't have a wide selection of options now. Come with me if you like. Or you can stay here with the kids, just in case something goes wrong and they need your protection."

She nodded. "I'll stay here with the weans, then." That gave Dylan serious pause. For the first time ever, the faerie was volunteering to watch over Dylan's loved ones instead of himself. She was that afraid of what he was about to bring from the other side. "Aye. I'll stay here. They'll need me if the spell goes awry, and there will be nothing whatever for me to do for you in that case."

Dylan's hand closed over the linen-wrapped bundle. "All right. I'll return when I've learned where Sarah is being held."

Sinann's only reply as he left the room was a couple of words in the old tongue, which he recognized as a ward against evil.

CHAPTER 25

To leave the castle in secrecy from both Mathesons and *Sassunaich*, and guarantee he wouldn't be followed, Dylan exited through the secret passage. He placed in his sporran the bundle of teeth and a black cloth, then hauled on the heavy bookcase. Reluctantly it opened, with much grinding of wood on stone. It was a wonder the thing had managed to stay a secret, as much as it took to open and close.

He then picked up a beeswax candle from the candelabra and yanked hard on the door to shut it behind him. The candle lit his way down stone steps that seemed to continue into the heart of the earth, the walls rough-hewn, solid stone. As he proceeded, his fingertips brushed the living rock walls and disturbed the cold dampness weeping from them. The floor of the tunnel was ankle deep in ice-cold water. When he came to dry stone and the floor began to rise, he knew he was on the mainland. The floor rose steadily, occasionally breaking up into shallow steps when the slope was too steep for walking.

At last he came to a heavy wooden door supported by mortared stones set in living rock, and set his shoulder against it to shove it open. Now he was in a cave behind a cluster of boulders. A burn rushed past beyond them, seeming far too loud and lively for the middle of the night, and he knew exactly where he was. It was the spot where the burn from the wooded hills to the north made a rapid descent for a few yards. Not quite a fall, but there was much white water tumbling over very large rocks.

Up one of the boulders he climbed, taking care on the moss and lichens. Then up the steep, forested hill from the burn and through dense thickets, to the track that ran from Glen Ciorram to the faerie tower. Stopping briefly to cut a number of willow sticks from a large, old tree, he then followed the track upward until it branched. He took the steeper branch to the top of the wooded hill.

The clearing on the summit was huge and well-used, marked in the middle by a large site for bonfires. This was the place where the clan celebrated festivals and holidays en masse, for it was of high elevation and had a wide exposure to the sky, yet was flat and large enough to accommodate many people. It was here Cait had jumped the Beltane fire the night they'd conceived Ciaran, and here Dylan had learned how well he belonged to the people of Ciorram. This year, however, there would be no festivals so long as the English were stirred up. Dylan went to the edge of the ashes and set down the candle and all his willow sticks, save one.

He knelt, and with Brigid he began to carve a series of slanted notches along the side of that stick. In Ogam letters, Ramsay's full name took up the entire stick. He set it to the side and laid the bundle of teeth next to it. With some wood and kindling left from the last bonfire, he lit a small fire among the ashes.

Once it was burning nicely, he stood and stripped to the skin. Every stitch, from *feileadh mór* to stockings, was laid in a pile off to the side, leaving only the crucifix and gold ring hung around his neck.

Skyclad now, covered only by the night air and as near to the sky as he could come, he took deep breaths to fill himself with it. Goose bumps rose all over him, and his pulse surged. He could feel every inch of skin where his body met the night, and it made him gasp with exhilaration.

It was time to focus. What he was about to do would take strength he wasn't certain he had, and if he failed to control the power, it could kill him. He knew this just as he knew he would die in a swordfight if he didn't kill the other guy first. Control was everything. He shook back his hair from his eyes and began.

Standing with his weight balanced, he threw his head back and in both hands raised Brigid toward the sliver of waning moon, low in the west. Silver light glinted from the hilt and blade. He focused his energy to his center and imagined the power of the moon entering Brigid and traveling down through his hands, his arms, to his body. It filled him, entering every corner of him until his skin tingled and his breaths came in rapid gasps.

He bent and put the willow sticks on the fire, leaving the carved one on the ground beside it. Willow represented death.

A thin line of dense smoke lifted straight into the air. Dylan took the cloth of black wool and held it in the smoke, then to his face as he breathed deeply the scent. The power of the willow joined in him with that of the moon and of himself. He began to sway as he focused.

Slowly, and in a low voice, in the old tongue he uttered a chant. Far older than Gaelic, it was a language he didn't speak but only knew a few special phrases Sinann had taught him for practicing the Craft. This chant was a request for death. Crossing over, nearly to the other side, was necessary to bring back Ramsay.

Over and over, he voiced the words and breathed smoke from the black cloth. The power in him grew, and he trembled with it. The air vibrated. More loudly, he spoke the words. A charge ran through him, a direct line from the sky to the earth. His back arched, and he threw his arms wide to the moon. The ground heaved. The air split.

He went cold to his core. Whistling wind blew straight through his bones. Sharp agony pierced them, and he uttered a cry. It took all his strength to stay conscious. Movement was further pain, but he bent for the Ogam stick and held it up to the moon.

Bestowed with its own power now, and marked with Ramsay's name, the stick was now ready to toss onto the fire. Dylan followed it with the bundle of teeth.

Now he had to wait, all the while struggling to keep the portal open without letting himself be blown through it by the currents of power. He reeled but stayed firm, standing before the fire as his mind searched for Ramsay. The air reeked of decay. He felt evil in him, turning the edges of his soul black. Despair crept in on him. The pain was hideous.

"Ramsay!" he shouted.

There was no reply but the whine of bitter emptiness.

"Ramsay!" The trembling became violent shaking. His body felt ready to pull to shreds with the strain. He reached through the passage with his mind, but when it touched Ramsay's, he wanted to pull away. More than anything, he wanted to yank himself back, slam the passage shut, and get as far away from this spot as he could.

Ramsay's soul was unspeakable evil, a morass of perversion, morally vacant. Like seepage, it entered the world through Dylan, leaving behind the gasping horror of things it had done as a man while still alive. In that moment, Dylan knew intimately what had happened to his wife. He was Ramsay. He saw her tears as he raped her, and heard her scream his name again and again, beseeching for rescue that would come far too late. He felt the resistance of her neck as the bayonet pierced it through, sticking into the table beneath. Her warm blood spilled over his hands. She struggled with her last strength. He was still inside her.

Dylan cried out, frantic to make it go away but helpless to unring the bell of knowledge. His chest heaved for air. Hot tears spilled onto his cold cheeks.

Ramsay's blackened teeth flew from the fire, whirled through the air, and arranged themselves before Dylan as they had been while in Ramsay's mouth. Two rows of bodiless teeth floated, surrounded by a ghostly, translucent image of Ramsay's former body. Dressed in his customary doeskin and silk velvet, he stood casually, looking about as if mildly interested in the high clearing. Insufferably blasé as ever, he then peered at Dylan with drowsy, hooded eyes.

Dylan struggled to keep standing. His knees longed to buckle. The cold was appalling. Breathing felt like frozen knives in his chest. "Where is she?"

Languid in death as in life, Ramsay replied with clicking teeth, "Who?"

"Sarah. Where's Sarah?" Dylan gasped as he weakened. He couldn't keep this up much longer.

Impatient now, Ramsay's incorporeal image drifted and swayed in the air. "What Sarah? Have you forgotten your whore already, then? She's no longer your one and only? Fickle you. I might not have bothered killing her, had I known you wouldn't give a damn."

Dylan spoke through clenched teeth. *"Where does Bedford keep the prisoners for the white slaver?"*

The teeth clattered and clicked with laughter. "Ah. That. I haven't the first inkling."

"Ramsay!"

More derisive laughter. "Oh, all right, I do. You've worn me down, imposing warlock that you are." He sighed. "I suppose if I don't tell you, you'll . . . what, kill me?"

Dylan's own voice was thready, weakening. "More than likely, you'll kill me instead. Right here. You'll take me with you into death, and I'll be at your throat till the end of time." He could feel himself being pulled to the other side. His flesh weakened, and it would be so sweet to just let go and make the pain stop. . . .

Ramsay sighed. "Well, then, we cannae have that. So I'll tell ye. Bedford's hiding yer Sarah in the Edinburgh Tolbooth."

"No, he's not. Truth, Ramsay. I've been in the Tolbooth. Try again."

"Aye, he is. There's another level of detention cells, below the ones commonly used."

Even if Dylan weren't dead certain there were no secret underground cells, he was absolutely sure Bedford was not hiding anyone there. He knew better than to think Bedford would run his illicit prisoners straight under the noses of his superiors, where the least slipup would cost him his career, if not his life.

He said, still holding onto Ramsay's spirit, "Thank you, Connor. I look forward to investigating the Tolbooth. You won't mind my giving you another call if I have any trouble finding Sarah, aye? You'll be glad to see me again, I expect, and you're not going anywhere that I can't find you. Forever."

There was a bit of a silence, then Ramsay said, his voice filled with real disgust, "Oh, all right. Bedford owns a bit of property outside Edinburgh, along the road to Glasgow. The old Robertson farm, known for its tremendous large barn. A great deal of room for things the Major cannae admit possessing."

Dylan clenched his teeth, resisting the pain, and said, "And billeting for about fifty men the Major can't admit hiring."

There was more chittering laughter from the floating teeth. "Aye, lad. Now, let me go lest ye die here before me and I will be forced to bear your uninspired company far longer than I could stand."

Dylan muttered, "By all means, then, go to hell," and he let his mind release Ramsay. The teeth whirled, picked up speed, and finally the image disappeared and the teeth fell to the ground. The passage closed, and Dylan collapsed before the waning fire.

It was a long moment as Dylan struggled to stay conscious. The world spun, and distances seemed deceptive. Changing. Then he crawled to the pile of his clothing. He pulled on his sark, shivering hard enough to make his teeth rattle like Ramsay's. Carefully he gathered the dead man's teeth together, mindful to find all twenty-eight of them, then he struggled to his feet and went to the bonfire ashes. He buried the teeth in the pit. Once they were covered, he stood, lifted the hem of his sark, and urinated on the spot to keep Ramsay's ghost from returning unbidden.

Still unable to calm his shaking, he bundled his clothes and dirk together to carry them back through the passage to the castle. He had no candle left and made his way by feel. The slimy cold and pitch dark went on and on. It seemed eternal. The weeping rock wall was deathly cold, and the water at his feet seemed to leach whatever warmth was left to him. The climb to the passage door in his office, moving upward through the earth, was like emerging from the grave, his shoulders nearly touching on either side and the ceiling low enough for his head to occasionally brush against the uneven stones. He came to the door at the top and shoved. Nothing happened. He groaned, and shoved harder. His knees trembled under the strain, and his left leg ached. The door budged. Dylan paused, gasping for breath, then shoved again. The door opened farther. He kept shoving until the door had opened enough for him to squeeze through, and he reentered the world. Trembling, he shoved the door closed behind him, screwing his eyes shut with the effort.

Though the fire was low, he went to warm himself by it and wrapped himself with his kilt for a blanket. The skin on his arms began to itch, and he scratched.

Sinann came, probably having seen him through the tapestry when he arrived. "*Och*, 'tis about time ye returned. I was beginning to worry."

"I was him." Dylan's fingernails dug harder into his skin as he scratched. "I was raping her. I was him, and he was killing her."

The faerie groaned. "Aye, lad. He came into the world through ye."

Dylan squeezed his eyes shut, desperate to rid himself of the image, but it was still there behind his eyelids. Cait crying. Calling his name. Choking on her own blood. *Dying.* "I felt her. I felt her die around me." The shaking took him, but this time it was more than the cold. "I was him, Sinann. I felt what he felt. I was him, and I was . . . I was killing her. I was killing her," he said through gritted teeth, "*and I liked it!*" He looked around the room, turning and looking, but finding no help. He itched all over now. His skin crawled, and he scratched. He wanted out of his skin, to get at the ugliness beneath. His fingers dug into his hair. Doubled over with the pain, he grabbed at his scalp. "Sinann, make it go away."

"I cannae."

The horror inside his head curdled his mind. He dropped his kilt to the floor, ripped the sark from his body, and threw it to the floor as well. He scratched himself all over, but not fast enough to keep up with the horrible itching. "I've got to get it out of me. Can't . . . I can't be like this. Not with the knowing. I can't know this." His skin was red now from the scratching, but he still itched. Burned.

Fire. He turned to the fire. "Burn it out . . ." He made for the hearth, ready to embrace the flame, to be purified by it.

"*Och*, no, ye dinnae!" Sinann leapt on his back, wrapped her arms and legs around him, and pulled him away with every bit of strength she had. Her wings beat furiously and she cried out for him to stop. He grabbed at her to get her off, for he didn't want to burn her, too. But she clung to him and continued pulling with all her might.

Dylan moaned as he acquiesced. "Let me do it. I've got to get rid of it." His body sagged. His arms dropped. All he could feel was the darkness inside him.

"Nae! Sleep! Sleep only will help. Sleep, Dylan, and be well."

He knelt by the hearth. "No," he said as her push made him want to yawn.

"Sleep, Dylan Dubh of Ciorram. Rest."

Sleep took him, and he collapsed before the fire.

W hen he awoke, he was quite surprised to find himself naked, on the floor in front of a well-kept wood fire in the Laird's office. *His* office, he remembered after a long, confused moment. He could barely remember coming back from the hilltop last night, and assumed Sinann had stoked the fire while he was asleep. It was high and bright, throwing a great deal of heat and flickering light. Even so, there was still a bit of a chill deep inside his bones, and he was glad for the blaze.

He was too groggy to even lift his head and might not even have awakened when he did except that Gracie had come into the room with a tray bearing a plate of meat and a *quaiche* of ale. One eye open and feeling as if he were observing the living through hell's passage, he watched her place the tray on the desk before the chair. Then she went to the arrow loop shutters on either side of the desk and threw them open. The room flooded with direct sunlight that streamed onto the floor in a great, bright wash.

Dylan groaned. Blinking, he sat up and reached for the wad of linen on the floor nearby. It was his sark, but it had been ripped to rags. There was a vague memory of himself tearing it off at one point or another. It was all very disjointed in his mind. Surreal. Somewhere in the images were things he knew he didn't want to see. They frightened him, though he couldn't remember what they were. He shook his head to clear it. Later. He would deal with them later. For now he shoved them to the back of his consciousness and tried to focus on what was before him.

The sark a loss, he set it aside and reached for his kilt. With the support of one of the chairs nearby, he pulled himself to his feet. He wrapped the kilt around his waist, holding it up with one fist, then ran his fingers through his hair to get it off his face. The horror of the night before lurked in the back of his mind, but for now it was safely tucked away and manageable. One hand on the mantel kept him from tipping over.

Gracie retrieved the linen rags from the floor and began to fold them neatly. The sark would either be repaired or, failing that, the cloth would be used as patches or kitchen rags. She said, without the least hint that she found it unusual to discover the Laird passed out naked on the floor of his office, "Good, ye're awake."

Dylan grunted. He might have slept another day or so, but couldn't wait that long to do what he had to do.

The castle servant glanced around the office and continued as she puttered, laying out Dylan's breakfast on the desk, "Ye'll be wanting to take a suitable bedchamber for yourself. If you like, I can have Artair's belongings packed away and his room given over to ye." She paused, and her voice took on a dark edge Dylan heard as warning. "Unless, of course, you've got your heart set on the Laird's bedchamber. In which case I'll need to find another for Iain Mór's poor widow—"

"Nah." Dylan waved off the issue. "I won't be disturbing Una. Give me Artair's room. One less flight of stairs to climb."

"Aye," said Gracie, apparently relieved the new Laird would continue to respect the Dowager Lady Matheson.

He continued, "And when you pack up Artair's belongings, have them readied for shipping. If he goes to prison, they'll be here if he's later released. If he's transported, we'll make sure he gets them." There was no need to discuss the possibility of Artair being hung. It existed, but even Dylan didn't want to talk about it. The young man had proven himself in a way that moved Dylan to deep respect, but there was nothing much to be done for him now. "Pray he'll need them, Gracie."

Gracie nodded as she finished with the breakfast and picked up the tray to return to the kitchen. "Is there anything else ye're needing?"

Dylan ventured to step away from the mantel toward the desk, feeling like a bag full of ill-sorted bones. "I'll need a ewer of fresh wash water straight away, please. But first find Robin Innis and tell him to gather the men in the upper glen at sunset for a *creach*."

She turned, wide-eyed. "On the MacDonells?"

He chuckled as he secured his kilt around his waist by tucking it into itself and made his wobbly way around to the desk chair, leaning on furniture as he went. "Aren't you the nosy one?" He sat in the red-upholstered chair and ate from the plate of meat. Surprisingly, the food was hot, and it was only then he realized how late it was in the day. The sun was slanting from the west, on its way toward setting.

Gracie made a disgusted noise. "I've served in this castle under four lairds now, and little has happened in it for the past half century I dinnae see nor hear. And neither have I spoken of any of it to anyone but my laird, whoever he may have been at the time."

Dylan swallowed and said, "All right, I'll tell you. It's not the MacDonells. In fact, we're going to Edinburgh." A slow grin crossed his face. "It's going to be a *creach* against the *Sassunaich*."

Gracie's eyes went wide, and she paled a bit. "Aye, sir." She took the ewer from the wash stand, and left the room while Dylan ate.

He chewed slowly, thoughtfully, gazing around at the desk. That Iain had died suddenly was apparent by the items lying about. A box of quills had a used one laid across one corner, as if set there briefly while writing. Iain's carved wooden pipe was propped against a stack of books, still filled with half-burnt tobacco. It brought an image of Iain, puffing away during a *céilidh*, listening as he struggled to keep the expensive tobacco lit. A melancholy crept in, and Dylan knew he would miss the Laird more than he'd imagined he could. Iain had been a difficult father-in-law, but he'd also been a respectable man and a good laird.

Near Dylan's right elbow was a rosary of ivory beads. He picked it up and let it dangle, draped over his palm. It was ancient. The ivory had darkened and chipped over its long life, but the gold corpus on the cross shone with a deep, polished luster.

Ciaran should have this. The thought came to him as if Iain himself had said it in his ear. Yes, Ciaran should have this. Iain would want that. Dylan decided he would save the rosary for the confirmation of Iain's grandson.

Soon Gracie returned with the filled ewer, a towel, and a fresh sark, then withdrew again for him to wash and dress. By sunset Dylan was feeling human again. He donned the silver King's sword, equipped himself for travel, and slipped away from the castle to meet his men.

Twenty men gathered in the dooryard of Dylan's peat house, still exhausted and hollow-eyed from the defeat at Glen Shiel. Many wore strips of linen to bind minor wounds, but Dylan could see in their eyes the glint of hope at the prospect of regaining their honor from the *Sassunaich*. Dylan's blood surged in anticipation of a successful raid. Failing to save Sarah was unthinkable; he would either return with her or die trying. The small band set off cross-country.

The walk to Edinburgh took five nights of dodging English patrols on the lookout for fleeing Jacobites. An encounter with Bedford would be disastrous, so they hid. The long summer days, marching to the solstice, were spent sleeping in barns and thickets, even though Dylan had his pardon with him this time. If discovered by anyone but the Major, he would present himself and his men as nothing more than drovers, all loyal to the Crown, on their way to buy cattle.

Sinann flew beside Dylan, just over his left shoulder, quiet most of the way. Her silence was a relief, for it was difficult to reply with the other men around. But during their last day before crossing below the Highland Line, she settled near him as he lay awake, thinking.

"Nae sleeping, lad?" She sat cross-legged next to him.

He shook his head. He'd hollowed out a spot in a thick bed of rotted leaves, under a spray of bracken. His men dotted the area, hidden as sleeping deer. None snored; all slept lightly, for they were no longer in friendly territory. Down here, it wasn't just the *Sassunaich* who would give them trouble. Lowlanders weren't overly fond of kilted Highlanders traipsing through their forests, cattle raids from above the Highland Line being so common.

Sinann said, " 'Tis a brave thing ye're doing."

Dylan nodded and closed his eyes. If she would shut up, he might sleep.

"Ye must love her a great deal."

Now he peered at her. In the lowest whisper he could manage, he said, "I've got to get her away from Bedford."

One of the men nearby said in a low voice, "*Och*, Dylan Dubh is praying. I dinnae ken whether to take it as a good sign or a bad one." That brought a general snicker among those who were still awake.

Dylan said to them, "I should hope you're all praying." That sobered the group, and he settled farther into his hollow.

To Sinann he said, "I've got to get her out of there. I can't fail again."

There was a hesitation from the faerie, then she said, "You blame yerself for Cait's death?"

"I swore I'd never let her come to harm." His chest tightened, and he fought off unwanted images. He forced them into the back of his mind, where he wished they'd stay. "I not only failed, but she died horribly. Terrified." He screwed his eyes shut. *"Alone."*

" 'Twas nae your fault. Cait's death was fated. You must understand that. You must also understand that the true reason you've come for Sarah is that ye love her."

Dylan opened his eyes.

The faerie said, " 'Tis high time ye admitted yer feelings."

"My feelings are none of your bloody business. But, fine, if you have to hear it, I love her. I want to love her better. She's smart, she's warm, she's pretty, she's . . . a generous lover. But most of all, she loves me to distraction. That means a lot."

"The love spell—"

"She could have shaken it off if she'd wanted. Just like I shook off Morrighan's spell. Sarah loves me because she wants to."

"She loved ye five years ago."

He sighed. "There was Cait then. Also, five years ago, Sarah didn't know me well. Now she knows me, in ways even Cait didn't until we were married. Sarah knows me, and she loves me anyway. My kids need a mother. Hers need a father. She needs a husband, and I need a wife. She loves me, and by God, I love her in return. I would be stupid not to love her."

There was a long silence, and Dylan closed his eyes to sleep, but

Sinann added, "You realize that, even should you find her alive, she may not be unharmed." There was an edge to the word "unharmed," and Dylan knew what she really meant.

"Aye," he whispered. He wanted it to not matter, but it did. It mattered a lot, and there was little he could do about it. Whatever he might feel, Sarah's own reaction to being "harmed" could change everything. She would think he wouldn't want her then. Things between them were already iffy; if she were "harmed," those things might never be righted.

"Ye'll marry her regardless?"

"Aye. If she'll have me."

"And if she should birth in March of next year?"

Dylan didn't want to think about that. "We cross that bridge when we come to it." Deep inside, were he to admit it, his wish was that she would already have been pregnant by the time she was kidnapped. But with the wish came the terror she might already be on the *Spirit* and have a baby en route to Singapore. This *creach* had to succeed before he could hope for anything at all.

D ylan knew the old Robertson place well, having hidden from pursuing authorities in the forest on the property more than once while working for Rob Roy. He'd never been inside the large building that served as a barn and storage for the manor house nearby, and of course had never been near the manor itself, but he had often traversed the surrounding forest. Rob had put in temporary safekeeping there many head of reived cattle. If Bedford owned the land, it was a well-kept secret, even among those with whom he did business. Dylan shuddered at how close he must have come to being seen and identified by Bedford while fleeing him those years ago.

The twenty Mathesons approached the stone building from the forest, Dylan finding a vantage point atop a boulder under a spreading oak tree. He lurked among the branches, relaxed but alert, and observed the comings and goings of the place during the day. Robin was posted at the other side with a small contingent, watching the manor house.

Dylan was elated to find the large pens outside the barn teeming with cattle. Closer inspection of the herd would more than likely reveal them as the ones taken from Glen Ciorram two weeks before. If they weren't, Dylan was still more than happy to take these in trade for the ones his clan had lost. In his head he began to plan the route they would take on the return trip with the herd.

There were men guarding the building with muskets and swords. Sin-ann popped back from counting them. "I put the force at more than thirty."

Dylan sucked air between his teeth with an irritated hiss. "Damn." The Mathesons were severely outnumbered and outgunned, for Dylan's force of twenty carried swords and dirks, with but three muskets and five pistols between them. "I'll need as much button-popping from you as I can get, aye?"

The faerie giggled.

"Did you find Sarah?"

She nodded. "She's with a dozen or so women and some children in a barred room high above the lofts. There are two ways to the second floor: those steps ye see there, and a wooden ladder inside the stable. The second floor, aside from the loft itself, is a labyrinth of offices, so once ye're there, I'll guide ye to the steps that will take ye above the loft."

"Is she all right?"

"Aye. Apart from some bruises."

"She hasn't been . . . *harmed*?"

The faerie's countenance darkened. "I cannae tell. It's a silent, frightened group in there. I heard nae talk."

Dylan fell silent himself.

Near the end of the day, his heart leapt to witness the arrival of Major Bedford, out of uniform. With him was Felix, riding the fractious young steed with the white markings. They dismounted before the barn entrance, and Felix took the animals through the large double doors to be stabled. Bedford climbed the steps along the outside of the building to enter a smaller door at a landing. It was early evening, but with the approaching solstice there would be light for a while yet.

"That's it," he whispered to himself. "We go now."

"Would ye rather wait till dark?"

He shook his head. "I want Bedford. We can't just hope he'll stay that long."

Just as he was about to slip down from his perch, a party of men, with Felix at the lead, rode from the double doors and galloped away toward the Glasgow road. Dylan grinned. He counted eleven fewer armed men against his Mathesons.

Robin approached and reported the manor house to be empty. The men moved on the barn.

CHAPTER 26

Dylan, wielding Brigid, led the attack, slipping from the trees and moving behind the sentry at the stairs. The plan was to take out the sentries quietly, but the barn was too skillfully posted. The attempt at stealth resulted in a musket fired by an alert guard in the pens. A divot of sod flew up at Dylan's feet.

He drew the King's sword and shouted an order for all to charge. The guard at the steps whirled and fired. The ball caught Dylan's kilt as he ran, tugging a piece from it but without touching flesh. Dylan ran down on the sentry, whose musket was now discharged. The man swung his musket as a club. Dylan dodged. The sentry reached for his sword. One stroke of the King's sword did the sentry in, and Dylan was spattered with his blood.

Two more sentries were taken out by Matheson muskets, and the first man out the upper door also was killed from the ground. He toppled over the side and landed hard. Mathesons ran up the stone stairs to meet Bedford's swordsmen halfway to the door.

Dylan gave a quick swipe to his face with a sleeve to clear the blood from his eyes, and took the rest of his men through the double doors to meet the stablemen inside. Pistol balls whined past their ears as they attacked in the lantern-lit dimness. Horses screamed with terror. Men shouted

and cursed as swords clashed. Dylan engaged a man and quickly dispatched
him with a slash across the gut, then glanced around for another opponent.
A hesitant defender then attacked, but after very few exchanges Dylan cut
the man's throat and moved on.

"Dylan!" Sinann cried, "Here! The ladder!"

He spun to look, then scabbarded Brigid and ran to scurry up the
ladder to the loft. All the defenders had gone to the floor, so the loft was
empty. Dylan shoved the ladder away from the loft so it toppled to the
floor below, then ran to the door that separated the offices from the barn
loft and threw it open.

The hallway was poorly lit and windowless. One small candle in a
sconce flickered at the turn a few yards away. He drew Brigid again, and
held the King's sword at *en garde* as he eased into the hallway. Every
sense was wide open, to detect the slightest hint of presence. Bedford was
up here somewhere, he knew, for there was no other way out except past
himself or his men.

A door slammed within the maze of offices behind heavy oak doors
and windowless walls. Dylan whispered, "Where is he?"

Sinann replied, "Third door. On the right. Just beyond the turn."

"Is he alone?" He listened carefully, but there were no sounds in these
rooms distinguishable from the noises outside and below.

"Aye. The offices are otherwise unoccupied."

"Does he know I'm here?"

"He kens he's become the prey."

Dylan gave a dry chuckle. "His ass has belonged to us since the day
he killed Iain's father." He went to the door Sinann indicated and raised
his eyebrows.

She popped out, then back, and replied to the unuttered question,
"Aye, he's still in there. He's drawn his sword." Dylan frowned and indicated Brigid. Sinann said, "Nae. He's not got a dirk. Not even a *sgian
dubh*, near as I can tell. He's standing in the middle of the room, straight
ahead. He's listening to the men below, through the window." The shouting outside was dwindling, as the number of combatants dwindled also and
the concerted attack became scattered sword work. Dylan could tell who
was winning, because the shouts were now mostly in Gaelic.

The faerie snapped her fingers and the door flew open. Dylan attacked
with a roar.

Bedford turned, and his eyes went wide, but he parried in time and responded with a lively assault of his own. Dylan stood up to him, and the swords clanged loudly in the small space. There wasn't enough room for the long weapons to be fully effective, which gave Dylan an advantage with his dirk. He parried high and came in low with Brigid. Bedford backed away in a hurry, gave a mighty swipe with his sword, and turned to run out a side door.

Dylan followed, and found himself in another office as Bedford dodged around a writing desk and some chairs and dashed through yet another door. Dylan followed, hoping Bedford might be fleeing into a corner.

In the next room lined with shelves full of ledgers, the Major tried to open a hallway door but found it wouldn't budge. He yanked and struggled with it, but it slammed shut with each attempt. He swore through clenched teeth. If he'd had a Goddess Stone, he would have seen the faerie above his head, holding the door closed with all her strength, wings beating wildly.

But he wasn't so equipped and quickly gave up on the door to charge Dylan. They clashed swords. Bedford locked hilts with him and shoved. The Major's desperation gave him an edge, and so Dylan was knocked aside. Bedford barreled past.

"Damn!" Dylan shook his head to clear it of the complacency that would be his downfall if he didn't start concentrating. He ran after his quarry.

Bedford made it all the way out to the loft, found the ladder had fallen, then turned to make his stand, sword *en garde*. Though his eyes were wide and frightened, he remained cool. Not a drop of sweat or a hint of perspiration anywhere. His long, aristocratic frame retained its perfect posture. Below, in the stable, there were still fights going on. The loft was scattered with loose hay, and at the far end were stacks of shipping crates.

Bedford said, "Matheson. Why aren't you dead?"

Without a word, Dylan attacked with all his strength, and Bedford defended with as much force. The Major succeeded in turning back the attack. Hitting hard with his sword, he backed Dylan almost to the door. When Bedford realized he couldn't get Dylan to return through it, he pressed close and punched him, then backed to avoid the dirk. Dylan, seeing stars, lashed out with Brigid but caught nothing. There was more room out here in the loft, and Bedford's disadvantage was minimal. With room to maneuver, he was a quick and ruthless opponent.

Head buzzing, Dylan shook away the bees, gasping for breath, and focused on the Major. He needed to gain time and piss Bedford off enough for him to make mistakes. Dylan's chest heaved as he said, "You're going to pay this time, you fucking limey. No more arrests. No more picking off the lairds. No more trafficking in people. I'm going to be rid of you."

A light of alarm flashed in Bedford's eyes as he realized Dylan knew of the white slave trade. *Pay dirt.* Bedford was rattled.

"Oh, yes," Dylan said with a snide grin, "I know the whole story. I'm not letting you out of here alive."

Bedford blanched. "You'll be hung for this. Trust in it."

A loud, barking laugh escaped Dylan before he could recover himself, and he windmilled his sword in an insouciant mulinette. "Let's take a reality break here, *Sassunach,* just for a moment. You're out of uniform, in a place known for harboring cattle thieves. I'm dead certain you covered your tracks coming here, and you'd best believe I did. By the time anyone of repute finds your body, the place will be dismantled and stripped, and your surviving reivers will be scattered to hell and gone, terrified of discovery and in search of employment. This place doesn't exist, and I was never here."

Bedford blanched.

Shouts came from the offices. They were in Gaelic. Dylan's men were searching the second floor. Dylan pointed his sword at his opponent and made little circles with the tip. "In fact, by the time your rotting carcass is discovered, I will be safely back at the *Tigh,* in possession of my lawful property, having just rescued a kinswoman from bad, *unidentified,* outlaw men who wanted to do terrible things to her." He tilted his head. "So bend over, Daniel, put your head between your knees, and kiss your ass good-bye."

In a flash of whirling steel he attacked. The swords clashed and clanged with another attack. He backed Bedford against a stack of crates, which tottered. Another attack, a stagger sideways, and a long, narrow crate at the top fell with the snapping sound of splitting wood. Dylan pressed, and Bedford was trapped. There was nowhere left to go but over the side of the loft. He defended desperately, but now Dylan was nearly on top of him. There was no more room to retreat. Dylan slashed at the Englishman with everything he had, and Bedford replied in kind.

"You," Dylan growled through clenched teeth that jarred as his sword clanged against his opponent's, "have pissed off . . ." another slash and clang, "... the wrong ..." *clang*, "... fucking ..." *clang*, "... guy." Dylan's fury reduced Bedford to little more than simply fending blows.

Finally Bedford wearied, and Dylan was able to knock the *Sassunach* sword away. It fell over the side of the loft and landed with a thump on the stable floor below. In the split second it took to focus again on Bedford's face, Dylan looked straight into his eyes as the Redcoat realized he was about to die. Dylan realized it, too, and wouldn't have stayed his hand even if it weren't already on its way to kill. Then the King's sword whipped across Bedford's throat in a flash of steel.

Bedford grabbed his throat in a futile attempt to stanch the blood, but it came pouring from between his fingers. He coughed, unable to breathe. It sprayed the air pink. He sank to his knees.

Dylan stepped back and wiped his face again to watch. There was no horror of having destroyed this man. Neither was there joy, but as the dying Englishman choked and bled, Dylan felt a quiet sense of rightness that a certain evil had been removed from the earth. Finally, Bedford's eyes glazed over, and he collapsed completely onto the floor.

Dylan looked around the loft for something on which to wipe his blades, and his glance fell on the long box that had broken open during the fight. A familiar shape was visible just under the lid. He wiped the blood from his weapons onto his kilt and scabbarded them both, then went to investigate. He stepped over Bedford's body, knelt by the box, and yanked on the lid. The broken wood pulled away easily from the nails securing it.

Inside, nestled in excelsior, lay the claymore. *The* claymore. Dylan recognized it. Alasdair's ancestral weapon, which Sinann had enchanted after his death and Bedford had stolen from her, lay before him. It was a gorgeous weapon—a symbol of Scotland and its history of brave Scottish men. Dylan reached out to touch it, reverently as he had—or would—on September 30, 2000.

"Dinnae touch that!" Sinann's voice was terrified.

"Why?" Dylan retrieved his hand and looked up at the faerie.

"It's enchanted, ye sumph, and means to take the next Matheson who touches it back in time to 1713. If ye touch it, 'twill take you. Then 'twill take ye again when ye touch it in the future. Ye ken, because I've told ye, that ye cannae exist twice in the same moment of time. Ye'll die if ye go twice at the sword's bidding."

"Oh." As Dylan gazed at the sword, a thought began to form that made his breath short and his skin tingle. What if he destroyed it? What if he took the box with the sword in it, carried it out in a boat, and dumped it in the middle of a loch so that it would never find its way to Tennessee? *What if he never touched the sword at all?*

"Sinann," he said, his voice low and quiet, "I could get rid of the sword so it would never reach me in America. I could fix it so I never came here. I could live out my life in my own time. No scars on my back, no musket balls through my leg, no grief, no pain, no living on the run, no living under the thumb of the *Sassunaich*, just teaching classes in my dojo. In peace." One finger picked at the splintering wood of the crate, absently pulling up a piece of it.

The faerie's voice was soft and sad. "Aye. Nae Cait. Nae Ciaran nor Sìle. Nae Eóin, nor Gregor, nor Sarah. Ye would never have known them, and yer children would never have even existed."

Dylan's chest tightened. "But I have it in my power to change it. I can make it all not happen. It's right here in my hands, Sinann. *I could change history.*"

"Can ye? Are ye certain of it? Do ye have it in ye to leave them? To turn yerself over to an existence without them? An existence without even knowledge of them?"

"I wouldn't know. I wouldn't miss them."

"Ye cannae say ye wouldnae feel an emptiness. You were meant to be here. You were born to be their father and Cait's husband. Ye cannae live yer destiny any other way."

He tried to imagine doing it—dumping the sword in a loch—but failed. She was right; he couldn't. He knew things happened the way they did for a reason, and he could no more throw the claymore into a loch than he could kill his children outright.

"As ye once told me," said the faerie, "sometimes ye do what ye do because it's the only choice ye can make. Because of who ye are."

He took a deep breath and let it out slowly. Then he set the lid back on the box and began tapping the nails back down with the small hilt of his *sgian dubh*.

Robin ran from the offices onto the loft, sword drawn, and skidded to a halt at sight of the dead Englishman in a pool of blood. *"Och!"* He took a moment to absorb the fact that Bedford was dead, then turned to Dylan and said, "We've killed or chased away the entirety of the raiders' forces. We'd best be moving along lest the others return."

"How many did we lose?"

"None. Keith Rómach has a bad wound in his belly, but he might live. The bleeding isnae much, and there's nae smell of bile. All the other injuries are slight, so far as I can tell."

"Escapees?"

"A few. They willnae be back, though, until we've gone, or until the others come. They ran, bleeding and frightened."

Dylan nodded. "Good." Relief filled him and he breathed easier, but they needed to move out quickly and not be caught with their drawers down by the remaining raiders. "Tell the men to start moving the cattle from the pens, and take them away toward home. And move smartly. I'll be along directly." Dylan's *fear-còmhnaidh* made a dash for the door to comply, but Dylan stopped him. "Robin, take this crate. And go see if there's a cash box anywhere in those offices there."

"Aye?" Robin peered curiously at the box.

"You know where Bedford's home is in London?"

Robin nodded. "He talked about it as if it were God's own country home." He glanced at the body again. "I expect he should have stayed there if he loved it so much."

"I want you to have this crate shipped there. To his son." Dylan knew nothing left in this building would ever make it to Bedford's heirs, and he needed to make sure this sword would be passed down to the Yankee who would one day let him hold it in his hands. "Whatever you do, don't open the box. Do not touch what's inside." Though Robin was a Matheson only on the distaff side, there was no sense in taking any chances. "Just send it. It's important. Bedford's son must receive this sword."

"Aye, sir." Innis was mystified, but Dylan knew he would obey the orders of his Laird, just as surely as the man would breathe. Dylan handed him the box, and Robin went back to the offices with it.

Dylan heard women's voices outside the stable door. He lay on the edge of the loft to find finger purchase on a beam below, then swung down to hang from it. He dropped to the stable floor and hurried outside.

A cluster of women and children were there, milling around, unsure of what was going on. There was snuffling among the children, and one of the women was asking nobody in particular what they were to do now. Dylan looked from face to face, but didn't see Sarah.

"Sarah? Sarah Matheson?"

There was no reply.

One of his men behind him announced to the women, "Everybody go now. Ye're free, and I would hie as far away as possible, as quickly as possible, before the *Sassunaich* return!" Nobody moved, and he said, "Go! Off with ye, now!"

The women began to move, and Dylan searched faces as they passed on their way toward the Glasgow road. Alarm grew. None of them was Sarah. "Sinann, you said she was here."

"Up the stairs."

He spun and ran up the stone stairs to the offices. "Where's that room, Sinann?"

The faerie directed him to the steps up to the third floor, which he climbed two at a time. Bursting into the room, past a splintered door crooked on its hinges, he came into a large, dim room. There were only a few high, barred windows.

He repeated under his breath, *"Sinann, you said she was here."*

"Aye, and she is. Look." The faerie pointed toward a pillar, and Dylan could now see a figure behind it in the darkest shadows.

"Sarah. It's me."

Her voice was low. "Aye."

He gestured for Sinann to leave. The faerie balked, but he insisted until she obeyed. When he was alone with Sarah, he said, "I'm sorry."

"Ye've nae need for it. Ye've done naught to be sorry for." The hard edge in her voice told him otherwise.

"I have. I kept you a servant when you should have been my wife."

She lifted her gaze from the floor, and now he could see one large, brown eye peek from behind the pillar, bright with tears and glittering with anger. Her kerchief was gone, leaving her hair to spill over her shoulders. Though her face was clean, her dress was dirty and torn from continual wear and rough treatment.

He stepped closer and continued, his voice as low and soft as it would go. "I came for you. While I was away fighting I missed you. Not for what you could do for me, but because I missed your company. I discovered I love you. I don't know why I never saw it before. Maybe I was afraid of forgetting Cait. Maybe it was penance for not saving her. I can't say. But I hope you haven't given up waiting for me. I hope you'll marry me."

Now she looked away again. There was a long, tense silence as he waited for a reply. Then she said, "You cannae want me now. It's far too late."

Disappointment shot through him. "You don't love me any more?"

Sarah sobbed and pressed a hand to her face, over her eyes. "I love you more than my life, and I cannae help it. But ye returned from the fighting too late."

He stepped closer, until he was just the other side of the pillar and he could speak in a whisper. "What did they do to you?"

She shook her head. "They did naught, for I found this piece of an old dirk over there on the floor." She reached into the pocket under her skirts and produced a tiny triangle of steel, about an inch long, and handed it to him. It was shiny and the edges were sharp.

He peered at it by the fading light from the high window, and frowned. "You didn't hold them off with this."

The angry edge sharpened in her voice. "I kent you wouldnae understand."

"What? What happened, then?"

"I cut myself. High on my legs. Then smeared the blood over my thighs. Fear of the evil humors kept them away."

A smile crept across Dylan's face. "You fooled them into thinking you were having . . . I mean, that it was your time?"

She nodded. "The blood dried, but that dinnae matter. They only needed to see it once, and they were off to bother the others. For there were plenty of others who dinnae care to draw their own blood. The men all left me alone, so fastidious they were."

He almost laughed, but stopped the urge in time. "Then, what's the problem? Why can't you marry me?"

Her mouth opened to speak, but no sound came. It took a long moment, but finally she was able to say, "It doesnae matter what happened. It matters only what is believed to have happened."

"I believe you."

"Nobody else will ever see the marks. The clan will be wary of me. Forever after, there will be whispers about me. The Laird cannae marry a woman of such repute."

He blinked. "How did you know—"

She nodded toward his scabbard. "Ye carry the King's sword. I saw

Iain Mór die. It wasnae difficult to guess. So I cannae marry you. I cannae put you in that position."

Dylan grunted. Though he knew she was right about the whispers, his twentieth-century sensibilities wouldn't let him give her up just for that. She was truthful and loyal, a good cook and a great mother, and she loved him in ways that boggled him. He would be a fool to give her up for any reason at all.

Slowly, he said, "I told you I love you. Nothing can change that." He reached out to lift her chin so she would look at him. "*Nothing*. A man could go far to find a wife clever enough to remain untouched in this place."

He reached into his sporran for the opal ring and held it up to catch what little light could be found. "I brought this for you, and I've been carrying it around for weeks. I bet it'll just fit you, because it was meant to be on your finger. It's your birthstone."

Tears streamed down her face, her eyes on the ring.

He continued, "We'll marry straight away . . . I mean, we'll be hand-fasted until we can find a priest. Your bairns will be mine. We'll have a long life together, you'll be my Lady, and anyone who wishes to give us guff about it will answer to my sword."

There was a long silence, but a light of hope grew in her eyes. "Do ye mean it?"

"I swear it. Marry me, or my life will be over." He took her hand to draw her from behind the pillar.

She hesitated for a long moment, resisting him, then stepped toward him. He brushed a wisp of hair from her face and as he did so ran his thumb over one eyebrow. "Do you doubt me? Have I destroyed all your faith in me?" Carefully, he kissed her. Then he slipped the ring onto the third finger of her left hand.

Finally she slipped into his arms. "*Och*, Dylan Matheson."

He kissed her, long and deep. Her body molded to his, filling his arms so well he knew she must be meant for them. His heart swelled and warmed, as it hadn't since Cait's death. It seemed the final missing piece of his soul now clicked into place, and he felt whole.

Holding her tight, he murmured into her ear, "Let's get out of this dump." Dylan guided Sarah down the steps and out of the building.

Off in the pens, the men were herding the cattle away into the gathering dusk, slowly but efficiently. With little fuss, the dark beasts lumbered along, prodded by the Matheson reivers. Hand in hand with Sarah, he watched and noted the number of animals. There were more than had been taken. The herd would restore the Mathesons nearly to what they'd had before Bedford's punitive acquisition.

Hoofbeats on sod came from behind, and Dylan turned to find a bridled but unsaddled horse, led by Sinann. She had it by the bridle, one hand holding either side of the headstall, flying backward as she tugged the horse toward Dylan and Sarah.

Sarah laughed. "Look! The *Sassunach* horse is wanting to go home with us!"

"*Och,*" was all Dylan would venture in front of Sarah. While his attention was on the horse, she fiddled with her hair, attempting to organize it with no kerchief.

Sinann said, "Ye're a long way from home, and 'twill be a long trail."

Dylan shook his head, not wanting to take what they had not come for.

"*Och,* dinnae be so stubborn. 'Tis a fine thoroughbred—even more fine a beast than the four that were taken from Ciorram some years ago. Take it, and be happy for yer bride, who willnae then be forced to walk home like a servant."

His eyes narrowed at the faerie, who knew where all his buttons were. But then he glanced at Sarah. She was braiding her hair at the back to appear more respectable. Her dark eyes shone at him in the twilight, and his resolve was gone. Uttering nothing more than a small grunt at the faerie, he acquiesced. He took the reins and a hank of mane, then lightly he swung aboard. A quick tug adjusted his kilt beneath him. Sinann settled on the horse's rump, back-to-back with Dylan.

"Come," he said, and reached down to help Sarah up in front of him. Arms locked with his, she gave a little hop and he was able to pull her up the rest of the way. She was unused to riding, but while following the cattle he wouldn't take the horse at more than a walk in any case. Sitting between his thighs as on a sidesaddle, she settled into his arms with her head on his shoulder. Holding her close, he felt the warmth of her ease into him. It went straight to his heart, then warmed him wholly. He kissed her hair, then urged the horse to a walk.

Following the cattle toward the Highlands, the new Laird of Ciorram spoke warmly to the woman who was soon to be his wife, of the future and of his hopes for the clan.

CHAPTER 27

It was a long but delightful walk from the pub in the middle of town to the castle they called *Tigh a' Mhadaidh Bhàin*. A slight breeze accompanied the summer sun, and the sweetness of flowers drifted to Barri now and again on the warm air. The short drive from the causeway to the gatehouse was lined with poplar trees that made a shady, leafy corridor. They swished in the breeze, sounding like a hushed conversation. Barri ventured through the archway by the gatehouse, staring up at the heavy wooden gate overhead as she passed.

It was so old! She could imagine ancient warriors with battering rams and catapults, trying to breach this barrier with much shouting and cursing. It was fascinating to realize this castle must have been built near the time of Edward I and Robert the Bruce, centuries older than any structure in any place she'd been before in her life.

Inside the castle, the drive made a circle in front of a large garage complex with three wide doors. The building looked modern, built of fieldstone to blend with the rest of the castle. It wasn't a very good match, though, for there was no mistaking the extreme age of the original, weathered stone.

The courtyard garden was a fantasy in roses, hedges, and junipers. Paths meandered here and there among the array of flowers. In the eastern corner was nestled an herb garden, throwing rich scents of sage, rosemary, and onion into the warm summer air. Between the flowers and the herbs was a path lined in boxwood, which led to a pair of large, carved doors. Barri approached it tentatively.

She looked around at the doorway for a bell of some sort, unsure whether to knock or what. She raised her hand, but before her knuckle could touch the wood, one of the doors opened. A young, uniformed maid smiled and curtsied, then bade her to enter. "This way, Mrs. Matheson."

Surprise shook Barri to her soles. "I was unaware I was expected."

The maid stammered a bit, then said, "My apologies, ma'am. Please follow me." Barri thought she might have been English, though she wasn't familiar enough with accents to tell. But the maid was easier to understand than most folks she'd met here, and her speech seemed less sharp.

The girl led the way through an entry where the walls were studded with wooden pegs, and on into a huge, echoing room of stone floor and wood paneling. A gigantic stone hearth occupied most of one end of the hall, with a small doorway next to it. The maid guided Barri toward another door at the other end. Barri couldn't help staring about like a tourist in a museum.

The walls were hung with a few oil portraits of men in kilts and women in nineteenth-century dress, and adorned with a number of swords and battleaxes. The floor was covered with the most magnificent, monstrously large oriental carpet Barri had ever seen. She half expected to find suits of armor standing about, but there were none. However, several iron-studded shields and sets of bagpipes graced the walls. Electric chandeliers of intricate crystal hung from the rafters threw ample light over it all.

They left the huge room through the heavy door at the far end. The maid spoke as they walked down a paneled hallway lit by electric sconces set at intervals along it. "Himself sent me to greet you at the door. He's asked to see you in his office."

"How did he know my name?"

The maid shrugged but whispered, "It's nae such a strange thing to happen here." Her tone was comforting, as if to say there was nothing to fear from strange things.

There was another heavy, wooden door, and another corridor. This hallway, being curved, had not been paneled and was lit only by a candelabra on a table at the end. The walls were stone, dank and earthy. Barri had the impression of being underground, and claustrophobia niggled at her. They passed a set of spiral stairs that rose to the right, then stopped at a door on the left. The maid knocked.

"Enter." It was a man's voice.

The maid opened the door for Barri, then waited to be dismissed.

The Laird's office was an odd combination of modern comfort and ancient trappings. Some of the incredibly narrow windows, glazed with rippling glass, were open to the beautiful weather outside. A fine walnut entertainment center stood between two of them, containing a television and stereo system, dark and silent. Like the Great Hall, this stone floor was covered in Persian finery, and by the fragrant peat-burning hearth stood two plush wing chairs upholstered in wine red. File cabinets stood against the walls, wooden but modern, and one decrepit-looking bookcase may have been original to the castle but was filled to overflowing with modern novels. Electric lights and sockets were served by conduit that ran along the base of the stone walls.

One section of wall between the old bookcase and a window was entirely covered by what must have been the famous tapestry of the faeries. It depicted an extremely large, red-haired and bearded man in a kilt, riding a unicorn through the forest, his plaid kilt sash flying behind him. He carried a sword in one hand and a white rose in the other, and following him was a small, white-clad faerie. The tapestry was obviously old, faded and threadbare, but just as obviously held an honored place in the room, for the view of it was unobstructed, and it was directly across from the enormous modern cherry wood desk. The desk stood before a wall bearing a display case. In that case, protected by glass, were a large silver sword and a silver-hilted knife, both in scabbards.

Standing by the tapestry was a man in his late forties. The Laird of Ciorram.

"Thank you, Janice," he said. The maid took her leave. He crossed the room and held out his hand to Barri. "Good afternoon. I'm Iain Matheson."

Barri took the hand, barely noticing. She couldn't take her eyes from his face. He was a handsome gentleman, but that wasn't what caught her attention. She studied him to know what it was that caught her eye, but it eluded her. His build was very tall and thin, and he dressed casually in slacks and a sweater. He had wavy brown hair, with a slight touch of gray at the temples, that curled gently about his ears. Through his fair complexion his cheeks glowed a bright, healthy pink. His eyes were quite blue—the color of the loch outside.

Though she couldn't put her finger on exactly how, he seemed familiar. Something in the way he carried himself, perhaps, or in the line of his brow. She blinked and told herself she was hoping too much, but the eerie feeling of familiarity persisted.

She said, "The maid called me by name. Did those men at the pub phone to tell you I was coming?"

A puzzled look flickered across Iain's eyes, and Barri knew he was about to lie. Kenneth always had that look whenever he lied. "Ah . . . aye. Yes. They rang. They said . . ." He glanced to the left, then recovered. "Aye. They said you were needing some information."

She nodded.

"Please, won't you have a seat then?" He indicated the chairs by the hearth and came to sit himself.

Barri turned toward the fire and noticed a number of framed photographs perched on the mantel. A woman and two boys at various ages smiled at her from them.

Iain answered her unasked question. "My wife and my sons. The boys are away at university, the both of them. Kate is in Dublin this week with her horses. She shows them. Does quite well, actually."

"Indeed? I've always had an affinity for horses, though I've had little opportunity to indulge it." She sat.

"Aye. Well," he sat also, "how might I help ye this fine day?" He glanced away again, this time looking as if he were listening. Then he said to Barri, "I'm told it's the legend of Dilean Dubh nan Chlaidheimh ye're after?"

She nodded. "Black Dylan . . . *Dilean Dubh* . . . what was the rest of it?"

"Black Dylan of the Sword would be the translation of the Gaelic. He was known for his swordsmanship and for having the darkest head of hair in the glen. How did you hear of him, all the way across the Atlantic? This is a small glen, and the Mathesons dinnae pop up in every popular history ye read." He paused as if listening again, then said in a lowered, muttering voice, "It wasnae my idea to give MacDonell the post. It's not like I can change it, either." His attention returned to Barri, and he said, "Our town historian is very highly focused on certain bits of history, ignoring other bits, which leaves some duties up to me."

Somewhat rattled by Iain's strange behavior, Barri nodded and said, "I heard the story from my husband's father, who'd heard it from a James Matheson who was an RAF officer during World War II. He'd said he was from Glen Ciorram."

A smile crossed Iain's face, somewhat wistful and in awe. "My father, perhaps. James Dilean Matheson, who was a fighter pilot, was my father. He served in the war, then came home to Glen Ciorram. It's been fifteen years since he passed away, rest his soul."

"Could you tell me about Black Dylan?"

He glanced to the side and nodded. "Oh, aye. There's very little I cannae tell ye about him. He was Laird of this castle for over twenty years during the eighteenth century."

Tears sprang to her eyes and she drew a deep breath. *Twenty years!* "He lived that long?"

"Aye. He was in his fif—" A slight breath of a pause, then, "Sixties. He was in his sixties when he died."

Barri swallowed the tears, both joyful that her son had lived so long and sorrowful that he'd eventually died. "He had children?"

Iain nodded, and said haltingly, "Eight. No, six. Aye, six. Two were stepsons, but the six were three sons and three daughters of his own that lived."

Grandchildren. She'd had grandchildren and never known them. The sense of loss surprised her, and her chest tightened. Suddenly she wasn't sure this was such a good idea. She cleared her throat and said, "Is he a direct ancestor of yours?"

That brought a bright smile of pride. "Aye, he certainly was. The Mathesons of Ciorram have enjoyed a strong line over the past centuries. Dylan Robert Matheson was my great-great-great-great-great-great-great-grandfather." Iain counted off the generations on his fingers to be sure he had the correct number.

"Black Dylan helped the people of Ciorram weather the immense social changes during his time. Though he couldnae have seen them through the entire century of the Clearances, he did lay the groundwork to turn an illegal still into the distillery, which is now the mainstay of the economy here. He was the first hereabouts to breed his sheep with the Cheviots to increase the wool yield, and encouraged industry here long before the Clearances forced folks off the land and into the cities or away to America and Australia. By all accounts, he paved the way for Ciorram to survive the destruction of the clan system on which they'd depended for centuries."

"Like he knew it was coming."

Iain blinked, then cleared his throat. "Aye. As if he did."

Then he leaned back in his chair and began telling a story about how Dylan had been arrested unjustly by the English. In great detail—far greater detail than one might expect from a storyteller nine generations removed from the subject—he spoke of her son's days as a highwayman, then as a Jacobite. He told her of Cait and Sarah, and of the children. As the afternoon progressed and the patch of sunshine moved across the floor, there were stories of battles and sword fights. Then Iain told how, in later years, Black Dylan had helped the clan dodge the bullet of English oppression in spite of being a Catholic and a former Jacobite.

"He was a Catholic?" Last time Barri had seen her son, he'd been a member of the Methodist Church and barely knew what Catholicism was.

Iain hesitated, and a look of doubt crossed his face. He said, carefully, "Aye. We're Catholic." There was a note of challenge in his voice, as if he expected a bad reaction from her. Barri then remembered the animosities between Catholic and Protestant were far more pronounced in this country than where she came from.

Thinking fast, she said, "Then it must have been difficult for him. For all of you, I imagine." Her voice was low and soft as she continued, "He must have been a brave man. A good man."

The tension left Iain and he nodded, glanced to the side again and back, then nodded and said, "He was a *great* man. Like Cuchulain, as some say, and I have it on excellent authority he was well-loved."

Barri had to look away, and gazed into the fireplace for a moment. When she looked back, Iain's expression had softened. She wondered whether he might know he was talking about her son. But she shook away the preposterous thought. He couldn't possibly.

He smiled and asked, "Would ye care to see where he's buried?"

A chill washed over her. Dylan's grave? Could she bear it? She could feel the blood drain from her face. "He's buried here?"

"In the churchyard. It's a bit east of here, a few miles. I could drive ye there, if ye wish to see it."

Barri opened her mouth to decline but paused and thought a moment. She shut her mouth and blinked as feelings warred with each other, flashing back and forth like flying swords. There were only two choices: to see the grave or not. If she went, she might break down completely and make a fool of herself. But if she didn't go, and left Scotland without ever seeing her son's grave, she would never feel right. It would almost be as if she'd deserted him. Finally she nodded. "Yes, I would like that."

Iain smiled and stood to reach for her hand.

The Catholic church stood on a rise just above the gravel parking lot that served it. Barri stared up at it as she closed the passenger door of Iain's Jaguar. It wasn't a large church, but it seemed nearly as old as the castle. A stained glass window with electric light inside glowed in the growing twilight, breathtakingly beautiful in reds, blues, green, and purple. She climbed the stone steps along the hillside to the churchyard. The far end of the property was scattered with gravestones. Before the church, along the walkway, there stood a painted sign that was old, dirty, and mildewed. In barely legible letters it said, Our Lady of the Lake Catholic Church—Service 1:30 P.M. Iain followed up the steps but hung back at the top as Barri passed the sign.

Nearly to the gathering of stones in the graveyard, Barri turned to see if he were coming and was struck once again by the familiarity of his presence. A quiver took her as the realization sank in she was looking at her own great-great-great-great-great-great-great-great-grandson, who was only a few years younger than herself. He didn't look like her. Neither did he look like Dylan, nor any of the other Mathesons she'd met in Scotland or the U.S. Nevertheless, the sense of connection was still there somehow.

He said, "Something the matter?"

"You coming?"

A smile touched his mouth. "Nae. I'll await ye here. Ye cannae miss it, it's the three white ones right in a row in the middle ye're looking for." He pointed with his chin, then stuffed his hands in his pockets.

As Barri turned, she hesitated as he spoke in a low voice not meant for her to hear. "Och," he said to the air, "I've seen it, as ye well know." She looked back at him to find him addressing a spot a few feet in front of him, as if talking to an invisible short person. There was silence for a moment, then he said, "I dinnae care. It's the right thing, and ye ken very well it's what he wanted, or he never would have asked for it to be done." Another pause, then, "I'll be here. Dinnae worry. It will be well." Then he fell silent and Barri turned back toward the graveyard again.

It wasn't a large yard, and stones were few. This wasn't the huge

Victorian sort of cemetery filled with rich folk outdoing each other with elaborate sculpture in granite and marble. But the well grassed-over area was scattered here and there with stones placed by moderately successful families experiencing changing fortunes over the centuries.

As Iain had promised, there were three identical stones near the center of the yard, of white marble. The small, worn markers were easily the oldest stones there, their edges rounded by weather and the writing on them slightly blurred to softness. Heavy thistles grew up between them. She was unsure whether the mass of prickly stems and fluffy purple blossoms was meant to be there, or had grown up from neglect. They seemed like weeds but echoed the thistle carved at the top of the center stone. As wild as they were, they seemed to belong more than did the white roses entwined on the rail fence by the hillside.

The stone on the left said, "Caitrionagh Sìleas Matheson, Beloved Wife of Dylan." And that was all. There was no other decoration.

The one on the right was carved in a slightly different hand, "Sarah Ross Matheson, Beloved Wife of Dylan." And that was all.

The center stone, in a hand that matched Sarah's, said, "Dylan Robert Matheson of Ciorram."

Barri knelt to place her hand on the soft, grassy ground before the stone. Dylan was here. Finally she knew what had happened to him. Something inside her, something that had been knotted up for two years, finally loosened. She whispered, "Dylan, I wish I could have told you good-bye. I wish you could have known how much I miss you."

She stayed for a few moments, remembering her son as he'd been when she'd known him and glad to know something of the man he'd become. The yearning to connect with him, the hope that the Laird who had helped his people through hard times had also remained her son, tightened in her. But the light was fading, and the air was turning chilly. Before standing, she reached over to pluck one of the thistles.

Behind the purple blossom, more writing on the middle stone caught her eye. Something at the very bottom of Dylan's marker was obscured by the thistles, and she carefully drew them aside.

There, carved on the headstone in the same ornate style as his name, were the words, "Hi, Mom."

She sat back on her heels, covered her face with her hands, and wept.